REALM OF RUINS

A Nissera Novel

HANNAH WEST

HOLIDAY HOUSE · NEW YORK

Copyright © 2018 by Hannah West
Map and family tree by Jaime Zollars. Copyright © 2018 by Holiday House
Publishing, Inc.
All Rights Reserved
HOLIDAY HOUSE is registered in the U.S. Patent and Trademark Office.
Printed and bound in July 2019 at Maple Press, York, PA, USA.
www.holidayhouse.com
3 5 7 9 10 8 6 4 2
Library of Congress Cataloging-in-Publication Data

Names: West, Hannah, 1990- author.
Title: Realm of ruins / Hannah West.
Description: First edition. | New York : Holiday House, [2018] | Companion to:
Kingdom of ash and briars. | Summary: Valory, an unlikely heroine and descendant
of Bristal, must battle the effects of a dangerous, time-bending resurrection spell
wreaking havoc on Nissera.
Identifiers: LCCN 2017028572 | ISBN 9780823439867 (hardcover)
Subjects: | CYAC: Magic—Fiction. | Time—Fiction. | Duty—Fiction.
Characters in literature—Fiction. | Fantasy.
Classification: LCC PZ7.1.W4368 Re 2018 | DDC [Fic]—dc23 LC
record available at https://lccn.loc.gov/2017028572

ISBN: 978-0-8234-4544-8 (paperback)

For Vince, my unflagging encourager through thick and thin

Nissera

rna

Mizrah
Sea

Perispos

Erdem

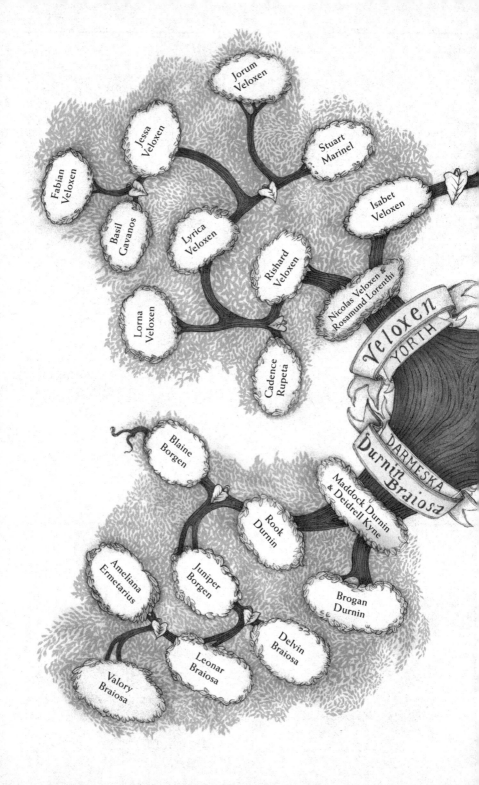

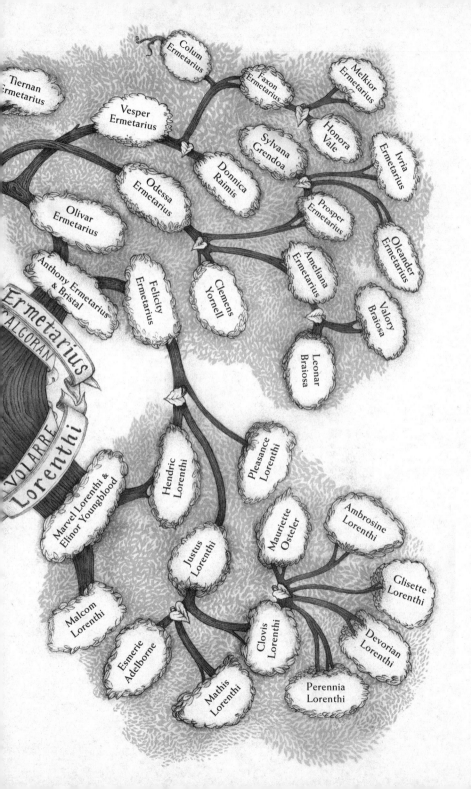

PROLOGUE

The first kingdom he destroyed by plague, the second by vanity and decadence. The third he destroyed by wielding its own craving for power.

But the new queens rebuilt the realm from its ruins.

And it will never be destroyed.

❧ ONE ❧

RAINDROPS tapped on my brow as I hastened across the soggy training grounds toward the academy. I shut out the sharp whispers pursuing me, but I couldn't outpace the enchantment that struck the small of my back.

Warmth danced between my shoulder blades as I fumbled with the ornamental clasp on my cloak, refusing to cast a sideways glance at the flames crawling up the fabric. But ribbons of heat licked through to my skin and gave me no choice but to drop my satchel full of books to roll in the mud.

My three assailants caught up to me. I lay on my back, gritting my teeth hard enough to crush them to powder.

"If you're going to spread disparaging rumors about a superior, Valory," said a wiry, wan-faced boy—my second cousin, Melkior—as he pinned my cloak under his boot, "you should mind your listener's loyalties."

I shot an exasperated look at the girl idling behind him. She was new to the elicromancer academy. I had hoped to make her feel welcome, but apparently Melkior had beaten me to it, and in return she'd given him her fealty. The offhand comment I'd made about him during Herb Magic lessons in the greenhouses had been noted.

Melkior hunkered down beside me, his eyes narrowing to slits behind a curtain of stringy dark hair. "You think I'm not worthy to be an elicromancer."

"You have your elicrin stone," I growled, ripping my cloak from under his heel. He wobbled and caught himself by planting a hand in the muck. "You've already proven yourself worthy. I simply said you make such waste of your gift."

"At least I have one to waste," Melkior sneered. He stood and signaled to the other two. I tried to scramble to my feet, but the boy, one of my dear cousin's rotating henchmen, lunged to pin my wrists. The girl made bloody hatch marks on my arms and face by merely flicking her finger through the air, as though my flesh were nothing but a scratch page in her notes dossier. My cloak and the sleeves of my gray scholar's tunic ripped to rags while I landed a glancing kick to the boy's stomach and stifled grunts of pain. I wouldn't give Melkior any more pleasure in his dark sport.

He let the torment go on much too long before he waved his friends away and drew close to touch my forehead, his milky-white elicrin stone aglow on the silver medallion around his neck. It was the only time the smirk slipped unsuspectingly off his face, when he concentrated on healing. My cuts closed up like ripped fabric under a deft seamstress's care.

I clambered up, eager to retaliate. But unlike those of the other pupils in my tier, my temper did not summon poisonous breaths from my lungs or a lightning bolt from the sky—or do anything magical at all.

Melkior knew this. His self-satisfied grin made his otherwise decent face look weaselly.

"If you're so superior, why are you still loitering around the academy?" I demanded, desperate to land a blow. "Don't you have more important things to do? Or do even the most sickly patients find your presence unbearable and beg for death to come?"

The girl swiped her hand through the air, slashing my cheek and lip. A growl rumbled deep in my throat. She cocked one thin brow as if to say she'd be happy to keep slicing me up like a juicy ham, but my cousin Ander jogged over from the nearby stables. The crest-shaped carnelian elicrin stone hanging above his navel captured the sunlight so as to twinge my pride a bit.

"Is he bothering you, Valory?" he asked.

"Is he ever not?"

Melkior's companions bowed their heads and shifted behind their leader. What was it about Ander that made him so regal and imposing? I possessed as much royal blood as he, and stood closer to claiming the throne than Melkior. But others did not instinctively bow their heads in my presence, much less do my bidding. In fact, they seemed to have no qualms about making mincemeat of me.

"I trust you will allow Valory to reach her next lecture *and* her birthday celebration on time, without further harm." Ander gave Melkior a pointed look, but it wasn't without pity. Melkior was the one cracked egg out of a dozen, the family outcast, and that hadn't changed when he became an elicromancer.

"Yes, of course. Are you quite all right, Valory? I admit that got out of hand." Melkior glared at his henchwoman as he said this. Her face flamed under Ander's gaze, and she hurried to pick up my satchel and books. She was not only a new pupil, but a peasant from a far village. Joining an elicromancer academy studded with royals was no doubt intimidating. I watched the realization dawn: she had too swiftly chosen her allies.

I would forgive her. Melkior's accomplices usually abandoned him after they realized that being royal didn't make one right.

Eyes down, she passed off my muddy satchel. Melkior placed a hand on my face to heal me, but I jerked back and spat blood onto his boot.

"Come on," Ander said, ushering me away. "You'll be late for your lecture."

We turned our backs on Melkior and his gang, strutting over the spongy grass. The rain clouds had begun to scatter, revealing a slate of cornflower blue. The palace stretched over the green fields, a pale mountain with a river running through it and wine-red flags waving sinuously from its parapets. The academic wing stood apart from the palace, joined to it by an arcade strewn with ivy.

"Melkior never learned why it was wrong to cut off a kitten's tail and regrow it," Ander said as we walked. "Since he can immediately fix something he's broken, I suppose it doesn't make sense to him not to break it."

"I don't care what does and doesn't make sense to him," I said, at last succeeding in unclasping my cloak. "His heart is a rock and his brain is a pebble. I don't see why the Water didn't just swallow him whole."

"Maybe it didn't want him." Ander smiled down at me, his fair cheeks ruddy. The levity in his gray eyes revealed that he hadn't a care in the world. He stood fourth in line to the throne of Calgoran, and these were untroubled times. "Perhaps he will have some use yet. With a gift like that, surely he will be useful whether he wants to be or not."

I shrugged, noticing as I did so that I smelled of sweat and sludge. Ander had just returned from a hunting trip planned in preparation for my birthday feast, but his dark hair still smelled of fine fragrant oils.

"Are you sure you don't want him to heal that cut?" he asked as we parted ways.

"I'd kiss a wild horse on the hoof before I'd let Melkior touch me again," I said, joining the other late pupils scurrying from one lecture to another.

Ander shook his head and strode toward the entrance to the palace, ignoring the fawning looks my peers cast his way. With a gentle dab at the stinging cut on my lip, I sauntered to my Elicrin History and Folklore lesson.

Professor Wyndwood had already begun his lecture and shot me a disapproving look from beneath feral gray eyebrows before proceeding. I draped my ruined cloak on a hook and hurried to my seat next to Knox Rodenia near the tracery windows. Most people I met were taller than me, but Knox's hefty build made him seem especially towering. He was strong yet a bit cushy, with kind green eyes, fawn skin, and agreeable features.

"I would say 'happy birthday,' but it doesn't look as if it has been," he whispered as I sank down beside him. "What happened? Was it Melkior? I swear, when I'm an elicromancer I won't let him get away with it. I don't care if he's royalty. He can't treat people like this."

"I'm fine," I said, extracting a soggy textbook from my satchel with a grimace.

"What about your ball tonight? You're going to go with your face like that and let him win?"

"He wins when anyone pays him mind," I hissed.

From the front row, Jovie Neswick sighed with annoyance at our commotion. She had never shown an aptitude for elicrin magic but was permitted to attend lectures due to her noble status and enthusiasm. Her tawny hair was always smoothed back in a painfully tight plait, pulling her parchment-pale forehead taut, and she was always, *always* taking notes. Sometimes I worried that there was no clear distinction between the Conclave's benevolence toward her and their justification for *my* presence at the academy. Hereditary magic didn't guarantee a gift—apparently—and there were plenty of people with no known elicromancer lineage who manifested gifts; but with a family tree laden with ripe magical fruit, I staked a greater claim to this seat.

The professor cleared his throat and glared at me and Knox. I clamped my lips together, tasting the tang of blood.

"Don't be like everyone else," Knox continued in a hushed voice when Professor Wyndwood resumed his lecture. "Don't absolve Melkior just because he's a Healer. I can feel the way he hurts people, tearing them down with words and bruises. I shudder to think what I'll sense from him when my gift is fully unlocked."

"Perhaps you'll better understand the motives behind the malice."

"I'm not sure I want to."

"Some Empath you are!" I teased with a wry smile that stung my split lip.

Professor Wyndwood nearly shouted to catch our attention. "Can anyone name the ages of Nissera?" he asked. "Valory?"

"The Archaic Age, the Heroic Age, the Mortal Age, and our current Age of Accords, sir."

"Very good," the professor muttered reluctantly.

"It might be sooner than we thought," Knox whispered after a moment.

"What?" I asked.

"My ceremony. The professors have agreed I'm ready for my elicrin stone. They've scheduled a hearing with the Conclave."

As we came of age, professors picked off pupils in my tier one by one like wild game on a hunt, pulling them out of courses and elevating them to a higher status. Once approved, each potential elicromancer stepped through the portal to a woodland pond rife with deadly, glorious magic. Upon contact, the Water tore each one under like a thief in the night, trapping its quarry under impenetrable ice.

If the Water considered you worthy, the ice shattered, and one of the shards became an elicrin stone offering greater power and control over your gift, as well as immortality.

If the Water didn't offer you an elicrin stone, it drowned you and swallowed every trace.

Whether the risk was worth taking was determined on a case-by-case basis by the Conclave, a collective of elicromancers and mortals who presided over the academy and acted as a gateway between us pupils and our ambitions.

"Already?" I shook away the shock and mustered a smile. "That's wonderful."

My tone contradicted my words. I glanced at the empty seat next to the window where Ivria had sat just weeks ago. Ander's older sister, my cousin and dearest friend, had been approved for her ceremony. Now the time had come for her to decide whether or not to brave the deadly Water in order to receive an elicrin stone, to test the unpredictable magic in her blood against her life.

Ander had excelled enough to obtain his stone early, while Ivria's lack of confidence had kept her at the academy well into her last term.

I wished I lacked confidence and nothing else. I knew the enchantments. I had excelled intellectually in all my studies: Astronomy, Cleromancy, Herb Magic, Curses and Forbidden Rituals, Deep Magic and Ancient Forces. Yet the absence of even a murmur of magic inside me meant I might never have the chance to put my expertise to use.

But Knox had received approval.

He and I had always been equals, never one a better student than the other. I had mastered knowledge but wavered in magic manifestation. He demonstrated a strong gift but lagged in his studies.

Now he would have his ceremony. He would touch the deadly Water, and it wouldn't kill him. He would receive an elicrin stone and become immortal the moment he reached physical maturity. He would put all the spells he had theoretically mastered into practice. To my left and my right would be nothing but empty chairs.

I would be stuck here with Jovie the mortal, and I would have no choice but to exit the academy in defeat and shame.

"What was the event that marked the end of the Heroic Age and the beginning of the Mortal Age?" Wyndwood asked. "Knox?"

"Um," Knox said.

I bit my tongue to keep from whispering the answer. Perhaps I'd given him too many answers.

"The Elicrin War?" Knox guessed.

"In a way," Wyndwood conceded. "After the peacekeeping cromancers defeated the rebels in the Elicrin War, they gave up their stones, and therefore their power and immortality. They subverted a flaw that has plagued elicromancers for ages: the temptation to think of ourselves as higher beings and use magic for personal gain rather than for the greater good. Of course, as long as the Water exists, so too will elicromancers, and so too will the temptation to subjugate mortals…but we have learned from history how to keep our kind in check."

While the professor lectured on, his rampant eyebrows helping to emphasize each point, I thought about the elicrin gifts, from prophetic visions and supernatural strength, to shapeshifting and self-duplication. There were so many gifts, so many flashing shades of jewel-like elicrin stones hanging from hundreds of throats.

Please, I thought, imploring the ancestral magic in my blood to catch. *Please let me be powerful.*

After the lecture, I crossed the arcade to the palace and was admitted by a stern-faced guard. Folding my cloak to avoid leaving a muddy trail on the crimson carpet, I ascended a grand staircase leading to the private quarters and traversed a corridor with portraits of dozens of members of the Ermetarius family. I wondered what it would be like to have lived over a century ago, during the Mortal Age, before elicromancy training became requisite education for the royal sons and daughters of the realm—before all three kingdoms in Nissera had established a sturdy peace. Back then

ture, and magic was a bright gleam in an otherwise

...er than a cloud of failed expectations hovering over

...ached the suite I shared with Ivria, I went to rap on the door that led to her private chamber, but paused just before my knuckles struck wood. My cousin had lately been more solemn than a grieving widow. She had not yet set a date for her Water ceremony. Most pupils began planning it the very hour they received approval from the Conclave.

Crossing our common room, I spotted Calanthe and trailed my fingertips along her wiry coat of hair. Ivria's gray deerhound, a gift from her brother, Ander, could often be found reposing in gentle dignity on her pallet by the fire—at least, when she wasn't tearing across the palace grounds or basking in the attention of her personal maid.

I opened the doors to my chamber, which held a grand bed that could have comfortably fit eight of me, though somehow I always found myself at its edge. Noticing my birthday gown at the front of the deep oak wardrobe, I felt a thrill of excitement.

Ivria's preferences often superseded my own when it came to my attire, resulting in the royal clothiers knotting me up in yellows, pinks, and periwinkles come spring. Winter tended to be an affair of deep-toned velvets and glistening jewels. But on my birthday, Ivria had made certain I would wear something I adored. A sheer silver material gathered over a cream silk underlayer, and from the plunging neckline to the shoulders of the gown, crystals clung to colorless gossamer.

"Do you like it?" Ivria appeared in the doorway, her raven hair tumbling around her shoulders. Her normally sharp gray eyes were as obscure as fogged windowpanes.

"It's breathtaking," I admitted.

The sunset was a simmering pool of blood orange through the west windows, and for a moment my cousin paused within the glow. When she stepped into my room, an ashen tinge washed across her porcelain face. She sat on the corner of my bed with a sigh, her lace dressing gown rippling around her feet. "Sit with me," she prompted.

When I obliged, she clasped my hands in hers, her knuckles turning white as bone. "You know you are a sister to me," she said. "Closer, even. We don't fight as sisters do. You are my dearest friend and our souls are entwined forever."

"I know that," I said, freeing one of my hands to close over hers in reassurance. "You look pale. Are you worried about your ceremony? You know you have nothing to fear."

"Of course not." She dismissed the notion with a wave. "I only wanted to wish you a happy birthday, properly, before all the commotion." She plucked a gob of dried mud from my braid and at long last noticed the swollen cut on my lip. "Melkior?" she asked, her misty eyes flashing like blades fresh from a forge. "I can make him heal you—"

"No, no," I muttered, daubing again at the bruised lump, which tasted of metal. "Ellen likes having her work cut out for her."

Ivria laughed. "I ought to get dressed," she said, then squeezed my hand and floated out of my bedchamber. I fought the urge to coax her back so I could somehow elicit another laugh. I hadn't heard her laugh for weeks.

But we'd be expected in the receiving hall soon. I would corner her after the celebration and pry her fears from her, remind her how fortunate she should feel to have earned access to the Water. I would do so more gently than Uncle Prosper and Aunt Sylvana, who grew agitated over their daughter's tarrying.

Ellen, my maid, attacked Melkior's handiwork with powder, concealing the swollen cuts as best she could. She rushed to plait my straight chestnut hair, the hair that made me stand out like a daisy in a rose garden of royal relatives. Most members of the Ermetarius line were tall and fair-skinned with ink-dark, wavy hair, including my mother. I would have felt like an impostor if my mossy eyes hadn't so matched those of my great-great-grandfather King Anthony, whose handsome portrait graced the corridor.

While I admired my gown in the mirror, Ivria returned, clad in deep purple silk embellished with fabric petals. Her curls had been painstakingly arranged with sapphire hairpins. She held an ornate wooden box tied with a blue ribbon—my favorite color—and donned a soft smile.

"Something you've always wanted," she said. But instead of offering it to me, she slid the familiar box onto the mantel. "Since you've waited this long, you can wait until after the party."

"Why? I already know what it is," I teased, eagerly imagining the intricate amethyst diadem, an enchanted family heirloom I'd always wanted to inherit. Grandmother Odessa had given it to Ivria instead.

"It doesn't match your dress." Ivria linked her arm in mine. "And you don't want to know what everyone truly thinks about you on your birthday, do you?"

My heart pattered. I both desired and feared the truth-seeing diadem, whose power derived from the retired elicrin stone nesting amid its silver whorls. With it, I might unearth the deepest insecurities of cruel people like Melkior, and practice wielding the knowledge to gain respect. But I might also confirm what I sensed from my family, something they all denied: that only prestige and power could earn their deepest acceptance—that I, not Melkior, was the cracked egg.

"You could have just let me borrow it," I said. "Grandmother Odessa won't be pleased you gave it away."

"She won't be pleased to hear you call her Grandmother either," Ivria said. And then her tone darkened a shade. "You deserve it more than I do."

As her gaze grew misty and distant again, I wondered: Was there something my cousin hoped I would see?

Or, in making me wait to open the gift, was there something she hoped I wouldn't?

❦ TWO ❦

WHEN we reached the receiving hall, Ivria hurried ahead, leaving me to make an ostentatious entrance as the guest of honor.

As the herald announced my name and I stepped through the double doors into the gleaming marble hall, hundreds of noble guests paused to observe my dress and hairstyle and murmur among themselves. Anytime Ivria made an entrance, the revelry would fall quiet and intakes of breath could be heard echoing off the pillars of the vast ballroom.

Garlands of blue delphinium decorated every archway and coiled up the bases of the shimmering gold candelabras. I felt so small walking across the glistening tiles, even though I was seventeen today and no longer considered a child.

I was reminded too keenly of this as I took my place across from my mother, Ameliana, and my field instructor, the cold, mountainous Victor, both of whom had expected me to demonstrate an elicrin gift well before my seventeenth birthday.

"Happy birthday, dearest," my mother said, her eyes twinkling over her wine goblet. Her gaze snagged on the powdered cuts on my face, but she only pursed her plump lips.

Becoming an elicromancer had halted her aging so that she looked but a few years my senior. I had never thought much of my relatives being older than their appearances would suggest—at least, not until recently. Coming of age made the subtle urgency to enter the Water ripen inside me.

I smiled at her and diverted my attention to the extravagant spread. My mouth watered over goose simmering in spices, sturgeon cooked in parsley and vinegar, stewed venison, honey-mulled wine, and rosewater-poached plums. But a soft tinkling drew my attention to the king's table on the dais.

Most kings who had reigned for decades would exhibit signs of aging: peppered hair, wrinkles, or a substantial gut. But Tiernan Ermetarius hardly looked a day over twenty-two. Recently, the Realm Alliance had determined that elicromancers would be permitted to stretch their immortality for five decades before surrendering their stones to age as mortals.

The light from the enormous chandelier glistened over the king's thick, dark curls as he stood and raised his goblet in my direction. "Tonight, we gather to celebrate the coming of age of my great-niece, Valory Braiosa," he said. "May your heart be as just, your mind as keen, and your spirit as joyful as your life is long."

"As your life is long," the crowd echoed, lifting their drinks in my honor.

At the table on the far side of the king's dais, Melkior kept his glass raised long enough for me to notice his vainglorious smirk. Despite the prickling of my split lip, a small burst of sympathy tested its wings inside me. Melkior's mother had died in childbirth, leaving his father to unfairly weigh that cost against the value of his son each day.

I took a sip of red wine to hide my grimace and broke our gaze. Ander, who sat to my right, waited until I had finished serving myself to begin heaping food on his plate. "Quite the toast," he said sardonically, carving a bite of venison with the stoic pride of a hunter who had felled the beast himself. "A rare show of emotion."

I laughed. King Tiernan tended to be brusque and taciturn, especially toward me, his great-niece, who stood only sixth in line for his throne, behind my mother as fifth—and that was without consideration to Ivria's and Ander's respective unborn children. "Right. I think I saw a sheen of tears," I added. "He was one sniffle away from naming me his heir apparent."

"Oh, you three," Mother said with feigned sternness. She'd included Ivria out of habit, but when I glanced from Ander to his older sister, I found her lips mashed together and no trace of humor in her countenance. Catching my concerned stare, Ivria stabbed a plum and nibbled dispassionately at the skin.

"Ander," I whispered. "What's wrong with her?"

"What do you mean?" he asked. Had he truly not noticed his sister's recent sullenness, the dread that seemed to stalk her like a shadow? He looked at Ivria and then concluded, "She probably laced her bodice too tight to eat anything. Wouldn't be the first time."

"Oleander," my mother chided, absentmindedly adjusting the gold chain that held her teal elicrin stone.

Ander succumbed and leaned toward his sister. "I'd wager Lord Davener brought you a grander gift than he brought Valory, even though it's *her* birthday," he said, gesturing at the gift table. "It wouldn't be the boldest thing he's done since he began courting you."

Ivria didn't acknowledge his attempt at cursory conversation. Her hand trembled as she lifted a cup of water to her lips.

"Speaking of courting," my mother said, "Valory, would you

please respond to the advances of young Lord Rodenia tonight? You're embarrassing him and yourself."

She made a request rather than a demand. She had to be careful with demands, as her power as an Imperator made those around her suggestible to them. She chose each word vigilantly before she spoke, and was often ordered by the Conclave to help settle mortal disputes or force a criminal to come peacefully into custody.

"Knox is my friend," I said. "My practice partner in combat lessons. Just because we're fond of each other doesn't mean—"

"Valory," Ander interrupted, his voice flat. "Come, don't be naïve."

"Victor," I said, turning to the large, quiet man. "Tell them the truth. Knox and I are merely fellow pupils who—"

"I'm your instructor, not a gossiping lady's maid," he responded.

I sighed at his tone, which left no room for argument. Only my mother could pry a word of affection from him. As a child, I'd admired Victor, how pragmatic he was about teaching me the principles of magical combat. He never treated me differently from the other students despite the fact that I hadn't manifested a gift.

But a few years ago—not long after we learned that my aimlessly wandering father had died of wounds sustained in a bear attack—I began noticing the looks my mother and Victor exchanged. And then I noticed their long absences from court events, her sudden refusal to let me sleep in her chamber even though I felt as though grief would swallow me whole.

Victor didn't have a title; therefore, my mother couldn't marry him without abdicating her bid for the throne—and mine—but that hardly discouraged their involvement.

"Don't make me command you to dance with him," my mother went on, half teasing. "If you don't, it will be a clear signal of disinterest."

"Fine," I conceded. "Since it's my birthday, I'll be passed around like the last bottle of mead in a siege regardless."

Indeed, before I could polish off dessert, I got swept away in a sea of dresses and slippers and shining boots, anchored only by sweaty palms and arms encircling my waist. Looking up to find Knox as my fourth partner was nothing short of a relief.

"You look beautiful," he proclaimed, breathless. I wanted to believe it was from dancing.

"Thank you," I said, but my inflection hiked to a question. We both cleared our throats.

"I know you didn't want to hear my news today," he said, studying my tactfully covered cut.

"That's not true at all," I scoffed.

"I'm an Empath, remember?"

I sighed. "I'm sorry. It's not that I'm not happy for you. I am."

"I know," he said with a sideways grin. "Buried beneath the bitterness."

"I am most certainly not bitter!"

He cocked an eyebrow.

"If being your friend after you receive your elicrin stone means having no secrets, I'm not sure I can suffer your company."

He rearranged our grasp so that our fingers interlaced and our palms met like lovers brushing cheek-to-cheek. A bright feeling raced through my gut, and the soft groove of my hand dampened. "What if we felt no need to keep secrets from each other?" he asked.

"What if we were to grow closer after I leave the academy instead of drifting apart?"

I swallowed and fixed my stare on his shoulder rather than his face. I had always liked Knox. But we were friends, nothing more. My thoughts and dreams fixated on one thing: inviting some hint of power to the surface and obtaining the immortality that would allow me to welcome each passing year instead of dreading it. If I did not receive approval from the Conclave by the end of my term at the academy, I had decided I would move to Darmeska to live with my late father's side of the family in their ancient mountain fortress. I knew I could survive the cold, the lack of palace intrigue, and the quiet of the hallowed halls—but not if I first attached myself to Knox.

"Do you think you would want that?" he prodded gently.

Ever superstitious about voicing my fear of failure, I dodged. "Um...yes, of course," I muttered in a rush. "I would like us to remain friends. I'm sure you will have so much to teach me, once you..." I trailed off.

Knox filled his broad chest with a deep breath, understanding the emotional barriers I was erecting between us.

"Are you afraid?" I asked just to close the gaping silence. "Of the ceremony?"

He shook his head. "I may be, when I'm staring at the Water. But not now."

Are you afraid? My question seemed to linger even after he answered it. Ivria's bone-white knuckles and haunted gaze loomed in my thoughts.

The fog in her eyes—it was fear.

She had held my hands. She had told me she loved me.

She'd given me a prized heirloom with the murk of melancholy behind her eyes. Each separate action did not strike me as strange, but together...together, they amounted to some sort of quiet farewell.

The song fortuitously drew to a close. Knox seemed to sense the worry spearing my chest and released me without question.

I stalked back to the table and found Jovie Neswick in Ander's seat. She wore a black dress with golden embroidered panels and an emerald the size of my fist at her throat. Flashy, nonmagical gems were the fashion among mortal courtiers, who tended to imitate immortals. But I suspected Jovie's was, in fact, a retired elicrin stone. Once the possessor of an elicrin stone died, the artifact often took on a second life as a sort of trinket. Some stones gave luck. Others might help you find love or protect your family. Most simply dimmed out completely after the death of their wearer, magical no longer.

"Have you seen Ivria?" I asked, searching for my cousin's eye-catching gown amid the revelers.

"She left a moment ago," Jovie said flatly. I followed her gaze and found Ander dancing with an elicromancer named Elythia Carrow. She was merry and lovely, with shiny brunette curls, a plump build, and full, red lips. "They're all so perfect, aren't they?" Jovie remarked, clasping the emerald between her thumb and ink-stained forefinger. "Ever young, beautiful, powerful."

"Elicromancers have problems just like everyone else," I said. "They're not perfect."

"You'd know better than any other mortal," she admitted.

Mortal. The word pricked. "Do you know where Ivria went?"

Jovie shook her head, fixing her round amber eyes on me. "She said she wanted to be alone. Do you want help looking for her?"

"No, thank you. If she said she wanted to be alone, then—"

"Then she probably meant completely alone," Jovie muttered, a dark look passing over her face. Perhaps it was envy of Ivria, or of my nearness to her, or both.

I brushed her off, knowing Ivria's edict didn't apply to me, and hurried out of the receiving hall. Outside the doors, I crossed paths with Uncle Prosper, who smelled of a successful hunting trip, like crisp woods and strong spirits. With dark hair, gray eyes, and a rigidly handsome face, Ivria and Ander's father looked similar to his uncle King Tiernan, but emitted warmth and vigor where Tiernan exuded ice and indifference. Prosper wore a yellow-orange elicrin stone that allowed him to emit a bright light so powerful it could permanently blind onlookers.

"Uncle Prosper, have you seen Ivria?" I asked.

"She mentioned she was feeling ill. She may have retired early. I'm sorry I missed the toast...I'm certain it was quite touching." Uncle Prosper squeezed my shoulder and offered a lighthearted wink before proceeding to the celebration.

Just as I lifted my layers of skirts to mount the curving marble steps, I noticed a glimmer on the wine-colored carpet down the west corridor and found one of Ivria's delicate sapphire hairpins. She hadn't returned to our rooms, then. I continued westward, brushing past pairs of guards clad in red tunics, each pointing me farther west when I inquired as to Ivria's whereabouts.

At the end of the corridor, I nearly tripped over Ivria's heeled purple slippers. I removed my own and hurried to reach the double oak doors leading out of the palace to the academic wing. The guards swung them open and I crossed beneath the stone arcade, bracing against the lingering chill of a waning winter.

The windows of dormitories occupied by nonroyal students glowed above. After a long period without much magic, the return of elicromancy to Nissera had stimulated a reawakening across the realm. Even in the most remote villages, you might find one or two folks with a promising elicrin gift. "Magic calls unto magic," my great-grandfather Olivar said the day he established the academy. "And we no longer fear it. We welcome it here, and we must teach the next generation of elicromancers to use it with integrity."

Magic these days was a neat and tidy thing, bound with ribbons and boxed up like the gift on my mantel. Yet I could feel the pull of a savage old magic strengthening with each step.

Laughter and lively conversations drifted from the upper stories, but when I found the door to the academy unlocked—and another one of Ivria's pins at the threshold—I proceeded into ghostly-quiet corridors and lecture halls. The academy was nowhere near as lavish as the royal residence. Metal sconces rather than ornate candelabras jutted from the walls. Instead of luxurious carpet, the surface underfoot was cold stone.

I called Ivria's name. Only my echo answered.

The halls that seemed so cramped between lectures now yawned, labyrinths of infinite shadow. Had I possessed an elicrin stone, I could have lit the darkness with an easy enchantment or whispered the lanterns aflame. But I was forced to feel my way along the smooth walls, listening to the distant laughter of the guards who stalked the academy halls at night. The sloshing of wineskins explained the ease with which Ivria had snuck inside.

The deeper I wandered, the more keenly I sensed an ominous presence.

A streak of white swept past me with a whoosh of soft air. I gasped, fancying a cloaked intruder in our midst, footfalls trained and silent—even though logic insisted it was only Professor Strather's white cat, known to roam the halls. A shiver scuttled between my shoulders, but it was only my imagination.

Yet the pull of ancient magic thrumming around me was real, and grew stronger when I found a certain door ajar, one that nearly always remained locked.

It was the room that held the portal to the Water.

Once, the Water had been difficult to reach, moving around the Forest of the West Fringe, cloaking itself, a capricious force of nature. But King Tiernan, a Portimacian, had erected a doorway spanning the distance and uncertainty. Now, mortals and pupils need not travel across the kingdom to hold an elicrin rite of passage. One could take a single step through the portal and arrive at the Water's edge. I'd passed through for Ander's ceremony just last year.

But there was a drawback to the convenience, which I'd never before pondered: immense danger lurked mere steps away.

The door creaked as if to contest as I pushed it fully open and cast a timorous glance inside. The circular chamber held no windows, yet muted moonlight spilled through the shadows. It came from the archway across from me, which led to a dense forest swathed in snow.

Ivria stood at the threshold of the portal, her graceful hands clinging to the frame. The shrill squeak of the door had announced my entrance, but she didn't acknowledge me.

"Ivria," I said. Her name left my lips a nervous melody.

She turned, exposing her delicate profile.

"What are you doing here?" I asked.

"I don't want them to see," she whispered.

"See what?"

She faced the portal again. Trepidation tingled through my limbs.

"You're missing my party," I said, hoping my insouciant tone would somehow reel her back to me.

"You don't care about the party," she said quietly. A stinging wind from the other side stirred the hem of her gown.

"I care about you being there."

"You can be at my party," Ivria said. "You can be the only one."

She took a deep breath. I lunged to grab her by the waist, but she had already stepped through the portal. The silk laces of her bodice slithered through my fingers.

I stepped through after her.

The sensations hit me in swift succession: cold beneath my feet, cold flurrying around me and landing on my eyelashes and hair, cold intimately caressing the skin exposed by my gown. The fragile smell of fresh snow brought back piercing memories of the months I'd spent wandering in the wilderness alongside my father, with only worn furs and shuddering flames to keep warm. He had spirited me away from my royal relatives, hoping I could live a life like his.

A pure white shroud covered the clearing and the surrounding woods. Several of these trees had once entwined to form a gate meant to keep out the unworthy, but the Conclave had done away with that. *They* were the ones who decided who reached the Water. Any fool willing to take her chances without their say-so deserved her fate.

My cousin traipsed, barefooted, to the shore of the black pond. She lined up her toes against the edge and let the icy wind toy with her hair, obscuring her features.

"Ivria," I whispered, softer than before. This place was both menacing and marked by ethereal beauty. I had only ever come here with a crowd of people in the daytime. But in the dark, it felt as if a mere sigh would echo for days and shake the snow from shadows best left undisturbed. "You don't have to do this. You're nervous. You're frightened. You're clearly not prepared for this."

"Will I ever be?" she asked.

"You don't have to be. No one said you *have* to do this."

"But I do. Or I will grow old while everyone stays the same. I'll shame our family."

Each word pierced my heart. I hadn't known Ivria harbored the same fears as I.

I took a step closer. The snow stung the tender pads of my feet. "Then do it properly," I answered. "You've received permission from the Conclave. Ander will want to be there, and Uncle Prosper and Aunt Sylvana. Grandmother Odessa will mount your head in the receiving hall if you don't invite her."

"I don't want them to see," she repeated.

"See what?"

Her lucid gray eyes met mine. My heart dove to my gut.

She didn't want them to see her die.

❧ THREE ❧

"IVRIA, you're not going to die," I said, chancing another step toward the magnificent presence looming before us.

"You know my gift," she said, facing the Water again. "I sense danger."

"Sensing danger and sensing death are not the same."

"I knew your father was going to die. No word from Leonar Braiosa for over a year as he rambled through the Brazor Mountains, and yet I knew the exact moment."

The cold felt like knife tips, though perhaps it was the pain I'd trained myself to tuck away like a broken, precious figurine.

"Let's go home, Ivria," I said, glancing at the dark archway behind us. Soon we could be warming before a crackling fire, explaining ourselves to relatives who would scold me for absconding from my own celebration. "Please?"

Ivria's pale features softened as she turned to me, eyes like twin moons in the night. I held out my hand to her.

But instead of stepping closer to grasp it, she extended her leg and pointed her toes, soaking the hem of her gown. Before I could even flinch, she skimmed along the surface of the Water, creating a tiny ripple.

A gasp tore out of my lips, jarring against the otherworldly silence.

After a few dreadful beats, an unseen force from below seized

Ivria by the ankle and dragged her into the depths of the Water, as merciless as a predator swallowing prey.

I shrieked and raced to the edge, my impulse to go after her warring with my knowledge of the Water and its ways. At first, the Water treated its chosen ones the same as the ones it would destroy: it pulled them under and trapped them beneath a solid sheet of ice.

Wait. See.

The ice began to form at the outer edges of the pond. Just as it had for Ander, it would emit a thousand glittering colors, then burst into a thousand shards. One of them would be an elicrin stone, which Ivria would retrieve and wear at her sternum all her long days like a prized royal jewel. A constellation of spells and enchantments would supplement her innate gift. She would be powerful, beautiful, unstoppable, a force of good in the world.

Wait. See.

Ivria was an Augurer, and only a fool would refuse to heed her warnings about impending danger. But her acute gift was exactly why she deserved to be an elicromancer in the first place. It was the reason she had received permission to try. It was the reason she wouldn't die.

Wait . . .

An unwelcome irony impaled my reasoning: If Ivria's spirit was attuned to imminent danger and, apparently, tragedy, then her belief concerning her own fate could be trusted. She would die. And if her intuition could not be trusted, then perhaps she did not deserve the Conclave's approval—which also meant she could die.

As the sheet of ice crept over the surface, hemming Ivria underneath, her last look of resignation haunted me.

I shot across the glistening barrier toward the black liquid center. My stockings offered little traction or protection from the blistering cold. I slipped and fell but managed to launch myself toward
the shrinking aperture, sliding on my knees and skidding to a stop
nearly within arm's reach of it.

A pale hand shot out of the Water, grappling with the slick ice. I
lunged for it, flattening my body against the surface and stretching
to clasp Ivria's shivering fingers, but the tips of mine barely touched
hers before hers slipped away.

I scrambled closer. My arm shot into the freezing Water of its
own volition to numbly grope for a limb or a handful of thick hair.

I latched on to a thin wrist, but the relief was ephemeral. The
ice was still closing in.

"Ivria!" I screamed, pounding my free hand on the rock-solid
barrier. But I knew, as I had always known, that the only force capable of breaking it was the elicrin power of the one trapped beneath
the surface.

The ice closed around my forearm, clamping down. I cried out
in pain but kept a desperate grip on Ivria.

Hold on, hold on, I commanded, but I knew that if I held on, this
unforgiving force of nature would break my bones. I would freeze
and die alone.

And whether I held on or not, Ivria was utterly at the Water's
mercy.

I released her and yanked my arm out of the Water, hoping for
the best. In the midst of the pounding suspense, an oblique realization struck me: I had touched the Water.

A bright light burgeoned at the center of the ice. I laid my hands flat on the surface as the light spread, seeping out around me. Was it for Ivria or for me? Which of us would prove worthy to receive an elicrin stone—and in so doing, survive?

Was it possible that both of us would?

A loud crack made me jump to my feet and whip around. A small fracture began to crawl through the ice behind me, growing and forking out like the roots of an ancient tree. The lines slithered and spread until they surrounded me and the only patch of solid ice resided just beneath my feet.

The cracks built to a loud rumble, barreling through the quiet night. I could feel the Water roiling and churning, its energy palpable, restless. I braced myself just in time.

Finally, the Water erupted around me like an inverted waterfall deluging into the black sky. My pedestal was a tiny vessel in its midst, and yet the Water did not toss me to and fro. As the deafening waves surged upward around me, my island held steady.

After what seemed an age, silence descended again, soft as a dove's wing. I inhaled deeply. The winter air burned my lungs, but it served to remind me that I was alive.

My eyes roved over the landscape. It had changed.

There was no Water.

All around my island lay smooth, black rock gleaming in the moonlight.

Survivors of the Water had explained what it was like under the surface. There should have been weeds and dirt, terrain one might find at the bottom of an ordinary lake. But there was only bald rock mirroring the lucent stars.

I didn't have long to take in the sight. A dense, sparkling fog drifted down and settled over the world like a fleece blanket. It wandered over my skin and sank into my pores. I sucked in a breath and watched the fog wind and coil its way toward my mouth.

As I absorbed it, I felt a deep, dormant part of me come alive with warmth, with light, with…power. It was as though the sky had soaked up the Water's magic and wrung it out for me in a soft mist.

For so long, I'd waited for my power to manifest, to strike something inside me like flint and steel. Now sparks flared within my spirit.

This was what magic felt like.

But ice snaked through my veins at the sight of Ivria lying motionless on the black rock, the silken folds of her dress sprawling like the petals of a crushed violet.

In the cold silence, the merciless truth struck me. I opened my mouth to scream her name, but no sound transpired. The pain tightened like a rope around my throat.

I climbed down from the slick block of ice, clambering over the sloping landscape to collect her in my arms. I pressed the cold fingers of each of her hands open, looking for an elicrin stone. One of the broken ice shards was supposed to be an elicrin stone in her grasp. She was *meant* to be an elicromancer.

Mashing my ear to her chest, I listened for a rhythm. But I could hear only my own blood pounding in my head.

"Ivria," I said, turning her face to me. Her black eyelashes fanned out around once-bright eyes. Beneath the rouge, her lips were bluish. I could feel the warmth leaving her cheeks with each fleeting moment.

Ivria had always shielded me and cared for me. When my mother had stopped dabbing away my tears, when she had stopped tucking me in to sleep, Ivria had not. But this time she'd needed me. And I couldn't save her.

I touched my forehead to hers. Hot tears welled over and slipped onto her skin. "What happened?" I whispered. "You were meant for this." A sob ripped out of my chest. I tore my gaze from her face and looked at the tranquil wood. "What happened?"

My hoarse refrain roared out from the clearing, shaking the boughs of the trees. Their branches and trunks twisted in on themselves and withered. The foliage on the evergreens drooped low, faded to brown, and drifted to the covering of fresh snow. I stared, aghast.

"Valory?"

Ander's call brought comfort and despair in equal measure. As long as I clung to Ivria, as long as it was just the two of us, I resided in my own universe of agony. Now I would have to invite others into this secret place, to expose and confront my wounds, to explain that I had touched the Water and survived without an elicrin stone.

I felt the warmth of Ander beside me. Gently, he peeled my hands away from his sister's corpse and went through familiar motions: searching for an elicrin stone, listening for a faint heartbeat. As he wept, he pleaded with her to come back.

Soon other figures became visible in the starlight. Some of them hesitated before stepping onto the rocky wasteland where the Water had once lain. One of them tossed a cloak around my shoulders and helped me stand.

As steady hands guided me back through the portal, I cast a

final look over my shoulder at Ivria. The sugary sound of her laugh tiptoed into my mind. I imagined capturing it and stowing it away in a snug, safe corner of my memories, where it would burrow deep, unthreatened by the passage of time.

For I could live a very long life.

Within the instant it took to return to the academy from the snowy woods, I was swept up in another dance. A partner with blurry features led me down the corridor and passed me off to another, and another. Each moved with more urgency than the last. My abandoned silver slippers were nothing but a whirling streak on the bloodred carpet in the palace.

I survived. But I don't have an elicrin stone. What happened?

Back in my bedchamber, the dance continued, coinciding with the rhythm of my hammering heart. I raised my arms so Ellen could trade my wet gown for a nightdress, stepped out of my stockings one foot at a time, and plunked down in a chair by the hearth. Someone asked me a question, but, like a shadow in the corner of my eye, I couldn't quite catch it.

"*Matara liss,*" my mother hissed, lighting the fire with words in the old tongue. As the warmth thawed my fingers and toes, I overheard her and Victor's whispered speculations.

"What happened?" my mother asked.

"One or both of them defied the tenets."

"Is she an elicromancer? I don't see an elicrin stone."

"Ask her yourself."

"She's stunned." My mother's hands fluttered nervously before landing at her temples. "We'll wait until she comes back to herself."

Servants brushed by me, stoking the fire and keeping their heads down. Ellen pitched a blanket over me and tucked in the hem with meticulous concern. Before she bustled away, the older woman looked on me with crinkled eyes and peeled a lock of damp hair from my cheek, tucking it back into my plait.

I felt a warm, hairy snout press into my palm and found Calanthe on the floor at my side. A soft whimper in her throat cut through the commotion of servants brushing in and out. The deerhound's ocher eyes moored my spirit.

"Valory." My mother's voice drew my gaze upward. King Tiernan stood in my doorway.

"Your Majesty," I croaked, standing to draw a curtsy.

His black brows dipped over eyes gleaming with questions. "A private word, please."

The gentle request sent servants and nobles alike scurrying from the room. My mother lingered, crushing her lips together until they lost color. "Uncle Tiernan—" she started, but he turned his stern features on her. With a rueful look, she darted out like the rest.

As she shut the door behind her, a last lone shiver traced its way up my back.

"Please, sit," the King of Calgoran said.

I stumbled back and sank onto the soft bed. Calanthe curled up at my feet, impervious to the commands of rulers.

Tiernan gripped the high back of the chair and slid it away from the fire before settling in across from me. I fixed my eyes on the maroon brocade velvet of his doublet, the same one he had worn at my party. Not even an hour could have passed since I'd fled the great hall in pursuit of Ivria. Had rumors of her fate already perforated the revelry?

He swept back a wayward dark wave and leaned forward. "What happened?" he asked calmly.

I expected to choke on the explanation, to sob uncontrollably, but the words flowed as freely as my tears. "Ivria snuck away from the feast to go to the Water. She believed it would kill her and she didn't want it to happen at her ceremony, in front of everyone. I followed her. I tried to stop her. And then something happened and the Water just...was gone."

"Is she the only one who touched it?"

"No. I tried to pull her out before the ice closed in."

He nodded slowly. "But she touched it of her own volition?"

A wave of indignation tore my gaze from the gold cross-stitching on his collar. I looked straight into his eyes, but they harbored no accusation. I didn't know much about the man behind the crown, yet his reputation was that of an impartial ruler. His blue elicrin stone, set in a gold medallion casing of twisted vines, seemed to reflect its wearer's cool temper.

"Yes, she touched it of her own volition." I cleared my throat. I could not, would not, dissolve into a helpless puddle until he was gone.

King Tiernan stood, paced to the door and back, and noticed the unopened gift from Ivria on the mantel. He tilted his head and lifted the box. Surely he wouldn't be so audacious as to open a birthday gift. Yet he untied the ribbon, let it glide to the floor. "The amethyst diadem?" he ventured.

I nodded, clenching my teeth. The anger that rattled through me lost its nerve and came out as a sigh.

The lid of the box creaked as he opened it. "Your great-great-great-grandmother's," he said, removing the sparkling silver circlet with its bulging jewel. It reminded me of a faraway time, of old magic and love poems lost to the ages. "Did you know this gem was Callista's elicrin stone?"

"Yes," I whispered, my bravery bolstered. "Its remaining traces of magic allow the one who touches it to more easily see the truth. So then, do you believe me, Your Majesty?" I longed for him to leave me in peace.

"Yes," he said. "Yes, even without this, I believe you. Though..." He trailed off, laying the diadem back in the velvet-lined box. He closed it and replaced it on the mantel. I stared down at my shaking hands as tears clouded my vision. "The trees surrounding the Water. They're destroyed too."

"I think...I think I did that," I said, pressing a palm to my heart as though I could isolate the grief there.

King Tiernan nodded again, curtly. "There will be a hearing the day after the funeral."

"A hearing?" I murmured.

"When an elicromancer or pupil breaks a tenet, there must be a hearing. May I make a suggestion I believe will benefit you? Give up your elicrin stone now. Don't wait for the Conclave to confiscate it. It will paint you as cooperative."

I tried to swallow but felt as though a lump of gravel had lodged in my throat. "I didn't receive an elicrin stone, Your Majesty."

King Tiernan's charcoal brows snapped together. Touching

the Water could lead to one of only two fates: death or elicro-mancy. There was no between, no half measure. Yet here I sat, empty-handed, no jewel glinting at my breastbone or hiding in my pocket.

An excruciating moment of silence passed and a dark fear began to ferment inside me, souring my stomach. The elicrin stone's function was to distill unmanageable hints of magic into a more potent magic that could be commanded and directed. The spells in Old Nisseran interacted with the stone to do the possessor's will. Without an elicrin stone...was there any hope of controlling whatever force had found its way inside me?

The king swept out of the room. As he exited the antechamber, I saw a flash of dark red tunics and glinting swords: guards. Either the king or the Conclave had posted guards outside my door.

My rigid posture collapsed and I lost myself in the roaring fire, whispering, "Ivria, what have we done?"

❦ FOUR ❦

PRING was cruel to come so early. During Ivria's funeral, the green-clad palace gardens smelled of sunshine and perfume. Warmth bore down on the shoulders of my black gown, but it made the rest of me shiver. Winter still lingered in every shadow.

My father's funeral had been in the dead of winter at his childhood home in the Brazor Mountains. I remembered being more preoccupied with the bitter cold slicing through my layers of fur and wool than I was with my grief. The blaze of his pyre had been, oddly, a welcome relief. Only when I found myself alone in the halls of Darmeska did the hollowness consume me, and by then it was too late to say a meaningful farewell.

My knuckles lost color as I gripped the balustrade of the bridge crossing the Roac River. The bright ribbon of water stretched away from the palace into the city, thinning before disappearing amid the distant shops and houses of Arna. Crowds of mourners lined up along the banks as far as I could see.

My mother and Victor stood at my left, their expressions somber as they stared over ivy-laced walls and meandering paths. On my right stood Ander with his parents and Grandmother Odessa. Uncle Prosper gripped Aunt Sylvana's elbow, stabilizing her as she shook with sobs.

I tore my eyes away from them and looked at the glistening surface below. Unlike the calm but deadly Water—the Water that had somehow evaporated—the Roac River bubbled and coursed and teemed with life.

The regrets swirling around the fresh memory of Ivria's death needled my raw, aching heart, as did the fear of the power inside me. In the past few days, my tears had singed holes in my sheets, left rust stains on the tiles of my room. I'd tried to use the simplest elicrin spell to light a fire, but it hadn't worked, and my subsequent frustration turned the grate and pokers to ash and smoke. I didn't know what sort of creature I had become. With outlandish magic and no elicrin stone, what *was* I?

The musicians' strings and voices finally tapered to silence as the long dirge ended. King Tiernan, who stood at the center of the bridge, began the blessing and a chorus of voices joined in. "May light surround you. May goodness follow you wherever you go."

I closed my eyes. Back upstream, where the river passed through an arcade of marble beneath the palace, the men holding Ivria's raft would now react to their cue and release it to the current.

The river lapped at the vessel's flanks as it made its slow journey underneath the bridge a few moments later. When I opened my eyes, I saw the pointed bow of the boat and the bundled wood that would become kindling on Ivria's funeral pyre. Then I saw the skirt of her silver gown, her hands crossed at her navel, the apples of her cheeks dusted with pink. A silver circlet ornamented her dark curls. She was the same—just as beautiful. And because of that sameness, I didn't think to trace her every feature until she had already passed by and hundreds of handfuls of white rose petals had launched into the air.

Downriver, beyond the crowds and the soaring flowers, the

undertaker and his assistants would halt the boat and burn her body on a pyre. She would return to us as ash.

The raft drifted away, vanishing amid the mourners who had lined up for a final glimpse of the beautiful princess.

The crowd around me began to migrate from the gardens toward the palace steps. I scooped up my skirts and turned, feeling the eyes of every palace guard upon me. My mother perched her hand like a friendly sparrow on my shoulder. "The hearing will clear all of this up," she said.

I moved with the throng, watching Ander's dark head bob above the sea of people. We hadn't seen each other in the days since the Water.

Once we reached the great hall, the family formed a receiving line. I attempted to press closer to my cousin, to draw from his strength and offer him a measure of mine. But Grandmother Odessa and my mother found their way between us. And then came face after face, hundreds of respects paid in whispered tones of sorrow.

Many of our elicromancer relatives, however distant, had materialized in Arna for the funeral. The royal generation of a century ago had been on friendlier terms than had been previously customary among the three kingdoms of Nissera. The resulting intermarrying of their children meant I possessed handfuls of royal and noble relatives, most with magic in their blood.

Three of my cousins from Volarre floated toward me as though a spring breeze carried them on an invisible chariot. Since I'd last seen the Lorenthi sisters, the eldest two had matured enough for elicromancy to halt their aging, making them nearly impossible to tell apart. They were all blond, fair, and willowy, including their brother, who was notably absent. While they offered their condolences and lauded Ivria's beauty and taste in fashion, I met eyes with Knox over the eldest's shoulder. He cringed and looked away. His gift of empathy made funerals especially difficult for him. I imagined all the grief in the room assailing his senses.

I snapped back to find the Lorenthi sisters studying the unadorned space at my sternum where an elicrin stone should have been. "You must visit us soon, Cousin Valory," the eldest said, her head tilted in a show of sympathy. "Know you have a home with us, if you find you're no longer welcome here."

No longer welcome here?

A sickly taste scraped up my throat. I glanced at Knox again and realized that hardly *anyone* had met my eyes since I'd emerged from my room, pursued by guards, to attend the ceremony. Most guests averted their gaze, focusing on the next person in line before they finished muttering respects to me. As I watched them warmly greet other family members, even Melkior, I had to wonder what version of events had circulated and what speculations had arisen.

I'd understood that the catastrophe at the Water was steeped in some measure of controversy. But I'd thought that after the dust settled, everyone would understand that I had only tried to save someone I loved.

I hurried to find Ander, dodging somber appraisals left and right. But when I squeezed his forearm to announce my presence, he shifted away from me.

"Ander…" I said, shocked to look up and see his jaw set and his gray eyes alight.

"Do you have no respect?" he demanded.

"What?" I asked, stunned to near breathlessness. How could he be angry with me? Did he think…did he think I had *hurt* Ivria?

There were elicromancers who could draw the truth out of people. The diadem could be used to detect flagrant deceit. I would stand on the dais and let the truth echo off the gleaming marble if need be. Not a single person could be permitted to doubt that I would have died in Ivria's place had the choice been mine— especially not Ander.

Aunt Sylvana turned to us with sluggish disapproval. Uncle Prosper said, "Not here, Oleander."

Ander's nostrils flared. He cupped my elbow and spurred me behind one of the massive marble pillars flanking the room. But by that time, his rage had broken down and reconstructed itself as sorrow. He shook his head. "She could have survived."

"I know," I said, choking up as I gripped his shoulder. "She seemed to think she had no choice, but she didn't have to—"

He wrenched out of my grasp as though my fingers were hot irons. Anger had taken his features captive once more.

"No," he said through gritted teeth. "I'm saying you shouldn't have gone in after her. She was *gifted*, Valory. You are not. When you touched the Water instead of trusting she would survive on her own, you ruined everything."

His accusation stole the air from my lungs. This Ander was a stranger.

"And now the Water has *dried up*," he went on, grinding the shattered pieces of me underfoot. "What will I tell my children when they age before I do? How will I explain to them why magic is not a part of their lives or their lineage?"

"Ander, I had to do something. She said she sensed her own death. She was never wrong."

"Exactly," he agreed sharply. "Her gift was sophisticated. She would have survived. It was natural for her to be nervous. Nerves don't mean anything."

"You didn't see her face. You didn't hear her voice." I realized by now we were both shouting, but I didn't care. "I couldn't let her die."

"You defied the tenets and touched the Water without permission. You confused it. You *broke* it. You showed no hint of an elicrin gift, yet you're the one standing here. It spared you and it killed her. It should have spared her and killed you, and everyone knows it."

Nearby onlookers gasped at the venom in his voice. I wanted to collapse in a heap, or spit in his face, but I stood motionless, fists clenched at my sides.

A seething strangeness started to boil inside me. The chairs and tables nearest us began to rattle. A tapestry on the wall ripped down, unraveling to tatters.

At first, Ander stared openmouthed at the effects of my unexpected power. Then his crest-shaped elicrin stone lit up and a protective crystal armor began to creep from his fingertips to his wrists and up his arms. I had only seen him engage his Armamenter gift during combat lessons at the academy. My pulse pounded in my palms and a primal fear set my blood ablaze. A chair snapped to pieces and clattered to the marble like firewood split with an axe.

"Get her under control!" I heard Uncle Prosper say. His voice cut through the haze of fury. Someone yanked my elbow and twisted my arms behind my back. A muscle in my shoulder revolted against the use of force and I let out a yelp of pain. The surge of unsettling power inside me abated, leaving me trembling.

"Let her go!" My mother gave a rare command, pushing through the crowd. Her teal elicrin stone flickered like lightning over the ocean. The guard had no choice but to obey and unhand me.

King Tiernan appeared out of nowhere, squaring himself between Ander and me. In court, materializing over short distances was seen as a display of vanity and laziness for elicromancers, but this clearly constituted an exception. The king's personal guard—a Neutralizer—appeared just behind him, wearing an oval elicrin stone of rough, grayish crystal.

"Settle down, Oleander, Valory," the king said.

Ander clenched his teeth, but the layer of impenetrable crystal crawling over his skin slowed and reversed. Engaging me in earnest combat would have amounted to unauthorized use of elicromancy, which warranted neutralization and a harsh penalty of surrendering his elicrin stone for five years.

I loosened my fists. Underneath Ander's anger, his grief was as raw as my own. Exhaling a rattling breath, I reassured myself that the Conclave showed more grace to pupils who could not yet harness their gifts.

Before I gathered words to make an apology or rebuttal—I wasn't sure which would emerge—my mother guided me toward the foyer. The ogling guests parted before us. She didn't speak as we hurried down the entranceway steps and stopped by one of the expansive arches leading to the gardens.

"I don't understand," I said as we crossed the terrace. "What is this?" I flattened my palms on my chest and looked at her, helpless.

"I don't know, darling," she said, sweeping a lock of dark hair away from her high cheekbone.

"What will happen to me?"

"You've always followed the rules and respected authority. You're not given to outbursts. The Conclave knows that."

Her voice didn't waver, but alarm crossed her face.

Victor jogged down the steps to catch up with us, his broad shoulders tense. "What were you thinking, giving that guard an unauthorized command?" he asked her.

"He was hurting my daughter."

"They could choose to punish you—"

"At most they'll confiscate my elicrin stone for a few weeks," she snapped. "It wouldn't be the first time."

Victor sighed, scratching his dark beard, and looked at me. "Your hearing will take place today."

"But she's supposed to have until tomorrow to prepare her testimony." Mother gripped his hand, eyes pleading. She needed him as I needed her: not at all, and yet in every way.

"We can't delay, not after that spectacle."

I bit down hard on my bottom lip. Whatever the vote came to, Victor would cast his in my favor. But he was just one person and not altogether eloquent. He would make a lackluster argument about what a rule-follower I was.

"Prosper will likely recuse himself and be replaced by another elicromancer," my mother said, taking on a look of determination as she turned to me. "Valory, listen. Go put on a very dull dress—"

"Is her wardrobe a concern right now?"

She ignored Victor and stroked my chestnut locks. "Have Ellen braid your hair the way she used to when you were younger. Write a statement and I will deliver it to the Conclave prior to your hearing. It will prevent you from misspeaking or becoming overemotional. Be calm. Be pliable. Say as little as possible. They just want to see that you can and will follow their commands."

My heavy heart somehow managed to flit like manic hummingbird wings. I had never thought to fear the Conclave. My fears had always revolved around embarrassing my prominent family, as my father had. Before his death, he had shown great proclivity for elicromancy, but he had refused to risk the Water and realize his potential.

My mother had just given me more commands in a few breaths than she had in years.

Perhaps my fears had been misplaced.

❧ FIVE ❧

AN hour after I handed over my statement, the Neutralizer came to collect me.

I wore a plain dark blue dress, one I might have donned to walk the grounds with Ivria and Calanthe or to shop in Arna without attracting stares. The box holding the diadem trembled imperceptibly in my hands.

I had seen the Conclave chamber before, though never with permission. Ivria, Ander, and I used to roam the vast palace looking for secret rooms or passages. But one day we seemed to know every closet and corner as well as you'd know a familiar book of children's stories. The mystery had vanished.

Tall lancet windows lined the back wall, overlooking the city to the south. Three steps led up to a dais with a throne and chairs on either side. While reviewing affairs of state, the king would sit on his throne with his advisors on the flanks. During Conclave meetings, the throne remained empty to symbolize the equality of all voices present. Within this room, there were no kings, no elicromancers, no powerless mortals—just ten people responsible for governing the academy and ensuring that its graduates adhered to the magical laws of the land. The Conclave answered not to King Tiernan, but to the Realm Alliance, the larger political union presiding over all of Nissera.

Despite the promise of unbiased governance, I couldn't resist categorizing the ten Conclave members into factions. There were five mortals and five elicromancers, five nobles and five without titles. One of the mortals had once been an elicromancer but had given up his stone as the tenets required and now aged normally. The commoners and mortals were here to hold their more powerful counterparts accountable.

My knees felt feeble as I stepped into the room and the doors slammed shut. The Neutralizer lingered stoically behind me. A record keeper scratched away despite the heavy silence.

"We have reviewed your account of the events, Mistress Braiosa," said Jovie's father, Glend Neswick, a bearded mortal with thinning ash-brown hair. He sat directly to the left of the imposing throne. "Do you have anything to add for the Conclave's consideration?"

I swallowed and spoke calmly. "My one and only aim was to save Ivria. I submit to any process required for you to be certain you've obtained the truth from me. I've brought the diadem holding Callista's retired elicrin stone, which allows the possessor to see the tru—"

"That won't be necessary." King Tiernan, sitting two seats to the right of the throne, beckoned the Neutralizer. The guard circled me and pried the box from my fingers. I opened my mouth to argue but instead clenched my teeth and let him take the gift without resistance.

"We cannot have someone on trial in possession of an elicrin stone, even a retired one with limited power," the king explained.

"Furthermore, your good intentions are not under scrutiny." Professor Strather, my instructor in Curses and Forbidden Rituals, raised her crackling voice. "Nor are the events of the night in question."

"Rather, we are here to determine the consequences for defying the Conclave's tenets," Neswick added. "All your life, you have been taught to revere and respect the Water. You were told time and time again that there is only one circumstance under which you may touch it: with the permission of the Conclave, once we've established that you possess both the magical capacity to survive and the moral fiber to be a leader in this realm."

Feeling off-balance, I raked in a deep breath. I could prove good intentions, but I couldn't argue against the result of my actions.

"In that case," I began, turning the word *pliable* over and over, "I will say that I have always respected the tenets. I never had any intention of breaking them, and would only do so in dire need. While my cousin fought to escape the Water..." I cleared my throat, blinking away traitorous tears. "I was not thinking of rules and consequences."

The despair of that night slammed against my chest, nearly evicting a stray sob. But I swallowed it like caustic medicine. Emotion, however appropriate to the occasion, suggested instability.

"I plan to comply with the tenets the Conclave has erected," I went on. "To continue my training so that I can learn to be an elicromancer above reproach, for as long as I hold—" I stopped short, realizing I couldn't swear on an elicrin stone I did not possess. "For as long as I live."

Professor Strather nodded her approval. She was one of my strictest instructors. I felt a trace of tension leave my shoulders.

An elicromancer with angular features and cutting blue eyes spoke up. "When one manages to peel away the emotional layers of what happened to you and Ivria—a difficult task on the day of her funeral, but a necessary one—the fact remains that you touched the Water. You disrupted the process of an approved pupil becoming an elicromancer, leaving great destruction in your wake."

The man did not speak the accusation that Ander had—perhaps decorum would not allow for such a conjecture—but I heard it all the same. And I began to wonder if it was true. What if my heedless decision, rather than any inherent unworthiness on her part, had caused Ivria's death?

Again, the record keeper dipped his quill and wrote on despite the silence.

"I must agree that her actions demonstrate not only a disregard for foundational tenets, but also a lack of trust in the Conclave's decisions," Neswick added. "We had already approved Ivria for her ceremony."

"Under ordinary circumstances, we would confiscate your elicrin stone," said the sharp-eyed elicromancer. "But as you mysteriously do not possess one, we will have to look into other options."

"She is only a pupil," Professor Strather said, drumming her fingertips on her knee. "She is permitted a strike on her record before facing punitive measures."

"A pupil is a child who has not yet entered the Water," said the other elicromancer. "She is eighteen years old—"

"Seventeen," I corrected.

"—and as her instructor, you have attested to her intellectual acumen as well as her grasp of the tenets. We must treat her as an adult and hold her accountable for her carelessness. She caused an innocent girl to die. Moreover, she demolished the source of all elicrin power, the consequences of which could very well plunge this realm into chaos."

Each word felt like a spit to the face. So much for decorum tying tongues and sparing me outright accusations.

A man with heavy-lidded eyes spoke up. "As a mortal, I'm concerned by the thought of letting a young woman with destructive magic and a disregard for rules leave this chamber with nothing but a slap on the wrist. The only answer is to imprison her, isolate her in a solitary cell, and forbid her to practice magic. At least until we know more about this power of hers."

I stared at him, mouth agape. By his tone, I might have thought he was suggesting sending me to the kitchens to scour pots. The idea of the palace dungeons had always disturbed me, ever since I was young and witnessed a crippled old thief being hauled off by guards. Ivria had comforted me by telling me that prisoners ate the same meals as us, and that the cells were no worse than the academy dormitories. Whether she believed it herself, I couldn't say.

"Forgive me, but this is absurd," Professor Strather said. "We must base her consequences on what she *has* done, not what she might do. Which one of us wouldn't break a tenet to save a loved one?"

"That is not how tenets work," the keen-eyed elicromancer said. "They are to be obeyed regardless of emotion or intuition directed by base instincts."

"Base instincts?" I cried. The Neutralizer who had escorted me here shifted his stance. I cooled my combative tone. "Please. I admit that I acted carelessly, but I'm not dangerous." The creaking of withering trees and snapping chair legs shot through my mind—the sounds of accidental destruction resulting from my anger. "To hold me prisoner, to forbid an elicromancer to practice magic—"

"The problem is that we can't be certain that's what you are," Neswick interjected, as somber as a royal portrait.

I was short a reply, but Professor Strather rushed to my defense again. "Inasmuch as she touched the Water, survived, and emerged with new magical abilities, she is."

"You must decide, Professor Strather, whether she is a fledgling pupil or an elicromancer, not whichever is convenient to your argument," Neswick replied. "Regardless, I think we can agree that decisive action is crucial to maintaining public trust in the Conclave. Punishment for breaking a tenet is harsh for that reason, and if we cannot confiscate her elicrin stone we must do something to guarantee public safety." Neswick turned to his peers. "I would like to bring the matter to a vote."

"Aren't we being a bit hasty?" Victor asked. He snapped his knuckles in the silence while I worried that he would fail to embroider his statement. But he continued, "Perhaps we should learn more about her power and how we might control it before going to such extreme measures."

"And do what with her in the meantime?" asked the mortal who had suggested imprisonment.

"Let us vote," Neswick said. "We can continue investigating, but we cannot simply let a tenet-breaker walk free."

"Especially one who has shown great propensity for destruction," the sharp-featured elicromancer added.

"Those in favor of the aforementioned penalties?" Neswick asked.

Five hands rose. The immense room seemed to shrink the way the palace had shrunk after the three of us children had probed every secret corner. Victor, Professor Strather, two mortals, and King Tiernan did not move.

The vote was split evenly.

"If you'll indulge me but a moment," King Tiernan said, leaning forward. "Ivria Ermetarius—may light surround her—picked locks to reach the portal and snuck in under cover of night. She did not set a date for her ceremony, and therefore the Conclave could not supervise the ritual or prevent a family member like Valory from indulging her protective instincts. Ivria may not be here to assume some responsibility for the night's events, but that should not leave Valory to take it all upon herself."

"What penalty do you deem appropriate, Your Majesty?" Neswick asked in a moderate tone that disguised impatience.

"She is a grieving girl overwhelmed by her magic. Locking her up, alone in the dark, angry and frightened, will hardly help her learn to tame her power. I propose that Valory remain confined to her rooms, with Brandar here acting as her personal escort, ensuring everyone's safety." He gestured at the Neutralizer.

"Nonsense, Your Majesty," Neswick said. "Lending her your Neutralizer would leave you unnecessarily vulnerable and exposed."

"I have plenty of talented elicromancers in my personal guard, Lord Neswick."

The outspoken mortal sighed but did not argue further. My heart leapt with renewed hope. I'd hoped Tiernan would champion my total freedom, but he could only shield me from so much before his defense reeked of familial partiality.

"Those terms are sufficient for me, barring any further incidents," said the keen-eyed elicromancer.

The Conclave took another vote. Only Neswick, the mortal itching to lock me up, and an elicromancer who hadn't spoken voted against King Tiernan's suggestion. And just like that, the colloquy ended.

Relief flooded over me, but on its heels came yawning emptiness. I'd walked into the Conclave chamber thinking I had only to convince them of decent intentions. Now I had to convince them I wasn't dangerous, when I was far from sure of that myself.

King Tiernan took the diadem box from his Neutralizer, whispering in his ear. After my great-uncle had defended me and kept me out of the dungeons, I dared not speak out. My freedom, my life, a second chance—these were all more precious than jewelry, even a magical heirloom given to me by Ivria.

Despite my lightened sentence, I began to feel like a prisoner as Brandar accompanied me to my rooms. I wondered blankly whether he would permit me any privacy, or if he would neutralize me at the first sign of a temper.

When we turned down the long corridor Ivria and I had shared with a few other female relatives and ladies' maids, I saw my door open. But it wasn't Ellen or one of the others. It was Melkior leading Calanthe away on a leash.

"What are you doing?" I demanded. Calanthe bounded forward a few steps and stood on her impressive hind legs to drape her front paws on my shoulders in greeting.

But Melkior yanked the leash and hissed a wordless rebuke. He swept back a lock of his near-black hair. "Ivria told me I could breed her. I have the ideal sire in mind."

"On the day of her funeral? Breeding her dog?" I tried to snatch the leather leash, but he jerked it out of my reach.

"I'm going to give Ander one of the whelps. To remind him of his sister."

A noise between a scoff and a feral growl ripped out of me. Even when Melkior managed to locate his decency, his methods of displaying it bordered on cruel. "Why not just give him Calanthe?"

"She's not mine to give. Ivria only gave me permission to breed her."

I gritted my teeth. Melkior treated dogs and horses with more compassion and respect than he spared for other creatures, as breeding and training them demonstrated status. His grandfather Vesper, younger brother to King Tiernan and Grandmother Odessa, had given him his own kennels and stables when he realized Melkior was capable of seeing these creatures as more than playthings to torment. But still, I couldn't let him take Calanthe away, for her sake and mine.

"Ivria would have wanted me to have her," I said, barely maintaining my calm. "If not me, then Ander. She didn't want to breed her. She probably forgot she ever said you could. She was just trying to show you kindness, and now you can show it to me for the first time in your life."

He pursed his lips, considering, but soon shook his head. "Deerhounds need to run. She shouldn't be cooped up in the palace. Besides, I can't give Ander anything short of the best pup from the best litter with the best brood bitch." He paused and cocked his head at me, his features carved of arrogance. "But I'll let you have second best. That is, if you promise not to rip it to shreds with your new pow—"

My fingernails bit into my palm. Twin cracks crept up the walls on either side of us. At first, Melkior stumbled away from me, pulling Calanthe with him. But I remembered the Neutralizer who stood a few steps behind me and cut a nervous glance in his direction. I released my fists and the cracks halted in their tracks.

Melkior arched a brow at me, then at Brandar, no doubt finding my limitations intriguing.

With a hint of a smirk, he brushed past me, taking Calanthe with him.

I stormed into the common room, startling the maids. Without a word, I hurried to my private chamber and pressed the door closed behind me, waiting a few beats to make sure Brandar wouldn't follow.

Rushing to the farthest corner of the room, I slammed my back against the wall and sank to the floor. My anger made the chandelier above me clank and rattle, but the burst was neither violent nor deafening. The metal quietly became flecks of ash that swirled high above me.

As they drifted over my head and shoulders like gray snow, I wept without restraint.

SIX

VALORY?" My mother knocked on my door, stirring me from sleep. When I opened my eyes, I found swirls of gray ash amid the moonbeams slicing through my chamber.

"Would you please step back?" I heard her say. "She's not going to fly out like a bird."

She opened the door and squeezed through, admitting Ellen behind her. I could see Brandar silhouetted by the fire in the common room just before she shut him out.

"It is not appropriate for a grown man to shadow a seventeen-year-old girl," my mother muttered, turning her light enchantment in my direction. Her elicrin stone held a steady, subdued glow. "I don't know why the Conclave couldn't have found—" She stopped abruptly and gasped, lifting her eyes to the cloud of gray and the black marks on the ceiling.

Ellen stared for a moment before setting a tray of food on the table and moving toward the hearth to start a fire.

"There's dinner for you," my mother said, stepping nimbly over the piles on the floor. She attempted to wipe clean a portion of my bed, to no avail, and settled for barely perching on the edge. "And your grandmother has arrived."

"I don't want to see her."

"From Darmeska."

"Grandmum?" I asked with a trace of hope.

She nodded. "Should Ellen let her in?"

"Yes." I straightened up as Ellen bustled to the door.

Few people in my life had wrinkled faces or fading hair. But my father's mother did, and she was more beautiful than the youthful elicromancers, like a crisp autumn dawn of auburn and silver. She took no notice of the sooty powder on the floor as she crossed to me and knelt at my side, folding my hands inside hers.

"Dear heart," she whispered. "I'm so sorry."

I extracted my hands to link them around her neck and shed tears into her gray-streaked red hair.

"I'm here," she said. Her lilting accent called to mind memories of the western mountains, the vast halls within the fortress of Darmeska, the wistful aroma of wood and dust. Her dignity went deeper than adornments and titles, than sparkling otherworldly jewels.

"Did I kill Ivria?"

"No, no, no. Hush." Grandmum sat beside me and pulled my head to her shoulder. "As much as the Conclave fancies they have the final say in who lives and who dies, there's no bending the Water to one's will. It has a will of its own. They can't force an ancient power to serve their purposes like a domesticated beast."

"How come Melkior survived and she didn't? That wretch."

"There's no knowing why Ivria failed the test. But as for Melkior—"

"The gift of healing is sacred, I know."

"I was going to say: that wicked boy needs more years to become a good man than most, so maybe fate thought to give them to him." She smiled and squeezed my forearm, but the smile faded too soon. "The expectations that haunt this place are what killed Ivria. And they're what drove your father away, though he loved you dearly."

A familiar ache returned. Like the royals of Arna, the people of Darmeska could trace their lineage to ancient elicromancers. Though magic ran thick in their blood, Darmeskans tended to keep their distance from the Water. And my father, a native Darmeskan, had felt no urge to become an elicromancer until he met my mother. He moved to Arna to attend the academy and marry her. His talent for fire-wielding won him approval from the Conclave, but he stalled his ceremony for years, humiliating my mother, who had begged King Tiernan to let her marry Leonar Braiosa without losing her bid for the throne. Tiernan had conceded on the grounds that my father could be considered "noble" as the son of two prominent Darmeskan elders.

But even with the family's blessing, the love between my mother and father soured. Not a week passed that she didn't beg him to touch the Water and realize his magical potential. They could barely share a word without arguing by the time my father decided to leave in the night when I was eight years old, taking me with him. He hoped to spare me from the constraints that accompanied the surname Ermetarius, from the inevitable choice to risk my very life just to gain magic.

We adventured in the Brazor Mountains for months, mapping out places where others had not yet dared go. My memories of that time lingered like a strange dream: the towering peaks, the crude shelters, the blood of fur-covered creatures staining my hands. Father and I stayed in the wilds until I caught wind fever and he brought me to Darmeska. Grandmum then convinced him to let me return to Arna.

As we said farewell, he told me I would always be a Braiosa, even if my mother succeeded in molding me in her immortal likeness.

For years after, he sent us a letter each time he stopped in Darmeska. Eventually, following months of silence, Grandmum wrote to tell us he had died of wounds from a bear mauling. He had survived just long enough to return once more to the mountain fortress, but was too delirious to write any farewells.

The next time I saw him, he was a corpse.

"There's a reason elicromancers surrendered their stones after defeating the traitors in the past," Grandmum said, yanking me out of my reverie. "Limitless power corrupts. This is the first time elicromancers have sustained peace as a ruling class. I fear what will become of the system now that confidence in their future has been ripped away."

I took in a shuddering sigh. "Half of the Conclave wants to imprison me for what happened."

"Fortunately, it's no longer their call to make," she said, giving my knee a firm pat.

"What do you mean?"

She rose and extended a hand. "Someone else has come to see you."

Shakily, I stood and we left my chambers, my mother trailing behind.

I entered the common room and found a striking man with eyes the color of soil after rain: Ambassador Rayed Lillis. His features were angular, sculpted by the clean lines of charcoal brows and a decisively kempt beard. On my visits to Beyrian over the years, I had gotten on quite well with the ambassador's younger sister, Kadri, who was now betrothed to the Prince of Yorth.

Ivria had been closer to the youthful Erdemese representative himself. When his country appointed him to replace his ailing father as ambassador to Nissera, I had begun to address him by his title, while Ivria continued to use his given name even after his boyishness had been polished away like smudges from silver. She might have wed him, but our family would have considered it daft for a soon-to-be-immortal woman to unite with a mortal man already half a decade older.

"Dear Valory," Rayed said, pacing forward to clasp my hand with his callused, russet-brown fingers. An enamel pin depicting the yellow-and-maroon flag of Erdem glinted on the collar of his wool tunic. "I could hardly fathom the news of Ivria's death. My heart aches for the loss and the devastation it's caused your family."

Tears clogged my throat. I gave a small nod in reply, grateful that he treated me like a grieving loved one rather than a rampaging murderer.

Grandmum sat on the sofa and crossed her legs, which made even the stoic Brandar double-glance. Highborn women in these parts wore gowns, except when training or riding, and crossed their ankles when they sat. But Juniper Braiosa had never yielded to our customs. She wore a knee-length shift over breeches and boots lined with fur, topped by an embossed leather coat. "You must eat, Valory," Grandmum said. "You're as feeble as a winter flower. Ellen, don't you have old tricks to make my granddaughter eat something?"

Ellen plunked the tray of food on the table nearest me. "Not for ten years now, Madam Braiosa. She's not usually hard to convince." My maid managed a modest smile and scurried off to make tea.

"You'll need your strength for the journey, dear one," Grandmum said.

"Journey?" I asked.

Rayed took a seat across from Grandmum and waited, stroking his beard. Clearly, they would withhold their plans from me until I surrendered and ate something for the first time in days. With a sigh of submission, I plucked up a chunk of bread and an apple. Ellen was thoughtful enough to bring simple foods that would settle my weak stomach. Mother had tried to tempt me with a buttery pastry yesterday and then commanded me to eat it, thinking she was doing me good. It had only made me sick. As I yielded to my hunger and bit into the apple, Mother looked rather resentful, alighting on a chair by the hearth and folding her arms. She did not much like the qualities Grandmum teased out of me, maintaining that I became defiant after my visits with her.

Grandmum nodded approval. The ambassador extracted a scroll from his coat and unfurled it, saying, "The Realm Alliance has ordered the Conclave to pass your case up to them. Queen Jessa has summoned the other Realm Alliance representatives to Beyrian to hear your testimony and determine how to move forward."

My nerves pulled taut as I took and studied the scroll, which bore a gray wax seal of balanced scales. The Realm Alliance was comprised of Nissera's kings and queens, prominent mortals, the Conclave members, and leaders from other lands. Grandmum and Rayed were both representatives. The inclusion of outlanders reflected Nissera's growing rapport with countries that had once avoided us due to our magical creatures and supernatural wars. When elicromancers had at last dwindled to only a few, nearby lands across the seas had begun to tentatively trade with us. After word spread that Queen Bristal and King Anthony had surrendered their elicrin stones and no elicromancers remained in Nissera, trade alliances sprang up like wild grasses.

Magic was reintroduced by my great-grandfather after Anthony and Bristal had passed on, and even then only under strict stipulations that would benefit all: elicromancers and mortals, natives and foreigners, kings and peasants.

I would have to face representatives of every one of these groups to explain the unexplainable.

"The Realm Alliance has the authority to overturn any penalty—or grace—the Conclave has rendered," Grandmum said, accepting briarberry tea from Ellen. The people of Darmeska preferred the bitter drink even to wine. "We will not rush through the trial as the Conclave tends to. You can expect to stay in Beyrian for at least a fortnight."

I swilled gulps of water and swished the last bit around my dry mouth. The Realm Alliance gathered at the most convenient hub for regulating travel and trade from distant lands: the southernmost royal city of Nissera. Beyrian was my favorite place to travel within the realm. Memories stirred my senses: I could almost taste the fresh oysters, smell the imported spices, hear the blends of languages and dialects, watch the blue sea whip up its gentle white foam. "When do we leave?"

"We have a few days' padding, but I'm keen to whisk you away from Arna before more trouble comes. I think we should leave tomorrow morning."

"Very well." I deposited the apple core on the tray. My stomach growled for whatever simmered inside the covered silver pot, but hope and fear seemed to knot my insides even more than despair. "I'll pack."

As I passed, Grandmum grabbed my wrist and gently pivoted me so we were facing. She rose and cupped my chin in her hands. "You have my grandmum Drell's fire and wisdom, her proud chin."

Somehow, I summoned a smile. Just as my mother's family would tell tales of my great-great-grandparents Bristal and Anthony, Grandmum would tell me of Drell and Maddock, my mortal ancestors who fought bravely alongside them in the war against the dark elicromancer Tamarice. They had defeated Tamarice and her armies from Galgeth, the dark netherworld to the west that only immortals could reach.

"Thank you," I whispered. "And thank you both for helping me."

"Thank King Tiernan," said Rayed, cradling his teacup. "He wrote the Realm Alliance a detailed missive on the night of Ivria's death to prevent facts mixing with rumors. The loss of the Water will affect the whole realm and beyond, not just elicromancers. Though the Conclave enjoys autonomy in many matters, King Tiernan insisted this should not be one of them."

I didn't miss the shadowed look the ambassador and Grandmum shared, the dark flash of worry and unuttered words in their eyes. Had King Tiernan feared I would not receive a fair trial from the Conclave?

"The Alliance could have sent a magical missive," I mused aloud.

"Did they dispatch you in person to ensure that the Conclave complied with the order?"

"Two mortals? One an old woman?" Grandmum snorted. "I should think not."

"We have no doubt the Conclave will comply." Rayed underscored his assurance with a smile that softened his clever features. "Not to worry."

Mother cleared her throat. "Will she be free to return when the trial is over? If she must be held captive, surely they will be reasonable and leave her with her family."

My teeth clenched hard on my lower lip as I imagined returning to *this*. I was fortunate indeed to be in the comfort of my own rooms, as vacant as they felt without Ivria. But the thought of coming back here, unable to use the magic I'd always longed to possess, hated and feared for what I had unknowingly done...

"We must hope for a better outcome than captivity," Grandmum replied tersely.

Rayed added, "Perhaps we can convince the other leaders it's a matter of age and discipline, that you will not be a threat with proper guidance."

I laced my fingers together, feeling a pulse of power thrumming under my skin. Brandar's blank eyes cut toward me with renewed interest. "If...if we are able to convince the Realm Alliance that I will cause no harm," I ventured, dropping my hands, "will I ever be permitted to use my magic?"

"Let's take it one day at a time," Grandmum said. "Tell the truth and everything will sort itself out."

I wanted to believe her. But I had told the truth to the Conclave and they had nearly voted to lock me away with criminals and murderers.

The only answer for now was to attempt to suffocate the magic I had always longed to possess—to appear unthreatening and untroublesome, even as everything inside me insisted I was neither.

The next morning, Ellen helped me stuff clothes into my trunk and wrestled down the lid so I could close the clasps. She had swept away the ashes while I slept, and now my room sparkled as if no one lived here at all.

Packing for a journey without Ivria's exacting opinion was no easy feat, and not merely because I lacked the eye for ensembles. I had to pack away my sadness too, and struggle to keep it closed.

Just after we stepped away from the laden trunk, satisfied with our work, I growled in frustration. "I meant to pack one of Ivria's gowns!"

"I already packed one," Ellen said. "The emerald with the waist clasp and lace underneath. I hemmed it for you."

"Oh, Ellen! Did you get even a wink of sleep?"

"I've got fairy blood in me, you'll recall, which means I've a knack for finishing chores in a twinkling." She lowered her voice and cast a sideways glance at the Neutralizer sitting in the common room. "Besides, I didn't feel right leaving you alone on your first night under...supervision."

With a wry smile, I said, "Don't worry about me, Ellen."

"I can't help it," she said, and bent to retrieve a small dagger from the bottom drawer of my wardrobe. My father had given me the weapon and taught me to use it during our months of mountaineering. Ellen pressed the leather-sheathed blade into my hands.

"Whyever would I need this?" I asked, brushing my thumb over the engraved hilt and cross guard. As I pinched the metal chape of the scabbard, I recalled how it felt to thrust that graceful, tapered blade into animal flesh. It would be as useless as a sewing needle against an elicromancer.

"Indulge your fretful old maid—there's a good lass."

I chuckled as I fastened the belt around my waist. "If it brings you comfort, Ellen."

Grandmum swept into my chamber. "Let's be going while the day is young!"

"Nearly ready, mistress," Ellen said. "Do you need your winter mantle, love?" she asked me, holding the fur-trimmed ivory garment by the shoulders. "You could still catch a chill."

"No, I'll be fine, I…" I trailed off. The memory of passing a white-cloaked person in the dark halls of the academy rushed back to me, buried and forgotten amid the night's harrowing events.

There had been no signs of foul play, no indication that the mysterious entity—perhaps a figment of my imagination—had anything to do with the tragedies that had occurred. But just like the figure slipping past me in the cold stone corridor, the remark slipped off my tongue. "I think I may have passed someone else sneaking around in the academy right before I found Ivria by the Water." I looked at Grandmum. "I know it wasn't a guard because I could hear them talking elsewhere. Should I mention it at my hearing?"

Grandmum frowned, her lips cinching like a coin purse. "You

should have already mentioned it to the Conclave. Their records on your case will be sent to the Realm Alliance."

"I'd forgotten until now."

Decades of wisdom puckered her brow as she considered. "Can you describe the person?"

"No, not really. All I saw was what looked like a white cloak, but it could have been—"

Grandmum jolted as though trying to rid her neck of a crick.

"What's wrong?" I asked.

Before she could answer, my mother swayed into the room, arms crossed. "I do hope this ordeal concludes quickly and favorably," she said, as though this trial were nothing but an inconvenience of my making.

A note materialized on my desk. Curiosity bloomed as I stepped forward to retrieve a featherlight parchment with gold trim. Breaking the pale blue seal with the imprint of a lily, I scanned the decorative handwriting and found a message from the three cousins I'd seen at the funeral yesterday.

"What is it?" Mother asked.

"An invitation from the Lorenthi sisters. They heard I'll be journeying south—"

"Already? I miss the days before magical missives started raging gossip."

"—and asked me to visit them at the palace in Pontaval."

"I don't think that's a good idea," Grandmum said.

"You'll be passing by Pontaval anyway," Mother said. "It's better than some seamy inn on the city outskirts. There are plenty of scoundrels ready to take advantage of a pretty girl from wealth."

"Valory ought to lie low," Grandmum argued, her eyes the shivery blue of a sunny midwinter day. "We can't risk another scandal erupting before her hearing. And the Lorenthi siblings are mighty scandalous, especially that boy Devorian—"

"Snubbing high-profile relatives is its *own* scandal," Mother cut in, fiddling with the chain that held her elicrin stone. "At least in polite society."

"We can discuss it on the way." I folded the parchment and tucked it into the pocket of my copper dress, putting the matter to rest. Mother and Grandmum's relationship was like a taut string on a lute; if you were careful, you could pluck around the discord to elicit a few agreeable notes.

Mother and Ellen followed us down to the mist-shrouded courtyard. Part of me wished Ander would appear, that he would apologize for wounding me with his accusations. But he wouldn't come, and I shouldn't want him to.

King Tiernan, however, materialized at my side as the coachman loaded my luggage onto the roof rack. Though I'd never admit it aloud, the elicromancer ability to be here one second and gone the next set my nerves on edge.

The dawn light cut across the king's rigid features as he placed his hand on my shoulder and steered me away from the others. "The Conclave must not discover what I'm about to tell you. In fact, no one should."

My heart galloped as he turned his pensive eyes on me. By default, I'd always thought they were as gray as steel. But now that he stood so close, I noticed they were more of a warm, gilded green—like mine.

"Brandar said he was unable to neutralize you yesterday," the king explained. "He attempted it twice, once when you cracked the walls in the corridor and again when you fled to your room. Fortunately, Brandar is loyal to me above the Conclave. Your secret is safe. He will give you as much privacy and dignity as he can while appearing to do his duty. But now you know how crucial it is that you manage your power."

"Yes, Your Majesty," I replied, my voice whisper-thin. "Thank you."

"I will see you in Beyrian for the hearing."

Before I could stutter out a reply, he materialized away. I shuffled back across the smooth courtyard stones, schooling my face to neutrality.

"What did Uncle Tiernan want?" Mother asked as Grandmum settled into the spacious covered carriage. Rayed had just arrived, his dark brown eyes surveying me with curiosity.

Too stunned to muster an adequate lie, I spit out a half-truth. "He wanted to make sure I wouldn't use my magic."

Even as I leveled my outward astonishment, King Tiernan's words beat like a war drum in my chest: *He was unable to neutralize you.* Neutralization was the first and last line of defense for the powerful Conclave. A Neutralizer was retrieved at the first sign of unfettered elicrin power—and if the tenet-breaker in question did not comply, the Neutralizer would confiscate her elicrin stone.

If I could not be neutralized, controlling me might come down to trading blows and spilling blood. And the blood would be mine, if I didn't learn to govern my power.

But if I did...I would be the *only* one who could.

This epiphany prompted me to turn around and march across the courtyard, my skirt bunched in my fists. I ignored the voices calling after me. On a sharp turn, I nearly clipped the base of a statue of Queen Bristal before hurrying over the stretch of green that bordered the eastern side of the palace.

The wooden gate leading to the kennels stood open. I flung it wide and searched the paddocks until I found Melkior and a kennel attendant in the midst of examining a male deerhound's teeth.

"Where's Calanthe?"

The yaps and barks that greeted me nearly drowned out my question. Melkior stood and draped his arms over the gate, his posture dripping with self-content. A jerk of his head made me look back to see that Brandar had pursued me.

"Last kennel on the left," Melkior answered. "But it would be bold to defy Ivria's wishes after . . . you know." He clicked his tongue. "Wouldn't look very proper."

The anger blistering in my veins threatened to awaken my unruly power. Instead of waiting for the rage to surface, I lunged at Melkior. My anger was not just toward him, but toward Ander, the Conclave, the scandalized funeral guests. With their faces in mind, I drove the heel of my hand into Melkior's nose.

The resulting sound was both wet, like a bare foot stuck in the mud, and brittle. His scathing snarl collapsed. He yowled a curse and lurched back, gripping the bridge of his bloody nose while he gathered the wherewithal to heal himself. The base of my palm ached with an impending bruise.

I walked on until I found Calanthe curled up in the corner of a large enclosure strewn with hay. When I unlatched the gate, she bounded ahead of me, soaring free from the confinement of the kennels. Melkior's elicrin stone glowed as he recovered and faced me, a spell poised behind his blood-drenched teeth.

But Brandar, in his deep voice, said, "Careful, boy," and stepped aside to let me trail Calanthe into the full light of the rising sun.

As though she knew my destination, Calanthe galloped toward the courtyard, grinding to a halt to grace my mother with unwanted kisses. I caught up and hurried to peck Mother and Ellen on the cheeks, bouncing into the carriage next to Grandmum before anyone could realize what I'd done and chastise me.

Calanthe jumped in and settled on the cushion beside Rayed. He arched a skeptical brow at her size but didn't object.

Brandar stepped up, saw Calanthe, and, with a sigh betraying a hint of a personality, squeezed onto the bench next to me and slammed the door. I smiled sideways at him, and his rigid mouth bent a little at the corner. The carriage started off, rounding the courtyard and gliding down the long tree-lined drive away from the palace.

As we jolted over the cobblestone streets of the city, Grandmum leaned close to me and quietly said, "Don't mention the intruder in the white cloak again. I've told King Tiernan, and he's the only one who need know."

"Why?" I asked in a small voice, the memory of my frightful trek through the academy overshadowing the joy of a meager victory.

The vestiges of youth in Grandmum's lovely face seemed to drain away, leaving her features pallid and sepulchral. "An artifact was stolen from a guarded cavern vault in Darmeska weeks ago. In the wrong hands, it could be dangerous, to say the least. The men who took it wore white cloaks and black masks. My fellow elders believe the unidentified thieves are part of a secret spiritual order called the Summoners, worshippers of an entity they call the Lord of Elicromancers. Your father encountered them on his travels and rambled about them on his deathbed. I thought it was the fever talking, but there have been other accounts."

"Why can't we speak of them?"

"So we can continue pursuing the group in secret. People are careless when they think no one's watching. And they were powerful enough to break through magical protections."

"What did the Summoners take? What are they trying to do?"

"You have enough trouble of your own, dear." She tugged the curtains on her side closed, the trenches on her forehead deepening. "Don't borrow mine."

❧ SEVEN ❧

HE flat farmlands swathing most of eastern Calgoran gave way to the rolling hills and woodlands of Volarre after a few days. I tried not to think much as I stared at the green wilderness, but neither hope nor sadness was easily banished from my mind. So I let hope lure me in. I fantasized about the warm, salty air of Beyrian while Rayed regaled me with how delighted his sister, Kadri, would be to see me, and the entertainment she had planned to cheer me.

As we neared the royal city of Pontaval, the palace where my cousins lived rose into view, perching atop a verdant hill with the city sprawling at its base. Grandmum shifted and groaned, massaging the muscles beneath her ribs while peering out the window.

"You don't *have* to sleep on another rickety inn bed," I said. "We can take the Lorenthis up on their invitation. Mother's right, you know. I can't afford to alienate my extended family." My reputation was already malodorous enough.

Grandmum flashed me a wary look. She was wise from her many years of leadership, studying and guarding Darmeska's history, and adjusting its laws to the modern age. But she was also obstinate as a pig in the mud. On the first night of the journey, I had tried to corner her about the white-cloaked men and she had demurred, withholding secrets about the stolen artifact. I couldn't crack her.

However, her aging joints and muscles must have hurt dreadfully because she muttered, "Oh, all right. But please act wisely around the Lorenthi siblings."

Satisfied, I relaxed in my seat and tugged my fingers through the tangles in my hair. I couldn't appear on the Lorenthis' doorstep a disheveled mess.

Calanthe groused with boredom from her designated spot on the cramped carriage floor. I had allowed her to run alongside us on deserted stretches of country road, but that didn't stop Grandmum and Brandar from expressing grievances over the lack of legroom. Though Rayed did his best to be a gentleman, even he had grown restless.

As we drew nearer the city, another palace jutted into the sky a smidgen south of the first. Volarian royalty had once resided there, before the elicromancer Tamarice cursed it. When Tamarice died and the curse was broken, traces of her dark elicromancy lingered like dust, or so it was said. Thus, the Lorenthi family built a new palace and the city shifted toward it, leaving much of the southern end abandoned.

After jostling uphill over cobblestones, we lurched to a halt in the palace courtyard, where attendants scuttled about like solicitous beetles. My cousins, perhaps warned of our approach, waited on a veranda branching off into two splendid stairways. The eldest, Ambrosine, wore a frothy yellow gown that puffed out from the waist like a buttercup. Glisette wore clingy light blue silk patterned with pink and purple flowers. Perennia, the youngest, looked like spring in subdued green crossed with sparkling emerald vines. I regretted wearing a sturdy traveling dress.

"We're thrilled you decided to come after all, Cousin Valory," Ambrosine said when we mounted the landing. She clasped my forearms and dusted a kiss on each cheek while Calanthe circled the three sisters, wagging her spry tail.

"Thank you for your hospitality, Your Highnesses," Rayed said. "We appreciate the opportunity to rest and refresh."

"It is our pleasure," Ambrosine assured him, grasping his hand and inviting him to softly kiss her knuckles. He obliged. "Valory, you should have tea with us in the garden."

"Yes, we'll leave you lovely ladies to reacquaint," Rayed said with a sly smile.

"Oh, but you *must* rejoin us for dinner," Ambrosine insisted, speaking more to Rayed than to Grandmum.

"Gladly," he assured her, while Grandmum massaged her sore muscles. With a flourish of his arm, an attendant led them into the foyer.

Perennia stepped in front of her elder sisters, her round eyes trained on me. "You poor thing. Every part of you is twisted with grief and guilt, I can tell." She latched on to my wrist. Her rose quartz elicrin stone pulsed with white light. Something dark inside me uncoiled and snuck away, leaving me feeling more peaceful than at any time I could recall.

"I'm sorry I didn't do that at the funeral," the girl said, stepping back. "You have to be careful, dismissing someone's sadness, even for a short time. Most people don't realize how important a feeling it is."

Perennia's statement held weight, considering she had borne her fair share of grief over the loss of both parents. A few years ago, the

King and Queen of Volarre had embarked on a routine diplomatic journey to Perispos only to be assassinated by a rebel group hostile to elicromancers. Most Perispi did not want our magic crossing their borders.

"Thank you," I said, mystified by how light I felt, as though I might drift away like a petal on the breeze.

"Come," Ambrosine said, eyeing the silent Neutralizer with annoyance. Gossip must have preceded my arrival, for they didn't question his presence, though she seemed to hope he would retire like the others. "You can bring your lovely dog as well. There's plenty of room for her to run."

The sisters ushered me through a glass-lined ballroom and across another veranda. The sun sparkled over a pond surrounded by trees with mauve flowers.

The Lorenthi sisters' idea of tea in the garden was more like a lavish sugarcoated feast. We approached a table laden with crystal platters and goblets brimming with pink wine, exotic fruits, and sweets topped with edible flowers. The princesses could not have gone to such lavish lengths purely for my benefit, but that was no surprise, since Volarian royalty was famous for its frivolity.

Without much ado, a separate table was set for Brandar on the far side of a low, flowering hedge and filled with fruit and cheeses. A harpist positioned herself nearby and began plucking. Brander sat and ate, paying us no mind. I was fortunate he had many years of experience keeping to himself while guarding King Tiernan. A less seasoned escort might have sat on me like a brooding hen.

A servant smiled as he slid out a chair and gestured for me to take it. My gaze couldn't resist clinging to his every flawless angle.

"Exquisite, isn't he?" Ambrosine asked, biting into a ruby raspberry.

I sat and the servant filled my goblet with sweet-smelling wine. There was no offer of tea. In fact, the silver tea service seemed perfunctory.

"What's the matter?" Ambrosine asked when I made no move to partake.

"I believe Cousin Valory thinks we're overextravagant," Glisette said, toying with her elicrin stone, a misty purple chalcedony.

"That's no fault of hers," Ambrosine countered, by way of defending me. "She's unaccustomed to enjoying herself. Arnans are so somber. They talk only of bloodlines and elicrin endowments."

"It will be fascinating to see what they do without their precious Water," Glisette purred into her goblet.

"As though it doesn't affect you?" I demanded. "Didn't you hope your children would be immortal, like you?"

Ambrosine patted my hand. "You can worry about the future all you like, Valory. But life strikes everyone with woe. So we laugh and we drink and we enjoy beautiful things. And you should as well."

The tension between my shoulder blades eased. I plucked up my goblet. "I suppose I shouldn't aim to convince you the loss of the Water is calamitous when I'm the one who caused it."

Glisette laughed and touched her crystal goblet to mine. "Precisely."

"About that..." Ambrosine began with a surreptitious glance at Brandar. "We did not invite you here strictly for the pleasure of your company."

My spirits drooped. Of course the princesses had other motives and felt no obligation to be coy about them. I was a curiosity, the subject of the realm's most lurid gossip. Death, destruction, undeserved power, and family feuds—disgraces orbited me like flies drawn to a fresh carcass.

"Devorian has shut himself off and is living a life of debauchery in the abandoned palace on the other side of the city," Ambrosine continued. "He's nearly seventeen and is meant to take the crown, but he refuses to return and accept his responsibilities as heir. We think you may be able to intimidate him with your power, and then use whatever leverage you have to convince him to return and embrace his role as King of Volarre."

I nearly snorted out my wine. "I have no control over my power, and I'm absolutely not permitted to use it right now. I'm awaiting trial with the Realm Alliance. If they learned I even considered trying—"

"You don't have to actually *use* it," Glisette said. "Its existence alone might intrigue him enough to allow you entry."

"Just listen, please, before you make your decision, Valory," Ambrosine cut in. "Not long after our parents died, Devorian decided to take up residence in that old palace. He needed room to breathe. We understood that. But it's been a year now, and he's supposed to have his coronation ceremony in a month. Our uncle is acting as regent and he's been civil so far. But if Devorian doesn't claim his birthright, Uncle Mathis will. And he's going to marry us off to his wealthy old friends and this whole court will become stiff and horrible and boring, just like him."

"Does Devorian know your uncle is pressing in?" I asked.

"He doesn't care," Glisette replied, flicking a flaxen curl behind her shoulder. "We've tried to reason with him, but he started refusing to see us. We dispatched a beautiful girl to talk him into coming home—his servants are always fetching beautiful girls from the town—but he discovered she was there at our behest and sent her back to us with no clothing but shoes. That poor girl was traumatized."

"How awful," I said, setting my glass on the table. Was he even fit to rule? I looked from Glisette to Ambrosine. "You two are older than him, aren't you? Does Volarre still refuse to pass a crown to a daughter?"

"Oh, Valory, you know very well it does," Ambrosine said, dismissing my question with a wave of her hand. "It's the one way we manage to be less modern than Calgoran. But it doesn't matter: neither of us wants to be queen. And before you go thinking it's because we don't want to sacrifice a life of play and luxury for drudgery and diplomacy, imagine—"

"That's why *I* don't want to do it," Glisette interrupted.

Ambrosine rolled her eyes and continued. "Imagine someone told you tomorrow you were to be Queen of Calgoran. Would you worry about leading your country to ruin, having not been properly prepared?"

"I would feel unprepared, yes, but I would surround myself with trusted advisors. You can change the laws, you can—"

"Don't be naïve," Glisette scoffed. "It took Queen Bristal changing the rules on your behalf. She won a war. She won the right to be a queen equal to her consort, and to demand that her daughters and granddaughters be considered viable heirs. But she still had to marry a king to change the laws."

"Let's not argue," Ambrosine said. "Regardless of the law, Devorian is more prepared to rule than we are, and it would take a lifetime of rigorous tutelage to change that. But the crown isn't the only reason we want you to convince him to come home."

She took a deep breath and pushed away her plate of delicacies. "That palace is...strange. Tamarice's curse broke when Bristal and the Realm Alliance defeated her. But there's a residue of darkness. Our family left it behind for a reason beyond building an opulent new home. And we think whatever lingers has influenced Devorian to involve himself in...unsavory pursuits."

"If he merely wants to bed whores and shirk his responsibilities, that's one matter," Glisette added. "But we fear he may do worse, that grief has transported him to a dark place. We don't know what he might be capable of, or whom he's entertaining. The only visitors he allows besides the girls are strange men in white cloaks and black masks."

I gasped. "White cloaks and black masks?" Were these the Summoners?

"That's what I said," Glisette answered. "Why? What's the matter?"

"My grandmother is searching for anonymous thieves in white cloaks and masks. She'll want to investigate—"

"Absolutely not," Glisette said through her teeth, though the rebuke was more impassioned than vicious. "She'll involve the authorities."

"Devorian needs grace, Valory, not punishment," Ambrosine added. "He's hurting. He's lost. I know he will make a good leader if we can pull him out of this spell. But he needs the chance to come back on his *own*, without force, or he will resent us forever."

I dug my teeth into my bottom lip. Grandmum needed to know what I'd discovered. But my reputation needed rehabilitating, and the Lorenthi sisters were too powerful to trifle with. Grandmum was right. I shouldn't have come.

"Have you tried using your gifts to force him home?" I asked, hoping distraction would help me squirm my way out of a pact of silence.

"I tried to take away his sadness," the youngest sister cut in. "When I touched him, he threw me to the floor."

"And there's nothing I can do as long as he's hibernating in there with magical barriers all around," Glisette said. "An icy gale wouldn't touch him."

"He covered all the mirrors so I can't use my gift to speak to or even see him," Ambrosine added. "We would never ask you to defy your sentence and use your power," she pressed, covering my hand with hers. "We only ask that you speak to him, reason with him. Make sure he's not up to anything...excessively questionable."

"What makes you sure he'll let me in, much less listen to me?" I was starting to feel cornered.

"He was a shameless gossip before he shut himself off," Glisette replied, leaning back to casually stroke the silver chain holding her chalcedony stone. "And any tidbits of news about you and the Water he gets from his servants won't be enough to satisfy him."

I shook my head. "I have to tell my—"

"Devorian will give her nothing," Ambrosine said. "He won't even allow her inside. *You* are more likely to get the answers your grandmother seeks, about the identities of the cloaked men."

"Try to speak to Devorian, please," Perennia urged, desperation clear in her small voice. "What harm could that do?"

"If it doesn't work, no one has to know you were involved," Ambrosine went on. "Then you can tell your grandmother about the white cloaks. We will resign ourselves to Uncle's rule and hope that someday Devorian returns to us."

A deep gulp of wine helped me stall for time as three pairs of blue-green eyes latched on to mine. I took my time swallowing, pondering Grandmum's wan expression when I mentioned seeing someone in a white cloak.

What business did the Summoners have here, and at the academy? What kind of artifact could have been stolen—something significant, dangerously so? Was Devorian involved? If not, why would the thieves visit him? Did they need aurions to fund their endeavors, or perhaps assistance from a wayward elicromancer flouting the tenets? Did they require Devorian's skill as an Omnilingual? Why hadn't Grandmum shared what she learned with the Conclave?

Curiosity and alarm entangled in my mind in an exhilarating dance. A stolen artifact, masked thieves, and mysterious visits to a recluse prince...this sounded like a treacherous plot in the works, something I should pass on to Grandmum without question. But the princesses believed she would be sent away from Devorian's lair if she tried to speak to him, and judging by Devorian's recalcitrance, any attempt on her part might obstruct *my* chances of securing an audience.

If Devorian might admit me, then I had an obligation to investigate in order to help Grandmum, to prevent an unnamed disaster that might take shape: perhaps a dark elicromancer's plot to oppress mortals, or a coup to overthrow King Tiernan, or Queen Jessa of Yorth. If I could stop an imminent terror and force Devorian onto his throne in the process, I would no longer be just the tenet-defying fool who dried up the Water.

"You'll need to sneak me out in the night," I said, my eyes tracking Brandar as he strolled through the garden, watching Calanthe sprint after a sparrow.

The princesses smiled conspiratorially. "That should be easy," Glisette said. "The difficult part will be getting you face-to-face with Devorian before he has a chance to say no. We must not give him an opportunity to refuse you."

"How?" Perennia asked. "The doors are barred, physically and with magic. Someone would have to admit her."

"I have an idea," Glisette said. "Devorian's most trusted servant goes to the pleasure house most nights to pick out a new 'guest.' We'll need to dress you to entice the servant."

"That seems like a game of chance. You said Devorian would *want* to see me."

"He will, I'm sure of it," Ambrosine said, frowning at her sister. "We don't need a silly ploy. If Devorian's curious about her, a simple knock should suffice. And if he's not, dressing her up as a whore won't help the situation. He'll just recognize her and throw her out."

Perennia bit her lip in uncertainty. She looked at Glisette, who shrugged.

"All right." Glisette turned back to me. "But if knocking doesn't work, just know that I *could* have made you look astounding and you *would* have been selected."

EIGHT

AS I followed the sloping cobblestone streets, I noticed a reek of refuse and potent perfume. Pleasure houses lined the outskirts of the south end, and just beyond them lay a depression of weeded rubble that functioned as a border to the old city.

Grateful to be wearing boots and my training breeches, I sidestepped puddles of stagnant water and piss, making my way toward a makeshift bridge that lay outside the boundary of warm light pulsing from the streetlamps. I cast an uncertain glance up at the prince's magnificent lair before crossing into the darkness of Pontaval's neglected quarters.

The princesses had offered me a horse and an escort, both of which I had refused. I didn't want to announce my approach too early. I'd considered bringing Calanthe, but she'd be more likely to take off after a rat than provide defense.

Yet I began to regret each choice that had led me here alone on foot. If even the pleasure houses remained within the limits of the new city, I wondered what kinds of sordid folks crept in the dark and called the old city home. My fingers closed over the grip of the dagger at my hip.

I could feel Perennia's enchantment beginning to wear off. The guilt and sadness that had been my constant companions since Ivria's death crept back, joining the fear that prickled up the back of my neck. The night breeze carried vestiges of winter's chill. I shivered.

But a sense of duty, and moreover, of desperation, struck anew. I clenched my fists, shook off the tightness in my spine, and walked on.

I sensed movement in my periphery but refused to peer into the forsaken shops and smithies. Whether rats or wretches, I prayed the inhabitants would mind their own business if I minded mine.

I thought the sense of unease would diminish as I approached the vast palace at the hill crest, but the dark windows, arches, and spires felt as watchful as the shadows around me.

There were no sentinels at the metal gates surrounded by wild gardens. In fact, the gates stood slightly ajar, one side straining away from the hinges. I sucked in my breath and slipped through the opening to prevent the telltale groan of rusted metal. Weeds sprouted from the cracked stones of the courtyard. The frayed flags topping the shadowy turrets swished in the wind. My feet longed to race downhill to the light and safety of even the seamiest alley of the new city. But I took a breath and ascended the steps leading to the grand entrance.

The tarnished gold knockers were nearly too high for my reach. I touched the cold metal with my fingertips, hesitating. What if the prince stripped away my belongings and threw me out, like the poor girl his sisters had sent? My sympathy for her was renewed as I realized how treacherous the path home must have been.

At least he let her keep her shoes, I thought, as a means of self-encouragement. Then I shook my head. The prince would sense my fear, and he would sniff out my bluff. *For whatever reason, the Water dried up beneath your touch*, I told myself. *The trees shriveled. The walls cracked. You do not fear a petulant prince.*

Bolstered, I seized the heavy knocker and banged it three resounding times.

I took a step back and crossed my arms, attempting poise.

The silence drew on and suspense scraped at my resolve. But at last, a slat in the door slid open and I saw the top half of a face with ruddy eyebrows.

"Are you one of the girls they sent up?" the servant asked, eyeing my clothing.

I considered saying yes. It might gain me entry. But I remembered the princesses' many ploys and said, "No. I'm Valory Braiosa."

A beat passed, and then the slat shut firmly. After a few dragging minutes of increasing disappointment, a metallic thud signified someone unlocking the massive wooden doors.

They swung open with a stout creak. Light spilled across the threshold, revealing an entryway so unexpectedly splendid that I let out a gasp. I would have thought that a prince living in self-imposed exile would let dust and filth devour the place, but everything was immaculate, from the royal blue carpet to the ironwork that curved with the sweeping marble stairs. The silver lily motifs ornamenting the walls had been polished to perfection. Even the servant holding the door wore a clean, pressed tunic of silver and blue. "His Highness is waiting for you in the library," he said with a bow. "I'll take you to him."

I stepped inside. The servant shut the door behind me, took my cloak, and led me upstairs. My palm didn't even collect dust as it slid along the banister. The paintings in the halls had either been restored or so well maintained over the decades that they showed no signs of dilapidation. Perhaps Devorian's father and grandfather had used this place as a secret retreat.

At last, we reached a set of double doors. The servant's knock was answered by a gasp and a giggle.

"Come in!" a male voice called, laughing.

The servant opened the doors and stepped aside, leaving me to announce myself. But the words fled from my mind as I took in the scene ahead.

A perimeter of towering shelves lined the vast library walls. A large desk faced glass doors, looking upon a balcony overgrown with roses. At the center of the library, where one might ordinarily find a statue or a precious ancient text on display, there was instead an enormous canopy bed. A constellation of velvet chaises and tables replete with trays of food and drink surrounded it. Several barely clothed women draped themselves in languorous poses—except the one who straddled the shirtless prince on the bed.

"Ah!" Devorian said, seizing the woman by her hips and setting her aside. He was revealed to be wearing only thigh-high breeches. "Dear Valory, have you come to join the revelry?"

His lover cursed in a language I didn't understand and collapsed back onto the bed in dismay. He answered her in the same language. His elicrin gift gave him command over all tongues and dialects.

"I should think not, considering I'm your cousin," I answered, clasping my hands behind my back and sauntering over to a collection of instruments. I wondered what the kings who had used this library in the past would think of its current purpose.

"Distant cousin," he amended, tossing back the dark blond

waves settling on his shoulders. His magenta elicrin stone caught the dim light. "If you rule out your distant relations, there will be no royals left for you to marry. But Calgoranians are more obsessed with elicrin blood than royalty these days, aren't they?" He hopped off the bed, strolled to a cart of liquor bottles, poured two tiny goblets of brandy, and offered one to me.

"I'm not here to take part in your decadence," I said, sinking into a high-backed chair and slinging my legs onto a cushion, determined not to allow the spectacle of bare skin to discomfit me. "I'm here to convince you to return home and assume the royal duties your sisters think themselves wildly incapable of carrying out. Your uncle is keen to marry them off to the highest bidders, and, well, you can guess what he does next, can't you?" I moved aside a tray of fruit and cheeses and picked up a handheld ornamental mirror lying facedown on an accent table. "Takes the crown, sits on the throne... you know the rest."

Devorian traipsed over to rip the mirror from my hand. My own thorny expression passed over the glass, cast in shadow and moonlight, before he plunked the reflective side back down on the wood surface. "To be clear, I didn't allow you in because I fear you or have any inclination to heed your advice," he said, sinking back onto the bed. The woman he had left behind clawed at his chest and covered his neck in fervent kisses. "I did so because I'm intrigued by what happened at the Water."

I tilted my head, locking him in a stare. "Maybe you should fear me," I said, my voice even.

Devorian blinked at me a moment, then laughed. "I always liked you, little Valory. You're so wry, so melancholy. And surprisingly dauntless. A Calgoranian woman of your standing ought to have shrieked and bolted at the sight of so much bare skin, yet here you are, sustaining an impressive façade."

I raised my eyebrows. "You are gifted, Devorian. Your elicrin talent for languages would make you a fine and industrious king. You could strengthen peace with outside kingdoms, establish relations with countries we haven't even dreamed of visiting. You could do great things, and you wouldn't have to give up your passions. A king can do what he wants behind closed doors."

"You think that hasn't occurred to me?" he asked flatly.

Springing out of the chair, I crossed the room to a portrait of a young Devorian with his parents and sisters hanging above the hearth. He looked so innocent, so docile. *Death coarsens us all.*

"Are you going to allow someone to steal your birthright?" I asked, trying another angle. I didn't want to bring up the men in white cloaks for fear he would show me the door. I whipped around. "Your parents would object."

His jocular expression froze over. "Let my uncle take the crown. He will be forced to step aside."

"By you? When you feel ready? Why not prevent him from claiming it in the first place?"

"It is not I who will overthrow him, cousin," he said, tearing away from his lover again to pace the room. With a tormented sigh, he flung open the balcony doors and stepped into the night.

I plucked a lantern off the desk occupied by a sleeping woman swathed in sheer fabric and followed him outside. Hundreds of roses flaunted their sanguine red and blush hues even in the darkness. They clutched at the balustrade and crawled up the walls.

"Lovely, aren't they?" Devorian asked.

I cupped a pink rose in my palm, minding the thorns.

"They're remnants of Tamarice's curse," he said. "Before it was broken, impenetrable briars surrounded the palace, and its inhabitants were stranded between life and death."

"Strange, that something so beautiful could spring from such wickedness," I whispered.

"All beauty is laced with darkness."

I released the petals and lifted the lantern to read his expression. "What do you mean, that someone else will overthrow your uncle?"

The single flame danced in his eyes. "You must know there are other kinds of magic besides elicromancy...ancient and fearsome, capable of awesome and unthinkable deeds."

Unsettled, I strove to penetrate the ambiguity with a straight question. "What kind of magic, Devorian?" I asked. "Who are the men in white cloaks, the Summoners?"

"What really happened at the Water?" he countered, his blond eyebrows playful. "If you tell me your truth, I may tell you mine."

"I have told it. I have *only* told it."

"Is that so?" he asked with a mirthless chuckle. "Ambitious yet powerless little Valory Braiosa didn't look at the Water and see... opportunity?"

"What do you mean, 'opportunity'?"

"You've striven your whole life to be worthy, watched your cousins prance through the academy with their showy magic. And then Ivria sneaks to the Water..." He trailed off.

The incredulity slid from my features. Perhaps I could use a lurid false confession to earn his trust.

I lowered the lantern, letting the shadows play on my face. "She snuck away, picked the lock, and went through the portal. All I did was follow her. As I stood in front of the Water, I knew I was meant to have power. And I knew that if I touched it, even if it was wrong, it would all look like Ivria's fault." True resentment slipped into my false admission. "The anger would roll off her back. Everyone loved Ivria. They couldn't punish me *more* than her for trying to save her."

"But then she died, and all the anger stuck to you." He clucked his tongue. "Inconvenient."

A sneer pulled at my lip. "What do your visitors want from you?" I demanded, hoping he would make good on our bargain.

With a canny look, he strode back inside. I followed. Once again, he spoke in another language—Perispi, this time—to request something of the woman sprawled across the desk. She sat up to face him with a feline smile. I sighed with impatience as he leaned down to kiss her mouth, biting her lower lip like a luscious fruit and seizing her small breasts. Just when I worried he was trifling with me, he purred in her ear and she slid off the desk, tendering a mischievous look in my direction.

Devorian sat in the chair and lifted the top away from the desk, exposing a compartment lined with blue velvet. Inside was a parcel as big as my torso, wrapped and tied with soft leather. He extracted it with great care and closed the secret cabinet, laying the large item down as gently as if it were an injured bird.

"Is this what the Summoners stole?" I asked.

"I know nothing of theft." With a graceful movement, Devorian loosened the tie and swept away the covering, revealing an iridescent slab of lustrous cloudy white, gray, mauve, and golden-pink. It reminded me of the inner layers of shells I used to collect from the beach in Beyrian. Minuscule engravings marred the mother-of-pearl surface.

"They want me to translate the runes," Devorian said.

"And what do the runes say?"

"This lost language is so ancient that it tests even my gift of tongues. I can sound out the markings, but I can't draw meaning from them. It's never happened to me before. I speak every language known to man." He ran his finger backward along a line of runes. "The Summoners asked me not to speak the entire incantation aloud. When I've finished parsing it out, they want me to participate in some sort of ritual."

"Do you know their identities? Can you describe any of them?"

"They wear masks," he said, salty. I glowered at his insufficient answer and he added, "No, I don't know who they are."

"What did they offer you in return?" Everything in me longed to ask what the incantation on this arcane tablet might accomplish. But Grandmum seemed to already know that, and I wasn't here to satisfy my own curiosity.

"They promised me a place of authority in a new world order. But that's not what interested me."

A new world order? "What did?"

The hungry gleam in his eyes perturbed me. Here he sat in a room of resplendent beauties, shielded from responsibility and free to pursue every luxury thanks to the privilege of his birth. What could these men offer him that he lacked?

"They told me precious little about the incantation"—he looked from the tablet to me, the spark in his eyes glowing ever more infernal—"but I gleaned more than they shared. There were whispers of an 'awakening.'"

For the first time since taking the princesses up on their challenge, it occurred to me that I had chosen the wrong path, a foolish path, and that I possessed neither the wisdom nor the aptitude to maneuver a ship headed for disaster back on course. I circled round the desk and spoke in as calm a tone as I could manage. "Devorian, resurrection rituals are forbidden to the utmost. Professor Strather said that even the darkest elicromancers of the olden days feared them."

"Because the rituals always go awry," he said. "But that's elicromancy. This is beyond, more, stronger, greater."

"Then we understand it even less." I glanced back at the portrait of his family, noticing two urns on the mantel. If his sisters realized he had taken his parents' remains and displayed them in his den of vices, they had spared me that unsavory detail.

Perhaps, at first, Devorian had hidden himself away to flee his duties as heir. But he stayed because the darkness of this place and the murmurings of his mysterious visitors had fomented a shadowy hope in his heart. He planned to resurrect his mother and father.

"Listen," I said, waiting until he severed his infatuated gaze from the tablet to continue. "Resurrection rituals multiply tragedy a thousandfold. Your parents are at peace. You wouldn't want to do anything to rip them from that, to give them back the misery of life."

"What about my misery?" he growled, eyes red-rimmed. "They were torn from me."

"Your sisters lost them too. Instead of closing yourself off, draw from their strength. Your parents are at peace in the land of light."

Devorian took deep breaths, glaring at nothing in particular. Everyone in the room watched his heaving shoulders with rapt attention. My fingers ventured to the edges of the tablet, smooth beneath my touch. When Devorian didn't react, I grasped it. It was large but slender, light enough to slide off the table without dipping with the weight.

I turned slowly, the urge to escape with this dangerous artifact racing through my bones. It would be a long journey back through the abandoned city, wondering if at any minute Devorian might catch up to me.

"What about Ivria?" Devorian asked, brusque, as I neared the library doorway. "What if this incantation has the power to bring her back?"

With an intake of breath, I turned back to him. "Devorian, I—"

"Imagine," he said, jumping nimbly from the chair. "This incantation is capable of bringing our loved ones back. But I'm the only one who can speak it."

I fought it. I fought it with all of my being, but it came to me regardless: a vision of Ivria rising from her ashes, smiling the way she used to. There would be a glow about her, a glow from the beyond, but it would fade as she settled back into her ordinary life. We would talk of everything and nothing, as we always had. She would be exactly the same.

But my father—he would have changed. He would no longer be a maddening ghost of a man, no longer restless and troubled. He would look at me and *see* me. He would know that I needed him more than he needed to escape the confines of a life he should never have chosen for himself.

Devorian tugged on the bottom edges of the tablet and gently pried it from my hands, striding over to the mantel that held his parents' remains. Realizing I had tumbled into a fantasy, I jolted after him.

"You know a resurrection spell would only bring back husks of your parents," I said to his back.

He whipped around, lips stretched into a sneer. "They call you Ivria's murderer, don't they? Not to your face, but they whisper it in their own hearts just as you whisper it in yours. What if you were her savior?"

"Enough!" I yelled, my voice hoarse with grief.

"Ivria doesn't have to be dead." He caught one of the nearby girls by the forearm and steered her in front of me. "Tell her Ivria's not dead," he commanded her.

"Ivria's not dead," she repeated blandly.

"Don't put this poison in my mind, you beast of a man!" I pushed past the girl to grasp at the tablet, but Devorian easily fended me off, twisting my arm hard enough to make me squeal. He ripped the tablet from my grip and flung me so close to the fire I nearly stumbled into the flames.

Devorian let out a piercing whistle, followed by a soft hum. His eyes traced the mystical runes as he held the tablet, firelight stretching his narrow features to wicked angles. He had begun the incantation.

Pushing off the mantel, I sprang forward and locked a hand over his mouth. I drew my dagger with the other and pressed the edge of the blade to the soft flesh of his throat.

After a breathless beat, Devorian began to laugh. My teeth locked together. I could become the fiercest, most cunning magician in the realm and elicromancers would still laugh at me. I wasn't suddenly fearsome because I'd gained power—I was a clumsy, hopeless creature who broke everything she touched.

I pricked the very tip of my knife through Devorian's pale flesh. As with Melkior, this physical release was the only tonic to soothe the anger that roiled through my veins, collecting magical vigor as it rushed to destroy.

"*Sararesth*," Devorian hissed in response, shoving my knife away. He turned on me and his magenta elicrin stone shone radiant. The women scattered to the far side of the room while a whip of light shot out from his stone and snaked around my wrists, binding them together at my navel. Devorian smiled a lazy smile as my knife clattered to the floor.

Then he started the incantation from the beginning.

"Stop, Devorian!" I yelled. But the prince only raised his voice to drown me out. The utterances grew louder and more haunting as he became sure of himself, looking up at the twin urns each time he had to pause for breath.

"Stop!" I screamed. My temper was heating as I fought against my bonds, the power inside me still churning.

But before I inflicted any damage, Devorian's shouting in the bizarre tongue quieted. He had finished the incantation.

We glared at each other as we drank in air. The light from his elicrin stone snuffed out, but the language lingered around us like echoes in a cave.

I watched helplessly as a crack crawled down the center of the tablet. With a deafening snap, the artifact split asunder and clunked to the marble floor.

Shadows passed by the balcony. We looked out to see a red moon partly masked by black clouds in a starless sky. The palace trembled as if responding to a faraway quake. Many of the women scurried from the room while others covered their heads and sank to the floor in fear. I knew my magic was not responsible for these disturbances.

"What have you done?" I whispered.

"I—I…" Devorian stammered.

"What have you done?" I roared.

The balcony doors slammed shut, shattering the glass. Bits of the ceiling crumbled and rained down on us. This time, it was no mysterious outside force, but the power that hibernated inside me. It ground across the rest of my being like steel against iron, and I wasn't sure which was stronger, which would eventually break into brittle pieces.

My power overcame me. It wreaked havoc on everything.

Then the world faded to black.

NINE

ABS of pain shot up my hands and elbows. The back of my head throbbed. I coughed and blinked my eyes open, seeing only broken glass, dust, and rubble.

The library looked like the site of a ferocious battle. The bookshelves had toppled, and stray volumes littered the floor. Blood gleamed on bits of glass around me. After dabbing the top of my head with my fingertips, I realized it was mine.

I pushed up on my elbows, fearing carnage worse than I could imagine. But there was no one. The prince's guests must have escaped before I turned the room to wreckage. Where had Devorian gone?

Fighting the faintness that made my vision tilt, I stood. My mouth was dry, which I attributed to the passing of time. The crimson moon could no longer be seen from the balcony, and tinges of dawn lurked outside the windows.

My soles crunched over the debris. The bed coverings were in tatters on the floor. The doors had been ripped from their frame. The urns had toppled off the mantel, their ashes scattered.

I did this.

The thought sickened me. Stepping around the tablet halves, I picked up my knife and passed through the open doorway into the corridor, where the candles on the sconces had burned low, their wax dripping like tears. But I halted and took a single step backward into the library.

Amid the wreckage, the marks hadn't caught my eye at first. They were distinct: five diagonal scratches on the stone doorframe, each the length of my forearm. What could have abraded stone in that manner? I ran my fingertips along the strange markings. An inexplicable terror bored into my belly.

"Devorian?" I called. His name tasted like a curse on my tongue after what he had done. His words had turned the moon to blood and blotted out the stars. The ashes from the urns were still just ashes. But had something risen from them?

I roamed the dark hallways in search of Devorian, one of his servants, anyone. I found only more rugged markings on the walls. Slow-building terror mounted inside me. Whispers seemed to come from the very walls, the candelabras, the portraits. I touched the dried blood on my crown and the sore spot beneath it, hoping the wound was responsible for these delusions.

Panic began to pound in my chest as I crossed another set of markings and followed them to the next, letting them guide me up more and more stairs until I wondered if I was imagining them too.

At last, I followed a cold stairwell to a tower, the highest by my estimation. Tears of desperation stung my cheeks.

The door at the top had been dismantled. "Devorian?" I tried to say, but his name was barely more than a whisper. Darkness filled the room. I recalled the tale of Princess Rosamund, how Tamarice had tried to kill her with a curse but instead trapped her in an unconsciousness between life and death. After Bristal destroyed Tamarice and broke the curse, she found Rosamund alive and hidden away in this very tower—a happy ending for the heroine.

I cleared my throat and said the prince's name again. This time, a shadow in the room shifted—no, not *a* shadow, but a mass of shadows. The handheld mirror I'd seen on the table in the library flashed with muted dawn light.

"Don't look at me," a gruff voice said. "Leave, unless you can undo this."

I gasped and staggered back, nearly tripping down the stairs. The voice was deep and ghastly, but it held a familiar dulcet quality. I squinted against the meager light of approaching dawn, discerning an enormous figure with a coat of bristling fur, hunched shoulders, jutting horns, and deadly claws that gripped the mirror handle.

"*I said leave!*" the creature bellowed, turning in my direction, its hot breath whisking loose hairs away from my face.

I ran.

My feet couldn't tread down the winding steps fast enough. I fancied that the creature—Devorian, I admitted with a bout of nausea—pursued me with haste, raking at the walls as it went. But even when I burst out the front entrance and realized nothing had followed, I felt no relief.

My capacity to ruin did not stop at inanimate entities.

I wondered whether it could be stopped at all.

I ran until I reached the warped metal gates and grasped the rusty bars, fighting to fill my empty lungs. When I flung a frightened glance over my shoulder, the front door gaped at me like a dragon's maw.

"What have you done?"

I whipped around. Ambrosine stood outside the gates, a silver filigree mirror like Devorian's clutched in her hand. Glisette materialized behind her. They both still wore dressing gowns and slippers. Devorian had shown them his face.

Ambrosine yanked the broken gate open and the rusted metal screamed. The wind tugged on her golden hair and strewed it across her face. "Turn him back," she said.

A loud clattering drew my gaze beyond the two sisters. The covered carriage we'd taken from Arna rumbled up the road. A second dose of dread leapt from my stomach to my throat like bile.

Glisette slipped past me and ran up the steps to the open doorway. But the broad door swung on its hinges and slammed shut in her face. "Devorian!" she called, pounding on the wood.

The carriage halted and Grandmum stepped out, her eyes like frigid pools. Perennia followed, blanching with obvious remorse. "I had to tell her everything," Perennia said to me. "Once I saw... saw..."

I swallowed hard and resisted the urge to cast my eyes at the ground. The horses took up a high-pitched, restless neighing, perhaps sensing the presence of an unnatural creature nearby. A chill hurried up my spine.

"Have you no sense?" Grandmum's voice teemed with restrained fury as she cast a long shadow over me.

"I—I was trying to—"

"Where's the tablet? Did they ask Devorian to translate it?"

"I tried to stop him," I croaked. Perennia must have told her about the men in white cloaks, and my clever grandmother had pieced everything together. "He read the runes aloud. He broke it."

Grandmum pinned her thin lips closed and pivoted on her heel.

"I'm sorry!" I cried, launching myself after her. "They begged me to talk to him." I gestured back at the princesses. "They said Devorian would never let you inside, much less listen to you."

"I wouldn't have needed him to listen," she barked, gripping the door of the passenger compartment. "If I had known, I would have retrieved the tablet with or without his cooperation. This is beyond your purview, girl. Did he recognize them? The Summoners?"

"No. They wear masks. All they told him was that they needed him to read the incantation."

"What incantation?" Perennia asked, shivering in her silk sleeves. "What was that quaking in the middle of the night?"

"How she's going to fix Devorian is the only question that matters!" Glisette yelled over her younger sister as she stormed back to us.

"Devorian performed some sort of resurrection ritual," I explained, frantic. "I tried to stop him and—"

"Resurrection ritual?" Perennia repeated. "You mean...he tried to raise our...?"

"Did it work?" Ambrosine asked, hope illuminating her face like a summer sunrise.

"You foolish girls," Grandmum said, looking from them to me. "You have no idea what he's set in motion."

I clamped a hand over my mouth as I weighed the urgency in her eyes. Peeling my hand away, I asked, "What? What does the incantation do?"

"Awaken something best left undisturbed. And no, not your mother and father," she snapped at the princesses, her tone wildly out of character. The rosiness fled from Ambrosine's cheeks.

"What did it awaken?" I asked, trembling. I recalled what she had shared with me about the Summoners: *worshippers of an entity they call the Lord of Elicromancers.*

"A great evil lost to memory," Grandmum answered, stepping into the coach. "But only Malyrra truly knows."

"Who's Malyrra?" I asked.

"The ambassador will make sure you reach Yorth," she continued, ignoring my question. "Bring the tablet and tell the Realm Alliance what's happened."

"What do I do about Devorian?"

"You've done enough. Someone will know how to right him."

"Where are you going?"

"To find Malyrra, if I can, among the fay," she replied, looking me square in the eye. "To ask them what exactly you and Devorian have unleashed on Nissera."

Had Grandmum gone mad? The fay were ancient ancestors of modern fairies, long extinct.

There was no time to ask. The carriage door slammed shut and the nervous horses seemed keen to answer the coachman's prodding. The silence felt thick in the wake of their hooves striking cobblestones.

The sisters exchanged fraught glances before ascending to the entrance. Knees feeble and head throbbing, I trailed behind.

Ambrosine knocked. "Devorian?" she called softly, her voice wavering, as though she feared as much as hoped he would answer the summons.

The slat slammed sideways. Amid the shadows, I saw a flash of sharp canines. The eye looking out shone a burnished yellow-gold.

The sisters screeched and stumbled back. Perennia braced herself and whispered chants meant to help lift dark curses. *"Hirafeth. Maras tacaral." Dispel the darkness. Restore what was.*

"Devorian," Ambrosine ventured again. "Did the resurrection work?"

"No!" he roared. "They're nothing but ashes. And I'm..."

His golden eye shot toward me. I cringed and fought the urge to scurry away.

Ambrosine clung to the open slot and emitted a sob. "Maybe Valory's curse will fade."

The word *curse* stung like a biting wind. Accidental outbursts of magic were one matter. A curse implied something else.

"Is there any word of the Water trickling back after she dried it up?" Glisette demanded, flinging aside the ridiculous train of her dressing gown to pace along the threshold. "No, because it's still a pit in the woods with no magic. *She* needs to undo this."

"I can't," I whispered.

"He's a deformed creature, you useless twit!" Glisette spat, but by the time she finished, oncoming tears had broken through her temper. She gripped my shoulders and shook me. "You can't leave without fixing this."

I shoved her away. "Don't you understand? You shouldn't have asked anything of me! I can *only* warp and destroy. What did you expect?" I was nearly snarling, jabbing my finger like a weapon, eager to blame anyone but myself. "You goaded me into this."

Glisette bared teeth that glistened like pearls, but the sneer soon slid off her face, leaving only despair.

Shame twisted in my gut. I raked in a breath and approached

the prince. "I'm going straight to the Realm Alliance, Devorian. We've both done wrong. For my part, I'm sorry. I never meant for this to happen. I want to fix this, and I will ask for grace on both our behalves. But I need to bring the tablet so they understand what we've set in motion."

A beat passed. The yellow-gold eye turned on me and the churlish voice ripped through the quiet. "You believe there's someone who can break this curse?"

"The Realm Alliance will know what to do. But I can't go empty-handed."

"Step back," he purred. "Turn around."

I retreated to the lowest step and did as he asked.

"All of you," he growled.

With a choked sob, Ambrosine turned her back on the palace. The other two followed.

A lock clicked and the heavy door swung open. I flinched when the broken tablet clattered on the threshold.

"Tell them I'm sorry," he said before slamming the door shut.

I whirled and started toward the iridescent tablet halves, but Ambrosine swept past me to pick one up and cradle it against her chest.

"What are you doing?" I demanded, snatching the other before she could.

"Mother and Father," Ambrosine said, looking at her sisters. "The Realm Alliance will want to undo this if they can. But what if the resurrection is still in process?"

"Didn't you hear the old woman?" Glisette asked. "That's not what this does. Besides, resurrection rituals don't bring back the person you've lost, just a shell that doesn't belong in the world of the living."

Tears tumbled down Ambrosine's cheeks. "Just to see them again," she said through a smile that prickled the hairs on my arm. She didn't care how they came back. "Can you imagine?"

"I won't imagine it," Glisette said. I stepped aside so she could close the distance between them. The cloudy purple chalcedony at her sternum swelled with white light, and a distinct chill laced through the breeze. I hoped she was prepared to fight for the tablet; I couldn't risk inciting another disaster. "And you shouldn't either. Mother and Father are gone."

Ambrosine resembled a cornered animal. The tiniest glimpse of light surfaced in her sky-blue elicrin stone, but she expelled another anguished sob and surrendered the tablet to Glisette, who handed it to me.

"Leave," Glisette said to me, her bright eyes merciless. "Don't show your face in Pontaval until you've fixed this."

Eager to oblige her, I hurried away with the tablets, once again turning my back on the havoc I had wrought.

~❦ TEN ❦~

AS we neared Beyrian, the city sprawling on a southern coastal inlet, I could taste the briny air and feel the sun's warmth, but I couldn't escape the recesses of my darkest thoughts.

A great evil lost to memory…

My attempt to salvage my reputation had only further demolished it, and I couldn't begin to imagine what Devorian—what I—had unknowingly summoned, though my mind did its best to dredge up dreadful ideas.

But the longer my guilt stewed, the more Grandmum's secrecy needled me, stoking a lick of anger. She had offered me tantalizing morsels of truth. If she had trusted me with the whole of it, I wouldn't have interfered.

I scratched oblivious Calanthe behind the ears and nudged my wayward satchel back under the carriage seat. A week ago, when we had left Pontaval behind, I had wrapped the stolen artifact in one of my nightdresses and shoved it beneath my other belongings.

Rayed had let me brood without interruption, even when I didn't emerge from my room at the last inn and forced us to tarry two extra days. As we traveled, he read books, scratched missives, and only occasionally peeked at me with concern. Brandar's inner life must have consumed him as mine did, for he rarely spoke but never seemed to tire of the silence.

Another magical missive appeared on Rayed's lap. He read it, frowned, and nodded as if agreeing to a command before leaning forward. His mahogany eyes were intent. "Queen Jessa plans to be discreet about Devorian's situation. She will steer the discussion toward solutions for the future rather than condemnation for what's already occurred. The Lorenthi princesses have agreed to stay quiet about their brother's plight so long as he faces no serious consequences for his actions."

"Why does Queen Jessa want to keep this quiet?" I asked. "Shouldn't she send someone to put Devorian to rights?"

"She has dispatched elicromancers to do so, but she doesn't want mortals to hear of his plight and become hysterical thinking elicromancers can't control their own kind. Governing is difficult when rumors fly wild."

"It's that simple?" I asked, doubtful. "No one besides Queen Jessa will know what I did to Devorian?"

"As you may learn, more matters are settled in the cloakroom than the communal chamber. It's just the way of things."

"Good," I said, relieved. "I don't know what the others would do to me if…"

"People fear what they don't understand," Rayed said when I trailed off. "As a child, I was frightened to leave Erdem for Nissera. I worried elicromancers might see my father as a lesser being to subjugate rather than a respected diplomat. Yet he was treated with dignity, and Kadri and I have flourished in Nissera even after his death. It was nothing like I expected, and I learned that very quickly. All elicrin gifts can be destructive until they're properly managed; it's how you came about your power that disturbs the others."

Rayed sat back, scratched his beard, and closed his eyes. At rest, his angular, clever features and prominent cheekbones seemed to soften, and I found myself feeling encouraged about my allies.

But as Beyrian appeared at the horizon, my nerves seemed to cinch tighter. Word of my latest mistake would only stay quiet for so long, especially if the ruthless, rule-worshipping members of the Conclave caught wind of it. And what of my next move? Scandal seemed inevitable so long as my magic stayed out of my grip like a wet, writhing fish determined to swim free.

The enclosed compartment began to feel like a prison cell. I yanked on the bellpull and the carriage gradually eased to a halt.

"I'll just be a moment," I said, disembarking and planting both boots firmly on the dirt road. My mother would want me to wear a dress, bat my eyes, and look altogether powerless, but this morning I had donned a fitted tunic, breeches, and shin-high leather boots. My sheathed dagger dangled at my hip. I felt helpless enough without a wardrobe to match.

I shut the door on Calanthe. She wouldn't wander off as long as there was a carriage to chase, but at rest I couldn't trust her not to fling herself after a rabbit. Noticing a patch of trees across the road, I fought through high grasses and clambered over the gray rocks toward it.

As soon as I entered the shade and raked in some fresh air, my worries ebbed a little. Since my companions probably already suspected me of doing it, I squatted to take a piss, steadying myself against a coarse tree. My fingers landed on sticky sap—but when I pulled them away, I found it was not sap.

It was dripping blood.

I hurried to pull up my breeches one-handed and glanced around me, pulse aflutter. In all likelihood, the blood belonged to a maimed animal that had already fled at my approach.

But then a low moan rose over the whoosh of the pleasant sea-borne breeze—a moan that sounded human.

Following the voice, I emerged from the other end of the tree patch and found a young man sprawled on an outcrop of smooth rock.

His left eye was bruised so badly it looked like an overripe fruit, plum purple against his light golden skin. He wore a tunic of shabby gray cloth bearing a fresh bloodstain, as well as a necklace made of twine and metal that held a gray-green gem I suspected of being an elicrin stone.

I took a knee beside him. He was in no shape to cope with the jerkiness of a materialization attempt—if he was indeed an elicromancer and able to materialize at all. He groaned again as I peeled back his shirt and found a vicious stab wound on his flank that could be fatal if not properly tended. If I could get him to an elicrin Healer at the Beyrian palace, or at least a talented mortal healer in the city, he would survive.

Extracting my knife, I rent one of my sleeves at the elbow and removed my belt to secure the fabric around the wound. The young man turned his head to peer at me through his good eye, which glistened the brown of barley wine.

"I don't suppose your elicrin gift is healing?" I asked under my breath. I leaned into my heels and negotiated my arms beneath his back. If he didn't have the wherewithal to cooperate, I would have to hurry back and ask Rayed and Brandar for help.

But he found the strength, and with a moan and a wince, he helped me help him to his feet, mumbling something so close to inarticulate that I barely caught it. "I suppose it isn't yours either?"

"Far from it," I muttered. "But I have a carriage and I'm on my way to the city."

When we staggered to the other side of the grove, Rayed and Brandar hurried to assist me without questions and we loaded the wounded young man into the carriage. Calanthe wagged her intrusive tail and licked the newcomer's swollen eye until I yanked her away by the scruff of her neck. I reached for the skin of water I'd stowed in a satchel and tilted the young man's head to let it drip into his mouth.

My traveling companions settled in next to me and the coach took off. It would take time to make our way through the crowded city to the palace on the shore, time I feared this boy could not spare. Instead of wishing Beyrian would stay minuscule in the distance, I willed it to rise up and meet us.

"What happened to him?" Rayed finally asked.

"There must have been a skirmish of some sort," I replied. "It seems the victor left him for dead."

The young man closed his good eye. I took the opportunity to look beyond his wounds and study his features. His hair was sandy brown but his eyebrows, beneath the dried blood, were a few shades darker. His nose was succinct and graceful, his jaw well defined. A small, dark mole decorated his cheek. I guessed him to be about my age, perhaps a bit older, on the cusp of elicrin immortality setting in. The deep purple bruising rimmed in splotchy yellow made it difficult to be certain of much except that he was a fine-looking fellow, and his contours only grew more pleasing the longer I scrutinized them.

Warmth blossomed in my cheeks as I realized that both of my companions were watching me watch him. Smoothing the crease of concern between my eyebrows, I slid back in my seat and looked outside.

At last, Beyrian rose up around us: the taverns, bakeries, inns, and market tents that welcomed travelers from the north. Beyond them lay residences, craft shops, and smithies, and beyond those lay the palace, which met with the edge of the vast blue sea.

But we wouldn't reach the shore anytime soon. Carriages, carts, pedestrians, and livestock jammed the overused and rutted streets. There seemed to be some sort of obstruction ahead of us.

"I'm not sure this poor fellow has any time to waste," Rayed said over the young man's rattling breaths.

"Is there not another route?" I asked, peering out the window.

"We're hemmed in." Rayed cracked the door to get a peek up and down the road. A jarring array of smells wafted into the compartment. Calanthe's wet nostrils throbbed in intrigue.

"We can take him to that inn and summon a healer," Brandar said, jerking his head. "May be his best chance."

"Yes, that'll do," Rayed agreed, exiting the carriage. "I'll go see what this nonsense is about up ahead."

I slung the ungainly satchel over my shoulder, unwilling to risk leaving the artifact behind in a bustling city. As I restrained Calanthe, and Brandar negotiated the wounded boy out of the carriage, I glanced up and noticed the sun inching higher in the sky. The hearing would start just after noon. I had time, but not much of it.

Gritting my teeth, I shouldered half of the boy's weight and we shuffled between stalls with pans of searing scallops suspended over blazing fires. The beggars at either side of the door to the inn didn't hold out their cups for a thesar, not after seeing the boy so bruised and bloodied.

Once inside, Brandar deposited the stranger in a chair and I wove through the tables toward the scruffy old man tending the tavern. "I would like to pay for a room for this fellow, and I need you to summon a healer." I pointed in the boy's direction.

The man squinted and pursed his lips, swaying on the other side of the counter. He reeked of ale.

"It's a simple request, sir," I said, plopping a pouch of silver aurions before him. "I'll pay you double to be quick about it."

The old man grabbed a pint and poured ale from the draught, managing to fill the mug without sloshing a single drop. "There you are, pretty missy," he said.

"No, I—"

"You can't rely on old Piers, here," said a nearby patron with a woolly beard. "Give me the coins and I'll fetch a skilled healer."

"Do you take me for an imbecile?" I demanded.

"Only trying to assist you, miss. Figured you were from elsewhere and I could save you the trouble of dealing with rotten Piers."

"I *am* from elsewhere: Arna, to be specific, because I'm an Ermetarius. Go find me a healer."

The man stood up, knocking his chair over on the way out. He stumbled over the doorstep before wandering off. Brandar pursued the man to ensure that he adhered to his quest.

Grunting a curse, I snatched the pouch of silver aurions and escorted my perspiring, delirious companion up the stairs. Why couldn't I have chanced upon hospitable folks? I had always found Yorthans more accommodating than my northern compatriots, but come to think of it, my royal blood had usually blazed me a path straight to the palace.

When I had managed to haul the boy to the top of the stairs, we encountered two women and a man conferring in the hallway. They refused to step aside until their sinister glares had probed us from head to toe. The coins jingled as I hobbled past. I realized I might have beckoned trouble by announcing my family name for the world to hear.

I knocked and tested locks until I found an empty room. The housekeeper hadn't tidied up, but I didn't see any signs of occupation. I laid the moaning young man and my satchel on the bed and opened the shutters. The carriages and wagons jammed front-to-end hadn't budged in the streets, but from here I could see a small crowd banding together to lift a wagon with a broken wheel, which must have caused the delay.

Embers glowed in the hearth, and I hurried to make the most of them. Crouching on the dusty floor, I nursed them to flame with my breath. Then I shoved past the hallway loiterers to fill a metal basin with water from the pump. I heaved it back upstairs and started it boiling. At the very least, I could clear the way for the healer to work quickly before I resumed my journey.

After rifling through drawers to find clean cloths, I tramped back down to the tavern kitchen, which I raided for salt and honey in spite of old Piers's incoherent protests.

Back in the room, I shut the door and dumped my supplies and my satchel on the bed. The young man's eyes fluttered, shining with fever.

I heard commotion and glanced out the window to find the carriages in front of ours moving into action. "Hurry, Brandar," I whispered while soaking a cloth in hot water. We had allotted plenty of time for delays, but if we couldn't find a healer soon this would escalate into a predicament.

"Are you expected somewhere?" The boy's voice was weak and quiet, but I detected a chuckle behind it.

"Sorry, I didn't mean for you to hear that. I'm expected at the palace soon, but I'm loath to leave until someone even remotely trustworthy arrives."

I approached him with the clean cloth and peeled his tunic away from the wound. He hissed. After absorbing the damage with a straight face, I let my gaze roam briefly over the taut landscape of surrounding skin. Though I'd grown up playing games with boys, studying alongside them, dancing with them, I felt as though I'd never come this near to one, not even when Knox had pressed his hand flush against mine. The scent of perspiration mingling with blood, the heat rising from his skin, made this stranger feel more *real*, as though I'd just realized the other boys had been statues and only he was flesh and bone.

"I've studied some healing arts," I assured him, though I refrained from sharing how briefly my Herb Magic lessons had touched on healing.

"Why the palace?" he croaked, then bared his teeth in pain as I dabbed the cloth on the wound. "Are you important?"

I felt my eyebrows hitch upward. "Not in the way I want to be."

"Are you an infamous outlaw?" The lilt in his accent reminded me of Grandmum's, and others from Darmeska, but its rural northern character was even more distinct. "An oppressed princess escaping your confines?"

I surprised myself by laughing. It felt strange, as if my esophagus were an old spout coughing up rusty water. "There's a little truth to both."

"Thank you for helping, princess outlaw," he muttered feebly, his eyes glazing over.

"What happened to you?" I asked, worried he might fade away if I let him. "Give me a tragic tale to tell in case I'm late. The worse it is, the more selfless and brave I'll sound."

"You have my permission to tell the important palace people whatever you'd like," he mumbled.

"Helpful," I snorted. I mixed salt into a glob of honey and began coating the wound with the ointment.

"*Gayr efthit,*" he cursed in a low growl when the salt met his torn skin.

"Old Nisseran?" I asked, proceeding in spite of the protest. Just as knowing how to stitch thread through fabric didn't make me a seamstress, knowing spells in Old Nisseran didn't make me proficient in the language. But I'd learned enough to easily recognize it. "Are you one of those elicromancers who learned more filthy words than spells and enchantments?"

"I know more than filthy words." His eyes fluttered as he started singing a song in the old tongue, his low voice cracking. The melody rang sorrowful in my ears, reminding me of songs sung at my father's funeral in Darmeska.

The boy seemed to choke on his own breath, the color draining from his face in a rush. I feared the loss of blood was dragging him to death's doorstep.

But that didn't explain the pale gray film that slid over his eyes from corner to corner.

I recoiled in fear but recovered to slather more ointment on his wounds and apply new cloths as bandages. Hopefully, a true healer would soon arrive to close the skin and address this unsettling fit of sorts.

As I dabbed the excess ointment from his facial cuts and bruises, his cloudy eyes cleared. "Are you all right?" I asked with relief. "I thought you were slipping away."

He blinked at the ceiling and mumbled something that sounded like, "You can do more than destroy."

"What did you say?" I demanded, but the sound of wheels and hooves clomping over stone—punctuated by Calanthe barking at the commotion from inside the carriage—brought on a pang of selfish urgency. I'd need to leave soon, healer or no.

"Mistress?" someone called, knocking on the door.

"Come in."

A middle-aged woman with ink-black hair and an umber complexion entered, wearing an apologetic smile. "I'm sorry about Old Piers. Didn't think much would happen while I left him in charge for half an hour. The healer will be here soon. I'll have a maid refresh the room and fetch anything you need."

I sighed with relief. In my haste, I nearly tossed her the whole bag of coins from my pocket. I glanced back at the injured boy. He seemed to have heard of me, but I didn't even know his name.

Concern and curiosity—plus something else unfurling like a ribbon of heat beneath my ribs—managed to prevail over my impatience. I dropped several silver aurions in the woman's palm. "This should be enough for his room and board and treatment. I plan to return tomorrow if I can. If you tend kindly to him, there will be more for you."

"He will be well looked after, mistress."

I doubled back for my things. One of the tablet pieces had slid out the mouth of the satchel. I stuffed it back inside and rushed out to the carriage.

❧ ELEVEN ❧

THE balmy air tasted of the ocean as we rattled into the palace courtyard. Through the carriage window, I saw Kadri Lillis perching on the edge of a marble fountain that depicted frolicking sea maidens.

Wary of allowing myself even a scrap of happiness, I put on a measured version of her broad smile and looped a leash around Calanthe's neck. I shouldered my awkward satchel and followed the others out of the carriage.

"Valory!"

"Kadri." When she embraced me, I smelled lavender in her dark waves and felt warmth on her sun-kissed russet shoulders. Calanthe forced her way between us to bestow a generous lick on Kadri's chin that made her laugh and stagger back.

"I'm so sorry I didn't come to Ivria's funeral," Kadri said, appeasing the giant hound by raking her fingers through her rough gray coat. "Or your birthday, for that matter. Elicromancers can be so discourteous, giving mortals no notice while they materialize from place to place. Rayed was only able to escort you because he was already traveling when the missive from King Tiernan arrived." She pursed her lips at her older brother. "You nearly made her late."

"Me?" he demanded. "It's your friend, not I, who goes out of her way to take in wounded boys like stray puppies." He gestured at my bloody tunic with its ripped sleeve. I was quite a sight.

"Oh?" Kadri asked, looking past me into the carriage.

"We found someone hurt on the side of the road...but we left him at an inn and summoned a healer," I said, absently picking his grimy blood from under a fingernail.

"I'll tell them you've arrived and see if they're ready for you," Rayed said, brushing past us.

Kadri turned to a nearby attendant. "Sir, you may please take her baggage to my quarters. And perhaps her dog for some exercise?"

"Still having trouble giving orders?" I asked, surrendering the leash.

She laughed. "I'm afraid so."

"Some queen you'll make."

"That's part of why I'm living here instead of at the embassy. I'm learning." Threading her arm around my waist, Kadri guided me inside the palace. Brandar pressed close behind, upholding the ruse that he could stifle my power.

"How is Prince Fabian?" I asked, largely to distract myself from the gnarl of nerves in my belly. We traversed a corridor lined with aquamarine panels and marble statues cradling books and instruments. In Arna, our statues clasped weapons and wore elicrin stones.

"He's holding a birthday celebration on his ship. It's moored in the bay."

"You didn't want to join your betrothed for his birthday?"

Kadri grimaced. "I can't set foot on a ship. Even if I wanted to return home to Erdem, I couldn't survive that sea voyage again."

"And Fabian isn't required to attend Realm Alliance gatherings?"

She scoffed. "Fabian can't be required to do anything. It's part of his charm."

We fell quiet as we approached a communal chamber, whose ranks of windows looked out on a vast balcony and, beyond, Beyrian Bay. Tiles of blue and bronze flecked the domed ceiling along with etchings of striking sea creatures. Tiered benches rose up from three sides of the central circular area of the room, where the floor held a mosaic rendering of a coiled sea serpent.

Rayed waved us inside and gestured for the tablets, which I handed off with a measure of relief. We filed through the open doors to lingering stares and murmurs.

"I'll find you after," Kadri whispered, gathering her midriff-bearing teal skirt to step up to the audience area.

A guard led me to a cordoned-off bench, and Brandar settled next to me. As little as I enjoyed having a shadow, surely he enjoyed being one even less.

The Realm Alliance representatives sat in the first row, forming a horseshoe curve around the center. These were kings, queens, generals, trade ministers, ambassadors from foreign countries, respected mortals. I followed the arc until I found King Tiernan, his phlegmatic expression securely installed. Neswick and the other Conclave members stared back at me, absorbed by my every move. I caught a glimpse of tawny hair and noticed Jovie sitting behind her father.

"Welcome," said Queen Jessa of Yorth, striding to the center of the chamber. "Thank you for answering the call in a time of crises and questions." She waited for Erdemese and Perispi interpreters to finish relaying her words before she continued. "Thanks to the brave heroines and heroes who came before us, the looming supernatural threats of ages past have been extinguished. We can now share fruitful trade relationships—and friendships—with lands that once feared us. Magic, however, is still unpredictable in nature. That is why, as Nissera's leaders, friends, and advisors, we have chosen to address the disappearance of the Water as a matter that touches the entire realm and our allies—not just elicromancers and the academy. I ask every Realm Alliance representative here to commit to responding in a way that reflects loyalty not to family, kingdom, or kind, but to the betterment and safety of all people in our sphere of influence."

Stares followed me like swirling flies I couldn't swat away. Queen Jessa became a safe point of focus. The cinnamon braids wound around her head accentuated her kindly young features. She was an elicromancer at least five decades old by mortal years, but of course remained youthful in visage. Her husband was a mortal from Perispos whose years had begun to etch lines on his face and thread silver through his hair.

"We summoned you here to discuss what tenets might need alterations now that the Water is gone," Queen Jessa went on.

My knuckles went white as I wrung my hands in my lap. *It spared you and it killed her,* I heard Ander say with cruel clarity. *It should have spared her and killed you.*

"But another urgent matter has arisen. Masked thieves stole an artifact, a tablet, from a guarded vault in Darmeska weeks ago. Darmeskan leaders tell us the thieves are a part of a secretive spiritual order called the Summoners, who worship a so-called Lord of Elicromancers. The Summoners brought the tablet to Volarre so that Prince Devorian, an Omnilingual, could read the forgotten runes inscribed on it. Devorian believed the runes could awaken the dead, an act of unthinkable—and forbidden—dark magic."

As Queen Jessa recounted what Grandmum and Rayed had written her, I wished I could close my ears to the sound of my own name cropping up with incriminating frequency.

"We must first and foremost attempt to learn the identities of the Summoners who delivered the stolen artifact to Devorian," she said after she had explained our altercation. "Even Devorian did not know the meaning of the runes he read—therefore we can't yet know the ramifications of reciting them. If the spell failed to raise his mother and father, what did it do? Who is the 'Lord of Elicromancers'? Hopefully, the tablet itself can help lead us to some answers."

She beckoned Rayed, who passed the tablet halves to Neswick and Professor Strather. The two of them frowned with scholarly curiosity and traced their fingers over the markings before passing them on to the sharp-eyed elicromancer from my hearing.

"Shouldn't we first discipline Devorian and Valory?" interrupted a man with a honeyed tenor. I followed the voice and found Mathis Lorenthi, Devorian's uncle, looking smug and boyishly handsome with golden hair tumbling in curls to his shoulders. "What sort of leadership would we demonstrate by coddling them like children? My nephew should be summoned to testify and speak for himself, like a man. He must face the consequences of breaking a tenet."

"I agree!" said Neswick with a thrust of his fist. "If we do not react to their defiance, we will set a dangerous precedent."

"We must remember that the last war in Nissera was waged by a single errant elicromancer," Mathis added, raising a pompous finger to emphasize his point.

My nostrils flared. Mathis was practically an usurper. His words dripped with selfish motivation. By forcing Devorian out of the shadows, Mathis would not only snatch the crown, he would reveal my darkest deeds.

"We are facing a threat that could be far more dangerous than two heedless young people, one of whom was still a pupil at the academy barely a fortnight ago," said the queen. Riding the wave of nods and affirmative murmurs, she continued, "So let us confront our greatest peril first. Valory, come forward and tell us what you learned about the Summoners from Devorian. Did he give any indication that he knew their identities? What led him to believe this incantation could raise the dead?"

Banishing anger and fear from my expression, I found Kadri in the audience and received a cringe of sympathy. With my pulse throbbing in my ears, I made my way across the tiled sea serpent, stopping on the bronze scales of its belly. I looked up and drew some calm from the view of the infinite sea. Down to the east sprawled the port with its jagged rock formations, stone buildings, and dozens of ships bobbing in cerulean waters. I reluctantly turned my back on it to face the audience.

But before I could speak, a voice cut clean across the open chamber. "Believe nothing she tells you!"

From the highest tier of benches, Ambrosine snapped to her feet, her lovely features cold as a frostbitten rose. She wore a simple mulberry dress, more mundane than her typical attire, and clutched a handheld mirror to her breast. My heart beat nearly hard enough to bruise my chest.

"The Summoners *did* contact Devorian," she said as eyes around the room alighted on her. "And they did give him the tablet with the incantation. But he never planned to join their ritual. He knew the runes were dangerous and was attempting to learn their identities before reporting them to the Conclave." She pointed her finger at me. "But Valory Braiosa was desperate. She extracted from her grandmother the truth that the spell on the tablet would bring about 'an awakening' of the dead. So Valory tried to use her power to force Devorian to speak the incantation. She planned to use it to resurrect Ivria and undo her greatest mistake."

The sickening accusation struck me like a stone to the temple. I grew dizzy, trying to comprehend her flagrant lies. But it all fit together, as simple as a child's puzzle: Devorian and his sisters had *never* fallen out of touch. He had been using the mirror identical to Ambrosine's, the one I'd found in his library, to communicate with them about the possibility of resurrecting their parents after the Summoners arrived. But they didn't know how to enact the spell without inviting harsh consequences, losing their elicrin stones... until the sisters caught wind of what had happened at the Water. Almost immediately, they beckoned me to Pontaval, pleaded with me to speak to Devorian, and assured me he would listen out of mere curiosity. And then he had uttered the incantation for the first time in *my* presence. The siblings had conspired to raise their parents and use my reputation as a cover for violating a tenet. I had been lured into a trap and set up to take the blame for their use of a forbidden spell, an abominable one.

"When Devorian resisted," Ambrosine went on, descending the stairs, her voice wracked with poignant anger, "she unleashed her dark magic on him."

My knees began to quake as she turned the mirror's face to the audience, exposing the creature my unbridled power had devised.

The roar that ripped out of Devorian's fanged, distended jaw erupted through the chamber. The audience released gasps of confusion and horror. Ambrosine tucked the glass back against her chest, whirling to face me with her lip curled in disgust. "Trouble follows Valory Braiosa wherever she goes."

"You liar," I whispered. "You lured me there! You asked for my help."

"Why would we ask for *your* help?" she demanded, calculated, ruthless. "You can only warp and destroy."

Hearing her spit my own words back at me churned up a toxic potion of magic and rage that clawed to act of its own accord. I felt a crazed impulse to bring the ceiling down on this trickster, to smash her golden head with glee.

Brandar sprang from his seat, coming between us. Extending his flat palm toward Ambrosine, he extinguished the light agitating in her blue elicrin stone. He turned to me, his normally expressionless eyes like points of spears. If I didn't rein in my power, everyone would know that a Neutralizer could not stop me. Chaos would follow. The men who already wanted to imprison me might bring worse to the table.

I tore my eyes away from Ambrosine and Brandar, finding aghast faces on all sides.

"Calm down, both of you," Queen Jessa said, her voice managing to break through the pounding in my head. "We will proceed in an orderly manner, allowing you both a chance to speak—"

"You wanted me to stay quiet about the curse she cast on Devorian," Ambrosine interrupted. "You're protecting her."

"I wanted to contain a volatile situation long enough for us to understand what the spell accomplished and how we can stop the Summoners' plans." Queen Jessa's even tone made Ambrosine's sound overwrought in contrast, but unmistakable whispers of doubt surrounded us.

"This raises broader questions of what Miss Braiosa might be capable of, Your Majesty," Professor Strather said, eyeing me like a wolf that might rip out her throat on a whim. "I must be candid: it was unwise to keep *this* from us." She gestured at Ambrosine, unable to find words to describe Devorian's condition.

"Where was the Neutralizer?" Neswick demanded. I felt more than saw the look Tiernan exchanged with his former personal guard.

"I snuck out from my bedchamber in the night without his knowledge," I said. "The princesses helped me escape from the balcony. I lost my temper with Devorian because I had tried and failed to stop him from saying the incantation. He broke a tenet in trying to raise the dead, and my reaction, I admit, was out of control—"

"She forced him to do the spell!" Ambrosine's protest tangled with other rising voices until each one became indistinguishable. Jessa tried and failed to reestablish order as the gathering of great and powerful minds collapsed into little more than a tavern brawl.

In the midst of the chaos, I cast my gaze beyond the open

chamber to the ocean and its patchwork of blue hues, imagining myself as nothing but a bit of driftwood washing away to oblivion.

But I noticed a storm cloud agitating against the otherwise immaculate horizon. I approached the windows, squinting at the growing gray curtain and the rugged white seam skimming along it. Just as I realized it was not a cloud, the pandemonium behind me fell quiet. More people filed to the windows. Jovie Neswick nudged past me, bursting through the balcony doors to a stop at the balustrade, where she stared in awe.

It was an enormous wave mounting, a faraway wall of roiling sea heading for shore.

❧ TWELVE ❧

BOOTS scuffled and squeaked as mortals absconded. Glend Neswick dashed onto the balcony to seize his daughter by the wrist and drag her toward safety, though she never tore her wide eyes from the impending disaster even as they fled. A few of the elicromancers materialized, including Ambrosine. The air sighed as they ghosted away.

The remaining elicromancers hurried to form a cluster on the balcony. I couldn't seem to flinch a muscle.

Kadri rushed to my side at the window, catching my elbow for balance as she nearly smacked into the glass. "Fabian," she breathed, beholding the busy port down below.

"*Sokek sinna!*" King Tiernan shouted, opening his palms toward the shore. The spell shot forth a shimmering shield from his elicrin stone. "*Acasar im doen.*"

The other elicromancers took up the chant, the stones in their medallions swirling with light. More shields bloomed. "*Sokek sinna. Acasar im doen.*"

They attached to one another, forming a barrier that spread— but slowly, like tree sap. At this rate, their magic might protect the palace from the surge, but what about the port?

"Our channels and seawalls aren't built for a wave of this magnitude," Queen Jessa yelled as the barrier continued to expand. Her son's name silently took shape on her lips.

"Fabian will materialize away from danger," her husband assured her.

"He won't leave his friends!" she shouted. "He'll go down with the ship before he abandons it."

Down in the bay, white sand climbed out of the water, depositing in dunes that formed a crescent around the vessels closest to the open sea.

"It's salt," Kadri said. "Fabian is pulling salt out of the sea."

The prince often used his elicrin gift to extract salt from seawater, providing supplies of both the precious mineral and clean drinking water to his people. His gift was useful and his efforts valiant, but I doubted the salt dunes would break the wall of water bringing us certain doom.

Kadri and her brother clasped hands, their identical mahogany eyes bright with both terror and resignation as the wave swelled and crashed closer, the din mounting from a distant exhale to a deafening bluster. The elicromancers' barrier seeped along the coast, capturing the land's edge in its desperate embrace, not quite reaching the port by the time the wave hung over us, blotting out the sunlight. My knees threatened to give way as I staggered back onto a bench and closed my eyes, listening to the thunder of water clashing against the magical blockade.

The pounding seemed to last an age. When I opened my eyes again, every elicromancer trembled beneath the weight of the vengeful sea but stood strong, arms outstretched and palms open until finally the calamitous force abated and the water washed back toward the endless blue expanse.

I stared aghast at the port, where the wave's pulsing rage

had engulfed Fabian's salt dunes, capsizing boats and crushing docks.

"No!" the queen cried out. The shield wavered as she materialized away. The other elicromancers collectively dropped their glimmering barrier and materialized down to the wreckage.

Shock hung like morning fog, until King Basil moved across the room. "We'll need every hand to help," he proclaimed thickly, and those of us remaining who couldn't materialize hurried after him.

Kadri bunched her skirts and darted ahead of me into the corridor, nearly colliding with a group of green-clad guards hurrying in the same direction. As I pursued her, a sickening dread lingered. Was the lethal wave an unfortunate coincidence? Or, like the blood moon and the quake, was it a link in a chain of repercussions resulting from the mysterious spell?

The memory of Devorian's incantation murmured wildly amid my feverish thoughts.

The scattered crowd passed through the east-facing gates and started across the bridge bending down toward the port. The settling water still thrashed against the seawall below. I caught up to Kadri and she clung to my arm while surveying the port wreckage from afar.

Whole ships had turned to floating matchsticks in the bay. One merchant ship had been ravaged on the rocks, its broken belly exposed. I could see bodies: bodies in the water, bodies amid the wreckage of the docks and the spilled imported goods.

She stared, unblinking. "He's gone."

I wanted to point out that Fabian could have materialized away at the last second, but I didn't want to tender false hope, and I couldn't seem to muster any sound besides a gasp of horror. Kadri bolted, her sandals clacking on the walkway.

"Be careful, Kadri!" her brother yelled after her.

Some buildings had been leveled by the wave, but the customs house and other stone structures stood intact. Rescuers braved the debris to seize victims beyond help. Queen Jessa used her gift of weightlessness to walk upon the surface of the water and search for her son. Another elicromancer used phenomenal strength to pull beams and planks from the bay and pile them on shore. My Neutralizer was helping overturn a capsized fishing vessel.

I jogged down vast steps and through another set of gates, arriving at the hub of the devastation. Steeling myself, I joined the soldiers sloshing through the rubble-ridden water that steeped the docks.

I hauled a dead young man to dry land by his elbows. As I waded through a mass of oranges and empty crates, haunting images of the red moon and black clouds drifted through my mind's eye.

Loud hollering drew my attention back toward the palace. "The prince!" A distant figure waved from the wet beaches, calling, "Prince Fabian! He's alive!"

Kadri stumbled out of the water. Relieved, I nearly followed, but knew that if I left, I wouldn't muster the will to return to the scene of the disaster.

So I aided the recovery efforts until nearly nightfall. Every man or woman, boy or girl with ghostly skin and dead eyes pierced me with a memory of Ivria until I could more easily recall her face in death than in life.

By the time I'd towed half a dozen corpses to the docks, watched loved ones' hopes turn to sorrow upon recognizing the dead, and saved a sorry-looking gray cat from drowning, my every muscle protested. The rosy sun burned at the edge of the world, and I wondered whether I would be permitted to sleep for days—sleep until time chipped away at the wretched feeling in my chest.

I sat on the remains of a dock and finished wiping the muck off some tightly sealed jars of spices and preserves I'd been able to salvage. With their rightful owners burdened by news of far greater losses, I had taken the liberty of offering some to grieving families and to an Erdemese employee of a wealthy merchant from Volarre whose ships had been destroyed. The Erdemese man had refused the meager gift, saying he could easily find work rebuilding docks and ships. "But I pity the old merchant," he added. "Three daughters to care for and now he's lost all his ships and fortunes. It's a good thing they're beauties, especially the youngest. They even call her Beauty. They'll still marry well without dowries, at least."

I'd watched him wander away, his hands deep in the pockets of his dripping coat, before he vanished among the broken hulls and tattered sails.

"It will be too dark soon. You'll injure yourself amid the rubble."

I looked up to see Jovie Neswick silhouetted in the night, the breeze flirting with her blue-and-gray skirts. The dock lanterns should have already been lit, but the nearest ones had been plucked up and tossed aside like weeds.

"It's no more than I deserve," I muttered. My stomach scraped at itself with hunger, and I deserved that too. "What are you doing down here?"

"I don't want to be the coward who can't bear to look tragedy in the face." Moonlight glinted in her long-lashed amber eyes as they gazed upon the ravaged port. Then, gravely, she peered down at me, clasping her hands at her navel. "But you're here because you fear you're responsible for this. I too believe this wave is linked to the awakening spell."

"But how?" I looked at the cool water lapping against the broken dock, carrying a cloud of ruined, ghostly linens. "What have I done?"

She gripped a post as the dock dipped with the tides. "I believe this is much bigger than you and Devorian. The very foundations of Nissera are trembling with some eldritch power."

A tremor worked its way up my spine. I suddenly wanted nothing more than to shuck off my wet clothes and crash headlong into a mattress. My thighs ached as I stood, a jar in each hand. "I suppose I should—"

"I understand why you don't enjoy my company." Jovie stepped over a broken board to block my path. "I mirror the parts of you that you do not want to see. We clawed and climbed our way through the academy like invasive ivy and wielded knowledge like a shield to compensate for magical shortcomings. But you don't have to resent me any longer. You have what you wanted."

I scoffed. "What I wanted? This is an illegitimate, insidious cousin of elicromancy. I'd rather have nothing at all."

"The Water chose you," Jovie insisted, excitement or envy scintillating in her amber eyes. "You were the last one it honored before it expelled the remainder of its power in a tired breath. If you judge yourself by the standards of elicromancy, try to play by their rules and use their spells, all while considering your magic some sort of lesser strain . . . you will be a failure as you've always feared." Despite the swaying of the dock, she stood erect and raised her chin. "No, you must brush all expectations aside, claim this with pride, and judge it by what it is rather than what it's not."

"Claim it with pride?" I nearly shouted. "How, when everyone believes I didn't deserve to survive, much less possess magic?"

My voice cracked, and with it both of the jars I held. A maniacal cry of frustration dislodged from my throat. I tossed the jars into the sloshing water and blinked at the sticky fruit preserves on my fingers.

Jovie stepped closer, speaking to my profile, her breath stirring hairs that had slipped loose from my plait. "The Water has always made the ultimate choice of whom to destroy and whom to exalt. And despite everyone's expectations, it destroyed Ivria and exalted you. You must accept what it has given you."

"How do I accept it when I don't understand it?" I asked, facing her. "When no one does?"

"I understand it." Hints of an exhilarated smile flitted across her face in the moon's silvery glow. "I've been pondering it for days. Instead of a trinket, the Water gave you what remained of *itself*: its power to destroy . . . and its power to transform."

I listened to the sounds of the sea and imagined it was the Water itself lapping against the inside wall of my sternum.

"Destruction and transformation," I whispered after a moment. *And when the two powers collide . . .*

I couldn't finish my thought, recalling Devorian the way I had left him: beastly, both terrifying and terrified, his beautiful palace in shambles.

"Just like the Water, you are an unpredictable and unruly creature. You are equipped to thrive even when the rules that govern our world change. You shouldn't care what they do to you, where they send you, what kind of punishment they impose. All you need worry about is mastering this power." Her fingers wrapped around my elbow, molding the cold, damp fabric to my skin. "Master it so it does not master you."

Jovie released me, pinched her skirts, and strode back down the unsteady dock into the shadows.

━❦ THIRTEEN ❦━

THE morning ought to have been gray and misty. But just as on the day Ivria floated downriver in a shower of blossoms, the sun flaunted its full glory, penetrating the sumptuous curtains in Kadri's chamber.

Hoping to slither away from yesterday as if shedding a hollow snakeskin, I writhed under the sheets and came nose-to-nose with Calanthe. Ivria had made her sleep on her own pallet, but as the silver deerhound stretched her long limbs and yawned with excessive relish, I didn't mind her disregard for Ivria's training.

"She's a gentle giant," Kadri said, stepping into view in a salmon-pink gown and archery gear from an early practice. She unfastened her leather arm guard and deposited her bow and quiver in the corner.

A maid offered me a glass of melon juice while another mopped up my muddy tracks and collected my wet garments. I brushed a wiry gray hair off the pillow and accepted the glass. "We've commandeered your whole room, haven't we?"

Kadri plopped down on a cushion by the window. "You can't commandeer what's been freely given."

As the haze of sleep cleared, I recalled my conversation with Jovie Neswick, as well as a fading dream in which I used my power to defeat whatever horror the spell had unleashed on this realm. Melkior, of all people, had presented me with a medal of honor. He had pricked me with it as he pinned it to my collar, drawing blood, yet I had felt no pain.

"How many are dead? Have you heard?"

Kadri stared at the rug, gliding her thumb along the rim of her glass. "Nearly three hundred presumed dead, but some may have survived like Fabian."

I might have guessed as many, but it was devastating to hear aloud. "How is Fabian today?" I asked, swinging my sore legs over the edge of the bed to reach the tray of cheese and honey-drizzled fruit on the nightstand.

"He's distraught over his friends and his ship, but he's the image of health. He keeps prattling on about a girl who saved him, a girl with white hair and crystal eyes."

I wrinkled my forehead in confusion.

"I know. I thought he'd hit his head, but the elicrin Healer said he's fine."

"Didn't he materialize to safety?" I asked.

Kadri shook her head. "He was prepared to go down with his ship, but someone intervened. I'm grateful to whoever brought him ashore, but if he's found a girl who can swim like an eel and loves the sea, my days as future queen may be numbered." She popped a grape into her mouth.

"But Fabian had the freedom to choose his own bride. He loves you, doesn't he?"

"We're friends. But from the day I met him, I knew he loved the sea more than he could love any woman. And the sea makes my stomach churn."

"Why did you agree to marry him?"

"Don't judge me."

"I would never."

"I'm marrying him so I can be queen. My country is beautiful, at least as I remember it, but Erdem doesn't have elicromancers who can heal diseases or grow healthy crops in a week. My people come to Nissera expecting equality, peace, and a life without sickness or hunger. But when they arrive at these shores, they don't know much of the language and have nowhere to live. They get lured to the pleasure houses or break their backs laboring for dismal wages. And when they get too old for either, they have to beg in the streets. When I'm queen, I want to make certain they can thrive here. Though I may never return to Erdem, I will be loyal to its people."

"I had no idea it was so difficult for them," I said, nibbling a bit of cheese. "It's good of you to make sacrifices for your people."

"It's hardly a sacrifice. Fabian and I don't burden each other with expectations. His life as an elicromancer will be far longer than mine. Who could expect him to pledge unconditional loyalty to a woman who will grow old before his eyes?"

Thoughts of mortality elicited the familiar pang of growing panic, but I dismissed it. Only time could prove my immortality, or lack of it.

"He doesn't expect me to remain devoted either," Kadri continued with an affable shrug. "He chose me because I never *minded* that his heart belonged to the sea. His amorous affections are shallow compared to his love of adventure. And to think how hard some have worked to win his favor..." She shielded her eyes from the sunlight and grinned crookedly at me. "I know this isn't very romantic. You probably think me too pragmatic for my own good."

"No, I..." I trailed off. In truth, I was flattered she would confide in me. I could feel our friendship probing its roots into richer soil. "I'm far from idealistic when it comes to romance."

"When I last saw Ivria, she said a fellow pupil was smitten with you."

I half-laughed, but my stomach tied itself in knots at the thought of Knox. "That might have been true before I ruined his future."

She looked thoughtful for a moment. "I don't know if you ruined anything. Maybe the Water was always a finite resource, and you just took the last of it."

"But Devorian—"

She dismissed my protest with a wave. "He deserved his fate."

"I suppose," I muttered, and washed down my breakfast with the melon juice. Through the cracked door leading to the outer chamber, I caught a glimpse of Brandar gazing down at the seaside through curtains striped the yellow and maroon of the Erdemese flag. "Do you know if I'm expected today?"

"Rayed said the Alliance won't summon you until afternoon." Kadri propped her chin on her fist. "And I won't be attending the memorial ceremony this morning, as it takes place on a blasted ship they somehow managed to round up. Unless you want to go, the morning is ours to do what we like with. We could explore the markets—"

"The wounded boy!" I said, recalling him with a start. The

wave had washed yesterday morning from my mind. "I promised to return and see if he's faring well."

"I'd nearly forgotten about the stray you took in!" Kadri leapt off the windowsill, suddenly animated as she exchanged her grass-stained boots for bejeweled sandals. "Shall we?"

"He could at least attempt to look less dour." Kadri glanced back at Brandar as we meandered through the market on the northeastern outskirts of the city.

Calanthe blazed an erratic path for us through stalls of seafood, flowers, and trinkets, investigating every distinct scent. I tried to steer her in the direction of the inn, but I didn't know one building from the next and the pressing crowds didn't give me much time to orient myself.

"Are we getting close?" Kadri asked.

"I don't know. I think so."

"Are you sure you can't recall the name?"

"Something to do with a ship, or fishermen, I think," I said.

"So, every establishment in Beyrian."

"We were in such a rush and he was badly hurt. I didn't even think to look. Perhaps Brandar recalls."

"Beautiful bride of the magnanimous prince!" A vendor bellowed at Kadri, trotting from his stall with showers of bracelets and necklaces displayed on his arms. He drew too close to us, his breath reeking of garlic. "Does anything strike your fancy? You have endured much, worrying for the well-being of your noble prince and your loyal citizens. You deserve to comfort yourself with the finest, purest pearls."

While Kadri summoned a beneficent response, I spotted the back of a sandy brown head inside a nearby doorway. The inn looked familiar, but sections of the walls had been lifted and propped open, enabling patrons to enjoy the fair weather. The name Anchorage Alehouse and Inn seemed as right as any, but the young man couldn't possibly have recovered enough to sit upright and toss back a pint.

"I think that's him," I said to Kadri. A gaggle of vendors had worked their way between us, and now her personal guard, who had been following at a respectful distance, stepped in to disperse them. Kadri grabbed my wrist and caught up to me. We laced through stalls of exotic fruits and approached the tavern.

This careless boy was my companion from the journey, to be sure—even Calanthe recognized him and beat her tail in greeting— but he was slurping down oysters without a single bruise on his face.

"You seem mighty well, considering you were on death's doorstep this time yesterday," I said, leaning an elbow on the counter.

He scratched behind Calanthe's ear and turned acorn-brown eyes on me. Without the swollen violet pocket around his eye, he was even more striking. "Good day to you, savior," he said. "The Healer they fetched turned out to be an elicromancer. Speaking of, we owe him three silvers."

"We?" Kadri echoed, lifting her eyebrows.

"Why?" I demanded. "I left nearly enough aurions to buy you the whole inn."

"I didn't ask to be brought to Beyrian and handed over to the most expensive healer in the southern kingdom." He licked sauce from his finger and tugged up the hem of his loose off-white shirt, exposing perfect skin without the slightest suggestion of a scar, stretched taut over healthy muscles. "Magic doesn't come cheap."

Disappointment dragged a scowl across my face. I dug through my purse, slapping three coins on the table. "Why are all elicrin Healers scoundrels? It's twisted. And why are you sucking down oysters if you're in debt?"

"You paid for my meals, remember?"

"Yes, I remember that and saving your life. How did you find yourself the victim of such an attack, I wonder? Was it perhaps your spirit of ingratitude that rankled someone enough to make them want to stab you?"

"I don't remember much."

"You don't remember how you were almost murdered?"

He shrugged. I looked at the gray-green jewel around his neck. Most elicromancers hung theirs on gold or silver chains in ornate settings, but his was set in crude, tarnished metal and tied with a leather strap.

"Well, now that we see you've managed to escape your tragic fate, we'll be going," I said. "Can I trust you to apply those aurions to your debt?"

"Why don't you beauties stay and help me polish off a flagon of wine? Then you can come along and make *certain* I pay my debt." He lifted a finger to flag down old Piers, who hobbled over with alacrity he hadn't bothered to demonstrate for me.

"*This* beauty is the future Queen of Yorth," Kadri said, pointing at herself. "And *that* beauty took the time to save your skin even though she was due to testify before the Realm Alliance."

"Testify? That sounds intriguing." The young man gave a subtle smile. I was bothered to notice the groove between his nose and top lip, the lips themselves, and the neat lines of his jaw. "Is the outlaw princess in legal peril?"

"You were more charming half dead," I said, turning my back on him and tugging Calanthe along. Kadri harrumphed and followed me.

"I know the language!" he called after me.

"What does that mean?" I asked over my shoulder.

"The one carved on the mother-of-pearl tablet. At least, I know *what* language it is."

I halted and turned. "It was poking out of my bag...you did that, didn't you? I was helping you and you looked at my things?"

"That's your response? You don't want to know what it is?"

Breathing deep through my nose, I marched back to him. "Of course I want to know."

He turned his profile to me and took his time with a deep swig of golden ale. "It's the tongue of the sea folk."

"As in...people who live by the sea?" Kadri ventured skeptically.

"People who live *within* the sea."

Kadri and I exchanged mystified expressions. An echo of Devorian's haunting hums and whistles flitted through my mind. He had said he could speak all languages known to *humans*, yet this one had thwarted his gift.

"They went extinct centuries ago." I said. "How would you know it's their language?"

He lifted his elicrin stone by the strap. It thudded against his hard chest when he released it. "Visions of the past."

As he indulged in another deep gulp, I connected this revelation to the fit that had overcome him while I treated his wounds. "Do you know anything else about the writing on the tablet?" I asked. "Your information could save lives."

"If you arrange an audience with the Realm Alliance, I might recall a few details."

"You're looking for a reward for information that could help innocent people?" Kadri asked. "How heroic."

He threw one long leg over the bench and turned to give us his full attention. "When she found me, I had nothing but an elicrin stone and the clothes on my back. A man needs more than one meal and an able body to survive. I'm sure the Realm Alliance can spare a few aurions if the information is so valuable."

The hollow eyes of waterlogged corpses seemed to pierce me yet again, and I bit back the saucy retort that I should have left this boy where I found him. We needed whatever help he could give.

"All right," Kadri said before I could reply. "We'll make sure you get an audience with the leaders and will communicate your expectations." She took a step closer and jammed a finger in his face. "But do *not* make fools of us."

"No, of course not," he said, and then turning to me, "Your reputation can't afford that, can it?"

I narrowed my eyes at him. If I hadn't seen the boy's wounds myself and stumbled upon him by chance, I would have thought he'd orchestrated our encounter. "Who are you?"

He swung his other leg over the bench and stood head and shoulders above me—startling, since I'd only seen him hunched over or lying prostrate. "Mercer Fye," he said with the slightest bow of his head.

"I'm Valory Braiosa...I assume you somehow already knew that."

"You *did* announce your name to the whole tavern yesterday." He looked at Kadri.

"Kadri Lillis," she said with cool arrogance. "Come with us."

Her black hair whirled like a cape as she started back in the direction of the coach. Brandar and Kadri's guard waited for us to pass before bringing up the rear.

The new addition made for a cramped journey back to the palace. I sat between Brandar and Calanthe on the open-top coach, while Kadri and the newcomer—Mercer, if that was truly his name—were separated by Kadri's guard, who rested a ready hand on the hilt of his sword by way of warning.

The domed roofs of the city, the crowds, and the occasional glimpse of the sea offered ample stimulation. However, I couldn't refrain from watching the boy in an attempt to read him. For the most part, he cast his eyes off to the side and wore a serious expression, but I could feel his gaze when I diverted mine. Our fleeting looks linked just once during the ride—which seemed inexplicably lengthier than our initial journey—and it sparked a visceral throb beneath my ribs. I attributed that to irritation.

"Let him be my responsibility, in case he turns out a fraud," Kadri said in my ear when we disembarked. "Take him to my lounge. One of the maids will find him something to wear." She tendered a mistrustful look at the boy before proceeding through the entry with purpose in her steps.

"Come with me," I said to Mercer.

"To see the Realm Alliance?"

"I'm meant to help you look presentable first."

Once we entered the palace, I slipped the leash from Calanthe's neck and proceeded at a furious pace. But I was wearing a pair of Kadri's sandals, which jammed painfully between my toes, and Mercer's legs were far longer than mine.

"You have quite the devotee," he said, drawing even with me as we turned on a landing lined with windows overlooking the sea.

In the corner of my eye, I saw Brandar mounting the steps below us. "He's a Neutralizer. I have a very dangerous power that must be kept in check."

Mercer didn't react. Such a comment should have piqued his curiosity. *Unless…*

I whirled on him at the top of the stairs. "But you already knew that, didn't you? In fact, you seem to know a great deal. When I wondered whether healing was your gift, you countered with a question as to whether it was mine. But as I don't wear an elic-rin stone, how did you know I possessed any gift whatsoever? And you said I had announced my name at the tavern, but I gave them my mother's better-known name of Ermetarius. Unless word of my misfortunes had met your ears already, you ought to have had no idea who I was."

"I told you, I have visions of the past, usually of eventful moments," he said, taking the last two steps. "The past could mean centuries ago or a fortnight ago."

"So, you're saying...you've seen me in one of your visions?" I asked. For some reason, it felt bold to look directly into his eyes.

"You *have* had an eventful fortnight..."

I charged onward toward Kadri's room. "Yes, I have. And now that I know you are aware of my struggles, there's simply no excuse for your toying with me and exploiting me as you have. If I hadn't found you only because I stopped to take a piss, I'd think that was your aim all along."

We reached the entrance to Kadri's lounge. I shoved open the doors and fought the inclination to slam them in his face.

"My aim was not to toy with you," he said calmly as we entered the domed room of colorful cushions and drapery. "People who are not born into privilege are trained for self-preservation. I've been selling information from my visions since before I even became an elicromancer, when they were weak and vague. It's how I've survived."

Resentment tempted me to interpret his presumptions about my privilege as an insult, but he wasn't wrong.

"Encountering new people usually triggers visions," he went on. "I know a little something about most people I meet. You are not unique in that respect." He had been soaking in Kadri's lush decor, but now he looked at me. "You did find me by chance. And thank fate you did."

Was that so hard? I wanted to ask. But instead, I took a deep breath and glanced up to find a maid plumping the cushions.

"Do you need anything, Mistress Braiosa?" she asked.

"Kadri said you could help find this young man something suitable to wear for an appearance before the Realm Alliance."

"Gladly." The maid smiled at Mercer and left the room.

I approached a gilded tray holding a variety of beverages and looked out across the balcony. In the bay, the memorial ship was returning to shore with black flags flying from its mast.

"Wine?" I asked, stuffing down the tendrils of dark feelings that lurked in my spirit.

"No, thank you."

I poured myself a glass, looking askance at him. "How long have you been an elicromancer? I've never seen you at the academy."

"Not long," he said. "I wasn't taught at the academy."

"'Not long' could mean anything to an elicromancer."

"I would have... I'm—I'm eighteen," he stammered.

"If you didn't go to the academy, you must have been trained by a certified instructor." I sat on a beet-red cushion and folded my legs. "Who was it?"

His expression turned opaque. "You wouldn't know him."

"I've met most of the instructors at some time or other. They tend to orbit around the academy—"

"He's not... part of all that." Mercer's nostrils flared. His smoldering eyes seemed to beg me not ask any more questions.

"Fine, don't tell me any more. I have enough on my plate without the obligation to report you to the Conclave."

Even as I said it, I knew I would never do such a thing. The Conclave used to feel like a neutral entity in my life, a hurdle to clear on the path to becoming an elicromancer. Now the institution felt like a suspended axe poised to land on my exposed neck. One wrong move and the axe would drop.

"You should at least register with the Conclave, if you haven't yet. They could confiscate your elicrin stone if they don't deem your training 'proper.'"

"I've been very well trained," he said.

That seemed to be the end of our discussion.

Kadri's maid returned and set clothes for him behind a semisheer partition. Mercer stepped behind it and wriggled out of his shirt, revealing sculpted arms and a strapping back. Though I'd already been acquainted with his bare midriff, my face warmed and I stalked to the balcony. But the image lingered long enough for me to note the difference between muscles like Ander's—formed by favorable lineage and combat lessons—and those like Mercer's, which, by appearances, had been built by hard labor of some sort.

He soon joined me on the balcony, sporting a light green tunic with golden trim, and new leather boots. "Shall we?"

"Yesterday at the inn, you said I could do more than destroy. What did you mean?"

He slid a finger into his stiff embroidered collar. "You saved me and cleaned my wounds with gentle hands. If you want me to praise your altruism for the Realm Alliance to hear, I'm happy to oblige."

"I'm not baiting you," I said through my teeth. "Just...is that all you meant?"

A canny look traversed his features. "Only you can answer the question you're really asking. Stop being a coward. Summon your magic instead of waiting for it to spew out of you like vomit."

I scowled at his vulgarity. "I'm forbidden to—"

"See? That face, there. You shouldn't be making that face when you invite it out to play. My visions showed me sadness and anger when your power emerged."

"You're suggesting if I merely smi—"

"I'm saying your magic must emerge on *your* terms," he said. "Now, are we going to see the Realm Alliance?"

❦ FOURTEEN ❦

MERCER and I did not speak as we descended to the communal chamber, pursued by the long-suffering Brandar.

Kadri and Fabian waited outside the entrance. "Your uncle Prosper is here," Kadri whispered when we approached. "He convinced them to hold a special vote on extending the age of surrender for elicromancers. He argued they should allow eighty years' possession of elicrin stones instead of fifty. He said yesterday's disaster reinforces how much mortals need elicromancers. They're voting on it now."

I glanced inside the chamber and found Uncle Prosper standing in favor of the vote he'd initiated. He looked as joyless as the day he had watched Ivria leave him forever. I could feel the tightness of his grief squeezing my own chest.

Diverting my attention to counting heads, I noted that Prosper lacked one vote to succeed. A mystifying relief swelled within me, stalked by guilt. Why wouldn't I want each member of my clan—save Melkior—to enjoy the luxury of long life? Neither Prosper nor Ander had wronged me, even if they believed I had wronged them. Prosper had sagely recused himself from my hearings.

"What's wrong with my brother?" Kadri whispered.

Rayed appeared ill at ease, wetting his lips, his deep brown eyes opaque. He stood, turning the vote, with a concise nod to no one in particular.

"That's a bit of a twist," Kadri said. "He voted against the last extension and it failed."

"That was before," Fabian said, scooping back his straight black hair.

Kadri cast a sideways glance up at her betrothed, whose sun-bronzed features were flat with ambivalence. To a young man who had barely begun to take advantage of his half-century aging pause, a few additional decades didn't mean much yet. But I knew older elicromancers would celebrate the news.

I wondered how Grandmum would have voted if she hadn't been off chasing fairies.

"The majority rules," Queen Jessa concluded. "The age of surrender will be eighty years from the day an elicrin stone is received...pardon me, *was* received. And as before, that is without regard for periods of confiscation based on conduct."

"I think we can go in now without interrupting," Kadri said, leading the way. Uncle Prosper averted his iron-gray gaze and brushed past me to leave. I would never again be his beloved niece, his daughter's dearest friend. I was no better than her murderer in his eyes.

"Valory." Queen Jessa pulled me aside. "It will please you to know that Prosper asked for lenience on your behalf. He agreed we should focus more on adapting to a world without the Water than on punishing you for the lack of it."

"He did?" I asked, warmed by the vestiges of familial allegiance.

"But he also suggested you distance yourself. The Realm Alliance needs every Neutralizer at our disposal right now, Brandar included. So we're sending you to live at Darmeska with your mortal relatives and forbidding you to practice magic. As the academy is dissolving, Professor Strather requires new employment. We have agreed that she will be your guardian, alerting us each time your power manifests. It's a more lenient sentence than some preferred...." She sent a glance toward the side of the room where Glend Neswick and Mathis Lorenthi sat. "And I suggest you accept it without resistance."

"Permanently?" I asked, exhausted by being treated like a double-edged blade with a hilt of thorns.

"For the foreseeable future." She touched my shoulder. "This is the best thing for you, dear. We understand you are of marriageable age and that it will be difficult to find a match away from court; we will allow you to return to Arna for holidays and special occasions, and of course, if a betrothal is arranged, we can revisit this."

Of all potential complications, marriage was furthest from my mind. Clearly, Queen Jessa had already discussed this arrangement with my mother, whose foremost priorities proved predictable and evergreen.

"Brandar and Professor Strather will escort you to Darmeska in three days' time, once the latter has made proper arrangements—"

"If I can prove that my power can do anything besides rend and destroy," I interrupted, "may I continue practicing under Professor Strather's supervision? If my magic becomes dangerous, she can intervene—"

"I suppose if..." Queen Jessa's lips flooded white as she locked them together, glancing warily at her colleagues. "If you were able to prepare a demonstration for us before you depart, I might have a chance of convincing the others. But you must not cause harm and

Brandar must agree to supervise. Tell no one but him that I gave you permission to practice."

"Thank you," I whispered.

Queen Jessa swept back to her place. Kadri waved me to the third row where she and Fabian were seated.

"What was that about?" Kadri asked.

"I'm being banished in three days' time," I whispered. "To Darmeska."

Kadri scowled. "I hoped you could stay here, but I suppose you're grateful the punishment isn't worse."

Queen Jessa summoned Mercer to the floor. I had stood in the belly of the mosaic sea serpent; Mercer straddled its neck as though poised to conquer it. He crossed his hands behind his back in a stance of casual readiness, looking important.

"My son's bride tells us you have valuable information, Sir Fye," Queen Jessa began.

"Yes, Your Majesty. I met Valory Braiosa on her travels yesterday and saw the runes on the tablet she carried. I don't speak the language, but I recognized it as the tongue of the sea folk."

Skeptical murmurs echoed off the walls of the chamber. On the other side of Kadri, Prince Fabian's bland expression gave way to curiosity. He stroked his chin and leaned forward.

"How do you know this?" the queen asked.

"My elicrin magic shows me visions of the past."

Jessa looked intrigued. "From where do you hail, Sir Fye?"

"A village in the mountains of northern Calgoran," he answered, reticent. "Near the Emlefir Pass."

"What else can you tell us?"

He cleared his throat. "The magic of the sea folk was based on bargains. The sea witches could not perform any magic, big or small, without a trade. It's possible that the tablet details some sort of contract."

"A contract now broken?" Professor Strather asked.

"It would seem so."

"Do you know anything about the Summoners, Sir Fye?" Queen Jessa asked.

"The Summoners, Your Majesty?"

"A spiritual order, very secretive. We know only that they worship their 'Lord of Elicromancers.'"

Something in the newcomer's countenance changed, darkened. "I've seen visions of a tyrant who once ruled in my region, who built his court in the heart of a mountain. Those loyal to him gave him that very epithet: 'Lord of Elicromancers.' There was all but no limit to his power. The people in my village still tell stories about him."

Professor Strather tapped her fingernails on her knee. "I've stumbled across legends of this tyrant who ruled from within a mountain before," she said. "A fellow pupil from my time at the academy collected oral tales from the rural north. They speak of widespread terror at his hand, and yet there is no evidence he was ever more than a myth. Mountain-dwellers tell all kinds of tales—"

"A myth he is not, that I can tell you," Mercer stated. "But unfortunately, not much more. My visions are piecemeal and outside my control."

"The professor is right," Neswick agreed, raking a hand through his sparse ash-brown hair. For once, he didn't challenge Strather. "Mountain-dwellers are too cut off from modern civilization for their own good. They are fond of their fables."

"What do your tales say, Sir Fye?" Jessa asked, ignoring Neswick's interjection.

Mercer fell silent for a beat before answering. "They say he could create plagues with a breath and tear the spirit from your body with a look. He twisted the minds of men until they crawled like beasts in confusion. His lies were like poisoned honey, and he was splendid and terrible to look upon. He could take any elicrin power from another and bestow it upon himself."

I repressed the shudder at my nape.

"This sounds rather farfetched," Mathis Lorenthi stated with a flourish of his hand.

"Indeed," Neswick grunted. "When did we resort to scraping riffraff off the streets to testify before this prestigious body?"

Queen Jessa shifted in her seat and subtly clamped her teeth in frustration, the demeanor of a woman beleaguered by inanity. At once I felt both pity and great respect for her, attempting to strike at a deeper truth while shoveling through petty grievances. "What would you require to stay in our pockets and inform us of any more helpful visions you experience?" she asked Mercer.

"I require no reward, Your Majesty."

Kadri and I traded bewildered expressions.

"Regardless," the queen went on, "you are now our guest, and we treat our guests well. Ask for anything you desire."

Mercer bowed his head.

The meeting adjourned. I wanted to ask Mercer what he was playing at, but Fabian jogged down the steps to catch him first.

"That was hardly a comforting testimony," Kadri muttered, fidgeting with her gold jewelry out of nerves.

Rayed approached, scrutinizing Mercer until he drew near enough to speak to us privately. He swung his intense gaze in our direction. "I don't trust our new friend."

"You hardly trust anyone, Rayed." Kadri ceased fidgeting, portraying a sense of calm. "I'm surprised you trust elicromancers enough to cast the deciding vote in their favor."

"This fellow seems to have stumbled into your path rather conveniently." Rayed addressed me, overlooking his sister's remark. "The odds of your encountering someone who could identify the language on the tablet when Devorian couldn't are slimmer than slim."

"Maybe more people are familiar with it than we think," I suggested.

"Perhaps. But is it not odd that you chanced upon him just days after the mysterious 'awakening'?"

"But *I* was the one who asked to stop the carriage and wandered away. He wasn't lying in the middle of the road waiting to intercept us."

"Even so, you can't tell me you accept his 'visions of the past' at face value."

"I've seen one overcome him," I said. "He had a fit and his eyes turned gray."

"Fine, but he was all too prepared to wax poetic about the 'Lord of Elicromancers.'" The ambassador shot an apprehensive look at

Mercer, who was watching us converse over Fabian's shoulder. "If this is not an incredible coincidence, then he is dangerous," Rayed whispered. "He is perhaps *the* danger."

"You mean...the one Devorian awakened?" I asked.

"If he was the powerful 'Lord of Elicromancers,' why would he need to lie and play us all for fools?" Kadri demanded.

"Maybe he's not as powerful as his legends suggest." Rayed laid a hand on my shoulder, clearly in earnest. "I fear he will take an interest in you and try to use you as Ambrosine Lorenthi did. You must be wary. As long as we don't understand what's causing these disasters or who is orchestrating them, it will be easy for an evil to use you as a tool or a scapegoat."

After a lingering look, the ambassador strode away. I pored over each moment with Mercer thus far, propping my interactions with him against the sinister backdrop of Rayed's suspicion. It created a disturbing tableau.

Slowly, I closed my fists and lowered them to my sides. I noticed Jovie Neswick across the chamber near the windows. The hazy sunlight glanced off her hair as she offered me a hint of a determined nod.

If there was a creature out there that could rattle the earth, toss the sea, and stain the moon, I would not get by with useless magic.

I cantered along tree-clad cliffs jutting over the sea until Beyrian was a speck in the distance. Veering into a patch of woods studded with rock formations, I glanced back to see Brandar lagging behind on his black palfrey. He winced at its twitching ears as though it might sling its head around and breathe fire at him. I'd heard some elicromancers could go years without mounting a four-legged beast, but most Calgoranians took too much pride in horsemanship to exchange a saddle for the simplicity of materializing.

When I reached the shade, a cool breeze dragged a loose lock of chestnut hair along my neck, making me shudder. I dismounted and led my borrowed palfrey to a sturdy pine, tying her with a lead rope from the saddlebag. Brandar had dismounted out of frustration and ceased pursuing me. What was the point of stalking me if no one was watching?

Hoping not to harm my mount if the Water's magic rushed too quickly to the fore, I left her behind, weaving through rustling branches and undergrowth dense with pale blossoms.

When I felt truly alone but for the chirping of insects, I stopped and inhaled the briny air. My magic had only ever lurched out of me unbidden. I needed to invite it, welcome the hungry wanderer instead of waiting for him to sneak in and murder me in the night. But would it accept the invitation?

All I knew to do was use an elicrin spell, so I decided to try a harmless one. I picked up a twig and whispered, *"Farhir astam,"* the duplication spell. The twig did not reproduce its identical. Nothing at all happened.

Glend and Jovie Neswick were right. I was not an elicromancer. *Destroy. Transform. Destroy. Transform.*
Transform.

I plucked an immature blossom wrapped in a tight bulb. As it lay on my palm, I closed my eyes, turning inward. There in the dark cavern of my being, I located my magic, a bright little stirring inside me, like the quickening of a babe in its mother's womb. *Come on*, I whispered to it, coaxing. *Please come.*

The petals brushed against my palm as they unfurled.

I opened my eyes and found the blossom growing, bursting as big as a lily though its siblings were the size of acorn shells. My mouth fell open in gleeful awe.

But I thought of the dainty pink roses clinging to Devorian's balcony, their petals soft as ladies' lips. I thought of thorns and curses, darkness and conceit. Fear struck through my spirit like lightning.

The blossom withered in my hand, its petals suddenly ashen and sharp as pricks on a thistle. I cast it to the earth. It left a jewel of blood on my palm.

Dense clouds passed overhead. A loaded wind creaked through the boughs. I turned to look north, away from the sea and its serenity, toward the remote mountains that lay far beyond my current horizon.

The sigh that emerged from my breast was one of surrender.

·❦ FIFTEEN ❦·

A GRAY curtain of rain coasted over the sky as soon as I stepped inside the palace. My stomach howled with hunger and my thighs ached from riding for the first time in weeks, but a supper with Kadri would soothe me.

My failed magical trial gave me peace at the thought of retreating to Darmeska. I would live at the edge of the mountainous northwestern wilds, a suitable home for a wild creature like me. My Neutralizer and I would be rid of each other, and I wouldn't have to face my family in Arna. Most importantly, whatever Devorian had done would be the Realm Alliance's problem, not mine. Grandmum was right; I had enough problems of my own.

But the serenity of resignation fled when the palace doors swung open behind me and I turned to find Glisette Lorenthi standing at the threshold.

"What are you doing?" I demanded, expecting her lovely features to contort into a sneer.

"I wasn't part of their scheme, Valory," she said as the guards shut the doors behind her. "I didn't know what Ambrosine and Devorian had planned for you."

I narrowed my eyes and studied her. Her golden hair hung limp and wet. You would think she'd never heard of traveling clothes; she wore a pale blue gown with a structured corset and a bejeweled sash. For security, no one could materialize inside the palace. She must have appeared just outside the gates in the driving rain, which gave me a petty sense of satisfaction. But her remorse seemed genuine—then again, so had the sisters' pleas for help.

"Let me take that, mistress." The approaching attendant was helpless to stop his eyes from clinging to Glisette's lithe form as he ushered her inside and relieved her of a blue velvet-coated trunk with silver lily clasps. It seemed she planned to stay.

"I heard about the wave," she continued. "I know it's Devorian's fault, and I want to help uncover what he's done. I still despise you for what you did to my brother. But I swear, neither Perennia nor I knew of the plan to blame you for the resurrection spell. We would have stopped it."

I was relieved to be standing a level above her as I considered this. Glisette had wanted to dress me as a whore so the servants would bring me into Devorian's lair—a silly and roundabout approach if she had known my visit with Devorian had already been arranged. Ambrosine was the one who'd told me to simply knock.

"If you don't believe me, I understand," Glisette added. "But it's the truth."

The head maid scurried into the foyer. "Your Highness, what a pleasant surprise! Their Majesties will be pleased to receive you. We have many out-of-town guests at present, so forgive us the few moments it will take to prepare your accommodations."

"Don't bother," Glisette said, slinging her wet hair to one shoulder. "Valory will share her room."

I opened my mouth to protest, but Kadri spoke up from behind me. "Valory is staying with me, but there's plenty of room for the three of us. Four of us," she corrected, sliding her hand along Calanthe's back. "Come this way. We'll get you dry."

Glisette followed Kadri, pursued by the enamored servant toting her luggage. Reconciling myself to three days in her company, I brought up the rear.

"How is Devorian faring?" Kadri asked as we walked.

"The elicromancers Queen Jessa sent have been unable to improve his situation so far, but Professor Strather materialized there early this morning to evaluate him," Glisette answered. "She doesn't believe it's a curse. Curses require malicious intent, and for one to be broken, the elicromancer who cast it must take the curse upon herself or die." I could almost *feel* the effort it took for her to suppress a disparaging look in my direction. I glared at the back of her head, doubly irritated at the way the ends of her honeyed hair had begun drying in effortless ringlets. "It's more like a lingering dark enchantment. Something with more power than a fairy jinx but less power than a curse. She believed it would wear off with a little help."

"Help?" I asked.

"She said noncurse dark magic can fade in the face of two powers to which we all must bow: love and time." She shrugged. "So we've tried to summon one of his former guests from the pleasure house, hoping maybe she'll see through his current state—and his prior state—to the man he could be. But none of them will go back to the palace, not even for a sack of gold, and Devorian wouldn't admit any of them anyway. He's ordered us not to interfere. So we just have to hope, I suppose, and wait."

"Hope and wait," I whispered as we arrived at Kadri's vibrant antechamber. I had much to learn about my magic, but knowing that I wasn't doling out malignant curses brought great comfort.

"That sounds like more good news than bad, at least," Kadri said, walking straight to the beverage tray to pour Glisette a cup of tea. "We haven't discovered much about the tablet, but we have someone who sees visions of the past and who told us what little we know. Valory found him."

"Are you sure he can be trusted?" Glisette asked, accepting a towel from the maid and dabbing at her hair. The barb buried in her question was open to interpretation, and I chose to ignore it in light of Rayed's theory about Mercer.

"No, we *can't* be sure," Kadri opined, "considering he's spent the better part of the day out at sea with Fabian." She watched the hard rain washing down the glass doors. "I thought the weather might bring them back in time to dine with us, but I should have known. Most people would need a respite from the sea after yesterday." Remembering the teacup in her hand, she offered it to Glisette and poured another. "Fabian insisted on holding a banquet two nights from now to honor his lost friends and 'to welcome new ones.' If *his* trust is any indication of Mercer's character, we have nothing to fret over."

"Does he…fancy him?" Glisette asked, barely attempting to tread delicately around what could be a sore topic for Kadri.

"I don't think so," Kadri replied, unperturbed. "Fabian is fascinated with the sea and Mercer told us that the runes on the tablet are the language of ancient sea folk."

"Is that so? Was he able to interpret the incantation?" Glisette set down her teacup and shed her wet gown to reveal thin lace undergarments. The head maid had fetched a robe from her trunk and now held it so the Lorenthi princess could slip out of her delicates and into the silky fabric.

Kadri shook her head. "No. And he can't summon visions at will."

"He sounds like an intriguing character," Glisette mused, sinking down onto a cushion. "Is he handsome?"

"Oh, very. Wouldn't you say, Valory?"

I grunted.

"Valory saved his life and he couldn't spare so much as a thank you."

"If anything, that will endear him to Glisette," I said, wincing through the soreness in my thighs to sit.

"You're right," Glisette sang with a cheeky smile. "I like him already."

A knock heralded a feast of dishes from Erdem: richly spiced vegetables, roots, and dips of yellow, red, and purple.

After we finished a dessert of cream-stuffed dates drizzled with honey, I combed my fingers through Calanthe's tail, thinking of Mercer again. His turnabouts from helpless invalid to smart-mouthed exploiter to amenable advisor certainly suggested a deceitful nature. Despite my renunciation of responsibility, curiosity reignited. If he was a danger, he wasn't only a danger to me. And if I was meant to leave in three days, I might as well use that time wisely.

Tipping a cup of steaming tea to my lips, I silently vowed to glean what I could about Mercer Fye.

Yet Fabian remained rather stingy with the Realm Alliance's guest, whisking him out to sea both days prior to the banquet. I visited with Kadri and took Calanthe to play on the greens while Kadri practiced archery, searching the horizon for a ship that didn't come.

On my final day in Beyrian, Kadri was invited to lunch with her brother at the Erdemese embassy, so I returned to my solitary retreat along the cliffs. I dug my hands into the crumbling dirt, exhuming brimming handfuls, and tossed it in the air, hoping it would transform into grains of sand before my eyes. But it showered down as bright sparks that consumed the grass in hungry ribbons of orange fire. I attacked the flames with a saddle blanket but singed one of my fingers in the process and left a plot of scorched earth behind me.

That evening, as Kadri lined my eyes with a black paste, I massaged the shiny streak of burned flesh. Ivria's emerald gown sprawled out on the bed, too beautiful for me, too beautiful for anyone but her. I stared at it so forlornly that when Kadri finished painting my face, she pressed a bright, soft skirt of royal blue into my hands. "It's a bit warm for that one anyway," she said. "You'd sweat like a cook in the kitchen."

The new ensemble revealed a band of bare skin at my waist, which Kadri decorated with a strand of gold beads. She donned a light green skirt and bodice of the same style and wrapped a gold draping with a sparkling fish scale pattern over one shoulder.

Glisette wore a sheer gown with embroidery in convenient places; two pale pink sparrows hid her breasts, and silver vines intertwined and merged at her pelvis. Over it, she donned a sheer cape that clasped above her cloudy chalcedony elicrin stone. Kadri dusted our hair with a shimmery mineral powder, and at last we began our descent to the ballroom.

A mosaic fountain at the center of the room flung its spray toward the domed ceiling. Vast windows and glass doors at the far end offered a generous view of the ocean and the incandescent sunset. They opened to a veranda lit with pierced metal lanterns. Bronze legs fashioned to look like kelp branches supported glass tabletops, and the chair backs at the head table were blue-green glass mimicking waves frozen at their peaks.

Thanks to his height, sandy hair, and proximity to important people, I had no trouble locating Mercer. He stood in a cluster of men including Fabian, King Basil, Glend Neswick, and Rayed.

"Is that him?" Glisette asked, latching on to Kadri's arm as a herald announced the three of us. "He's so lovely it's downright wicked."

Fabian and Mercer broke away from the group to greet us. Though Fabian charted a straight course to his fiancée, his gaze loitered on Glisette thanks to her gown—and what lay beneath.

"My bride," he said, pressing a kiss to Kadri's hand. "I feel as though I haven't seen you in months. Only two days and I've forgotten how beautiful you are."

"And I nearly forgot you existed," Kadri jested, her dark eyes glimmering.

Fabian put a hand to his heart. His elicrin stone sparkled a bright citrus green. "You wound me. And whom do we have here? A Lorenthi princess?" He touched Glisette's knuckles to his lips.

"You can't tell me apart from my sisters, can you?" Glisette asked, her voice barely more than a purr. "Honestly, after all the times we played together as children? You and I were almost betrothed before child betrothals went out of fashion."

"Of course. You're Glisette. I should learn to listen closely when a flock of beautiful ladies enters a room. Cousin," he said, laying a kiss on my hand as dispassionately as if he were stamping a seal on parchment. "Forgive me for not greeting you with warmth at the Realm Alliance gathering."

"You're cousins?" Mercer asked. I had nearly forgotten that fact myself.

"Third or fourth," Fabian explained. "Practically every Ermetarius is a cousin of anyone with another royal name. The war against Tamarice united our ancestors, and most of their children 'united' as adults."

"Your visions didn't offer that up?" I asked Mercer. He offered a guarded smile in return.

"You must be Mercer Fye." Glisette extended her hand to Mercer, and he pressed his lips ever so softly to her skin.

"Let's sit and eat," Fabian said. "I've survived on wine and brandy for days."

"So that's what you've been doing out at sea," Kadri teased.

"That's not all we do. We explore the islands, tell seafaring tales, play drinking card games . . . and punish the losers in *most* interesting ways." He offered her his arm. "Good thing you weren't there; you might have been tossed overboard for a swim."

Kadri visibly shuddered at the thought as he escorted her to the head table.

Glisette nestled her hand in the crook of Mercer's elbow. He presented the other arm to me. I used the contact as an opportunity to study him as though I could harvest his deepest secrets from a lingering look.

"Have you seen any other visions that may prove useful?" I asked him. "Anything further about the Lord of Elicromancers?"

"I wish I had."

"Isn't there something you can do to arouse a vision?"

"As I explained before, I get 'aroused' rather spontaneously." One of his brunet brows hitched a mischievous arc. "You witnessed it yourself...when I was sprawled out on a bed, utterly at your mercy."

The hint of a smile at the corner of his mouth made my neck flush with heat. Glisette peered around his chest at me, her eyes almost menacingly full of intrigue.

"It's not what it sounds," I hissed at her, untangling my arm from Mercer's.

When we reached the table, Fabian remained standing while his guests settled into their seats. He clinked his knife to his glass goblet to grab their attention and said, "I am pleased you are all here. Normally my mother and father like to welcome our guests, but tonight it is my privilege. We all suffered losses in the rogue wave, and our city and country suffered a great wound. We have honored friends and strangers who made their graves in the depths. Tonight, we honor restoration and recovery. We honor new friendships. And we honor those who risked their lives to save others, even those who are not present to accept our gratitude."

Kadri pursed her lips. Fabian finished by raising a glass in salute, and after we all drank in unison, Kadri whispered, "He was out there looking for the girl who saved him. He's obsessed. He fancies she's a fisherwoman or a water sprite, I suppose."

As Fabian sat, he shot a glance toward the scarlet sun dipping over the sea.

"Have you heard from your grandmother?" Rayed asked me as he fished a lobster tail onto his plate.

"Not since she left Pontaval," I answered. Her final rebukes lashed me again, a burning stripe across my mind. *You foolish girls. You've done enough.*

I cleared my throat. "Have you received a missive from her?"

"No," Rayed muttered, his comely face creased with concern. "But she's a highly connected and clever woman. She reminds me of my own grandmother, my *dahtara*. I'd count on Madam Braiosa knowing more than we do by now."

"You're probably right," I agreed. My resourceful grandmother might very well dig to the heart of Nissera's predicament before others even knew where to break ground.

I cleared my throat as the conversation tapered off, sensing the weight of Mercer's attentions on me. I dared answer them with a glance, only to find him and Glisette engrossed with each other. Glisette was using some sort of palmistry party trick as an excuse to trace her fingers gently over Mercer's upturned hand behind their wine goblets. Kadri and Rayed had begun quietly bickering across the table in their native tongue, so I resorted to staring at my food as though studying a masterpiece portrait. Finally, when the remnants of the meal were cleared away, I moved with the listless crowd out to the veranda.

Kadri linked her arm in mine while Fabian, Mercer, and Glisette traveled as a flock ahead of us. "With silver dust in her hair and blue eyes, she resembles Fabian's mythical mystery savior."

I snorted. "Glisette would have hauled sinking trunks of jewels and silk to safety before reaching a hand to help."

Kadri hiccupped with laughter. "You're jealous."

"What? No, you are. I'm comforting you."

"I don't care what Fabian does as long as he doesn't tempt people to pity me. But he is most certainly tempting them tonight."

I watched Glisette lean back on the balustrade, laughing, fingers spread across Mercer's breastbone. She slipped her other arm through Fabian's as though she might drift away if unmoored from either's touch.

"I suppose I should reinforce my claim," Kadri sighed. "People are already gawking at the three of them."

She approached the others, but I kept my distance. The act of adoring the fascinating elicromancers from afar was hardly new to me and left a bitter taste in my mouth. I thought of Jovie Neswick and that wrinkle of longing between her brows as she'd watched Ander dancing with one of his kind.

Setting off in the opposite direction, I wove through clusters of people toward wide steps leading from the veranda to the beach. I noticed Brandar as he propped his wineglass on the balustrade, positioning himself to convince those watching that he was keeping an eye on me. We shared a conspiratorial glance before I journeyed down to the beach, pausing a few steps from the sand.

The salty twilight breeze swept back my hair and carried a gray-and-black gull feather with a white tip, which I caught and pinned between my thumb and forefinger under the diffused glow of a metal lantern. There was something about the risk of testing my power here, near all these people, that made the magic within me froth up like sea foam, effervescent and pure.

The pale tinge at the feather's tip snuck down the fringe and took on a luster. The texture of the shaft crystallized beneath my touch. With sheer, dumbfounded admiration, I realized that the feather was hardening into a silver cast of itself.

My chest swelled with pride. If I could do this again, tomorrow, in front of the leaders, I could convince the Realm Alliance to let me continue practicing. I wouldn't have to lie to them. Unlike my father, I could return from my isolation, triumphant and ready to take on a role befitting my station and studies. I grinned madly at the stars that lit up the dusk.

Then a twinkle caught my eye from among the rock formations between the flank of the palace and the shore. I squinted into the darkness and thought I glimpsed a massive gull perching on a rock, perhaps the very one whose feather had molted and drifted my way. But this figure was far too big, even bigger than a swan, and the light emanating from the palace reflected off its form in odd and unbirdlike ways. As if in a sudden panic, whatever it was flung itself off the rock, making a quiet splash below.

Cocking my head to the side, I hesitated for a moment before tucking the feather into my neckline and jogging down the final steps to the beach.

I picked my way over white sand and rocks until I reached the bigger formations. I had to hike a bit to reach the creature's perch, venturing ankle-deep into cold pools of water to access footholds. By the time I found the spot, night had set in and I had to feel my way through the shadows where lights from the royal residence didn't quite reach.

My fingers groped along wet stone until I approached a little lagoon carved out of the rock, partially illuminated by lantern light from a balcony up above. Whatever I'd seen was probably long gone, considering it either swam or flew, and I had ruined the hem of Kadri's skirt. I plunked down on a ledge and pulled the silver feather out of my bodice to study it in the peace of my alcove of solitude.

Another glint of white flashed in my periphery. It could have been a fish splashing out to nip an insect, but I wasn't convinced. A strange suspicion led me to lower myself to my hands and knees—Kadri would never let me borrow anything again—and stare deep into the pool, heart flittering.

For a moment, the only traces of a presence in the lagoon were the faint ripples sloshing. And then a pale shape emerged from the dark end, where light from the balcony didn't reach. My eyes adjusted to the moonlight again and I gasped.

The head and shoulders of a woman rose above the surface. Hair so fair it was almost white framed a pale face with shockingly blue eyes, and faint silver scales dappled either side of her chest from the water to the hollows of her collarbones.

Her human aspects appeared small and delicate, but the tail that composed her lower body nearly circled the perimeter of the pool, ending in vibrant flukes with flowing tendrils. The silvery blue at her hips gradually deepened to a saturated violet along her tail, whose thick scales glinted like coins in the moonlight.

❧ SIXTEEN ❧

WORDS stuck in my throat. The creature, wearing an expression of cautious vigilance that mirrored mine, did not move. This gave me time to recover from shock and think of the mother-of-pearl tablet that had yet to be deciphered. What if the creature departed and chose never to return?

I froze, fearing that a flinch might banish her to the infinite darkness of the open sea.

But a foot scraped on stone behind me, and in one swift movement her supple body heaved over the ledge into the black water below.

I whirled around, readying a curse for my ever-present Neutralizer. But I found Mercer, his features clear in the light from the balcony.

"Was that a—?"

"A sea maiden!" I planted my hands on the ground and clambered to an upright position. "No one's seen one in nearly a thousand years and you scared her off."

To get a view of the sea, I had to maneuver my way past him on the narrow ledge. The familiarity with which my body was forced to skim across his should have coerced him a step sideways, but he didn't budge. Looking out from the ridge and scanning the tides below, I saw no hint of my quarry. But the toe of my sandal caught on the uneven surface, nearly pitching me to the rocky swells below. Mercer gripped my upper arm, tethering me to safety.

I ducked away and started on the treacherous path to the beach. Somehow, I managed to reach level ground with nothing but a few scrapes and a broken sandal strap. I could feel Mercer traipsing behind me, finessing his way over the jagged route with ease.

"She didn't flee or attack when she saw you," he said, passing me up and turning to face me, spraying my shins with sand. "That means she's sociable toward humans. She might come back."

"I'm guessing you've had plentiful visions of sea maidens to inform your opinion?" I asked, stopping at the base of the stairs to snatch off my broken sandal.

"I'm sorry. I only followed you because I thought something might be wrong."

"On the contrary, I—" I reached to retrieve the seagull feather from my bodice and realized I'd left it at the lagoon. It occurred to me that Mercer must have been watching me to notice me wandering off. My feelings about that landed somewhere on the vast spectrum between flattered and suspicious.

"After the banquet, I'll find a way to get my hands on the contract," he said. "We'll sneak back and see if she returns."

"Why must we sneak?" I asked, gripping the banister. The banquet guests had gathered in clusters on the landings; some were parading drunkenly down the beach in the other direction. "Don't we want the Realm Alliance to know she's here?"

He combed back his wheat-brown hair. "At best, humans view sea people as specimens to study. At worst, trophies. If word gets out, someone might try to hunt her down. And a conflict with the sea folk is not pleasant. In my...at times, sea folk wreaked havoc on anyone who dared wade in deeper than the ankles. During the worst periods of human–sea folk relations, there were pods of them sabotaging travel and trade at every port."

"Oh," I muttered, thinking of the sea maiden's magnificent tail. A splendid sense of mystery and *otherness* had glimmered about her. It made me shiver as the breeze trailed its lukewarm fingers across my nape.

"They're just like us," he went on. "They protect their own and hold grudges when they can't. Hopefully we can find out what that blasted contract says before something else happens. She might even speak a bit of Nisseran, if she's as sociable with land folk as she seems."

"But—"

"Meet me back here when the guests are gone." Mercer hurried up the steps to the veranda.

When the music and the hum of conversations finally stopped competing for dominance, Kadri and Glisette prepared to retire. I muttered an excuse about having lost a bracelet on the beach, and they blinked their bleary eyes before starting upstairs without me. I hadn't seen Brandar since he'd watched me descend to the shore, and in the midst of the revelry, no one seemed to consider my need for a custodian.

The sky had cooled to the black-blue marking the wee hours. The metal lanterns swayed in a wind that skimmed across the sea, and by their light I wandered back down the beach until I found a quarter-moon-shaped rock on the shore.

Despite my fear of unknown creatures teeming in the deep, I sank my feet into the salt water, letting it sting and then soothe the blisters I'd earned hiking and dancing. I scanned the peaks and arches jutting out from the beach but saw no white hair or shimmering scales. There seemed little chance the sea maiden would appear again.

Mercer joined me after a quarter hour, toting the tablet halves in a blanket. Their smooth ridges and iridescent swirls gleamed purple and gray in the moonlight as he uncovered them and hunkered next to me.

"Did you have any trouble?" I asked.

"Not at all. Fabian helped me."

He had so easily earned the prince's trust. "Why did you misrepresent your objective the day I found you at the inn?" I asked. "You said you wanted a reward, and then you turned it down. Did you simply want somewhere to stay and meals to eat?"

Mercer tilted his head. "I didn't want to seem too eager to share what I knew, or you might have thought me mad and made sure I never set foot in front of the Realm Alliance. Pretending to want something in exchange gave me an excuse to withhold the truth from you so I could give it directly to the leaders."

"What is the truth?" I asked. "Are you who you say you are? Mercer Fye, an elicromancer from a northern village so remote its name isn't worth mentioning?"

"I am who I say I am," he said. "And I've seen what I say I have."

"So you truly believe Devorian resurrected the 'Lord of Elicromancers'?" I asked, pedaling my feet through the water.

"Don't call him that unless you want to sound like one of his blind followers," Mercer said in a low voice. "But stars help us if that's the case."

"How do you know so much about the...?"

I stopped abruptly, for his body had gone rigid. His shoulder blades pressed together and the gray film slid over his eyes. I bit back a gasp of shock.

This could be a trick of elicromancy, I thought. *Mercer Fye could be a fraud meant to make fools of us all.*

"She's coming back soon," he said, blinking the clouds from his eyes. "The sea maiden."

"Do your visions predict what's to come, as well?" I taunted. "Are you conveniently a *Prophet* now?"

Mercer's expression was opaque.

"Who are you, really? What do you want? Tell me the truth."

"I'll tell you. But you won't believe me."

I pursed my lips, inviting him to test me.

"I *am* a Prophet," he said. "I don't have visions of the past, but of the future."

"Why wouldn't I believe that? My cousin was an Augurer—"

"Just listen," he said, gesturing for me to hush. "My visions of the tyrant weren't visions. I lived through his reign."

"What are you saying? Just be forthright!" My tone rose to a desperate crescendo. I had only hours left in Beyrian. I wanted to use them wisely: either getting answers about the contract or practicing for my demonstration.

"I lived during what you would call the Archaic Age, and back then the—"

"The Archaic Age?" I laughed, but it sounded terse and forced.

"The Archaic Age ended over a thousand years ago. The people of that time didn't even speak our language."

"No, they didn't. But the boy who grew up watching the future play out behind his eyelids did. He had to learn to listen, otherwise he would never understand his prophecies. Some were just plain visions without significance. Others were revelations of events that would change the course of history."

I scoffed, refusing to relinquish my skepticism. "You're saying you survived the Heroic Age with its Elicrin War, and then the Mortal Age as well? I've never heard of elicromancers living that long, not without turning to dark magic eventually and then facing execution for treason."

"I'm eighteen years old. That I didn't lie about." So melancholy was his tone that a corner of my mind realized that the thankless boy I'd encountered slurping oysters at the inn was only one sliver of a whole person, an intentionally exaggerated sliver.

I shook my head as though the information would settle better with a little nudge. "If that's true, how did you get here?"

"I'm trying to answer that myself." He splashed water on the back of his neck.

"I've heard of portals that span both distance *and* time," I murmured. "One of my ancestors could open them. Perhaps you passed through one?"

"I don't remember. I was wounded and unconscious. I didn't even know I should use this language until you addressed me first."

"So what *do* you know about the Lord of Elicromancers?"

He massaged his forehead. I could see him shoring up the will to speak about what he'd endured.

"In my time, he established dominion over the north from his court at Mount Emlefir," he began. "One day, he was nothing, no one of import. Before we could blink, he had overtaken the Brazor Mountains and was well on his way to dominating the whole realm. Mortals suffered under his rule, and the magic-kinds he captured were worse off. He would twist and torture them, make them his servants and set them against their own kind. He made elicromancers perform dark magic on his behalf until they decayed from the inside out. Many killed themselves when captured."

Mercer faced the sea again. The moonlight harshened the rigid set of his jaw. "My elder brother, Tilmorn, was one of the first elicromancers he took. We didn't know much about the threat at the time. Travelers and rangers said the Emlefir Pass was no longer safe and that the villages closest to it were like towns of ghosts. But we didn't put a name to the danger until a gang of ragged soldiers came to our village to bid Tilmorn visit their king's court. They bore a royal summons, though I had never heard of their king, nor did I recognize his sigil. His name was Emlyn Valmarys, and he had declared himself 'King of Nissera and Lord of Elicromancers.' His soldiers carried a gray banner with a white moth emblem. It was almost comically presumptuous at the time. Tilmorn laughed and called him the 'Moth King,' but agreed to answer the summons in order to gauge the potential enemy and strip him of his power if necessary."

"Strip him of his power? What do you mean?"

"Tilmorn's elicrin gift allowed him to take and bestow other elicrin gifts, but he used it carefully. Sometimes, he would conduct mutual trades or take from an elicromancer who abused their power. He made a trade with an Omnilingual so I could understand and learn the language from my visions—the one we're speaking now. I couldn't hold both gifts at once as Tilmorn could, so he made me an Omnilingual after each vision, taking my power of prophecy upon himself—which was a relief. The visions could be frightening. . . ." He trailed off and shook his head. "In addition to possessing his extraordinary gift, my brother was a skilled warrior. He feared no one, especially not a handful of soldiers with dull blades and cracked shields. So he answered the imposter king's call. And soon after that, the terrors began."

The mournfulness in his voice was beyond what anyone could muster for a ruse. My suspicion deserted me. Of their own volition, my fingers encircled Mercer's forearm. "Did Tilmorn die?"

"Far worse. Tilmorn's power was the only one he couldn't trade. It was his and his alone, but the Moth King subjugated him. By either manipulation, torture, or both, the royal impostor turned a noble, fearless man into a servant who would strip any 'disobedient' or 'traitorous' elicromancer of their power and bestow it on his overlord."

My heart thudded in the base of my throat. I thought of my mother's gift, the way her commands influenced the actions of others and the harm it could do if wielded without restraint. And she was just one elicromancer.

"Every attempt to overthrow Valmarys failed," Mercer went on. "Mortal armies snapped like arrows on boulders against his forces. Elicromancers would secretly invade his fortress at Mount Emlefir and never return, and then his power would wax greater. Elicromancer leadership forbade me from trying to save Tilmorn, knowing that if I attempted a rescue mission without a foolproof plan, I would only become a tool to help Valmarys crush more innocent creatures."

"Did your prophecies not warn you what would happen when Tilmorn answered the summons?"

Mercer shook his head, turning away from me. "They tried. The frightening visions that came when I was young depicted Tilmorn's torment in brief, startling flashes. There was no detail, no context, unlike many of my other prophecies. But they were horrifying. He took the burden on himself, enduring them without complaint. And then he gave me back my power and went on living his life as though he had never seen these hints of his fate."

"He must have been very brave," I whispered. "And the Moth King very strong to subdue someone like him."

"Valmarys's power seemed to have no limits. We did everything we could to stop him. All of us: the mortal kings and their armies, elicromancers, even the fay. We all fought, but our numbers were dwindling and we were abandoning hope. It seemed there was nothing our enemy couldn't do on a whim. The fay and the sea folk began to retreat to their hideouts in the forest and the open sea. They had little interest in the fate of humans. It was only the elicromancers left protecting the realm, and we were doing a poor job of it. Half of us found ourselves serving our enemy, and those who evaded him didn't trust one another. That's how skilled he was at dividing us; the mere suggestion that some of us could be his servants in disguise tore us apart."

He clenched his hands until his knuckles turned white. I could almost hear the pulse of sorrow-tinged rage thrumming inside him.

"And then one day, while we were gathered in our hideout in the woods," he went on, "the leaders said they had an idea, a way to trap Valmarys and his servants in their mountain court. For centuries, possibly for all time. But the ritual would take great sacrifice. They said we would have to 'bargain.' It wasn't elicromancy. But they wouldn't tell us the nature of the ritual, for fear the Moth King would find a way to stop it. Trust had worn thin."

This time, when he flicked water onto his face and combed it through his hair, the act seemed desperate, an attempt to remind himself of his new reality.

"Do you think this contract was what the leaders were talking about?" I asked, tracing the runes with my fingertip. "The bargain?"

"That's what I fear."

"But you don't know?"

"We weren't supposed to know anything about the ritual beforehand. But the night we were to perform it, I received a vision. I saw the Moth King bleeding to death, the life leaving his eyes. I saw his court collapsing around him. My vision meant that someone was strong enough to destroy him, forever, not merely restrain him."

His voice trembled with exhilaration. A palpable sense of hope—dangerous, costly hope—set my heart pounding.

"I tried to reason with the other elicromancers, to tell them there had to be another way, something to prevent the Moth King from tormenting a later generation. But they had set their minds. They accused me of attempting to divide the few of us who remained against one another. They thought I might be working for the Moth King in exchange for Tilmorn's freedom. I don't think they understood that the Moth King needed Tilmorn in order to remain strong, that Valmarys would never let him go, no matter what I could offer in return. They thought I had exaggerated Tilmorn's role to convince them to attempt a rescue mission. I was in the midst of arguing when one of them stabbed me cold. They tied me down, spoke of disemboweling me." He shook his head, as if he barely believed it himself. "I heard someone I thought of as a friend say what a shame it was I had betrayed them, but that at least I would be useful. I started losing consciousness...."

"Is that the last thing you remember?"

"I think...someone saved me. I've tried over and over to recall what happened, but all I remember is a skirmish in the dark, and someone lifting me onto their shoulders. The air grew brighter and warmer, and then they laid me down on the grass, cursed, and ran off. Then you found me."

Silence folded around us, until I drew in a gulping breath. "What happened to Tilmorn? Did he die?"

"I don't know, but I hope so," he answered. "He would be free of servitude. And if the Moth King *has* returned, he'll be less powerful without Tilmorn."

I shook my head. "Why have so few people heard of him? If he was terrorizing the whole realm and turning elicromancers into slaves, why does nothing remain but tales in the north and followers in white cloaks?"

"Elicromancers must have wiped the memories of mortals so they could recover from the devastation, so that mortals would trust them to set everything right. But it sounds as though the truth lingered through generations, possibly through the lines of the elicromancers who pledged fealty to the 'Lord of Elicromancers.'"

I considered this. "Do the Summoners wear white cloaks to pay homage to the moth insignia—?"

My last word evolved into a squeal. Something latched on to my ankle with a touch so light it could easily have been seaweed snaking a path through the tides that licked my knees.

I lurched back and found the sea maiden's silver-white hair unfurling like a lily pad in the black water.

❧ SEVENTEEN ❧

THE creature trained her wide eyes on us. After a few beats, Mercer found the wherewithal to calmly reach for the tablet pieces.

"*Il samenef?*" he asked. "Do you understand me?"

She tilted her head and emanated a whistle that dove to a hum. The sound was similar to those Devorian had expressed when reading the tablet, but far more graceful, like a bird's song.

Mercer fit the tablet halves together and held them for her to see. As she read the runes, her pale eyebrows shot together in a rather human expression. Then her starry eyes latched on to mine with sudden fierceness.

"What is it?" I whispered.

Words in her language bubbled forth, melodic but urgent.

"What do we do?" I asked Mercer. "She can't speak to us."

The sea maiden propped her torso on the rock and gripped my wrist. Cords of strength ran under the pale, silvery skin of her arms. She seemed docile, but with one effortless yank she could send me to sleep in the depths.

Yet she merely opened my hand and set a silver feather on my palm—my feather—giving me a long, knowing look. Then she opened her other hand, and inside it lay a smooth pebble. After a pause, she plucked the feather out of my hand and set the pebble in its place.

"A trade?" I asked.

Her small fingers traced the arch of my bare foot before sliding up my calf and thigh, bunching up my skirt around my hips. I jerked away and she jerked away in response, sending ripples to caress the stones.

Considering that gestures were our only form of communication, she was likely illustrating her desires. I smoothed my skirt back over my legs. "I can't. I don't have that kind of power."

She furnished the feather again, a rebuttal to my argument. And then she swept her eyes toward Fabian's balcony with such longing that I understood why she wanted this.

I gestured at the balcony. "Fabian is betrothed. He's going to marry my friend."

She blinked at me. I scooped up Mercer's hand, interlaced our fingers, and jabbed them in her direction as a demonstration, but a silent plea remained in her blue eyes. I shrugged defeat.

She ducked back underwater. "Wait!" I started, but she resurfaced and plunked a larger pebble down on the crescent-shaped rock where we sat. Prying my hand open, she took the small pebble from me, touched it to the large one, and held it to her chest. Then she passed the feather over the large pebble and gave it to me.

"What? What does that mean?"

"The trade requires a third party," Mercer said. "She knows you can't do what she wants on your own, and she can't translate the tablet for us. You need a sea witch to broker the trade."

"A sea witch?"

"Their version of elicromancers. Except the sea witches deal in bargains and they usually charge a tariff for their services."

"I'm not going to agree to a bargain if I don't understand the terms."

"Then I suppose we won't know for sure that Emlyn Valmarys has returned until he takes over your city and calls himself king."

I scratched at my hairpins, which were by now in disarray. "What sort of tariff?"

Mercer slid his knuckles along his chin in thought. "You could offer something sea people can't easily obtain."

"You mean like silk or jewels?"

He snapped a finger. "I know just the thing. Agree to the trade and I'll be back soon."

"Oh...all right," I said as he dashed off, leaving me alone with the sea maiden.

She waited, those blue eyes like raindrops on bluebells, patient and pleading. I twisted the shaft of the feather between my fingers and chewed on the inside of my lip. Then, forcing myself to think of no consequences besides saving lives, I offered her the silver feather and held out my hand for the pebble.

Joy beamed in her eyes. She plopped the pebble down and gave me a sign to wait here—just then I noticed tiny pale webs between her spread fingers—and dove back into the water, the lissome blue and violet tendrils of her flukes scattering droplets on my face.

Mercer returned and sat on a little bulge of rock above me, cradling a hefty jug of brandy. My eyes had started to feel heavy when he whispered, "Here they come."

My sleepless joints creaked as I stood up. I looked and saw amid the gulping black tides one silver-white head and one golden-green drawing near. The familiar sea maiden approached first and gripped the edge of the rock. The witch kept her distance, narrowing pale eyes at us. A tattered gray-green fluke coiled out of the water, and a frayed strip of fishing net held colorful shells in her hair. By the time she drew near enough for me to see a necklace of human foot bones strung together, I'd taken an instinctive step back.

"Stay calm," Mercer said. "As long as we can give her something she wants, she won't hurt us."

"Such as our *bones*?" I whispered.

Unlike Fabian's savior, whose oddities were easy to overlook thanks to her glittering beauty, the sea witch was a haggard creature with hollow eyes. The burnish on her bright green scales had faded in patches to a lusterless gray, and scars marred her arms and chest. She beckoned me forward with fingers that were membranous and charted with veins.

Reluctantly, I dropped to one knee and planted my hands on the damp, gritty rocks. I heard Mercer shuffle closer.

The sea witch gripped my chin in her long fingers and searched my eyes before noticing the tablet next to me. Recognition washed over her features and she croaked something in their strange language, but unlike when the young sea maiden spoke, it sounded like a song spoiled by out-of-tune instruments.

In her other hand she cupped a large shell with an iridescent inner layer bearing spiral patterns of green, brown, silver, and blue. Tiny characters like the ones on the tablet had been etched onto the surface. The sea witch released my jaw, leaving impressions from her tapering fingernails.

"What if she wants my power?" I whispered to Mercer. "Or my legs? What exactly am I trading?"

"It will be fine," he said. "You'll be none the worse for wear."

"How do you know? Oh, right," I mumbled with a sideways look of resent. "Visions."

The sea witch offered the shell to the sea maiden. The younger creature trembled as she whistled into the hollow of the shell. The etchings of the contract glowed, and when the sea witch passed the shell to me, new ones had formed.

"I don't know..." I started.

"Try repeating what she said." Mercer knelt beside me.

I was put off by his eagerness to surrender me to the mercies of a lovestruck maiden and a human-hating witch, but I remembered his brother and everything he had lost. I latched on to the echo of the noise still bouncing in my mind.

"*Hmmaaaaweehooohwut*," I attempted, but the sea witch chastened me with a wagging finger. She repeated the sound I'd tried to emulate and pointed at the sea maiden. Then she pointed at me and beckoned.

"Your name?" Mercer suggested.

Speaking into the hollow of the shell, my heart aflutter, I said, "Valory Ermetarius Braiosa."

More runes formed on the tablet. The sea witch clamped her hand around my chin again, pried my lips open, and curled her long forefinger inside my mouth, drawing out a wisp of sparkling vapor. It was like when the Water had gifted me—or cursed me—with its magic. But it had produced enough fog to cloak a forest clearing, and the sea witch took just a tendril, which swirled and floated into one of two open vials clanking against the bone jewelry between her scaly bosoms. The clear water in the vial became an elixir that glistened like captive starlight, which she gave to the maiden.

Fear shone in the maiden's eyes as she tipped the elixir to her lips, but she drank it all. When the vial was empty, the sea witch extracted a rod of light from her yellow-green hair. As she had done with me, she gripped the sea maiden's delicate chin and pried her mouth open. By the time I realized that the witch planned to cut off the young maiden's tongue, the deed was already done. My scream would have cut through the quiet night if I hadn't clapped a hand over my mouth. The sea maiden darted under the surface, moaning and trilling.

The moist organ wriggled and glowed in the witch's grasp. Her cavernous eyes looked upon it as a weary traveler might look upon a feast. I tasted bile in my throat. Even Mercer, who had certainly seen worse in the dark days that had befallen him, tensed next to me.

The witch sliced the tongue in two. One half she forced into the other vial, where it disintegrated into flecks of radiant light, creating an elixir that looked just like the first. She dipped the shell with the runes into the sea and swirled the other half of the tongue inside it. It too became a glowing potion, which she swallowed in one swig. Light beamed out from her gullet and a dark smile stretched her overripe features. When she spoke the sea language again, her voice was gliding and nectarous.

The witch snapped the second vial off the strap around her neck and gave it to me. With horror I studied the starry elixir, but the sea witch chirped something at me that was as sharp as any utterance I'd yet heard in their language. I steeled my churning stomach and swallowed. It tasted like salt and fire as it singed its way down my throat.

"Can you understand me?" the sea witch asked.

"Yes," I answered in disbelief, and the sound that emerged from me was unnerving and strange.

"I require a small fee for my services."

"Um," I said, my hand shaking as I brushed a loose lock of hair from my face. "Mercer, hand me the..."

He shoved the jug of brandy into my arms. "Brandy," I finished, cringing as I offered it.

She snatched the jug from me, uncorked it, and inhaled its aroma. "I accept this as partial payment. But I want something else."

Mercer tugged on my arm. He assumed we'd completed the trade. The far reaches of the sky hinted at a rose-gold dawn, but the sun wouldn't rise quickly enough to usher this bizarre creature back to the underwater caverns and forgotten sea bottoms before I had paid my fee in full.

She fastened her gaze on me for what I hoped would be the last time. "I want your fondest memory of the beauty of the land above. Not of the shore or the surface of the sea. Nothing I can see with my own eyes."

Relieved, I closed my eyes and reached inside. The first memory that emerged was of crashing through the forest with Ander and Ivria, pinning myself to trees and crawling in the undergrowth as we hid from one another. Afterward we had plopped down to eat plums on a luscious grassy knoll. The palace was just a blot in the distance. Juice trickled down to our elbows and dried like baked sugar in the noonday sun.

The second memory was from my journeys with my father in the mountains. I was packaged in furs upon furs as we stood on a lonely peak overlooking a snow-dusted pine forest with no end.

I could surrender neither of those. I summoned another memory of Calgoran's majestic beauty, one untethered to someone I'd loved and lost. "I'm ready," I said, and felt her fingers touch my temples. I focused only on that memory, hedging out the more precious ones, until it faded away.

"I was one of the witches who struck this bargain," she trilled, releasing me. "An elicromancer had heard a great sea legend, how our mothers once tamed a terrible god of the deep by placing him in a deathlike slumber within a sea cave. The elicromancer summoned the witches—a few of my sisters spoke their language back then—and asked if they could create such a spell to tame the Lord of Elicromancers. My sisters told him it would require blood and suffering."

"How does the spell work?" I asked, breathless.

"When our mothers tamed the sea god, they chose someone to sacrifice. The chosen one suffered much and deeply, for her guts had to be strewn out and tied in knots while she was alive. The greater the evil, the more knots one must tie to trap it. They tied only one for the sea god, as he was a mere beast. Then one feeds the knots to the quarry. This is simple with a sea beast who eats without thinking, but not so with a clever man with many enemies he fears might poison him. I warned the elicromancer of this before we drew up this contract to trap the Lord of Elicromancers in his domain."

I hadn't imagined magic more viscerally revolting than the mutilation of the poor sea maiden, but I was wrong. I choked back the taste of bile again and asked, "Who did the elicromancers sacrifice?"

"They had one of their own."

"So you provided the magic needed for the ritual, and they chose one of their own to sacrifice. But you said it was a bargain. What did they give you in return for helping them?"

"In order to trap their enemy with our magic, their kind would cast a spell hiding sea-dwellers from land-walkers. That way they could no longer hunt and kill us."

"Why did you make the contract breakable? Why not just agree upon those terms in perpetuity: the safety of your people for the safety of theirs?"

"Nothing is eternal," she said, gripping the rocks with claw-like fingernails. I imagined those nails dismantling prey and had to force myself not to balk. "All sea witch magic must be written as a contract, and every contract can be broken. Even the sea beast will rise one day, when tales of it are forgotten. Anyone could read the runes etched on hidden surfaces in the deep and unravel the blood magic."

"The contract has been broken. That means the Lord of Elicromancers has risen?"

"That is what we warned your kind would happen. We told the elicromancer to guard the contract and revere its power." She unlatched her claws from the rock, signaling that our time was limited. "But the lives and memories of humans are brief, and their legends become twisted and forgotten."

The sea witch dipped underwater with her spoils. Her torn flukes surfaced with a quiet splash, and then she was gone.

Dawn sketched a glowing ring around the edge of the world. As I glanced at the tablet halves, the runes arranged themselves into words that made sense, reflecting what the sea witch had said.

"Can you read it now?" Mercer asked.

From shoulder to fingertip, my arms began to tremble. The moist air suddenly seemed scarce and incompatible with my lungs. My mind dove into dark recesses, into the waking of a loathsome, undead being breaking free from newly opened depths, tearing its age-old, decrepit body from the shadows, ready to avenge its fall from power.

I gathered up the broken contract and stood, a queasy weight tossing in my stomach. When I could no longer abide it, I bent double and vomited on the sand.

Mercer gathered my sweat-dampened hair until I finished. I washed out my mouth with salty water and haltingly explained to him what the sea witch had told me. While he listened, he looked out across the sea as though he wanted to toss himself into the waves and let them carry him away.

"I wonder ... I wonder if you were intended to be the sacrifice," I muttered, reaching out toward him. I stopped short of touching the soft fabric of his tunic and instead plucked the tablet halves out of the sand.

"They must have succeeded in sacrificing someone else," he said.

A burst of growing daylight lit his eyes, turning them to burnished ocher.

"Perhaps you got caught up in this bargain somehow, trapped through time."

"I don't know. I only know we have to tell the Realm Alliance. We have to make a plan. We can't let it be like last time."

Though nearly blinded by the array of colors at the horizon, I noticed the sea maiden on the seaward side of a dune near the palace steps leading to the ballroom. In the shadows, she twisted and writhed, grappling with the change the elixir had initiated. From tendrils to pelvis, her shimmering tail ripped clean in two as though following a seam. She had no voice to scream, but I could see silent agony as her scales became bleeding scabs and flaked off to reveal milk-white skin. At the end of it all, she was naked, and quite human, with only her silver hair to cover her body.

She climbed to her feet, wobbling, then stumbled just far enough to drape herself at the base of the steps leading from the beach to the palace veranda, in full view of servants and guards.

I jolted forward, but two guards in green had already noticed her and hurried to assist. Soon after, Fabian started across the veranda above, his hair messy and his banquet clothes rumpled.

"Mercer?" he yelled, traipsing out to the balustrade and squinting at the rock formations. "Valory?"

"Why is he looking for us out here?" I whispered.

"When I needed his help getting the contract, I implied that our 'research' was just an excuse to get you alone," Mercer explained. "I told him I was meeting you on the beach."

"Someone said there's a naked girl out here," Fabian called out. "You two can subject the gulls and fishes to your naughty acts, but my guards deserve more respect!"

I started to emerge—I couldn't let *that* rumor spread unchecked— but paused as I considered what would follow the telling of our tale. Yes, we had obtained information that would help the Realm Alliance. But would anyone believe us? Or would they suspect us of lying, plotting in secret? Mercer had stolen the contract, albeit with Fabian's help, and that would diminish any trust the Realm Alliance had in him.

In the light of a new dawn, one that heralded my departure, even Queen Jessa's demonstration plan seemed tenuous—it meant revealing to my enemies that I had defied orders and practiced my magic, and that Brandar had not fulfilled his duty. If the Neutralizer's loyalties were called into question, it might bring Nissera's leadership to doubt both King Tiernan's and Queen Jessa's loyalties as well, and would endanger my most precious secret: that Brandar's gift could not be used to restrain mine.

"We have to change our story," I said. "To something more believable."

Mercer blinked at me, incredulous. "We can't sully the truth with a single lie," he said, stressing each word. "I came out of nowhere and the Realm Alliance already has reason to mistrust me for that."

"I'm not going to be punished for doing something that's actually *helpful*."

"This message is too important for you to muddle it just to avoid a slap on the wrist!"

"A slap on the wrist? Half the Conclave wants to throw me in prison! If I stroll in and tell them that I meddled and used my magic to obtain a sea witch's help, I might as well put the manacles on myself!"

"And you fancy your fate more important than the whole of Nissera?" he demanded, securing a grip on both halves of the contract. He was strong enough to pry my hands off, so I tore the object out of his reach, nearly toppling to the uneven rocks underfoot.

I felt a strange sense of loss at the idea of him thinking me a horrid person, yet I remained committed to my argument out of self-preservation. "I've no idea why I'm appealing to you for mercy! You risked my life. That sea witch could have taken anything from me, anything at all, and you encouraged me to make the bargain regardless."

"Because I knew everything was going to be—! Argh!" His explanation devolved into a gnarl of frustration, but the commotion from the veranda drew our attention. Fabian had noticed the nude woman at the base of the stairs and was in the midst of shrugging off his rumpled tunic to cover her, murmuring gleefully that she had saved him from the flood. Through the ballroom windows, a maid spotted the two of them and clunked down a tray of dishes to untie her starched apron. She hurried to meet them and arrange the pristine fabric over the sea maiden's bare skin. As she whisked the creature away for the sake of propriety, Fabian watched in awe, sifting a hand through his thick, dark hair.

Before I could insist that we hide the contract, Mercer ripped the halves from my hands and started toward the steps. With a small shriek, I balled my hands into fists and hurried after him.

"There you are," Fabian called as we approached the veranda, me glaring at Mercer's broad back. The prince clapped his hands down on Mercer's shoulders. "Did you see her? The girl who saved me?"

"If that was her, then yes, we saw plenty of her," Mercer replied with the hint of a mischievous chuckle. He was like a flag flapping in a vigorous breeze, displaying a new side every time the wind changed. Had I seen his true crest and colors in the dark of the night?

"I must ensure she receives a proper welcome," Fabian said, but rushed footfalls made him trail off. A guard sprinted through the ballroom, dodging displaced chairs and maids collecting used plates and goblets.

"My prince," the guard said, without the usual song and dance of begging for pardon. "You're needed at the front gates. Urgently."

Wide-eyed, Fabian pursued the guard. Mercer and I shared an uneasy glance and followed. My bare foot and sandal alternately smacked against the marble as my heart quickened. Did yet another disaster await us? Would I hear that Arna had burned to ash and its people with it, or that a blizzard of such strength had swept over Darmeska that even its ancient ramparts couldn't stand against it?

Once we'd crossed through the palace to the front entrance, we jogged down the steps and darted across the courtyard toward the open gates, where a throng of servants and guards waited, parting as the prince approached. Fabian stopped suddenly before we reached the center point around which everyone coagulated. I smacked into Mercer, nearly slipping on a pool of liquid underfoot, and gripped him by the elbow to regain my balance. His muscles went rigid under my touch.

I took a step back, my bare foot squelching as I peeled it away from the slick courtyard stones. When I managed to peer around Mercer's shoulder at the spectacle ahead, I issued a horrified gasp.

A man lay on the ground, his face mutilated with gashes. The skin of his chest and legs had been clawed to ribbons. His clothing dangled off him in bloodied tatters. The wet substance underfoot was his fresh blood.

I might have failed to recognize Brandar if not for his cloudy gray elicrin stone.

~§ EIGHTEEN §~

HE Neutralizer drew ragged breaths. His end approached.

Fabian froze, but Mercer shoved the tablets against my chest before dropping to his knees beside Brandar.

"Is there a Healer?" I yelled at no one in particular, my voice sounding distant.

"We've sent for her," a guard said.

After a protracted breath that I thought might be his last, Brandar fixed his blue eyes—one of which blossomed red with burst vessels—on Mercer, then rasped out, "Trap...they're coming for you."

A torrent of terror rushed over me. I wanted to ask what he meant, but Mercer clenched his jaw and scooped a supportive arm under Brandar's back. He didn't beg for clarification. He must have understood the warning. "Go in peace," he whispered. "*Portil waena fir sironoell.*"

Someone pushed past me, their soles sloppy on the wet tiles. The Healer knelt over Brandar, her elicrin stone shimmering with white light, but she was seconds too late. A haze had passed over his eyes. His lips hung slack after ejecting a final breath.

Sharp tears burned the bridge of my nose. No one deserved to die in such agony.

"What's happening?" I asked Mercer as he pressed Brandar's eyes closed.

"It was a materialization trap." Mercer stood and attempted to clean one grimy palm on the other, to no avail. "I've seen wounds like this. This is one of the Moth King's tactics to isolate elicromancers from one another. It worked before."

I shuddered as I thought of that mysterious between-place that elicromancers could step across to reach their destinations. It was common knowledge that highly skilled elicromancers could create barriers to block access to certain places, or to designate paths within that unseen stratosphere. But I hadn't known they could set deadly traps. As I dared to study Brandar's lifeless body lying at the foot of the open metal gates, I noticed a pattern among his wounds: they were all lacerations slicing in one direction.

"The traps catch victims in the midst of materializing," Mercer said, as Fabian and I ripped our gazes away from the gruesome sight to listen. "The only way to escape is to materialize away, and depending on how you're trapped..." He shook his head. "I've seen elicromancers cut to bits after materializing out of snares or cages. There's no way to know what paths they intersect until someone's been caught in one."

"Warn all elicromancers in the city not to materialize until further notice," Fabian called to a guard, his commanding tone teetering on the edge of hysteria. "We'll send missives to Arna and Pontaval as well."

I hoped my family would receive word in time. I couldn't ponder the idea of my mother or Ander meeting the same fate as Brandar. "Who's coming, Mercer?" I asked.

"The Moth King's servants must have heard about my talk with the Realm Alliance," he said, removing the tablets from my grasp.

"They're going to want to stop me from spreading word about Valmarys's return while he gains a foothold. We have to act fast."

Rayed emerged from the crowd and strode toward me, casting a watchful glance at Mercer. The mixture of sand and blood rubbed gritty between my toes as he pulled me aside. "You need to leave now," he said. "Lie low. Don't go to Darmeska."

"But I—"

"Brandar was one of the only people capable of controlling you, Valory, and now he's dead under suspicious circumstances."

The implication hit me with the weight of a cliffside crumbling. "Are you saying the Realm Alliance might think I...I killed him?"

"No one's going to believe this violence was perpetrated by an ancient dead tyrant when you're right here, flesh and blood—not to mention the rumors that you're defying orders by practicing magic."

"But I haven't hurt..." I sputtered. "I would never—"

"Don't you see?" Rayed growled, baring his white teeth. "Whoever killed Brandar wants to cover their own tracks by making you look guilty, and they might succeed if you don't escape. It seems the Lorenthis inspired a far more dangerous person to emulate their tactics. And I would bet my life that someone is standing here in this courtyard, a wolf in sheep's clothing giving the orders."

"Mercer was a victim of the Lord of Elicromancers," I insisted, my eyes charting a course to his grim face. "If he could just explain—"

"Did he encourage you to use your magic?" Rayed asked.

"He..." Again, my gaze found its way to the mysterious boy from the past. He crossed his arms with the seriousness of a commander ready to deploy his restless army for a long-awaited battle. "Jovie Neswick did too, and Queen Jessa...."

I regretted the words even as they spilled out. Jessa had asked for my discretion and I'd blurted out our secret at the first opportunity. "We can explain everything," I finished.

King Tiernan would tell the Realm Alliance that I had no reason to murder Brandar, seeing as the Neutralizer couldn't *actually* neutralize me. Perhaps disclosing this terrifying truth would be the only way to secure my freedom.

"Please, Valory," Rayed begged, shaking me by the shoulders. "If you trust me in the least, flee before one of the Realm Alliance leaders who suspects you of wrongdoing has you arrested on suspicion of murder."

The thought of Glend Neswick's adamant pursuit of justice made me turn and hurry across the courtyard, shoeless and ragged and stained with a dead man's blood.

The curtains were drawn around Kadri's bed. Glisette slept on a sofa, her face and arms still gleaming with smeared cosmetics. As I stuffed my belongings into my satchel, Calanthe plodded at my heels, panting in anticipation of her early-morning sprints across the palace yards.

After tearing off my stained clothing, I pulled on breeches, a lightweight tunic, and boots, barely taking the time to scrub my feet with a wet cloth. Without comment, Kadri's maid rolled the soiled skirt into a ball, either to launder it or to toss it in a fire. I asked her to give Ivria's emerald dress to Kadri in exchange for the garments I'd ruined.

As I arranged my dagger at my hip, Glisette began to stir. I paused, hoping she would drift back to sleep, but she blinked at me, rolled up on her elbow, and purred, "What were you and Mercer doing last night?"

"What do you think?" I demanded, shouldering my satchel.

"You weren't doing *that*," she said with ruthless confidence. "You were on a secret mission of sorts. You're not going to Darmeska, are you? You're going on an adventure."

I didn't answer as I leashed Calanthe.

Glisette launched herself from the sofa and shimmied out of her robe. "I'm going to need to borrow some plain clothes. Didn't you have a shirt that was too baggy across your chest? I think it would fit me."

I reached for the door handle while she sifted through the suitcase I was forced to leave behind. But the door swung open without my help.

Mercer stood at the threshold, breathless, bursts of golden fire gleaming in the brown of his eyes. "There are riders coming through the city," he said. "Bearing a gray standard with a white moth."

My heart seemed to simultaneously dive to my belly and leap to my throat. I thought of Mercer's brother, Tilmorn the warrior, and the emissaries sent to escort him to the Moth King's court—if that was indeed true.

"Won't the guards shoot them down?" I asked as Calanthe

shoved by me, relying on her tremendous size to win Mercer's attentions when whapping him with her tail didn't work.

"I couldn't convince Fabian to give the order," Mercer said, gently nudging the hound away by the snout. "The guards won't attack a small band of riders unless they prove hostile. And by then it could be too late for us to escape."

"Us?" I demanded.

He peered over my head at Glisette, who had pulled on one of my gray tunics and now squirmed into a pair of my breeches.

"We have to go. I'll explain later." Mercer put a hand on my shoulder and attempted to steer me out.

"Don't manhandle me," I said, jerking away. "Maybe in *your* time it was fine to fling ladies about like sacks of potatoes, but now it's considered rude."

"In *his time?*" Glisette repeated, flicking her blond ringlets out from under her tunic collar.

Mercer gritted his teeth and squared himself in front of me, but he didn't touch me again. It occurred to me as he loomed like a storm cloud that he could be dangerous if he desired—and that was without regard for the gem around his neck.

"I heard the ambassador. I know he doesn't trust me, and I don't blame him. I truly don't. But I told you everything and I thought you understood."

I paused, my hand on the doorframe, and shook my head. "I don't know."

Without another word, Mercer caught Calanthe's leash and tugged it from my grasp, charging down the corridor.

"Don't you dare!" I screeched, storming after him.

When I lunged for the leash, he turned on me. The intensity in his eyes took me aback, but it melted quickly and he let out a sigh. "My visions put me a step ahead of everyone else. They can make me single-minded and impatient. I promise you I wouldn't have risked your life with the trade if I weren't certain you'd survive in one piece to...to..." He trailed off.

"To what?" I asked.

A dizzying realization sprang up. *I saw the Moth King bleeding to death, the life leaving his eyes*, Mercer had said of his prophecy. *My vision meant that someone was strong enough to destroy him, forever, not merely restrain him.*

"To—" he started again.

"To kill the Moth King?" I asked over him.

I longed for Mercer to laugh at the thought. But he maintained his somber expression. "Yes."

There was so much packed into his answer: hope, resolve, pity, fear. But I couldn't see beyond my own fear to forgive him for being the bearer of this news.

"Why didn't you tell me?" I asked feebly.

"There's not much more I *can* tell you. I didn't recognize you in my visions of the Moth King's demise until I had another one at the inn."

"You're sure?"

"Yes," he said with a step in my direction. "I saw you twisting a knife in his heart. You have no idea how much hope and confusion that sight brought me. I didn't know who you were, or where

I might find you. But you're here, and the Moth King's servants are on their way, and you're likely wanted on suspicion of murder by now. So we have to go."

Orderly footsteps—several pairs of them—thudded nearer. At the very least, the Realm Alliance would want me for questioning. And with Neswick involved, I knew that wouldn't end in them turning me free. I had no choice but to escape now and strategize later.

Mercer started off, trusting I would follow. Long-limbed Calanthe nearly dragged me through the lesser-trod passages we pursued. A rogue set of footsteps chased us the entire way with panic-inducing persistence. I pushed through the burning in my lungs until we ended our trek at a door that swung open to reveal a glorified closet with wood paneling.

Prince Fabian and two guards waited for us. For a fleeting second, I thought I'd been lured into another trap. But one of the guards shoved a panel and it swung open to reveal stairs.

"I couldn't secure horses on such short notice, and this was all the coin I could get without raiding the vault." Fabian shoved a jangling bag into Mercer's hand—aurions for the journey, no doubt. "Fortune be with you."

"Thank you, Fabian," Mercer said, slipping the purse down the neck of his bloody tunic, the same from last night's banquet. They patted each other's shoulders as though they'd been friends for years. The thought of leaving Kadri behind without so much as a farewell smarted.

"Wait!" someone yelled, and I stuck my head out the door to see Glisette pursuing us in overlarge boots she had clearly persuaded a servant to hand over. Her blue velvet trunk banged against her thighs. "I'm coming with you."

"You can't—it's a—coming after us!" My protest was inarticulate, and she dismissed it as such.

"I made it my mission to help fix this," she said, breathless. "You could always use another elicromancer on your side."

"Just hurry!" Mercer growled, jogging down the stairs. I followed him and shortly emerged among the jagged rock formations beneath Fabian's balcony, in the lagoon where I'd first seen the sea maiden. The salty air reminded me too acutely of the nauseating sea witch elixir.

Mercer leapt over a jagged ledge with ease. I suspected this was not the first time he'd been forced to make an escape in a pinch. Calanthe and I scrambled after him, but Glisette materialized beyond the rocky terrain to wait for us where the sand met the stone path leading to the gardens.

"Don't materialize!" I heard Mercer snap. The coin purse had slid into the belly of his tunic, resting on his belt. Without regard for how ridiculous he looked, he jumped off the final ledge and landed next to Glisette. "Someone's laid traps."

Calanthe and I caught up to them, her athletic prowess putting me to shame.

"Traps?" Glisette demanded.

"The Neutralizer died from one," Mercer explained, swinging open the garden gate.

"Is that what the blood is all about?" she asked. Fear burned raw in her voice. "I need to warn my sisters."

"They'll hear soon enough. Fabian will make sure of it."

Magnificent hedges traced their way along elaborate fountains and ivy-strewn pavilions. Waterfalls tumbled into a private swimming beach for palace guests. The archery field where Kadri often practiced stretched vivid and green alongside the shore. And amid all that grandeur, there was not a single guard. I assumed we had Fabian to thank for that.

The morning shadows turned the sweat on my neck cold as we hurried through the garden, casting glances in every direction before slipping through the outer gate, which stood conveniently ajar.

On the other side, we found a grim-faced Rayed. To my shock, he drew his sword. The naked steel sang a high note as he trained it on Mercer with a deft flick of his wrist.

Mercer reacted before I could—I felt a tug at my hip when he snatched my dagger from its sheath just as Rayed glided forward to make his blade softly kiss the skin of the boy's throat. Mercer held the point of my knife just beneath the ambassador's exposed underarm. They had maneuvered themselves into a deadlock quicker than I could have uttered the word.

"Ambassador, what are you doing?" I asked timidly.

"Why won't you leave them alone, you parasite?" he demanded of Mercer. "They've suffered enough of your lies and nonsense. We all have."

"Don't make me use my advantage against a mortal," Mercer said in a low voice, his elicrin stone illuminating with a warning flash.

"And what advantage would that be, exactly?" Rayed demanded, nearly nose-to-nose with Mercer. His grip on the blade tightened until his tendons bulged, tense and dangerous. "The ability to 'twist the minds of men until they crawl like beasts in confusion'? To tell 'lies like poisoned honey'?"

"Whoever we're running from will catch us if you two don't stop comparing cocks," Glisette snapped.

"He's the one you ought to run from," Rayed sneered.

"Let us pass, Rayed," I said, managing to sound calm despite the thrashing of my heart. "It is *my* choice to go with him. Any consequences will be mine to face."

They stared each other down for a few more beats. Mercer was the first to lower his weapon. He offered me the hilt and I sank it concisely in its sheath. Teeth bared, Rayed slid the blade away from Mercer's throat.

Brushing past Rayed with defiance etched on his face, Mercer led us down a sloping cobblestone path. We crossed the main thoroughfare before turning into an alley crowded with laundry lines and barrels of fish and crates of chickens. We jogged with the rising sun at our backs, navigating the tight, unfamiliar streets. Many stared at Glisette's flowing golden hair until Mercer stuffed several thesars into a young boy's hand and swiped the hat off his head, offering it to her.

"Do the people chasing us have to do with the Neutralizer's death?" she asked me as she tucked her curls into the cap.

Fear knitted my lips together, but I squeaked out a small "Yes" and continued on.

Dark shapes filled my periphery to the right, and I glanced down the alley to see riders traveling down a parallel road, moving toward the palace. The crowds around them fell to such a hush that even from afar I could hear the canter of their horses' hooves. The riders neither crept nor charged through the city—no, they rambled, shoulders relaxed and chins held high as though Beyrian *belonged* to them, as though the streets had been paved for them. There were six riders, one a standard-bearer who turned to look down our alley as he passed.

An eerie, pale moth fluttered across the tattered fabric he carried.

Under the rider's hood, one eye glowed an opaque, milky white. A patch of skin around his lip was dark gray and rimmed with red lesions, nearly resembling a wide, crooked smile. I caught a flash of the same sort of pestilence on a band of exposed skin between his glove and sleeve.

A lump of terror bobbed in my throat. Everything inside me wanted to crumple and cower and hide because I knew what he was: a blight, an elicromancer who had performed enough dark magic to begin rotting from the inside out. But I focused on a rogue curl bouncing gaily from Glisette's hat and continued following her one step at a time, until we could no longer see the riders.

The alley curved and widened to a dirt road as the buildings on either side of us shrank. We meandered our way through a herd of spotted cattle and crossed a bridge over a river roaring toward the sea. By the time we slowed to a walk on the far side of a craggy hill, a shaft of pain cut through my ribs and my legs felt like limp wineskins.

"They were blights," I said to the others, gulping for breath.

Mercer merely adjusted the strap on his broad shoulder with a grim expression. Glisette stopped in her tracks.

"But how would any dark elicromancers have escaped the attention of the Conclave long enough to become a blight?" Glisette asked, winded. "Are you sure that's what you saw?"

"I'm sure." My hand shook as I wiped away sweat trickling past my ear. "It means the whole city is in danger."

"We need to keep moving," Mercer said, cutting his elegant features west.

"We need to turn back and warn them," I argued. "The disease could spread. There's no remedy for mortals, none except the gift of elicrin healing."

I thought of Melkior. Fates help us if he was one of our only hopes against a ravaging plague—but if that was the case, I'd drag him to do the grim work myself.

"We can't risk the riders catching us," Mercer said. "Getting you safe is our goal."

"People will die," I said.

"Why getting *her* safe?" Glisette demanded, but Mercer ignored her.

"For as long as the Moth King lives, there will be atrocities we can't stop. They will happen to innocent people. It doesn't help to cut off one head of a many-headed serpent. You have to stab it in the heart."

"So we're supposed to just let this happen?" I asked.

"It's too late to warn them about the blights. Fabian will warn the Realm Alliance about the Moth King and explain to them why you needed to run. I told him everything. We'll get the help we need to end this."

Mercer hadn't looked back at me once, so I yanked his arm and forced him to face me. "We can't—"

"If we go back, we may save a few lives," he said. "But I'm not risking yours to do it. Every day Emlyn Valmarys breathes is a day people die."

"You don't care about Kadri or Ambassador Lillis or Fabian or those people we just passed." My voice was hoarse with anger. "You only care about vengeance."

He stepped closer so that I had to tilt my head up to look him in the eye, which made me feel powerless. "I have fought this fight already," he said. "I have seen this realm ravaged by the Moth King's rule. I sawed off the head of the serpent only to see it sprout a new one with sharper teeth. Every day I refrained from attempting to rescue Tilmorn. Every day I worried after Lundy and the baby. But every day I left home to fight, to plan, to help. And now you are our greatest hope for freedom."

"What...?" I started, feeling a peculiar wrench in my gut at the mention of a woman and a baby.

"I don't know how I got here or how I found you," he went on. "But I have, and we must do what we were meant to do. Trust that I would not arbitrarily leave this city to its fate." He gestured back at Beyrian, his eyes red-ringed with unshed tears. "But for once I have a clear path. I know this demon. I know his ways. Let's tear him down."

I cast my gaze to his boots but found the courage to look up at him again and nod slowly, even as panic thrummed in my blood.

With a deep breath, Mercer turned westward.

"What is *happening?*" Glisette asked, stomping across the rock-strewn grass to follow him.

Neither of us answered her. I latched on to Mercer's mention of these people from his past. It was hard to imagine that he'd started a family during such a bleak time, and his occasional flare of boyishness seemed to preclude paternal experience. But the Archaic Age was a long time ago, and things had been different then. People used to wed and conceive earlier. Before healers had produced contraceptive tonics, a childless relationship between man and woman, like what my mother and Victor sustained, must have been rare.

I should have felt emboldened and encouraged by Mercer's certainty, but instead I felt as though the hands of fate had decided to wrap around my throat and squeeze. I missed Grandmum. I ached for her to assure me that the stories of the Moth King were mere myths. Her wisdom and common sense would dismiss Mercer and his vision. Devorian and I had acted foolishly, but surely we had not made the most monumental mistake of the last thousand years.

But Grandmum wasn't here, and I couldn't dismiss the sorrows and the fury of the young man trudging ahead, or the hope he seemed to have placed in me.

And if I couldn't dismiss them, I would have to sell myself fully into his trust—to go where he bade, do what he commanded, and accept his prophecy and, therefore, my fate.

"We need to find a safe place to stop and send a missive back to the Realm Alliance before the routes are compromised," Mercer said.

"Maybe Tully?" I suggested, drawing up the familiar map of

Nissera in my head. "It's a small outlying village to the northwest. We can get everything we need at the market."

"Sounds fine," Mercer said before muttering *"Aphanis inoden"* under his breath to conceal our trail. I silently chided myself for not suggesting the spell first.

Calanthe cantered alongside us with aplomb while thoughts of home weighed heavily on me, as well as questions I couldn't answer: Would the riders go to Arna? Was my family safe? How much of the realm might have already fallen prey to this unseen tyrant?

NINETEEN

WE approached Tully at the brink of dusk. As townsfolk and traveling merchants broke down their tents in the market square and packed up leftover wares, our eyes prowled for anything resembling a meal. My stomach roared with an appetite earned by slogging across the wilderness. It distracted me so that I'd finally stopped looking over my shoulder for a glimpse of riders in the distance.

Mercer had offered Glisette a laconic explanation of the sea witch contract and the task set before us—namely, getting me face-to-face with the Moth King. I felt Glisette's sense of wonder shift to distress as she learned the significance of the contract her brother had broken.

She'd been silent since. I wondered if she regretted coming along, but she walked on as the sun dipped low and shadow-tinged clouds skimmed across it.

Mercer secured us lodging in a crammed public house and sent a missive to Fabian explaining where the Realm Alliance could meet us. The one room available was a musty attic with a table but no bed, only sacks stuffed with hay and wool blankets. It came with nut bread and bean stew, brought to our room and served with a helping of inquisitive stares.

We ate ravenously. Calanthe made even quicker work of her

portion than I did of mine, wetting her wiry mustache, licking her chops, and begging for a nibble of bread when finished. I gave in.

After wordlessly wolfing down his stew and bread, Mercer pulled a map of Nissera from his pocket and unfolded it on the rickety table, ironing it down with his fingers. He'd scrawled various notes to help him marry his knowledge of an older Nissera to this new, more populated one.

"We will have a long and arduous journey to Mount Emlefir," he said, voice hushed. "Without the ability to materialize, the trek through the Brazor Mountains will be difficult. But I'm sure roads are better than they were in my time. With the Realm Alliance's troops and supplies, we might make it."

Glisette met my eyes as we waited for him to tack on a "quickly" or "without trouble." He didn't.

I traced a path to Mount Emlefir, straying east to brush across Arna. I missed my home with its green flatlands and hills and forests. I even missed the cursed snows of deep winter and the way the stars seemed to twinkle brighter in cold air.

"Or we could avoid roads altogether," Mercer said, eyes sparking. "King Tiernan creates portals from one place to another, does he not? He could make a way for us to reach the Moth King's court, protected from ambushes and traps."

A sudden fear seized hold of me, fear that I was not ready to do what needed to be done. "I don't—"

"And when the Realm Alliance is ready, their army can follow us through the portal to Mount Emlef—"

Mercer stopped abruptly as the gray film slid over his eyes. His chest rose and fell with a rapid rhythm. The color washed from his cheeks.

"What's happening?" Glisette asked, nearly knocking her chair over as she tried to distance herself from him.

"It's a vision," I whispered.

It endured just long enough to invite worry. After nearly a minute, Mercer blinked the mist away from his eyes and drew in a deep breath. "Darmeska," he said finally. "Valmarys's old court in Mount Emlefir is nothing but dust and crumbling ruins. He wants his new court to be magnificent. He's going to invade Darmeska."

"He won't be able to," I said, fury and pride filling my chest. "The fortress is impenetrable and they've enough stores to endure a five-year siege."

"This is no ordinary elicromancer," Mercer said. "We need to update the Realm Alliance and ask for King Tiernan's help before Valmarys cuts off communication and travel between the cities. His first goal will be to isolate each power."

He looked feverishly about as though more writing supplies might suddenly appear in a puff of smoke, then stood up and struck his head on the low ceiling before stomping out of the room.

Glisette kneaded her temples and used the *tharat insaf* spell to turn her lukewarm tea into wine. "This is so much to take in."

Mercer returned and dragged his chair back to the table with his toes as he plunked down. He scrawled out his message and muttered the spell that inhaled it into the magical missive routes.

There was no shortage of thick woven blankets and we succeeded in making a comfortable pallet, though the three of us hesitated when it came time to determine where to sleep. Calanthe settled down first, listless as ever. With a wry smirk acknowledging the forced intimacy of our sleeping arrangements, Mercer lay on the far end nearest the small window.

I sank onto my meager slice of the pallet next to Calanthe, my head by Glisette's dainty feet, which were dotted with blisters she hadn't mentioned.

With a huff, I extinguished the lantern flame. In spite of the sounds of breathing around me, I felt more alone than ever, skewered with worry for those I loved.

We woke at the crack of dawn to scour the market. Before we'd even choked down breakfast, a jolly man had offered thirty silvers for Calanthe and a cobbler's wife had tried to buy Glisette's hair, nearly taking a knife to it before Glisette could squeak out a refusal.

"Rub some dirt into it, won't you?" Mercer joked, but it rang humorless. No reply had come from Fabian, Queen Jessa, King Tiernan, or anyone else.

I almost feared their reply more than the lack of one. What would it say? That the realm's armies were ready to march? That King Tiernan could create a portal for me to go to Darmeska this very hour? Would I stand on the ramparts of the fortress city, challenging the Moth King to try to take what didn't belong to him? Would soldiers have to die so that I could stand face-to-face with him?

My stomach contorted in fear for the hundredth time. This dilemma was a barrel rolling downhill, picking up great speed—with me stuck inside.

Hurried hooves striking earth made my heart lodge in my throat yet again, but it was a coach hurtling up the dirt road from the south. It jerked to a stop at the edge of the market square and Kadri popped out, sporting a bow and quiver packed with neatly fletched arrows.

Calanthe strained at the leash to greet her and I stumble-stepped after. Kadri waved the coachman along. He bowed his head and snapped the reins, leaving us in a cloud of dust.

"I saw your message to Fabian," Kadri said before I could ask her why she'd come. "The Realm Alliance isn't coming to your aid."

Mercer swore in Old Nisseran, pacing several steps to calm himself.

"The leaders think one of you killed Brandar," Kadri continued, eyes haunted with dark circles. "Neswick has a silver tongue."

"He convinced the Realm Alliance?" I asked, my mouth suddenly dry as dirt.

"He did," Kadri answered. "But they're more concerned with the plague than they are with capturing you. At least for now. Hundreds of people fell ill with sores and fever yesterday and the palace elicrin Healer was found beheaded."

A fresh wave of terror washed over me. The blacksmith at the forge across the street fanned the fire with her bellows and I jolted as livid flames answered. I thought of the boy whose hat we'd taken, one of many innocent people who would fall victim to a deadly disease.

"They plan to stop all traffic in and out of Beyrian by noon," Kadri said. "I'm lucky to have made it out."

"What about Fabian and Rayed?" I asked. "They just let you leave?"

"Everyone thinks I boarded the last ship for Erdem before the quarantine. I had to sneak away without even bringing my horse."

"What about our second message?" Mercer asked. "Did it reach King Tiernan?"

"I didn't see or hear of a second message, but King Tiernan returned to Arna yesterday morning anyway. Elicromancers are desperate to get to their homes before more materialization traps crop up."

"What did Fabian tell the Realm Alliance?" Mercer asked.

"Everything. I wrote to you last night. Did you not receive my missive?"

"No," Mercer said darkly. "The missive routes must be compromised."

"Then I have more news." Kadri raked her teeth across her bottom lip. "Valory...Neswick twisted everything Fabian said until it sounded plausible that you were behind the chaos. He thinks that when your father encountered the Summoners on his travels in the mountains, he converted to their thinking and passed their creed along to you. In his mind, you planned to resurrect an ancient evil, and Mercer *is* that evil in disguise. He echoed Ambrosine's accusation that your grandmother helped you set up Devorian to take the fall for breaking the contract. He said Brandar knew you were practicing your magic and that's why you killed him."

I felt as though the wind had been knocked out of me. "Jovie told me I should master my power before it mastered me. She's the only way Neswick could have known."

"But what would they have to gain?" Kadri asked.

"I..." I shook my head. "I have no idea."

"Those who don't believe you plotted this seem to think you're a victim of Mercer's wiles," she continued, her mahogany eyes searching my face. "Queen Jessa believes both of you are innocent and telling the truth. But she is vastly outnumbered."

I wished to sit down. "So both the Realm Alliance and the Moth King's men will be after us?"

"We'll have to take obscure paths to Darmeska, through the Forest of the West Fringe," Glisette said, snatching the map from Mercer's breast pocket. "The roads are heavily regulated. There are guard outposts everywhere."

"You two would be much safer if you returned to your families," Mercer said, looking from Glisette to Kadri.

"I am here to right my brother's wrongs," Glisette said defiantly.

"Sending me back to the city would mean condemning me to die by plague," Kadri added, resituating the bow slung across her back. "Besides, I'm a fine shot."

"You're mortal and therefore a liability," Mercer pointed out. "You're one more mouth to feed and one more set of footprints to track."

Kadri fluidly slipped the bow off her back, nocked an arrow, and let it fly so close to Mercer's head that it ruffled a lock of his sandy hair on its way to skewering a slab of meat in a stall about fifty paces away.

"Ho there, missy!" the shopkeeper yelped. "You'll need to pay for that!"

"Go on, Mercer," Kadri said through an acerbic smile. "Please elaborate on how useless I am."

"I'm going to buy a sword." He sighed, extracting a few silver and gold coins and dropping Fabian's purse into my hands. He stalked toward the smithy. "Please talk some sense into your friend before she ends up dead. We're leaving in a quarter hour."

"I'll need boots that fit," Glisette said, peering warily at the cobbler's wife.

"What about your engagement?" I asked Kadri as we filed into the market crowd weaving through the stalls.

"The king and queen approved of my decision to return to Erdem until it's safe in Beyrian. When that time comes, Fabian and I will marry as planned."

"Not if you're disgraced when they catch you keeping company with the likes of us," I muttered. *That is, if any of us survive.*

"Fabian isn't exactly in good graces either. The Conclave confiscated his elicrin stone, though I'm sure it'll only be for a few weeks. In the meantime, he's decided he's useless and escaped out to sea with his 'little foundling,' the girl who saved him. I didn't even have a chance to tell him I was supposedly departing for safer shores. How do you pack to part with civilization?" she asked, readily changing the subject.

I thought of my father, of the laden bags we'd carried over snow and jagged rocks. His feet had been as sure as a mule's, while mine slipped and stumbled often. The songs he would sing rang with melancholy through the thin mountain air. I remembered trying to guess what he searched for—perhaps hidden treasure, or a long-lost friend. But when he taught me to navigate by the sun and stars, I realized how aimlessly we wandered. My father was looking not for a place, a person, or a thing, but for a purpose he would never find.

I recalled the supplies he used to carry: waterskins, dry food, bandages, cloaks, lightweight bedrolls, a pot, a pan, flint, and tinder. After making the rounds at the market, Kadri and I joined back up with Glisette, who'd had the foresight to buy a garden trowel. When Kadri asked what it was for, Glisette said simply, "Privy digging. We must leave no trace," and moved on to the next stall. "I do enjoy luxuries," she added, noting our surprise. "So much that I will happily hunt down anyone who poses a threat to them."

I shrugged and traded a few thesars for a packet of sage ground with salt for freshening our teeth, bars of wood ash soap, and rags for menstruation. Glisette was proving surprisingly stalwart, but I didn't want her—or me—to become sore company in the absence of basic comforts. Years had passed since I'd survived the wilderness.

We loaded down bags with our spoils and crossed the market to the forge, where Mercer was speaking with a girl just younger than me and a burly, middle-aged man. The girl's hair was dark blond and bundled in a sensible braid, and her nose was dusted with freckles and streaks of soot. She held an unadorned longsword with a leather grip.

"Smiths in the city outfit the soldiers," she was telling Mercer. "My uncle and I just make tools, locks, horseshoes, and the like."

Mercer noticed us and said, "The only sword here belonged to her father. She's asking a higher price for it. Do you mind?"

"How much?" I asked, digging into the significantly lighter coin purse.

"Five more silvers," the bearish man said. "Right, Pearl?"

"Two is sufficient," Pearl replied, and I gave her the coins. She offered Mercer the weapon. "This didn't just belong to my father, but to his father's father, who fought for Queen Bristal against

Tamarice on the Lairn Hills when he was barely old enough to wield a sword."

"Perhaps the strength and valor of its past owners will give me strength," Mercer said. His gaze lingered on hers before he accepted the sword and belted it around his waist. "I'm not sure whether you've heard, but a contagious disease is making the rounds in Beyrian proper. Beware of strangers."

"Strangers like you?" the girl asked with a sideways smile. "Who look like they belong in a royal court in fancy clothes?"

Her uncle cleared his throat. "We should get back to work."

"Fortune be with you," Pearl said to us.

"And with you," Mercer replied.

With that, our little caravan headed to the edge of the market, where only a few humble dwellings separated us from a vast wilderness of hills and woods.

"You can stay with us until we're three days clear of Beyrian and the plague," Mercer said to Kadri. "We'll deliver you to a crossing and you can catch a coach to a safer city."

"Why?" Kadri asked. "Because I'm not an elicromancer? You can't materialize anyway."

"We're attempting stealth," Mercer argued, "not gathering an army of recognizable princesses to flaunt."

"Are we that ostentatious?" I bristled, gesturing at my plain brown breeches and dusky blue tunic, ignoring the fact that neither Glisette nor I had quite scrubbed off the sparkling minerals caked on our skin.

"If you keep impaling slabs of meat with arrows, the answer is yes," Mercer said.

"I'm not recognizable outside the capital," Kadri said calmly. "I think you'll find me amenable to the trail and, dare I say, useful."

Mercer looked from Kadri to me. I nodded approval. Like a compass needle oscillating as it settles closer to true north, I sensed him aligning with me. "Did you happen to bring enough coins to buy a horse or two?" he asked her.

She scoffed. "Not quite."

"Then we'll walk for now, until we can steal horses in the cover of night," Mercer said.

Mercer and Glisette cast spells to cover our trail while I commandeered the map and plotted our path to Darmeska. It was hard to believe that Professor Strather and I were supposed to have already embarked on our tedious journey to the very same place.

We didn't stop walking until the last dregs of daylight drained from the western sky. Low hills began sprouting from the flat wilderness, and my legs burned with overuse.

When we stopped to make camp in an escarpment at the base of a green slope, I sought privacy to relieve myself, gulped water, and built a fire. Glisette tried to make herself useful by setting the kindling aflame. Her spell roared up robust flames, licking outside the circle of stones I'd arranged.

"*Matara sarth,*" Mercer said, extinguishing the fire and tossing dirt on it for good measure.

"Why did you do that?" Glisette demanded.

"We'll save the risk of bigger fires for cooking and keeping warm. Tonight we just need a little light." Mercer whispered to what was left of the heap of twigs and coaxed a tender flame from them.

After we rolled out our pallets, I doled out jerky, apples, and flat, dry bread, then tore my meal into bites for Calanthe. Aside from the occasional wild game or foraged berries and mushrooms, most of our meals would have to be plain and serviceable.

Glisette whimpered as she pulled off her boots and found raw blisters. I hauled myself over to the supplies and hunted for salve and the roll of woven fabric I'd bought for dressing wounds. But when I sat next to Glisette, Mercer said, "Better off saving the bandages."

This brought a sick feeling to the pit of my stomach, which in turn roused my anger. I stomped back to the bags and tucked the bandages away, then dropped onto my bedroll by the fire.

"I'm sorry. I'm not your keeper. Do what you will." Mercer tucked his sword beside his bed, settled under his blankets, and closed his eyes. He stopped fidgeting first and thus Calanthe heaped her hairy warmth next to him instead of me.

Kadri was asleep by the time I lay down. Glisette had applied conservative dabs of salve to her blisters and curled up with her hands tucked under her cheek. I closed my eyes, but I couldn't help envisioning Neswick and Jovie returning to Calgoran with their tales, poisoning my own people against me. The gossip was all too easy to imagine. *She always did have a hard time accepting her lack of magic. Studied so hard, that one, and trailed Ander and Ivria everywhere they went, as if she could soak up their gifts just by breathing the same air. I'm not surprised she found some way to use dark magic to get what she wanted. She may even have murdered Ivria. She's always been bitter.*

I hushed these thoughts and blinked at the stars, tracing the constellations in hopes of lulling myself to slumber. But the sheer enormity of the universe unnerved me and made me feel small and powerless, so I turned over with a huff.

Mercer opened one eye. "If you don't sleep, tomorrow is going to be a flogging."

"Reminding a sleepless person of why they need to sleep is *always* helpful," I grumbled.

He chuckled and closed his eye again.

I'd thought fleetingly of the woman he'd mentioned, but now that we were practically alone, I heard myself ask, "Who's Lundy?"

Both of his brown eyes opened this time.

"You mentioned her and a baby," I said.

Silence stretched through the seconds until they felt like hours, but he finally said, "She grew up with us in Aldirn. That was our village. She was two years younger than Tilmorn and two years older than me. The three of us were always together. From the time we were children, everyone teased her about how she'd never be able to choose which Fye brother to marry. She loved us equally and in different ways, it was plain to see. But once I became an elicromancer, I wasn't content to live a simple life in Aldirn like Tilmorn. I wanted to sharpen my gift so I could one day serve as an advisor to the King of Calgoran. I didn't want to marry, I wanted to go on adventures. And I didn't love Lundy the way she did me. But Tilmorn did, so they wed. She was pregnant when the Moth King's men took him."

"And you helped care for her and the baby?" I asked.

He nodded. "And it was my pleasure, even though times were hard. But Lundy wanted more than I could give. She wanted me to be a father and husband. She even wanted to tell their son that

I was his father so he wouldn't feel the lack. We assumed Tilmorn wouldn't return the same man, if he ever returned. But lie to the boy and tell him I was his father? As though Tilmorn had never even existed?"

He stopped, cleared his throat before continuing. "I refused to let the boy's true legacy be forgotten. I said I would help provide for the two of them and keep them safe until my dying breath, but part of keeping them safe was wresting the realm back from the monster that had taken Tilmorn. I felt it was my first duty. I materialized to the elicromancer hideout in Yorth often, until I'd seen too many people die in traps. I asked Lundy to come to Yorth with me so we'd be farther from danger. But Lundy refused. The last time I saw her, she hated me for being willing to leave without them. But I had to."

"You don't know what became of them, do you?"

This time, he didn't try to force down the weakness in his voice. "No. Thanks to the elicromancers' contract with the sea witches, I assume they lived out their lives until they died of old age. If Halmer inherited Tilmorn's elicrin blood, he might have survived the Water."

"Halmer," I said, trying the name on my tongue. "There was a famous Halmer who fought in the Elicrin War, but it was centuries after your time. He had the gift of stealth and conducted most of the reconnaissance missions before the good elicromancers defeated the traitors. He was one of the oldest elicromancers at that time, and one of the few from his generation to remain loyal. They say time corrupts, which is why we have an age of surrender for elicrin stones."

"Was Fye his family name?" Mercer asked.

"No," I said, regretting that I had spurred erroneous hope. "No, it was something else. I'll ask Glisette tomorrow to see if she remembers from history lessons." Though I doubted I would bring it up again.

Mercer closed his eyes. "We should sleep."

Disheartened, I turned over to look at the stars again. But before I could glare into the void of sleeplessness once more, I said, "Halmer Gladforth."

Mercer jolted to a sitting position, hair perking out in all directions. "What?"

"That was his name."

"Gladforth was Lundy's family name." He laughed in disbelief, and the sound was round and full. It made me want to laugh too. "That can't be coincidence, can it?"

I found myself smiling. "I doubt it."

"That's unbelievable," he said, breathless as he spread out on his mat and tucked one hand behind his head. The other rested on the exposed hollow space between muscle and bone above his pelvis. I thought of those brief minutes when I had permission to touch his bare skin, how distant that reality seemed at the moment. "He was a little lad to me just a few weeks ago. A war hero . . ." The joy faded from his voice. "How did he die? In battle?"

"I believe he gave up his elicrin stone with the others after the war. He would have lived out the rest of his days among friends who aged as mortals after giving up their stones, probably in Darmeska."

"She didn't pass on our name. Everything I did . . . I was striving to protect their futures. I couldn't give her what she wanted. But I thought I could give her something more important."

I didn't know what to say. Words hung unspoken in the air, but none of them were right, so I didn't pluck them until a new thought crossed my mind. "Did the blacksmith remind you of her?"

"Yes," he said, lying back down. "Lundy was strong and sweet-natured. She liked hard work and good ale and company. She wasn't afraid of anything until everything was taken from her."

"I'm sorry," I said.

"We've all suffered loss," he said, his throat bobbing.

"Why didn't your visions show you Lundy and Halmer?"

"They don't exactly heed my wishes."

"I suppose not, if you know so much about me yet so little about them."

He didn't reply, and I sensed a sudden coldness coming from his bedroll. The fire began to dim and I watched flecks of ash swirl in the smoke.

"We're crossing into Volarre soon?" he asked.

"Yes. We'll reach the border before nightfall day after tomorrow. There are two bridges that cross the gorge, and one of them is the main road. We should take the narrower, less-used bridge and steal horses after we've crossed."

He didn't say anything after that. Calanthe left his side to curl up at mine and warmed me as the night grew cool. I drifted off to sleep.

✦ TWENTY ✦

ORE and more trees cropped up over the next two days.
Soon after crossing the border into Volarre, we would be
free of the open fields and able to lose ourselves in the centuries-old
trees. Upon reaching the Forest of the West Fringe, we could disappear entirely.

At last, we approached the deep chasm of the gorge that followed the border. A glance from the edge offered dizzying views
that made my knees feel as though they would drop out from under
me. The grass gave way to steep rock ledges, none navigable. We
hadn't come upon the narrow bridge yet, but I assured the others it
should be just around a westward bend.

Clouds flew by on a quick wind, casting shadows across the
dramatic landscape. We stopped for an early dinner, which Kadri
declined. I realized that she hadn't eaten breakfast either. It struck
me that her abstinence had nothing to do with appetite and all to
do with proving her value on this journey after insisting to Mercer that she would not be dead weight. She had combed any wild
bushes we'd passed and kept a sharp eye out for game and berries
even though there was plenty of food for her.

"Kadri," I said, coming alongside her and dodging her bow tip.
"You need to eat something. We're not strapped for provisions."

"It's the principle. I promised I would be an asset, not a burden."

"If you grow too weak to walk you *will* be a burden."

"I'm far from that," she said. "And we're almost to the wood-lands. There will be plenty of game there."

"In the meantime, eat something. Please?"

She didn't reply, but I decided would take up the battle again at the next meal.

We walked on without seeing any bridge at all—yet I was sure I hadn't led us astray.

"What's it like in Erdem?" I asked, to distract myself. "The land? Is it green?"

"In parts, but other regions are arid. It was rainy and muddy where we lived and there were violent storms. Mountain ranges separate inland Erdem from the coasts and from Perispos, and there aren't many passes through. When the mist rolled down in autumn, it felt as if there was no escaping that wall of jagged mountains. But it was beautiful on sunny days, and *oh!* The spices. You wouldn't believe them. I know we have imports from Erdem here, but the colors and flavors aren't the same. There were whole markets in Dogahn dedicated to spices and nothing else."

Kadri's eyes took on a dreamy quality and she got lost in her thoughts, presumably of food, while Glisette stopped short. "I don't think there's a bridge," she announced.

I turned around. "There is." If I'd made an error—though I was sure I hadn't—I planned to fall on my sword. "We shouldn't be far...."

"Did you see that pile of rocks at the bottom a few minutes back?"

"That little dam?" I asked with a sinking feeling.

Glisette shook her head. "I think it was the bridge. Someone destroyed it. Maybe Mercer and I could levitate us across."

"It's a hard spell to maintain for that long and I'm not willing to risk it," Mercer said. "We need to take the main road." I didn't miss the way he gripped the hilt of his sword, or the way his gray-green elicrin stone seemed to glint with rapt attention to his movements.

"Or skirt the gorge completely," I suggested.

"There will be blights waiting for us no matter which route we choose. We may as well go the quickest way, over the main bridge. We're closer to the road."

"So whatever we do, we *will* face an ambush?" I asked.

Mercer's eyes sparked with resolve. "It's not an ambush if you expect it."

My nerves hummed as we reached the point where the dirt road running north to south met the gorge running east to west. All we had to do was cross the bridge and pass beneath the guard tower. Then we'd be in Volarre.

"What about the concealing spell?" Glisette asked, tucking her hair into her cap. Her curls' clean shine had dulled. "We could sneak across?"

"Some blights still have enough magic to sniff out spells," Mercer said. "Let's just hope the only eyes in the tower belong to Realm Alliance guards. We can pay a toll and be on our way."

"Paying a toll to get into my own kingdom!" Glisette harrumphed.

"If they're blights, you and I can take care of them," Mercer said to her. "I've fought and killed many blights," he reassured us when

Kadri and I shared a panicked glance. "We'll rest easier knowing we've picked off a few of them."

A peddler with a wagon in tow appeared on the road, heading north like us. "Let's see what happens," Mercer suggested, stepping back into the trees. "Get ready to come to his aid."

The peddler passed underneath the guard tower, receiving nary a greeting. He paused for a moment on the other side, perhaps curious as to why he hadn't seen a face in the window or guards posted at the passage, and then moved on.

"Are the towers always manned?" Mercer asked.

"Ours are," Glisette said.

"Same in Calgoran," I said.

"It's likely compromised, then," Mercer said. "But we can't stay here forever."

"I agree," Glisette said. "I would rather face them in the light than wait for them to steal upon us in the dark." She clamped her sparkling elicrin stone and its elaborate pendant between her fingers.

We started forward, cautious, Kadri quietly drawing back an arrow. My gaze clung to the windows of the tower where I expected a pale, wasting face to appear, probably with a leering grin that would haunt my dreams.

I gripped my dagger hilt as we took the first step onto the bridge. Any other day, the depth of the drop on either side would have unnerved me, but I trained my attention on the looming and eerily empty tower.

And then we came upon it, crossing under the shadow of the archway with no trouble. My mind danced with the hope that we'd somehow outsmarted the blights or outrun them.

But we saw the flagpoles at the far end of the bridge, and that hope fell to pieces.

The blue flag of Volarre with its silver lily lay in a heap at the bottom of the right post. The green flag of Yorth with its bronze sea serpent lay tattered on the left. Two gray banners had been raised, each bearing the sigil of a white moth. And a bloody corpse had been bound to each pole.

A cry of horror slashed its way out of me as I recognized the dark blond hair and leather apron of the body on the right, and then the gray hair and sturdy build on the left: the blacksmiths from Tully.

With a roar of rage and sorrow, Mercer drew his sword and sprinted to the open tower door. But other than the hollow echo of his boots on the stones, there was only silence. The guard post was empty.

"It could still be an attack," Glisette said, her eyes scanning the sparse trees lining the road.

It would have been a fine time for blights to attack. The dagger shook in my hands. I couldn't have even gutted a fish with my shock-weakened muscles. But it didn't matter. No attack came.

Calanthe loped forward and sniffed at the red-stained grass around the posts, scaring away the birds pecking at the bodies.

I trod onward out of a sense of duty and the others followed. Gruesome details became clearer with every step until a blur of warm tears blocked them out: discolored faces, missing fingers, bloody ropes tied around wrists and necks. I took a step off the bridge and stumbled to my knees in the dirt, my chest filling with sobs so intense I couldn't find air to breathe.

A hand squeezed my shoulder. Lingering whiffs of Kadri's lavender perfume covered the smell of death.

Mercer winced up at Pearl's body. "They haven't been up there long," he muttered, averting his eyes. "Scavengers would have…" He trailed off, sparing us. "The blights could still be nearby."

"Their fingers…" I said.

"Clean cuts," Mercer rasped. "Not scavengers."

"No," I said, shaking my head as if the movement might jerk me out of this nightmare. The blights had tortured and murdered these people because of *us*. The creatures somehow discovered that we had lingered at the smithy in Tully, and perhaps assumed the blacksmiths could provide information regarding our whereabouts…or they had slaughtered these innocent people merely to show us there was no escape. Either way, they had to have known that we would recognize their bodies and that this horror would hit us hard.

Holding his breath, Mercer sawed at the ropes around Pearl's ankles. Pretending I was made of steel like my dagger, I started sawing at the ties binding her uncle's body. "*Umrac korat,*" Glisette whispered, slashing a finger through the air to slice the ropes too high for me to reach. She and Mercer caught Pearl's lifeless body with a levitating spell and set her gently on the ground before moving on to her uncle.

I wiped my tears with my sleeve, stood up, and retrieved the trowel from the saddlebags. I marched past the bodies down the road—ignoring a strewn and bloody tunic that must have belonged to one of the the guards manning the tower—and dove into a patch of unsullied grass, attacking it ferociously in an attempt to dig a grave. I dug desperately, making little progress while Calanthe licked away my tears. When my power started acting up without my control and the nearby tree roots rotted and shriveled, Glisette seized me by the shoulders and backed me away.

She and Mercer calmly chanted together in Old Nisseran, their elicrin stones bright, and the dirt churned and poured upward until two deep and perfect graves yawned up at us.

The blights could have waited for us. They could have made sure to attack us.

But the terror was enough for now.

~§ TWENTY-ONE §~

THE anticipation of an ambush hung heavier in the air with every step we took and every league we put behind us.

Mercer and Glisette mumbled protective spells under their breaths. Our sleep was restless. None of us struggled to rise at dawn each day; we were already awake. We didn't even mention stealing horses from the few lonely residences we passed, knowing that our mere presence could be a death sentence for those who dwelt within.

Since encountering the bodies, Kadri hadn't skipped a single meal, and true to her promise, she had delivered a brown hare, a pheasant, and a few handfuls of unripe blackberries. But I could hardly tear into the meat without thinking of the flesh of the innocents we'd doomed with nothing more than a friendly encounter, the strewn parts of the Yorthan guard whose only crime was to man the wrong post at the wrong time. The Volarian guard had been left to die of the disease and was still breathing—barely—when we found him farther down the road.

He had asked for mercy and we had given it to him. Kadri's shot was the kindest way, and she made tidy work of it.

Approaching the Forest of the West Fringe should have relieved us. Here we could more easily hide, and the magic of the ancient forest might abet our protective enchantments. But the blights could hide in the age-old shadows too, and mask their steps beneath the eerie creaking of old trees.

The boughs were so dense and the trees so tall that we had to make camp an hour earlier than when we trod hills and fields. It was Glisette's turn to keep watch, but when I collapsed on my bedroll, it was with my hand on my dagger and my eyes open. My muscles somehow remembered what it felt like to use a dagger every day in the wilderness, to wield it as naturally as I'd wielded a quill at the academy. My hand recalled the feeling of dragging the blade through hide and readying it in answer to the faintest threatening sound. Mother would have hated to know that these reflexes had survived my return to proper palace life. It surprised even me that my bizarre upbringing had proved useful.

A chill wreathed through the air, licking up my arms and neck and through my hair. It felt predatory.

I looked toward my companions. Kadri and Mercer were asleep, or at least appeared to be. Calanthe curled up in a massive heap of wiry gray hair next to me. Glisette sat with her back to the warm fire, but a shudder crawled between her shoulders.

The memory of Devorian's twisted features came unbidden: the bent shoulders, the rawboned fingers and ragged claws. If he hadn't ventured down the selfish, dark road of trying to resurrect his mother and father, maybe the Moth King would have remained imprisoned and dormant forever.

But a secret pity for Devorian bloomed in my heart. I remembered how close I had been to believing I could resurrect Ivria.

I closed my eyes. Rather than thinking of Devorian or the blacksmiths or the plagued citizens of Beyrian, I listened to the leaves rustling and tried not to think at all.

A low growl yanked me out of sleep. I blinked my eyes open. The ancient forest chirred and whispered around me, as full of darkness as the belly of a beast.

Another vibrating growl rumbled deep in Calanthe's throat. My eyes adjusted, and I distinguished her silhouette standing at full attention with hackles raised. I reached for my knife and scanned the perimeter. But when my hand jerked in the direction of my weapon, a vicious snarl tore out of Calanthe's throat. Her shining eyes were locked on mine, not an approaching predator.

I froze. I heard others stirring and saw Glisette stand up, a white light beaming out from her elicrin stone. Her first thought had also been to comb the shadows for an assailant.

"Calanthe?" I whispered. The hound's muscles locked in an aggressive stance. Though she was bred to take down stags and stood a head taller than me on her hind legs, I had never feared her. She'd never once displayed her teeth or even frightened a stranger with a soft warning growl.

I opened my palm in a gesture of submission, slowly reaching out to pet her snout. But instead of bowing to nuzzle my palm, she lunged and caught my hand and wrist between her teeth.

I screamed as numbing pain shot through me. My attempt to wrench away from her clamped jaws only heightened it. Now I could feel the warmth of blood and the deeper sting of betrayal. With my free hand, I clenched her long snout and tried to yank her teeth from my flesh.

"*Nagak!*" Glisette cried out, ripping Calanthe away—taking a chunk of my flesh with her—and smashing her into a tree.

"No!" I screamed. I wobbled to my feet only to see milky-white eyes twinkling from under hoods around the perimeter of our campsite. Putrid sores shone in the soft light. This was the ambush we'd been awaiting.

My pulse throbbed in the torn flesh of my hand. Calanthe lay limp on the mossy bedding of the forest floor. Mercer withdrew his sword with the *sing* of metal. Kadri notched an arrow on her bowstring, her chest heaving.

"*Maranil foraen,*" hissed one of the six hooded figures, and a piercing sound jabbed like a needle through my head. My unharmed hand shot to cover my ear, but nothing could muffle the excruciating ringing.

Glisette reached out and curled her fingers, evoking a bracing wind that sliced through the trees. The torturous sound tapered off, but as I shivered in the driving wind, it seemed Glisette's counter was even more unbearable than the attack it curtailed. My breath billowed out in a fog that rushed away. The wind felt like icicles pricking my skin.

The chill finally receded and Glisette was ready with a next spell, one that wrenched a blight's joints in all directions. Mercer hobbled forward—was he wounded?—and shouted "*Matara liss!*" Light bloomed from his elicrin stone and bright flames engulfed one of the blights. The creature squealed like a suckling pig and sank to the ground while another jabbed the same spell at Glisette, who countered with "*Asas nila!*" to block the retaliation. I knew from Professor Strather's class that blights could exercise only a dim version of elicromancy, but despite this, they were dangerous and tenacious opponents. These ones seemed especially so.

One of the blights singled me out and charged, but a long blade squelched through its sternum, skewering it from behind.

The blade ripped out and the blight fell. Mercer stood in the shadows, his bloody sword ferocious in a stripe of moonlight.

Meanwhile a blight rushed Kadri, wielding a jagged knife. She drew an arrow at the last second and pierced it through the shoulder, which angered more than injured it. I knelt to fumble for my dagger, barely dodging a spell intended for me, and crossed paths with Kadri's attacker. With the help of the light flashing from Mercer's elicrin stone, I lodged my knife in the blight's neck and gave a good yank on the arrow, twisting it through muscle and flesh. Dark blood oozed from the knife wound, which also should have been fatal, but the creature ripped the blade out and bared its jagged teeth, raising the knife to puncture my heart and end me.

I heard a whoosh and a felt a sharp pinch along the edge of my ear. One of Kadri's arrows pierced straight through the blight's eye. The creature released me, staggering back.

Dark blood spurted across my face. I spat it out, barely ducked beneath the blight's swiping arm to grab my dagger, and lunged to sink the blade in its gut. Another arrow whistled over my head, catching some of my hair as it struck the blight between the ribs.

"Kadri!" I yelped, tearing my hair as I jerked free.

"Sorry, I thought he was mine!"

I eased off her prey, barely disengaging in time to duck an unfamiliar spell that withered the pad of moss I'd only just occupied.

"*Sokek sinna.*" Mercer blocked the blight's next attack with a glowing shield, coming alongside me with his sword raised and one rusty manacle trapped on his wrist. It seemed their orders were to take Mercer alive and kill his companions.

Mercer swung the empty manacle and brought it down on the blight's face, then stabbed it through the chest with his sword, coaxing spells from his elicrin stone—one of which turned the creature's jagged knife into nothing but a gray wisp of fog when it struck skin.

Mercer turned and slashed at the blight Glisette had disabled, carving at the grayish flesh until gruesome entrails emerged from what should have been a mortal wound—but the creature was still fighting back.

"*Bifreat nargon,*" uttered a gravelly voice behind me. I knew what was coming before the spell hit, but knowing did nothing to stop the burning beneath my flesh. My fingernails raked across my skin, unstoppable. I dropped to my knees in agony. Even my wounds itched like mad and I couldn't bring myself to show them any mercy.

I looked up to find a blight with one white eye. Its body was hollow and thin, but it easily kicked my slick, wet knife out of reach.

Everything went slow as the blight clamped its hands on my temples, poised to break my neck. One side of its face revealed the elicromancer she had once been: a proud, bright-eyed woman, a human. But the other half had decayed to expose a raw cheekbone and rancid molars. A murky, colorless elicrin stone swung at her concave chest. Had the Moth King forced her into servitude? Or had she elected to deal in dark elicromancy knowing full well it would, little by little, turn her into this creature? Could the same happen to Mercer if he was captured?

As if responding to a silent plea, Mercer called my name, a bright light shining from his chest, casting his features into stunning relief. I found his gaze and thought fleetingly of the warmth and safety of my hearth at home in Arna. Out of the corner of my eye, I saw Glisette covered in filth and blood, a wicked gash bleeding over one eye. Kadri lay sprawled on the ground, her bow more than an arm's reach away as one of our enemies raised a spear to pin her body to the soil. Calanthe lay in an unconscious heap by the tree. I couldn't let them suffer, let them die. The very thought triggered a zealous rage.

The world went oddly quiet as the blight tensed to break me. The peace and the rage that washed over me intertwined, one and the same. *A peaceful rage*, I thought, though it sounded nonsensical. My spirit was so still, so untroubled, that I even noticed a moth drawn to the embers of our dying campfire.

A moth drawn to flame. I would be the light, the flame, deadlier than I seemed. This Moth King could never guess how I'd burn him.

My bloody hands opened in a gesture that might have looked like a plea for mercy. But I locked eyes with the wasted elicromancer touching my face, curled my fingers, and snapped my wrists away from each other. The creature's neck broke.

The crack of breaking bones echoed around the campsite. Bodies thudded to the ground, and somehow I knew they were only the right ones.

For a moment, I stared, mesmerized by the slick blood on my hands, my wrists and fingers contorted. The power still battered inside me, a heartbeat so wild it broke free from any rhythm. I stood and met the wide eyes of my companions.

"Is anyone badly hurt?" I asked, searching their faces in the dark. When no one replied, I stepped over the blight and knelt next to Calanthe, locating a hard knot above her ear. When I trailed my finger over the wound, she stirred and blinked up at me, then tried to tenderly lick the bite she'd inflicted while under some sort of beguilement. I steered her away from the smears of infected blight blood and felt down her ribs, hips, and legs.

"I'm sorry," Glisette said. "I had to do something."

"Are you all right?" Mercer asked Glisette, cupping her face to examine the cut above her eye.

She chuckled gallantly. "It's just deep enough to hurt my ego."

He turned to Kadri. "Did they make enough contact to infect you?"

"I don't think so." She scanned her shaking limbs. "But my blood is rushing so hard I don't think I'd feel it. I'll go to the creek and wash off."

"Valory?" Mercer asked.

All three of them turned my way. I didn't miss the awe illuminated in their eyes, and for the first time I saw it: the understanding that we weren't just undertaking some foolhardy, hopeless adventure for the sake of it. We were here fighting, bleeding, suffering, because I was meant to touch the untouchable, destroy the indestructible. My power had a purpose.

"That's going to need sewing shut," Mercer murmured.

I cast my eyes down to my trembling hand, almost surprised to find I was still vulnerable to bodily wounds. A hunk of flesh was missing and blood dripped to the soft forest floor. "Have you given stitches before?"

"Not while wearing an iron manacle." Mercer staggered over to gently encircle my wrist—it looked like a twig in his large grasp—and inspect the wound. "It's not going to be pretty."

"What happened to your leg?" I knew how to slather a wound with herbs and apply simple dressings, but my prowess didn't cover broken bones.

"Hard whap from a bludgeon. I can walk it off."

We started down the rocky trail to the creek we'd passed earlier. Downstream, Kadri scrubbed furiously at her skin. The cold water washing over my wounds made the pain almost too much to bear while conscious, but I filled a bowl of water for Calanthe and cleaned the contusion on her skull before I let Mercer bribe me with wine in exchange for treating my wound.

"This is what I bought it for," he said. I bit my cheek as he tugged the needle through my flesh. He nudged the wineskin back to my lips. "Just keep drinking."

When he finished, he started a fire to burn the bodies. I drank until the pain detached, until the strange, buried notions lurking in cages at the edges of my mind broke free to roam as they pleased:

I was dangerous, destructive, deadly.

And instead of leaning away from that truth, I threw it on me like a glorious mantle.

❦ TWENTY-TWO ❧

HE next morning brought a spring rain. We crossed paths with the blights' horses and Kadri managed to catch one by the reins, but it was wild-eyed and manic, marked with lashes. My heart ached for the innocent creature swept up in the enemy's cruelty. However, we couldn't afford an overexcited packhorse. Kadri slipped off its gear and released it to the woods.

Mercer's leg bruised up riotously and the jagged stitches on my left hand looked and felt no better than advertised. Glisette agonized over the cut trailing from her brow to the apple of her cheek. Calanthe seemed a bit dazed and slow. I wished I had left her with Ander, regardless of our discord. She might even have been better off in the kennels as Melkior's prized bitch.

But then again, Arna might be in a worse state than Beyrian. The thought made an acrid taste rise in my throat.

Something had changed since the encounter with the blights last night, besides our mismatched troupe being worse for wear. The others used any excuse to cast a sidelong glance my way. There was hardly a rearranging of a heavy bag on a shoulder that did not lead to a stare in my direction. They began to defer to me on matters that had naught to do with my handy recollections from geography lessons.

When we stopped to lunch on yellow-tinged mushrooms,

roasting them on sticks, I sat on a log perch and stared fixedly at the campfire until my mushrooms browned around the edges.

"How did they find us?" Kadri asked. "Weren't the spells covering our tracks?"

Glisette gave a one-shouldered shrug. "There are ways to negate them. But that's harder than casting them. No blight should be powerful enough to do it."

"They were stronger than any blights I've met," Mercer said, "almost as if they still had elicrin gifts...."

He trailed off as something sparked in his eyes, embers of hope. "Elicrin gifts," he repeated in a whisper. "Do you think it's possible someone else could have been trapped with the Moth King all this time?" he asked me.

"I suppose, but the sea witch didn't mention it. Do you think...?" I let the question hang.

"Tilmorn once took a gift from an elicromancer who used it for ill and placed it in an abandoned elicrin stone," Mercer said, his hands trembling where they rested on his knees. "He wanted Lundy be immortal. She was afraid to even touch it, but theoretically, if Tilmorn awoke when the Moth King did, he could have reanimated the blights' stones. It would explain why they were so hard to defeat, why we couldn't shake them off our trail. Tilmorn could have made one a Tracker to counter our protections, and given small gifts to the others. Normally killing a blight is like killing a walking corpse."

"Who's Tilmorn?" Kadri asked.

Mercer's eyes were wide and intense as they met hers. "My older brother."

A lump formed in my throat. If Tilmorn could give even the wasted blights power to hunt us down, what more could he do to us?

I didn't want Mercer to suffer the same loss again, but I hoped his brother was long dead.

"I think we're nearing my family's summer cottage," Glisette said. The cut across her eye might have added a dangerous edge to her beauty if she hadn't been constantly smearing it with globs of salve. "If we're up against another powerful foe, then at the very least, we need supplies and horses to finish the journey. It wouldn't be far out of the way, and very few people know of it."

Mercer winced at her use of *foe* but said nothing, staring into the fire.

"You need a 'summer cottage' when there are two palaces in Pontaval?" Kadri chortled.

"My father liked hunting in the woods," Glisette replied matter-of-factly. "And you know the old palace in Pontaval is cursed."

"You Nisserans and your curses, blights, and undead tyrants," Kadri grumbled. She squeezed her mushrooms to test their tenderness and stuck them back in the heat. Her normally vibrant skin had lost some of its color and her lips were dry and cracked. I wondered how this journey had taken its toll on me, other than the obvious wound and layer of grime. "I'm beginning to wonder why I didn't get on that ship."

"There's a mirror there that Ambrosine enchanted to look in on Pontaval," Glisette pressed. "We could ask Perennia if there's any news. We're so isolated, we wouldn't even know if the Moth King was dead as a doornail by now."

I unfolded the map. Glisette circled the fire to point out the location of the hidden summer cottage. She had waited until the last possible moment to mention the detour, until we were practically on top of her family's woodland property, at least as far as ink and parchment were concerned.

Since our visit to the market had resulted in disaster, I hadn't considered reentering civilization, not as long as we had plenty of dried meat and shriveled fruit. But the idea of baths, a Healer, and horses to finish out the journey made the brief detour difficult to refuse.

I looked to Mercer to help me make the decision. He had been less imperious since we'd found the bodies of the blacksmiths and the guards. I wondered if he felt paralyzed knowing innocent people might meet cruel fates whatever direction we turned. If we couldn't so much as sneak through an alley without dooming those we passed, the burden of making decisions hung heavy, and now it hung on my shoulders. I wanted to tell him I didn't mind his imperiousness *sometimes* and to stop treating me like a commander, but he was too consumed in thought.

"I'm not sure it's worth the risk," I said, feeding Calanthe my last toasted mushroom.

"We would put everyone we meet in danger," Mercer added. "Including your sisters, Glisette."

"We could use a concealing spell," she said, growing desperate. "There might be news from Arna or Darmeska...."

The last argument was a low-hanging fruit. Confirming Mother's or Grandmum's welfare would ease the tension that had taken up permanent residence between my shoulder blades. I missed home and the comfort of family. Perhaps I would wake up from a lingering dream and Ellen would toss open my curtains at dawn's first light. I would eat a hearty breakfast with Ivria before going to lectures...

"How easy is it to reach the mirror?" Mercer asked, his face coming into focus again.

"Easy enough," Glisette said. "There's one in my father's old trophy room. And we could find a garden tool to get your manacle off."

Mercer stretched out his hurt leg and frowned at the rusty hunk of metal hanging from his wrist. Earlier, when I'd watched him and Glisette put their heads together to try to magically break the manacle without snapping his arm in two—and her subsequent salving of the raw skin when they came up short on ideas—I'd felt an irksome ache and imagined myself in her place, exploring more than just his wrist with my touch.

I knew that ache. It had tried to emerge before, when young men like Knox had scattered hints about their interest, but I'd stifled it.

Now it was as if a tight knot had loosened with a single tug. I recalled when I'd opened Mercer's tunic to treat his wounds, the way his lips parted slightly in an admission of pleasure when Glisette had boldly traced his palm at the banquet. I scattered and reorganized these images in my thoughts until his bare skin was unmarred, sweaty with something other than fever, and that look was meant for me.

But Mercer met my eager gaze with grim consternation. I glowered at the fire again and said, "I say we wear concealing spells and break into the stables for a tool and horses. But I don't think we should contact Pontaval. We shouldn't put ourselves or others in danger for the sake of news."

"But we need to know if—"

"If you want to materialize home, Glisette, no one will think less of you," I snapped. "A quick forgetting spell and you're back to noonday drinking and a love affair with your vanity mirror."

She rose to her feet and threw her roasting stick in the fire. "You'd like that, wouldn't you? Too bad for you, I'm not a coward. Too bad for you, I face the consequences of my actions instead of running away. You ran away from Arna after you destroyed the Water, then you ran away from *my* city after you cursed my brother and all his servants."

"I 'ran away' to try to undo his evil. And the servants fled. Devorian was the only one there when I left."

"I spared you the details, but no one has seen or heard from any of them, not his cook nor his doorman nor anyone who served him. That palace is full of whispers. Things move without being touched. I saw it for myself when we took Professor Strather to try to lift the curse."

"She said it's *not* a curse."

"Well, it's not exactly a delightful fairy charm, is it?" she cried. "And with all the tragedy you leave in your wake, suddenly you care about putting my sisters and our servants in danger?"

I clenched my fists. My injured hand seared with pain. "You're the ones who asked me to confront Devorian. We're both trying to fix this, but you won't stop treating me like the villain. If either of us had known I was capable of turning him into a monster, you wouldn't have invited me to Pontaval and I wouldn't have come. But we must come to terms with where we are, or—"

"Or what, you'll snap my neck in half?" she demanded coldly.

"Kadri, are you all right?" Mercer asked suddenly, staggering toward her.

My anger dissipated when I noticed Kadri's glassy eyes and glistening brow. A shiver came over her, rattling her shoulders. Our clothes were damp from rain but the air was muggy, far from cold. A horrible realization loomed.

Mercer bent and touched the back of his hand to Kadri's forehead. "She's feverish. Could it be the mushrooms?"

"They're just goldencups," I answered. "I've eaten them a hundred times."

"I caught the blight disease," Kadri mumbled, dragging her eyes up to look at me. "I'm going to die."

"No, you're not," Mercer insisted.

"Kadri," I whispered, sinking to my knees beside her.

"Back up." Mercer pressed his hand against my sternum and pushed me away. "We don't know if you can catch it."

He had been right: a mortal companion was a liability—a liability who had saved my life last night.

"Is there an elicrin Healer at the palace in Pontaval?" I asked Glisette.

She nodded vigorously. "Yes, one who would risk materializing if I asked him. He's been caring for us since we were born."

I knelt next to Mercer and swept Kadri's hair away from her brow. "We're going to get you help, Kadri."

She blinked languidly and didn't respond.

"That settles it," I said bleakly, reaching for my pack.

Glisette levitated Kadri, leaving Mercer and me to carry the bulk of the luggage. He used a spell that made the heavy loads feel lighter. A sedate Calanthe lagged behind.

"You haven't received any prophecies since we started our journey?" I asked him as we trailed along a river with waterfalls at every turn. The summer cottage wasn't far, but I couldn't bring myself to look at Kadri's ashen face until we could see it in the distance.

"No, nothing important, really." I didn't miss Mercer's attempt at nonchalance.

"You seem bothered."

"I have plenty to be bothered about." He clamped on to a tree to protect his injured leg while he maneuvered his way over a slope carpeted in lush purple wildflowers.

"I'm not suggesting you smile and act downright jolly," I said, resituating the bedrolls on my shoulder. "But that eagerness you had to get this done and over with...it's lessened. I can't help but suspect you've learned something new you don't want to tell us."

Mercer glanced ahead at the others. "We should keep going," he said. "I don't want to slow them down when Kadri is in a bad way."

"We'll catch up," I said, sliding the packs from my shoulders. "If there's something that changes the outcome of this, I deserve to know. We all do, after what we've been through."

I crossed my arms, forgetting about my wound just long enough to scrape it against my opposite elbow and emit a pathetic cry of pain. Calanthe turned to peer at me inquisitively from beneath bushy eyebrows that, oddly, reminded me of Professor Wyndwood from the academy. I almost laughed, but it would have come out sounding delirious, so I refrained.

"Let me see." Mercer limped back to hook one hand behind my elbow, dragging me forward one gentle shuffle-step until my chest nearly pressed against his ribs. He lifted the bandage to examine my stitched wound. His sudden nearness made coherent thought disintegrate. "I'd say you still have several days before we need to remove them."

"Several days? Just until the stitches come out?"

"Have you had to live with even a bruise before now?" he demanded. "Or does royal life protect you from all pain?"

I slid my hand out of his grasp and padded the bandage back over the wound. "It does, unless you despise the only elicrin Healer you know and never ask him for a favor."

Mercer let out a long breath, his broad chest collapsing. "Forgive me. This injury is making me sore company."

As he turned to follow the others, I caught his wrist. "Mercer—"

"Fine," he said. "I'll tell you."

My heart cantered in response to his admission that there *was* something to tell, something kept from the rest of us.

"I've seen glimpses of this before, in my past life. I ignored them. There were more urgent visions I needed to heed. But the other night, after we found the bodies at the border bridge, this vision fleshed itself out. Maybe the blood provoked it, I don't know. I don't know why they come to me."

"What was it?" I asked, wishing I possessed some sort of mechanical crank to force the words out of him at my pace instead of his. Was I going to die killing the Moth King? Would I not kill him at all?

"I saw you in a marble courtroom. There were broken bodies. Humans, not blights. There was blood pooled on the floor, and dripping from your dagger. You walked through the blood to the steps of a dais and sat on the throne. I heard whispers. The dead were your own people. Calgoranians. They would call you Queen of Widows thanks to the corpses left in your wake."

"What?" I asked with a mirthless laugh. "Why would I ever...? How do you know they were people of Calgoran? Did they have it stamped on their foreheads?"

"I just knew. It's what the vision wanted me to know. I'm sorry. "

"Do you realize how many people would have to die for me to take the throne?"

"Maybe it occurs far in the future, when those people are gone and you are still here, with no elicrin stone to surrender in order to die as a mortal. But it does happen."

"Surely not every vision you've had comes true."

"Is that what you want to believe while we're deep in the forest with a trail of bodies already behind us on our way to bring an ancient oppressor to justice—because *I* saw it happen?"

The harshness of his tone took me aback. He acted as if I'd already done this heinous thing.

"I could never kill with abandon," I whispered desperately, searching his eyes. "I know my power brings that into question. But I'm not a murderer."

His stiff expression softened. Underneath the callousness there was only pain, and it brought my own tender feelings to the surface.

"Am I immortal?" I asked.

"You hadn't aged a day in that vision. I've had another vision in which I saw you watch someone else give up their elicrin stone, and you looked the same then as well."

This long-awaited consolation struck me with awe. I was like the others, at least in this one way—like *him*. The shaft of loneliness embedded in my soul seemed to shrink.

For a moment I sensed an invisible, taut tether between us, a force pulling at our twitching fingertips, making our hands long for each other's wounds. My touch could destroy, but it could also comfort and restore.

"I do the best I can with this gift," he said, "but prophecies are as much a burden as a boon, and I've misinterpreted before. I don't *want* to see dark visions come to pass. But when there's something good…" His hands found their way to my shoulders. The warm weight of his thumbs on my collarbone made my heartbeat strike in the base of my throat. "…like you ridding this realm of the Moth King forever, I can charge ahead of everyone involved and act like a stubborn ass."

"I want you to act like a stubborn ass again," I said. "I want you to stop spurning me as if I'm a villain. The others can treat me like one, but not you. You brought me here."

"You're right," he said, catching hold of a loose lock of my hair. The golden sunlight set its red tinges aflame as it slid like silk between his fingers.

Suddenly aware of his actions, he looked at his hand as though it had betrayed him and stepped back.

"From now on, I'll tell you everything I see. I swear."

He turned to catch up with the others.

✦ TWENTY-THREE ✦

THE summer cottage might have been modest by Lorenthi standards, built of plain gray stone and wood. But a misty, roaring waterfall swelled behind it and a nearby glass greenhouse burst with colors in the sunlight.

We picked our way over the wet growth and slick rocks until we could peer down at the cottage, perching alongside the river as it tipped and fell over the cliff with abandon.

Glisette carefully set Kadri on her feet and held her upright when she staggered on the spongy patch of green. "I'll make sure there are no surprises awaiting us," Glisette half-yelled over the din of the waterfall, gently touching the cut on her eye. She did this about once a minute when her hands were free, perhaps expecting the wound to have miraculously healed since the last time she checked. "There are only a few servants who live on the property. Avoiding them should be easy."

"Be quick," I said to her, batting my eyes against the cool spray. "We don't want to be their death sentence like..." I didn't finish, thinking of what our tarrying back in Tully had cost.

With a curt nod of understanding, Glisette slid her rear down a mossy slab of rock to reach a lower foothold and disappeared with the help of the concealing spell.

Kadri groaned as Mercer propped her up. A sore with a dark tinge had begun creeping along her neck. I swallowed hard, assured myself a Healer would be in our presence soon, and supported half her weight. Mercer emitted a barely suppressed grunt of discomfort as he wove under her other arm and gripped my shoulder, casting a concealing spell over us with a quiet utterance of "*Seter inoden.*" None of us smelled delightful, and the heat of Kadri's fever blazed right through her clothes and made my tunic stick to my skin. If it hadn't been for the spray of the waterfall across my face, my stomach might have heaved.

Calanthe emitted a pitiful whine and hunkered down in the grass at the end of her leash, begging me not to go. "See you in a minute, girl," I said.

We batted away dewy leaves and stepped carefully over slithering weeds until we reached level ground. There, we followed a garden path flanking the cottage, hedged with aromatic blooms. I recalled that Glisette's mother had possessed an elicrin gift for growing plants and used to tour the farms in Volarre once a year to give the crops a boost. The thought made me miss my own mother terribly, even though she wasn't the most nurturing of souls.

We peered around the corner at the front of the cottage and saw dozens of windows with pale curtains flung open. Glisette waited in the doorway to wave us inside.

"I'll stay out here with Kadri," Mercer said. "No sense in exposing the servants to the blight disease."

"Look for garlic in the vegetable garden," I said, as though any such humble remedy had any hope of easing her suffering. "It's cleansing."

He nodded and released me, ending the concealing spell's hold over me. "The servants are in their quarters eating," Glisette whispered. "Come this way."

The entryway boasted a rustic stamp of Lorenthi opulence, featuring antler chandeliers, grand stairs, and paintings of golden-haired beauties in crowns. I heard far-off chattering and the clinking of pots and pans. I hoped the servants couldn't hear the groan of the door as Glisette closed it behind us.

We tiptoed up the stairs. Through a window overlooking the garden, I could see Kadri propped against the fence and Mercer on his knees, poking around for something to help her.

At the end of a hall carpeted with furs—how I yearned to dig clean toes into their luxurious folds—Glisette flung open two heavy oak doors and revealed a dark room bedecked with smooth black eyes in mounted heads. There were gorgeous bows, even prettier than Kadri's, and arrows with bright fletching. An expansive mirror with a scrollwork frame spanned the far wall.

I hardly recognized myself within it. Scrapes and dirt smudges marked the face that looked back at me. My mossy-green eyes looked keen above flushed cheeks, but my auburn-tinged brown hair hung damp and stringy.

Glisette squared herself in front of the glass. "Mirror, show me Perennia's antechamber."

Our haggard reflections bloated, rippled, and faded. A new image splashed across the glass, the image of a sitting room with plush blue fabrics. A maid hummed while attacking the furnishings with a feather duster.

"Where's my sister?" Glisette asked, startling the girl enough that she tripped backward.

"She—she might be in—in Princess Ambrosine's rooms, Your Highness," the maid stammered, catching herself on the back of a chair.

"Send the elicrin Healer to the summer cottage at once," Glisette commanded.

"Yes, Your Highness." The maid managed an ungainly curtsy as she fled the room.

"Mirror, show me Ambrosine."

The image shifted. I wondered if materializing felt like this, dizzying and disorienting. Ambrosine's face appeared in the glass. As her surroundings fell still, I gasped. Royalty lent itself to a certain exhibition of wealth, but everything in the eldest princess's chamber went so far beyond the usual extravagance that I could do nothing but blink, dumbfounded by the garish sight. There was a trunk brimming with precious gems, furs sprawled across the floor, airy silk gowns with bejeweled trains spilling from the wardrobe.

Ambrosine herself wore a garment of thousands of diamonds strung together by colorless threads like some sort of delicate full-body armor. A mantle of white feathers with gold and silver tips graced her shoulders. Jewels twinkled in her hair and at her neck, looking so heavy that I marveled at how she remained upright.

"Glisette!" she cried, barely lifting a hand of greeting. The stones of her gown chimed as they kissed each other. "We've been so worried. Why are you at the summer cottage? You look positively ragged. And Valory... I hardly recognized you. You look *beastly*." Her pale eyes glimmered.

"Don't be smart, Ambrosine," Glisette said. "What is all this?"

"Gifts from a suitor. What do you think of this diadem?"

"It's a bit understated."

"Is it really?" Ambrosine managed to lift her arm enough to follow the golden arches with her fingers.

"No! You look absurd."

"Absurd?" Ambrosine demanded, waving a hand at the mirror. Her elicrin stone must have changed the surface before her back into a looking glass. She patted her blond curls and turned her chin at a proud slant, inspecting every pore and angle.

"Ambrosine!" Glisette snapped.

Ambrosine waved her hand over the mirror again. "Ugh. Can't you two at least take baths? I can practically smell you from here."

By some miracle, she gathered the ambitious train of her gown and turned away from us. "Oliva!" she called, and a maid emerged from the lavatory with a crystal perfume bottle. While she showered Ambrosine in fragrance, the princess clasped her hands and said, "Help me select one of these gowns for my sister."

"Yes, Your Highness," the woman said, eyeing the cascade of glittering riches.

"I know we often toy with potential suitors, Ambrosine, but we've never let the ruse go this far," Glisette said. "The most we've ever gotten was a pretty necklace or a horse. You're going to let Uncle think you're willing to be traded off?"

"Nothing's carved in stone," Ambrosine said. "My suitor is coming to meet me in the flesh soon and I'll have a chance to assess his character. If you catch a coach home now, you'll be back in time for the welcoming ball. But don't you dare look more ravishing than me." She narrowed her eyes and screeched in shock before Glisette could deny the invitation. "What happened to your face?"

Glisette cupped a hand over the cut, which she'd been guarding with a swoop of greasy hair.

"Have you received news from Darmeska, Ambrosine?" I asked.

My question was swallowed by a squeal as Perennia appeared in the doorway and rushed to the glass, her glossy blond waves fluttering behind her. "Glisette! Are you all right? When are you coming home? I thought you'd died! We hadn't heard from you since before the plague in Beyrian. And with the Realm Alliance saying it's not safe to materialize, we've been so worried."

"The Healer, Glisette," I whispered. "That's why we're here."

She'd already used our crisis as an excuse to stray from the plan. I wasn't going to let her wander far.

"There's something you both need to know," Glisette said. "When Devorian read the incantation, he broke a contract that bound an elicromancer—"

"I don't want to talk about Devorian." Ambrosine cut her off with a dismissive gesture. "Just come home. Uncle is making certain every last detail of the welcoming event is spectacular. He even had the floors of the biggest guest suite replaced with black onyx and pearl glass."

"They're gorgeous," Perennia said. "I can take the hand mirror so you can see for yourself."

"Last I heard, he wasn't pleased with our frivolous spending," Glisette said. "He canceled my most recent clothier order before I left. Where are these funds coming from?"

"Uncle tripled the tolls along both borders," Ambrosine said. "Better for keeping the fever off our soil anyway."

"Tripled?" Glisette echoed in surprise.

"Don't Volarians rely on farm produce from Calgoran?" I asked.

"Yes, and...?" Ambrosine demanded.

"Volarre has had a dry decade and your soil hasn't been yielding well since your mother died. Raising the tolls could prompt a famine."

"Over a few thesars? It's hardly an egregious cost for using well-kept roads."

"Why don't you just use *those* to pay for the ball?" Glisette asked, gesturing at crystal bowls of cut and polished sapphires.

"That would be untoward, selling gifts from our guest of honor!" Ambrosine shuffled to the wardrobe, her skirts revealing precarious silver shoes with vines climbing up the heel. She selected a flowing midnight-blue gown studded with diamonds and sapphires and returned to the mirror. "This would be striking on you, Glisette."

Glisette's blue eyes went starry as she admired the garment. It looked as if someone had yanked a cloudless night from the sky and sewn it into a dress.

"Have you heard from Arna or Darmeska?" I interrupted again.

"No, but I've been busy," Ambrosine said. "Go to Uncle's study and ask him."

"I'll do it," Perennia said, hurrying out of the room.

"Are there cases of the plague in Volarre?" I asked.

"The fever will die out before it spreads all the way to Arna, Valory," Ambrosine said, guessing the motive behind my inquiry. "Don't borrow trouble when you cause enough of your own. I wouldn't be surprised to hear you started the wave *and* the fever just by sneezing in the wrong direction." She laughed like garden chimes in an ominous wind. "But I know what they say about you isn't true. You don't have the gall or the wit to take down the Realm Alliance. You've stumbled into your misfortunes. You actually believed we sent you to Devorian because we thought you could help him."

Sweltering anger filled me. I wished I could torch her room and all its flagrant riches. "A tyrant elicromancer from long ago has returned to Nissera," I said in a low voice, brushing off her barbs for the sake of brevity. "The blights, the plague, the traps, the intercepted missives, they're all his doing. If you care about your kingdom, then warn your uncle, have him mobilize the Volarian branch of the Realm Alliance army to Darmeska—"

"You're sounding a bit unhinged, Valory, and you look it too." Ambrosine waved a hand and whisked away the sight of her chamber to show me my reflection again. My muddied green eyes sparked with fury, but despite their depth and seriousness, I was still small of stature and far from intimidating. "Some quiet days in your prison at Darmeska would do you good," Ambrosine went on in a supercilious tone of mock pity, somehow both blasé and cruel.

"She's telling the truth!" Glisette yelled. "We fought off blights just last night. Devorian resurrected the tyrant, but Valory is going to put all this to rights. She's going to take him down."

"We've warned them, Glisette," I said. "It's not our fault your sisters won't listen. Kadri needs us."

"We can send guards to escort you home, Glisette," Ambrosine said. She held the gown she'd offered against her own collar and let it flood around her ankles. "I know it's not safe on the road, but we can ensure that you arrive without harm." She somehow made everything fade from the mirror but Glisette and the sparkling garment. "This can be your homecoming present."

For a beat, Glisette lost herself in the imagining, parting her pillowy lips in shameless self-admiration. The garment seemed to move with her in the reflection, and even her jagged cut appeared to fade. She straightened her shoulders and turned her head from side to side, examining the refined beauty beneath the grime.

But Ambrosine ripped the manufactured image from the glass. She reappeared in the frame with narrowed eyes. "On second thought, maybe pink is more your color," she muttered. "I might just wear this one myself to meet Lord Valmarys."

"Valmarys?" I said, a wave of weakness spreading from my belly to my knees.

"Emlyn Valmarys?" Glisette clarified, shaking off the spell that had ensnared her.

"Yes. I'm surprised you know the name." Ambrosine sounded pleased. "He owns a large estate and several mines in the Brazor Mountains. He's a private man, rather coy, but one of his servants brought him a likeness of me, knowing it would interest him. My beauty has given Lord Valmarys the will to venture into society. I'd never heard of him, but apparently he is greatly respected in certain circles—"

"When did you say he arrives?" Glisette interrupted.

"He keeps making promises to come and doesn't deliver. My guess is he must be hideous if he elects to avoid civilization. He's supposed to arrive in a week, but he might claim to be busy and send more dresses and jewels."

Glisette grabbed my wrist and steered me out into the corridor. "What if we traveled straight to Pontaval to meet Valmarys?" she whispered, shutting the door softly behind her. "All of this could be over. We could end this on our terms, get the upper hand...." I started to argue, but she squeezed my shoulders as if to transfer her resolve to me. "What you did to the blights...I've never seen anything like that before. You're ready to face him, Valory."

"What if your sisters warn him we're coming?"

"They'll listen to me. She said we could have a guard escort back to the palace.... This is *ideal*."

"She doesn't even know if he'll keep his word to show his face. Or maybe she does—and this is a trap."

"Fate is on our side," she insisted. "This is an opportunity. I can't be the only one who's bone-weary of this journey."

I let the possibility play out in my mind's eye, but guards following Ambrosine's orders were guards who couldn't be trusted. "Make sure the Healer is on his way and let's go," I said, my tone leaving no margin for argument. "We've already stayed longer than we ought."

Glisette's lip twitched with a prelude to a snarl, but she relented and flung open the trophy room door, positioning herself in front of the grand mirror again. "Ambrosine, make sure Ethion is on his way to the summer cottage—" she started, but the eldest princess had disappeared.

"Ethion is traveling to the border to help block the fever," Perennia said, stepping into view. "He departed just after he finished Ambrosine's cosmetic skin treatments this morning. We only have mortal healers right now. And I asked Uncle about incoming missives, but we haven't received any besides the ones from Lord Valmarys, not since the news about the materialization traps that came from the Alliance."

"The Healer's gone?" I asked, feeling tears rise in my throat while my hope plummeted like an anchor. I couldn't let Kadri become another corpse buried behind us on this perilous journey.

"What do you need him for?" Perennia asked. "Your face, Glisette?"

"No," she scoffed, but covered it again. "Kadri Lillis is dying from the blight disease. That's why we came."

"Oh," Perennia gasped. "I don't know if it will help, but Mother planted a white astrikane tree in the greenhouse at the summer cottage before she died. She taught me to tend it, but I haven't been to the summer cottage since we heard about the traps. The astrikane might not heal Kadri completely, but it could prolong her life."

"Thank you," I breathed, grateful to have something to seize. The rare, magical leaf was renowned for bringing on pleasant visions and healing the mind. While it certainly wouldn't harm Kadri, I wasn't sure it would help. "Come on, Glisette."

"Ambrosine wouldn't listen to us, but you must, Perennia," Glisette said, desperate. "Emlyn Valmarys is the architect of everything that's happened."

"Even the Water drying up, and Devorian?" Fear shimmered in Perennia's eyes, which she flicked from Glisette to me.

"No," Glisette barked. "I mean, yes, clearly the Summoners had their own plans for the contract, and Devorian fulfilled them in some backward way. But the wave and the blight disease and the traps—"

"There are rumors that…that Valory is trying to take on the Realm Alliance," Perennia murmured, casting her gaze to her toes.

"They aren't true." Glisette altered her stance to block me. Oddly, her unflagging loyalty flattered me. "I've been at Valory's side practically since I left you. I trust her."

Perennia expelled a nervous breath and trembled as she said, "Valmarys's envoys just materialized here. Is that why they're brave enough to materialize? Because the traps won't hurt them? I've wondered about that. What should I do? Have the guards close the gates?"

"Listen to me," Glisette said, pressing a hand to the glass. "Pretend nothing is wrong. They haven't hurt you yet. Act as you have the other times they've come."

"Don't leave me," Perennia begged.

"We must—" I started, but Glisette spoke over me.

"I won't."

Perennia picked up Ambrosine's gilded hand mirror and gave a command that shifted our point of view so that we were peering up at her from the smaller glass. As much as I wanted to, I couldn't begrudge Glisette this moment.

Perennia pointed the mirror out the window. Four figures crossed the courtyard: three men in black tunics and a small woman in a ragged dress.

These were not blights, but living men with swords at their hips. A pair of them carried a trunk overflowing with jeweled bracelets, diadems, and necklaces.

The leader boasted broad shoulders and a purposeful gait. His right hand rested on his sword pommel and a smoky elicrin stone nested at the center of a palm-sized medallion around his neck. In his left hand, he clasped a chain connecting to manacles that held the petite woman captive. As she drew closer, I saw that she was barefoot and her dress was nothing more than a burlap sack. She had auburn hair and elegant, pointed ears, and she was wearing an elicrin stone—though that didn't last long. The leader ripped the chain from her neck and tucked it into his breast pocket.

I grew dizzy as Perennia traveled out of the room, down the corridor, to the banister overlooking the circular entryway. She seemed to be discreetly holding the mirror alongside her lilac skirts.

Two guards swung the doors open to welcome the men inside. The whole household seemed to have congregated in the entryway to watch them cross the threshold with their tokens of admiration.

"If Lord Valmarys sends more gifts, he'll have to buy us a whole new palace to put them in!" Ambrosine laughed, tossing back her long tresses as she reached the ground floor. The leader caught her hand and kissed it. "Who's this?" she asked, eyeing the small, red-headed woman with tapered ears.

"Your Highness," the leader said, his voice gruff with a rustic northern accent. "You look most alluring. Lord Valmarys will be pleased you're enjoying his gifts. It also pleases him to offer you one of his own fairy servants to answer your every whim."

"I don't believe it," Ambrosine cooed, circling the woman. "Full-blooded fairies are supposed to be extinct. How exquisitely small she is! But why is she chained?"

I closed my eyes, thinking of Grandmum and her quest to find the fay. If they were in danger, then she must be too.

"Her kind can be fickle. But if you treat her well, you will earn her loyalty." As the broad-shouldered leader spoke, he slid a discerning gaze across the horde of servants and cast his eyes upward to the landing. His dark blond hair was cropped short on the sides and grew long down the middle. Even from afar, and despite a thick blond beard, I could see the scars raked across his face, the hunger for blood in his eyes. But the angles of his brow, nose, and jaw held a familiarity that yanked on my heartstrings.

I clenched Glisette's wrist. "It's Tilmorn," I mouthed in awe. "He did survive."

Here was the man who could give and take elicrin gifts so easily. He had given the fairy slave a gift and stone just so she could materialize to Pontaval.

"Do you mind if I have a look to ensure that the accommodations will suit my lord?" Tilmorn asked, eyes combing the crowded hallway. I could see the cunning in his expression barely concealed by cordiality—just before Perennia shifted the mirror deeper into her skirts.

"Be my guest," I heard Ambrosine reply. "We still have preparations to finalize, but I think you'll find everything most suitable. Do you know when Lord Valmarys will grace us with his presence?"

"He sends his regrets that he won't be able to visit next week, but he vows it will be soon. Where are they?"

"Where are who?"

My heart clenched like a fist.

"Your sister and her friends," Tilmorn replied.

Glisette went rigid and slowly reached to grip my wrist.

"Oh, she's at our family's cottage out west," Ambrosine replied, examining the fairy's every feature while casually spilling our precious secrets like cheap perfume. "She used one of my enchanted mirrors to contact us. I told her your men would see her home safely. I'll be desperately relieved when she's not off gallivanting with people of ill repute."

"It would be our pleasure to escort her home." Tilmorn's deep voice was sonorous, effortlessly thundering. He must have taken the gift of an Omnilingual, just as he had given it to Mercer long ago. "It's a dangerous world, especially for a beautiful young woman of high standing. Simply point me in the right direction and we'll deliver her here as soon as possible."

Glisette's fingernails dug into my forearm.

"Beautiful?" Ambrosine repeated. "Do the peddlers sell portraits of my sister as well?"

Glisette whispered, "Mirror, as you were."

Our obscured view of the palace entry rippled and our reflections returned to the glass. The trophy room fell as quiet as a winter night before the first snowfall.

"What do we do?" she demanded.

"We run," I said, bolting for the door. "Cover our trail, snake through the forest to lose them."

"We can't—"

"Tilmorn serves the Moth King!" I shouted, no longer minding if the servants could hear me. "He can evade the materialization traps. Ambrosine told him our location and he materialized to Pontaval right then. He could be here in seconds. I knew this was a terrible idea."

"But Perennia—"

"Will be fine as long as she plays along!" Realizing that Glisette would have to be dragged away from the cottage, I steered her to the door. But she dug in her heels and shrugged out of my grasp.

"Unless they were only keeping my sisters alive so they could learn our location. If they no longer need them, they might kill them."

"What can we do to help them, Glisette? If you want to risk materializing to Pontaval, that's your choice. But if you don't get eviscerated like Brandar, Tilmorn will capture you. You saw what the Moth King's servants are capable of, what they did to those poor—"

"Yes, I saw it!" Glisette screamed through her teeth. "That's why I can't leave my sisters to suffer."

"I'm getting the astrikane and we're leaving. You can come with us or stay."

Behind Glisette, the mirror undulated again like the surface of a pond. Perennia appeared in Ambrosine's room again, her pale hands splayed on the glass. "Ambrosine told them where you are," she whispered, a sob caught in her throat. "They're coming. Run."

"Are you all right?" Glisette asked, and I had no doubt the righteous anger ringing in her voice could inflict worse damage on her enemies than the Moth King had so far inflicted on innocents.

"Yes, I'm fine. I'll keep playing along," Perennia insisted. "I love you. You have to go. Go now."

"Perennia!" Glisette cried.

"Mirror, as you were," Perennia whispered, and disappeared.

Glisette turned and crossed the trophy room. The black eyes in the mounted heads seemed to glint with warning, as though the final image they had glimpsed—of a ruthless hunter stalking his prey—still haunted their empty husks.

If we could reach Mercer in time, if Tilmorn could see the face of his brother, we might stand a chance.

"He'll have to come in the front because of the materialization barrier," Glisette said. "We'll go out the back."

But heavy, deliberate boots in the hallway struck terror in my heart. Glisette and I froze, our heartbeats deafening in the quiet, breaths strenuously hushed.

The handle turned. The door unleashed its warning wail. And there he stood.

Tilmorn wore a handsome black wool tunic with silver clasps, but his boots left mud on the pristine floor. Now that I stood but a few paces from him, I had no doubt that he was an excellent warrior, trained to fight and survive. If Mercer had never told me the nature of his brother's power, I would have feared this man nonetheless.

A pure light burst from Glisette's elicrin stone, but as her lips formed a spell, she froze, locked into place by an unseen force, her eyes enormous with dread. Then the same rigidity worked its way through my own muscles.

Our hands dropped to our sides. Our feet shuffled together. The light in Tilmorn's elicrin stone danced as he toyed with us, manipulated us, forced our bodies to move without our permission.

Step by calm step, my feet brought me back to the mirror, obedient to Tilmorn. Glisette's stiff form went through the same motions at my side.

Mercer, please, please come looking for us. You are the only one who can save us.

Tilmorn towered over Glisette, who stood a palm's length taller than me. Even his neck looked immensely powerful. His paces were measured as he circled behind us, sending a brigade of shivers skittering over my scalp.

But it was Glisette he approximated. He stood behind her, studying her reflection. "You must be the rogue sister," he said in his low voice. His eyes resembled Mercer's, but a deep darkness dwelt within them. It was like glimpsing opposite sides of the same pair of gold aurions. "Those curls," he mused, flicking one of her honeyed tendrils. "What man hasn't been brought to his knees by a girl with yellow hair?"

His thick arm reached around her shoulder, following an arc that suggested he might use his power to caress her breasts. *No, no, no, no.* Astounding curses would have exploded out of my mouth if my tongue hadn't been glued to the wall of my teeth. *This can't be how this mission ends,* I pleaded. *With rape and torture and death.*

But it was Glisette's elicrin stone he sought. With his hand hovering over her chest, he curled his finger and beckoned the white light within her opaque purple chalcedony. It burgeoned and coiled out in a bright tendril, snaking through the air to nest in Tilmorn's smoky gray gem.

"What about you, lovely?" he asked. Taking one step, he overshadowed me and flicked the laces of my tunic collar, opening a gap that exposed the hollow area beneath my sternum. A scream that I couldn't release built up inside me like steam in a kettle.

Tilmorn smelled of icy wind, smoke, and the bitter briarberry tea that Darmeskans partook of every hour of the day. He must have come to Ambrosine straight from the mountains. I wanted to shut my eyes and crumple where I stood, but all I could do was breathe, breathe in that scent that confirmed the captivity of my father's people, the claiming of their home by an enemy.

"You're the one who dried up the Water," Tilmorn said, his mountain accent thick as congealed blood. "The one who could end the reign of the Lord of Elicromancers."

Nauseating fear swept over me. We had spilled dangerous secrets to the Realm Alliance through Fabian and our missives, desperate to convince them of the truth so we didn't have to do this alone. I'd thought even the most selfish people in that chamber would act nobly with so much at stake. But we'd given more than we gained.

The Moth King knew of me, and what I was meant to do.

Tilmorn turned his palm up and beckoned. I felt a nudge inside my ribs. As soon as he found a way to extract my power—or realized he couldn't—he would destroy me. He tried again, and that nudge inside me became more of a thud that left me fighting for air.

He frowned in dismay. Was there anything remaining of him besides loyalty to this manipulative Moth King? I longed to remind him of Lundy and Halmer, of his brother who had fought to bring him home. Speaking their names might constitute magic beyond any he traded in.

A shout rang out from the garden. It sounded like Mercer. My heart soared with hope, but then I heard the sounds of struggle: shuffling steps, singing blades, and elicrin spells bandied back and forth. The Moth King's servants had come for my companions.

Just as panic and the pounding of my power against my ribs robbed me of breath, Tilmorn stepped back and slid his sword from its sheath. This ignited terror in my every vein, though my body couldn't even flinch in response. It was a simple sword with a leather-wrapped grip and plain disk pommel, crafted for one service alone.

Tilmorn's calculating expression showed me that I posed too great a threat to be given mercy. I could move only my eyes and chose to close them, terrified to see him reel back to strike me down, terrified to see the horror on Glisette's face.

But he didn't bear down on me. The blade didn't pierce my heart or lodge in my neck.

I opened my eyes and found Perennia's image in the mirror, her teeth clenched in concentration. Her hands reached out, trembling, as though lifting a heavy crown, and her rosy elicrin stone swirled to life.

The cunning in Tilmorn's eyes dissipated. His broad shoulders relaxed. I thought Perennia had to touch to take away anger, sadness, guilt, fear, distrust—but perhaps her power simply worked best that way.

Glisette and I were able to shake off his control. "Give my sister back her power," Perennia said in a soft, soothing voice.

Tilmorn did as she asked. Glisette snarled at him, the light churning vengefully as it nestled back inside her stone.

Tilmorn lurched in response, showing his teeth, nearly breaking free of Perennia's grasp on his emotions.

"I can't hold him for long," Perennia said. "My power is weaker from here."

"We should kill him while we can," Glisette growled.

"Mercer could get him on our side," I argued. "He could help us defeat the Moth King."

Tilmorn didn't react to his brother's name. My faith in his redemption had wavered as I'd watched him prowl and loom over us. That faith now vanished altogether.

"Take his elicrin stone and go," Perennia said. "Make sure he never finds it."

My heart throbbed again, but this time with exhilaration. Tilmorn was a major source of the Moth King's power. Without his ability to trade elicrin gifts, he couldn't give the Moth King whatever gift he desired. For a glimmering moment, I imagined tossing that powerful gray stone into the thrashing waves off the western cliffs. This was the solution. We could spare Tilmorn's life so that Mercer could reunite with his beloved brother—yet castrate his elicrin magic so that he could no longer aid the Moth King in butchering the realm.

But when I stepped forward to seize the medallion, Tilmorn ripped away from Perennia's control and charged to meet me, the dim light glancing off the deadly steel of his sword.

I cringed and covered my face as the blade swung down to cleave me in two. Its edge bit into my forearm and I screamed in anticipation of agony. But the sword stopped before it rent muscle and bone.

I cradled the torn flesh and dared to look up. Perennia's shoulders shook as she regained wavering control over Tilmorn. Her piercing eyes turned bloodshot. She wouldn't be able to spare us a third time.

"Find the astrikane and get out!" she shouted.

"But—" Glisette started.

"I know you can stop Lord Valmarys. Just…do it before it's too late."

Glisette hauled me to my feet and pushed me out the door.

TWENTY-FOUR

WE burst outdoors to find Mercer covered in blood but standing, alive, unharmed. An exquisite relief overcame me. Tilmorn's two henchmen lay limp in the grass, their blood splashed liberally across patches of flowers. Mercer's sword made a loathsome wet sound as he withdrew it from one's chest. He slid the medallions encasing their elicrin stones from their throats.

Kadri leaned against the garden gate, staring feverishly at the mess before her. The sore on her neck had grown to the size of my thumb and was as discolored as a rotten fruit.

"Run, run, run!" Glisette yelled as we hurtled down the path. She yanked Kadri to her feet. Warm wetness seeped through my fingers where they pressed tight on my fresh cut.

"Where's the Healer? What happened?" Mercer caught me and tried to peel my hand away so he could see the source of the blood. Had he not seen Tilmorn?

"No Healer. Just one of the Moth King's men," I replied in a rush. "Help Kadri. I'll follow you." I sprinted to the greenhouse, rampaging over the weaving paths with my heart walloping in my ears. The sun emerged from behind the clouds, casting rainbow beams through the ceiling on a single young astrikane tree tucked inside an ivy-trammeled gate. Most of its bright white leaves had shriveled without Perennia's attentions.

I mounted the gate and grimaced at the pain that gored my

arm. My bright blood smirched the dead leaves as I foraged. There were only a handful worth taking and I stuffed them into my pocket.

I struggled back up the slippery foliage alongside the waterfall, not daring to look down at the cottage. When I reached the ledge, I expected to scoop up half of the supplies, untether Calanthe, and hurry to catch up with the others. But there was nothing: no Calanthe, no packs, not even a solitary piece of dried fruit for us to split four ways—three, since Kadri probably wouldn't be eating anytime soon. The others stood dumbstruck.

"Where's Calanthe?" I demanded.

"We don't know," Glisette said, panic raw in her voice. "Did you see anyone besides those two, Mercer?" She gestured at the bodies below.

Mercer shook his head as he lowered Kadri to the gray grass. Sweat drew dewy red rivers down his blood-spattered forehead. "Not that I saw. But..." He bent over, studying the impressions underfoot. "There are multiple sets of footprints here. Bigger than either of yours."

Glisette raked her fingers through her dingy hair and looked warily over her shoulder at the cottage. But she noticed something, tilted her head in curiosity, and sprang forward to pluck an item the size of an aurion from a trench in the grass.

"What is it?" Mercer and I asked in unison.

"I don't know," she said, handing it off to me. From the back, it was clear the object was a broken pin. I stopped putting pressure on my forearm wound to turn the pin over with a bloody fingertip.

The enamel surface showed a yellow-and-maroon Erdemese

flag. I glared at it. "Did either of you notice Kadri wearing this?" I asked, passing it to Mercer.

He shook his head and Glisette muttered, "No."

I took the pin back and studied it, baffled, until the truth struck like a thunderclap.

More matters are settled in the cloakroom than the communal chamber.

Rayed Lillis had uttered those words to me on the way to Beyrian.

No one's going to believe this violence was perpetrated by an ancient dead tyrant when you're right here, flesh and blood—not to mention the rumors that you're defying orders by practicing magic.

He had said that in the courtyard, near Brandar's mutilated body.

I kicked a solid rock and the caged thing inside me clawed its way toward freedom. A wave of destruction slashed out of me, splitting the smooth face of the boulder and withering the verdant vegetation surrounding us.

Why? The question seemed to sear holes in my head. The betrayal stung as sharply as the gash from Tilmorn's blade. But I had no time to linger and parse out past suggestions of Rayed's treachery.

I flung a wild glance at Kadri. What if she had helped him, had lied to us in saying no one from the Realm Alliance was coming to our aid?

I could hardly ask her now.

A wet wind whipped over the grass. "We have to go," I said. "Cover our tracks."

"We can't leave without the supplies," Glisette argued.

"We have no choice! They're gone."

"And what do we do about her?" she demanded, gesturing at Kadri. Her skin held an awful tinge of sallow gray and the whites of her eyes flared with red veins.

I sifted through the damp leaves in my pocket and produced the white astrikane. "We have this, at least."

"What's that? Astrikane?" Mercer demanded. "Well, at least she'll have pleasant delusions while she's dying and we're growing too weak to help her."

"It's the best we can do," I barked. "Here, Glisette, put one on her tongue and another on the sore."

Mercer set his jaw. "If I go back to the cottage and finish off Valmarys's servant as I did the others—"

"He's not like the others. That's why we have to move. Do you need help with Kadri?"

Mercer didn't reply. He limped back to Kadri and held his hands over her, palms up. He looked like Tilmorn trying to beckon our power. I flashed Glisette a look that I hoped would communicate how foolish it would be to mention Tilmorn right now. Mercer would get himself killed, along with the rest of us.

"*Nagak nerenin,*" Mercer whispered. A levitation spell evoked his elicrin light. Kadri's chest bowed out and she was spirited into the air until the toes of her boots floated just above the ground and her head drooped back. Mercer slowly reclined her until the spell suspended her horizontally about five hand heights from the forest floor.

Glisette tenderly crossed Kadri's arms over her chest and whispered spells to cover our tracks. I led the way onward, taking sharp, random turns as an extra precaution. But the unfortunate truth was that we needed to make our way to the nearest village or we wouldn't survive, and those pursuing us knew that.

"Rayed Lillis betrayed us," I said aloud. "That pin with the Erdemese flag is his."

"That's an absurd leap," Glisette said. "There are countless Erdemese citizens in Nissera."

"But Rayed has one just like it. And he convinced me to leave Beyrian."

"Yes, because Brandar's death looked bad for you."

"It looked even worse when he persuaded me to run." I put too much pressure on my fresh wound and hissed at the pain. "And it was the same hour that the blights came for Mercer. The plan was to sour my reputation and capture or kill Mercer." I thought for a moment, pulling at this terrifying thread. "Rayed said someone was taking advantage of my misfortunes, using my reputation to cover their own deeds. He accused Mercer, and I thought he truly mistrusted him. But he was driving a wedge between us, making me fear for my well-being so that I would flee, which was practically an admission of guilt considering the circumstances."

"But Rayed's a mortal," Glisette pointed out. "He couldn't have materialized to the summer cottage, and how else could he have arrived in time to steal from us?"

"Maybe he followed us?" Even as I said it, I realized how unlikely it was. If he had followed us, he would have seen Kadri and realized she had not embarked on her ship. And somehow I knew, even as I questioned everything else, that he would never do anything to hurt her, would never leave her sick and without supplies.

"What would be his motivation?" Mercer asked, clearly intrigued by the theory, though not quite sold.

Each realization became a rung on a ladder, but I wasn't sure where it led. Rayed Lillis possessed power, relative wealth, respect. *More matters are settled in the cloakroom than the communal chamber.* The damning observation looped through my thoughts.

"He was compromised," I said, cupping the gash on my arm again. The blood had dried sticky on my fingers, soaking the bandage wrapped around my stitched hand. "He voted to extend the age of surrender for elicromancers. He cast the *deciding* vote. He's under someone's heel. But who could it be? Someone who wants to see me fall, who wants my fall to obscure their own rise to power. Someone who's working for the Moth King and wants him to succeed. Perhaps Glend Neswick. But what would he want with an extension, as a mortal?"

I thought back to my short visit at Yorth. I didn't remember seeing Rayed and Neswick fraternizing, but perhaps they'd kept their distance on purpose. I nearly felt sick wondering if Rayed had been working on behalf of Neswick when he first arrived in Arna to rescue me from the Conclave's sentence.

"And then we have the Summoners," I said, my mind navigating its own treacherous path as my feet charged over the forest floor. "Those who believe Valmarys is the 'Lord of Elicromancers.' Perhaps they aren't isolated mountain-dwellers clinging to their tales, as Professor Strather and Neswick himself suggested. Maybe they are more sophisticated than that. Maybe there's a reason they must wear masks—because we would recognize them."

They listened without comment as the details of my suspicion unspooled, so I charged on. "Neswick occupies a seat on the Conclave and the Realm Alliance. After Ambrosine manipulated me into taking the fall for Devorian's mistake, it gave Neswick ideas. Rayed himself suggested as much. They say the best way to lie is to tell as much of the truth as you dare, and he told the truth: that someone was looking to ruin me."

"If Glend Neswick is a Summoner who wanted you to be blamed for the Moth King's deeds, why would he send blights to kill all of us but Mercer?" Glisette asked. "And if the blights were sent to kill Mercer the morning of Brandar's death, why did they try to take him last night?"

I inhaled deeply, stopping to turn my face up to the green canopies that shivered in the damp breeze. "New information changed their minds about both of us. Valmarys was content to let me live in exile, using me as a cover for his actions until he gained enough power that the Realm Alliance couldn't stop him. But then Fabian told the Realm Alliance everything, including Mercer's vision of me. Once the Moth King learned of my supposed destiny—from Neswick or Rayed—I was too dangerous to leave alive, and Mercer too useful to kill. I wager the blights would have taken you captive as well, Glisette, as your gift could be stolen and given to the Moth King."

"And Tilmorn would have killed me after he stole it—" Glisette muttered, then gasped, realizing her mistake too late.

"Tilmorn?" Mercer echoed. I heard him stop in his tracks.

I closed my eyes before finding the courage to turn around. When I did, the stalwart hope on his face wrenched my gut.

"Was it Tilmorn back there?" he demanded.

I felt the urge to grip his hands, in part to restrain him— but only in part. "Yes. It was. He tried to kill me. He took Glisette's power. And he knows that I am supposed to kill the Moth King."

Mercer lowered Kadri and turned to retrace our trail to the summer cottage. Glisette caught his arm. "You can't, Mercer. You'll die."

"This is the chance I've been waiting for."

"Mercer." Her graceful hand molded along his jaw and she stepped closer to him. Seeing him soften at her tenderness sent a spear of envy through me. "I can stop you from leaving, but I'd rather not have to," she said. "We need you. You're the one who knows the Moth King's ways."

I looked down at the blood caked in the basins of the knuckles on my marred hand.

"He's not the man you knew him to be, Mercer," I said, finding it beyond difficult to look back up at him.

Mercer slid Glisette's hand away and turned his ire on me. "I know he's not the same. But all I've wanted is a chance to break through the Moth King's manipulation, to remind him of who he once was, or at least try—"

"He didn't even flinch at the sound of your name."

The moment the words escaped, I wished I hadn't said them. Pain worked its way across his pleasing features. But something about my ruthless tone made the truth sink in. His shoulders sagged.

"So, what happened?" he asked. "How did Tilmorn know you were there?"

"Ambrosine," I breathed, relieved that Mercer wasn't about to charge back to meet almost certain death.

"She didn't think she was betraying us," Glisette rushed to say. "She thinks Valmarys is a doting suitor, that his men were willing to escort me safely back to Pontaval. She didn't share my location initially because she was hoping to lure his envoys to her with more gifts. It worked. And now she and Perennia are in danger."

"Tilmorn could have killed your entire family already if he wanted," I reassured her. "He hasn't."

"Valory's right," Mercer said. "If that's what the Moth King desired, it would be done. He finds his pleasure in other ways."

"Torture?" Glisette asked feebly.

"Sometimes," Mercer said. "But other times, it's corruption. Subversion. Making the mighty fall on their own swords."

Glisette nodded, staring at her worn boots. "We should keep moving."

Kadri groaned, and the horror of our situation came bearing down. We were stranded without food. Calanthe had been stolen, fate willing by someone who would care for her. Rayed had betrayed me. Kadri was dying.

"If Rayed... Do you think Kadri...?" Glisette whispered, losing her nerve before voicing the suspicion.

"I'll assume not, for now," Mercer said. "She couldn't hurt us if she wanted to, and I don't think she would want to."

He worked off one of his boots and tore at a hole in his threadbare stocking until the fabric ripped. He limped toward me, barefoot on his wounded leg, and folded my tunic sleeve beneath the makeshift bandage for extra padding. I stifled a whimper as he knotted the stocking.

"What do we do?" I asked.

"We get as far from here as we can," he said. "We go to another town for supplies and hope to find an elicrin Healer. We press on to Darmeska." He looked from me to Glisette. "And we don't trust *anyone*."

The color of Kadri's skin began to improve hours after we administered the astrikane. By the second application the next morning, the hard lines of suffering around her mouth had softened, which offered a bit of encouragement amid the harsh landscape of despair. Like Mercer, I found it hard to believe she had plotted our demise.

Glisette and Mercer took turns levitating Kadri, but it wearied them. I could tell it required concentration, almost more than they could spare on another day of journeying on nearly empty stomachs. I blazed the trail, trying to stop my magic from leaving a path of wilted, faded foliage.

I missed Calanthe loping on ahead, hunting for prey. Why would Rayed's master have taken her? She didn't offer protection, except maybe from wolves, and wolves were the least of our worries. She wasn't much of a hunter either. Had he done it to save her, knowing her mistress was about to be murdered?

Rayed must not have known that Kadri accompanied us. No

matter what he had done to me, he would die a thousand deaths to save his sister.

My hunger soon surpassed my desire to divine his motives. The few berries we'd found weren't enough to stop me from fantasizing about the stocks of food sitting in the kitchens at the summer cottage. Glisette had made a rock look and taste like a hunk of bread, but nibbling on it helped nothing. The spell only made it *seem* like sustenance.

"How far are we from the nearest town?" Mercer asked.

I glanced down at the map, which thankfully had been tucked in a pocket of my tunic when the supplies were stolen. "We won't make it before nightfall. We'll reach the road, though."

"And ask for a ride?" Mercer asked.

"No one's going to take Kadri," Glisette said. "Word of the plague has gotten around."

"For a leaf of white astrikane they might," Mercer said.

"Even the saddest folk won't chance their life on a happy vision," I said, glancing back at Kadri. I wondered what she was dreaming about, what joyous truths might be revealed to her under the influence of the astrikane. Blue astrikane from Galgeth was pungent and gave frightening visions, while its rare Nisseran counterpart was said to offer glimpses of hopeful truths or possibilities. "Besides, it appears to be helping her. I don't want to give a single leaf away, not until we can find a Healer."

"We have these elicrin stones." Mercer dug in his pocket and extracted two silver medallions, one holding a ruby and the other an orange sunstone. Now that their possessors had died, they were probably no better than trinkets—to anyone but Tilmorn, at least.

Callista's amethyst diadem had remained powerful even after her death, but many elicrin stones dimmed out, magical no longer.

Under ordinary circumstances, we could probably find a mortal who would pay a high price for their beauty. But no coachman or mortal healer would risk death by plague for a bauble.

"I'm hungry," Glisette whined. "How come we saw mushrooms left and right back when we had plenty of food in our packs?"

Kadri muttered something unintelligible. I looked back at her ghostly figure floating above the sprawling growth of the forest floor. Mercer stopped to lower her to the mossy ground while I trudged over the crushed weeds, keeping my distance.

"Don't get close to me," she mumbled.

"We can't catch it," Glisette reminded her. "Well, we don't know about Valory. That's why she's over there."

"And…" Kadri blinked again, staring at the beams of evening sunlight wedging through the dense branches. "Where are our things? Calanthe?"

"Stolen," I muttered, exchanging a glance with Mercer. "During an attack."

Mercer helped her sit up. "We'll find supplies. We're not far from a village."

She dabbed at the sore along her neck, peeling off the white astrikane leaf before Mercer could stop her. "I had wonderful dreams," she said. "Not to offend, but I would rather have stayed in them. Is it bad?" she asked, tilting her chin so he could look at her neck.

"It looks a little better," Mercer said, evading the actual question.

"We couldn't find a Healer at the summer cottage, but white astrikane seems to be helping for now."

"I want to stand up," she said.

Mercer supported her shoulders. "I don't think—"

Kadri waved off his naysaying and planted her hands on the ground, lifting herself to a crouch. She closed her eyes, swallowed hard, and, with Mercer's help, found the strength to stand.

"We're set to reach the village after nightfall as it is," he said. "We should carry you."

"I'd rather walk than float."

Her deep brown eyes rose to meet mine, golden in the dusky light. "I thought you were gone," I managed to say through the pressure in my throat. I couldn't bring myself to ask if she'd taken part in her brother's plot. If she hadn't, news of his betrayal might weaken her again.

"I couldn't let myself be a mortal liability, could I?" she asked, giving Mercer a sideways look. He grinned in response. A thrill fluttered through me.

"Let's keep moving," I said, remembering my hunger. If Kadri was recovering, that meant she would need food soon, and more than a few blackberries.

As we walked on, Glisette tiptoed along sprawling roots and caught up to me. "It adds up, doesn't it?" she whispered. "Ambassador Lillis betraying us. But I was thinking...he would only have done so for good reason. I know that much about him. Perhaps he was threatened."

"Perhaps," I responded. "It doesn't excuse what he's done."

Her eyes skimmed across the darkening horizon. "Even his outright treachery doesn't vex me as much as Ambrosine's infatuation with the Moth King's trinkets. Not because I'm surprised, but because of how easily that could have been *me*. If I had stayed in Pontaval, I would have been dazzled by those trunks of gems and silk. And I wouldn't think twice about raising the tolls. I didn't even know that, about... about the famine." Absentmindedly, she patted the scab over her eye. "But walking in on that spectacle when I did... Ambrosine looked vulgar and vain." She expelled a long breath. "Only an elicromancer with a very special gift could produce that many precious gems. And I hope I never meet that elicromancer, or I might end up like Ambrosine. She almost pulled me in...."

I was thankful for the shadows of dusk that concealed my expression. "What you did matters more than what you might have done."

❧ TWENTY-FIVE ❧

E found the road just before dark. It wrapped like a brown ribbon around a tree-covered hill that otherwise looked identical to all the other tree-covered hills.

Kadri's bout of strength didn't last long. Mercer had to give her more white astrikane as we edged west along the road toward the village of Greenglen.

The village square was dim and lifeless, aside from the lanterns burning around the statue in the square. But dozens of campfires winked among circles of peddlers' wagons tucked between the village and the border of the forest.

"Do you smell that smoking meat?" Glisette asked as we looked on the glen from the shadows of the woods. "I'm going to steal us some."

"There are so many people," Mercer said. "It will be hard to get away with stealing food and sneaking around."

"What are you saying?" Glisette asked.

Mercer sighed. "I'm exhausted and hungry and the night's getting cold. Kadri will need warmth, and if we're going to have a fire it might as well be one of thirty fires rather than a lonely little one in the woods. We'll cause *less* of a stir if we keep our heads down and camp on the fringes than if we go traipsing around taking enough food and bedrolls for four people."

"But it could—" I started.

"I know, whoever's following us could be dangerous to them," he admitted wearily. "But they're travelers. They'll be gone soon. And look: some beggars have joined the camp. They'll think we're nothing but vagabonds."

"We certainly smell like vagabonds," Glisette snorted.

"I agree with him. No stealing," Kadri said. "The belly of one who asks for bread is fuller than the belly of one who steals it."

"That astrikane is making you sound quite transcendent, Kadri," Glisette teased.

"It's an Erdemese proverb," Kadri said, her shadow swaying. "But it did come to me in a vision a few moments ago. My mother said it. She smelled like jasmine."

"*I'm* not going to defy the wisdom of a white astrikane apparition that smells like jasmine," Mercer said. "We'd be asking for trouble."

"We can't just—" I started again, but a recurring pang of hunger squelched my argument, so we seamlessly joined the sparse outer circle of the sprawling camp. No one paid us much mind, not with elicrin stones tucked out of sight and lovely locks tied in filthy braids.

An old woman offered us a bit of bread while a little girl served soup to all the beggars. We sat far enough away from the flames of our modest fire to obscure our features.

While Glisette helped Kadri eat for the first time in days, I bought supplies from a drunken peddler, trading one of the elicrin stones for packs, bedrolls, and food. As he opened the panels of his wagon, I saw uncanny likenesses of the three Lorenthi princesses and a slightly outdated likeness of Devorian painted on miniature wood panels. When the peddler asked if I was traveling with anyone, I pointed indiscriminately and wandered around in the shadows flanking the camp before rejoining my companions.

Mercer was speaking with an elderly man when I returned. I watched Mercer comb a hand through his dark blond hair, the movement accentuating the lean length of his body. They laughed as they talked, which brought a pinch of worry to my chest.

"You two seemed friendly," I said when he returned.

"He wanted to know how I got so lucky as to travel alongside three beauties with golden, red, and raven hair. I told him one of you was my wife and the other two my mistresses, but I wouldn't let on who's who."

"My hair's not red," I said, because it was the only response I could think of that wasn't a chastisement.

"It's red when the light hits it."

When Mercer found the three of us watching him, he averted his attentions to my purchases. "He said there's a well in the square. Did you buy skins?"

I delved into the packs and handed him the empty water pouches.

"I'll be back," he said.

"None of us should go off alone," Glisette said.

"I'll go," I said. "There were miniature portraits of you and your siblings in that wagon."

"You should have bought them all so no one would see," she said. "They can't be more than an aurion apiece."

Mercer and I couldn't help laughing, and even Kadri let out a halfhearted giggle. "More like a copper thesar," I said. "And that would have drawn even more attention."

Glisette rolled her eyes. "Just go get some water, will you? I'm parched."

While Mercer and I wandered toward the village, I suddenly wanted words to fill the silence, but didn't have any to offer. I felt his glance skim over me and saw his lips part, but he closed them and rubbed the back of his neck.

He soon cleared his throat. "Tomorrow we'll arrange a coach for Kadri, whatever it takes. She'll arrive in Beyrian in time to be treated by the palace Healer."

I stopped in my tracks. "You want to send Kadri back?"

"We don't have a choice. So far, her illness has forced us to take a dangerous detour and slowed our pace by half."

"Our injuries haven't exactly doubled our speed either."

"It's not just that. The astrikane is keeping her alive, but can it cure the disease? We'll run out soon, and we can't just pick it like a wildflower. Even if she recovers, we may encounter more blights. What then?"

"But the guards may not let her back into the city."

"Her status in Yorth will all but guarantee her entry and healing. If she were to keep pressing north with us...at the border of Volarre and Calgoran, that much is not guaranteed, if she even survives to reach it."

I rubbed my eyes, exhausted, feeling I could curl up in a hole and die. "I see your point."

"Will you talk to her?"

"I'll try. In the morning."

As we skirted the edge of the camp, a soft melody sung by a feminine voice glided toward us. The words were in another language, but each one moved me more than the last.

Mercer recognized it and softly sang along, his voice tired but still tuneful:

> *"Kor iknor il efrindaren*
> *Kor elenis il efrindaren*
> *Pren olisthar var lenis den*
> *Eft magar int glinnis var hessen*
> *Kor shinavar ah sera norn*
> *Ef glithila tis var eshal fiorn"*

"Old Nisseran?" I asked, glancing around to place the origin of the heartrending song.

"Yes," Mercer answered.

I scanned the thinning crowd and found a young beggar woman by a lonesome fire, watching us from underneath her hood. I bit the inside of my cheek and walked faster to escape her gaze.

"What does it mean?" I asked Mercer, catching up to him.

He stopped and turned to me, his barley-brown eyes softer than I'd seen them. "'Through the night I search for you. By the dawn I search for you. Under summer fire and winter snow, my footsteps mark the meadows and the hills. Through forests deep in lands unknown, I call your name and hear the wind.'"

"That's what you were singing when I was helping you?" I asked, my voice feeble. I realized I had stepped closer to him, and instead of moving away, he had answered my boldness by spanning the same distance. He stood so close that I could see the fine lines etched into his lips.

"We enjoyed each other's company more in those harrowing moments than we have in the many harrowing moments since," he said. "Why?"

"Because you were vulnerable and grateful instead of argumentative."

"Or maybe it's because you were helpful and obliging instead of stubborn." He smiled, reaching out to rub dirt from my cheekbone. Surely I was imagining the lingering caress.

"The song is, um, sad," I muttered, walking on to escape him.

He paused in the dark before following. The grass of the glen turned to cobblestones beneath our feet. The village square was silent and dark, but not in the threatening way I was accustomed to in the recesses of the mighty forest.

"There's the well," I said, striding past the statue at the center of the square. Leaning on the stone ledge, I lowered the bucket into the depths. When I brought it back up and it overflowed with fresh, cold water, I couldn't resist splashing it into my mouth with abandon. I took another deep gulp and slid the bucket toward Mercer.

"*Il samenef Nisserali?*"

The voice behind me startled me so much that I choked on the water and fell into a coughing fit while I furnished my dagger. I twisted around to find the beggar woman who had been singing and watching us. I'd seen no one behind us, nor had I heard any footsteps.

"What do you want?" I demanded when I could speak again.

The woman slipped off her hood, revealing nutty-brown hair

and a face pale for a wanderer. She gave me a steady, fearless look, not even acknowledging the dagger before she turned back to Mercer and repeated her question.

"*Ris, ef samenil*," he answered.

"*Efrindaren eft linathir.*"

"We don't have any coins to give you," I said.

"She's looking for her daughter," Mercer replied.

"Well, she followed us and I don't like it."

"It seems she only speaks Old Nisseran," he said. "That's strange, isn't it? And I feel as though I've seen her before."

"You said yourself we shouldn't trust anyone, and I agree." I tried to force him back toward the camp, but the woman spoke faster, recapturing his attention. Mercer furrowed his brow and rubbed his knuckles along his chin. I barely recognized any words, but when the woman reversed a concealment spell and an elicrin stone appeared around her neck, I recognized the threat.

"The Moth King sent her," I said, pointing my dagger at her throat.

The woman hooked her arm through my elbow and twisted until I had no choice but to surrender my weapon. With a flick of her wrist, she impaled it through an empty cask outside the tavern across the street. The cask rolled over the cobblestones until it struck the base of the statue with a hollow clunk.

"*Ef gemeren ilen heval*," she said fiercely.

"She said she's not going to hurt us," Mercer said, unfazed by the exchange. "She keeps mentioning her daughter."

"*Eft linathir*," she repeated with a fervent nod. "Bristal."

"Bristal?" I repeated.

"I know her. I know her from somewhere," Mercer said, narrowing his eyes. "But it can't be right."

"What?"

"I think she's the one who saved me. When I was...meant to be the sacrifice."

An outrageous theory struck me. I tried to dismiss it, but it lingered. "Wait," I said, peering at her elicrin stone in the vague lantern light. Just as I suspected, its facets gleamed the stunning color of amethyst. "No. No, this isn't possible."

"Do you know her?" he asked.

"I've never met her. But I think she may be my ancestor."

"Someone from Arna?"

"This is ridiculous, but..." I decided to try the name. If I was wrong, she wouldn't know how mad I'd been to even think it. "Callista?" I ventured.

Shock registered on her face, and then she smiled in disbelief. "Callista," she agreed, her hand on her heart.

I laughed in astonishment. "This is not possible," I repeated.

"Who is she?" Mercer asked, impatient.

"She's...she's Queen Bristal's mother, but she came from a time long before Bristal waged war against Tamarice. Callista created—creates—portals. Not just from one place to another, like King Tiernan, but from one time to another, as I told you once before. If she saved you and that's the last thing you remember..."

"It means she sent me here," Mercer finished.

She cocked her head, waiting for an explanation.

"But she doesn't seem to recognize me," he went on. "She hasn't mentioned our encounter."

I massaged my forehead, utterly confounded. "All right..." I muttered. "She doesn't remember you...perhaps I'm wrong. Unless...unless this is *before* that for her."

"What?"

"So, in my time, Callista is long dead. That elicrin stone she's wearing is nothing but a piece of jewelry, a family heirloom Ivria gave to me before..." I trailed off. "Yet here Callista stands, and there's that elicrin stone. Maybe in *her* lifetime, saving you hasn't occurred yet. She could be going anywhere, or any time after this."

He answered with nothing but a dubious look.

"She was born before the Elicrin War," I explained. "Some five or six hundred years ago, after your time. She didn't use her gift much because it muddles things, obviously. But during a dangerous battle, she opened a portal for her daughter, Bristal, and sent her through to keep her safe. Amid the chaos, Callista didn't know where—or rather, *when*—she'd sent Bristal. After the war was won, she went looking for her through time. Which is what she's *currently* doing. Looking for her daughter."

Callista waited patiently while we discussed this, nodding at the sound of Bristal's name.

"Do you know if she ever found her?" he asked.

I shook my head. "No. She stopped looking and went back to her own time, where she gave up her elicrin stone to age mortally with the other victors from the war. But we could tell her where—I mean when—Bristal is."

He turned to speak to Callista. I'd always found Old Nisseran delicious to listen to, perhaps because I only knew spells and a few old songs, which made me think of the entire language as powerful and whimsical. But I had heard more shades of it since meeting Mercer, and it sounded so fluid and complex on his tongue.

"I told her we could help her, but not until she answers our questions," he explained.

As the two of them launched into an animated conversation, I took the opportunity to examine my forebear. The roundness of her features hadn't been handed down through the generations, but I took pride in the few similarities I found. Callista was known to be an incredible warrior, fearless, and honest. Her power was too awesome to live on in her abandoned elicrin stone, but the residue of magic it did hold reflected her noble nature.

"She hasn't visited my time yet," Mercer said, confusion wrinkling his forehead. "She's never heard of the Moth King."

"Maybe we're the reason she goes back," I suggested. "Maybe this moment changes everything."

"You think she knows to save me and opens a portal for me because... we're here now? *I'm* only here because she sent me."

"And she sent you because you're here. The two don't have to be mutually exclusive, do they? If you weren't here, I wouldn't have known that I should kill the Moth King."

"So we need to tell her where to go. But she's on a mission to find her daughter. Why would she care about what's happening in a time that doesn't concern her?"

"I know her legacy. She fought against traitor elicromancers who threatened to conquer Nissera. She risked her life for this realm's peace and freedom. She'll do it again."

Callista watched us, her eyes perceptive and curious in the lantern light.

"What if I ask her to go back even further?" he whispered. "What if she could go back to when the Moth King was just a child, to when he was vulnerable, if he ever was, and find a way to kill him before he establishes his reign?"

I shook my head, feeling more and more certain of what we needed to do. "No, you have to tell her what we know has happened already. Tell her to interrupt the sacrifice and stop the elicromancers from killing you at the hideout in Yorth. Tell her to create a portal to send you through to the sixty-fifth year of the Age of Accords, day"—I did the math in my head—"ninety-three. She has to send you to me so I can save you."

Mercer loosed a breath of disbelief. The wonder of it all, the chance and fate, seem to strike us both at once.

He spoke to Callista again. Her dainty eyebrows drew together as she listened. I continued to admire the reality of her presence when Mercer turned back to me. "She understands. Now, tell her about Bristal. Explain who you are. I'll translate."

"Bristal was my grandmother's grandmother," I said. "She was raised as an orphan in a small village after you sent her away. She got kidnapped and taken to the Water by people who wanted to exploit her magic, but she survived and became an elicromancer, a Clandestine who could take on any form. She resisted and defeated a dark elicromancer who waged war on the realm."

Mercer related this to Callista while I spoke. I watched the revelations register on her face.

"She was a hero," I continued. "In fact..." I turned to glance at the statue in the center of the square. It depicted a young woman with a spear in her grip and an elicrin stone hanging from her neck.

Her long hair streamed in a ghostly wind. "That's a statue of her going to battle."

Callista's mouth dropped open as Mercer's explanation caught up to mine. Her eyes filled with tears as they rose to regard the statue in the dim light. She stepped forward to run her fingers across the name inscribed on the statue's base.

Mercer and I looked at each other, awestruck. Callista hurried back to us and clasped my face in her hands, searching it. She whispered something I could tell was as bittersweet as the song she had sung.

"She says she sees her in you, and knows it's the truth," Mercer said. "She's been searching for Bristal to bring her home. But now that she knows what became of her, she'll stop searching. Leave her where she is."

"Will she go back to save you?" I asked.

Mercer relayed the question to Callista. The dreamy, lost look in her eyes faded. She donned a sober expression and looked back at the likeness of her daughter. She said slowly, "*Ris. Pren ef drenniar fir eft eglen var shevnen magrar elicrin.*"

"She said she will," Mercer said. "And after, she'll return to her own time and give up her elicrin stone."

I didn't know this woman, this foremother of mine, but I felt a sense of loss at the idea of a farewell, perhaps due to the question budding in my mind: What if I could take a step back through time, just one small step, and stop Ivria's death? What if I could stop the eradication of the Water?

As quickly as the thought sprouted, a wiser part of me tore it from the soil and ground it underfoot. If the Water remained, I would not have this power meant to contend with the realm's greatest enemy, the power that led Mercer to see my role in this. And I would not know Mercer himself.

Callista fit a hand on each of our shoulders. Her grip was strong. "*Lon yerwev,*" she said, and kissed my brow.

She approached the statue. I could only see the back of her head, but I sensed she was smiling, filled to the brim with emotion. Then she slipped away, agile and swift, disappearing down a narrow strip between two buildings.

Mercer and I hurried after her. By the time we turned the corner to glimpse through the portal to the past, nothing remained of it but a shrinking sphere of glimmering light.

Lon yerwev. Be brave.

The twitters of the dawn birds seemed to echo Callista. I stretched, dismissing the regret brought on by the sense of a squandered opportunity. I knew Callista would not have allowed Mercer or me to travel back and undo what was already done. If she wouldn't even go back in time to undo losing her daughter in the first place, then she knew a heavy cost came with convoluting history.

A succulent smell drew me out of my thoughts. I opened my eyes to find Kadri hunkered down by the fire, roasting a plump rabbit on a spit. A bow and a quiver crowded with white-tipped arrows lay at her side.

"Did you go hunting?" I asked, my voice husky with sleep.

"I did," she said, defiance obscured in her placid tone.

"You're supposed to be resting."

"I was hoping to prove my worth so you wouldn't be rid of me like a pair of torn, crusty stockings," she said. Afterward, she bit her bottom lip and avoided my gaze.

"How did you know—?" I asked.

"The astrikane." She attempted to subdue a feverish shiver. "It's the only vision I've had that's been less than delightful. It must have really wanted to warn me I was about to get packed up and shipped back to Beyrian."

"I'm sorry, Kadri," I said, glancing at Mercer for a little help. He was still asleep, of course. "I promise, I intended to convince you. We weren't going to tie you up and force you. Where did you get the bow?"

"I traded for it."

"*We*," Glisette amended, returning from refilling the skins. "We gave the peddler an astrikane leaf and a lock of hair from each of us." She ran her fingers through a short, blunt section behind her ear before tucking it away.

Instinctively, I reached up and found that a lock of my hair had been cut from my nape. Swallowing hard, I told myself this was not the time to engage Glisette in argument. She resented me for failing to tell her about Callista before she had departed forever, citing the fact that she too was a descendant, though she couldn't quite determine how many *greats* came before *granddaughter*.

Glisette and Kadri both crossed their arms, inviting me to rebuke them. I snubbed the bait, choosing instead to appraise our surroundings. The morning still looked like night. The sky was a gray-purple bowl trimmed with fire, the moon nearly perfectly round but for a sliver of darkness cutting into it. The camp of strangers we'd chosen to imperil thanks to the urgent aches in our bellies remained sleeping and shrouded in mist, but I knew not for long.

"How many astrikane leaves do we have left?" I asked.

"Three," Kadri answered.

"Three?" I repeated. "And have you been treated this morning?"

Kadri shook her head. That strange pallor roosted behind her russet cheeks, and her black hair had relinquished its enviable luster. While Glisette watched the roasting meat like a wolf watching a lamb frolic, Kadri refused to look directly at it and breathed through her mouth to block the smell.

"Kadri…" I said softly, and she faced me, her remonstration crumpling. The sore on her neck didn't seem any better than yesterday, and I thought I smelled a staleness. I fought the temptation to hide my face inside my collar. "I will not bury you out here."

"I know," she said, wrapping her arms around her knees. "I understand."

Unfortunately, the decision wasn't ours to make. We waited by the road long enough to snatch the attention of a coach traveling south, but it already bore two passengers. The driver insisted he would travel no farther than the border due to the danger of illness, and he doubted any drivers would feel differently. "Besides that, I've heard the border tolls are getting steeper, and a dead elicromancer's jewel won't satisfy the guard," the coachman finished, sealing Kadri's fate.

As the snap of reins whisked the coach down the rutted road,

Glisette said, "I hope the Moth King gives Ambrosine a magnificent horse that shits right on her shoes."

"It'll more likely be some sort of mythical gryphon," I muttered sourly.

"All the better. Should we wait for the next coach? We can walk back to the village and buy a portrait of me and I'll start giving royal commands. I've missed wielding power."

"Not to underestimate your influence, but I don't even think a threat of execution could have forced that driver over the border," I said.

"So, what now?" she asked.

The three of us looked at Kadri, who seemed to want to curl into herself like a hibernating creature.

"We walk," Mercer said, massaging sleep from his eyes.

"And we don't trust anyone," I said, echoing his mandate. "Unless that anyone happens to be an ancestor who walks through portals from one age to another. Or an elicrin Healer we stumble upon in the depths of the forest…"

"If this journey has proven anything, it's that the unexpected can happen," he said.

Kadri slipped an astrikane leaf onto her tongue and waited for us to plunge into the tight-knit greens of the expansive forest.

Kadri only slowed us down when the visions overcame her. A shiny seal of dreaminess would slide across her eyes and she would snake around the trail the other three of us had blazed, murmuring to apparitions and smiling at phantoms. Rayed's name tore out of her lips once in anger and distress, and we understood she had seen a vision of his betrayal. Glisette explained the attack at the summer cottage in more detail, and I didn't have to look back to know that the news of Rayed's treachery came as a powerful shock to Kadri.

She was quiet after that and somehow kept pace, which fooled me into forgetting that an astrikane leaf was plucked off and used each day—until we had arrived at the third day and none remained and there was no forgetting it.

On that day, my mind began to proffer strange visions as well. It wasn't for lack of food or water; with Kadri's bow and the fresh streams that carved through the forest, we made do.

But I began to fancy that the trees grew taller and wider as we walked, and that they spread farther apart, each the undisputed ruler of her own kingdom. Flitting shapes visited my periphery without lingering to introduce themselves. The flowers and toad-stools in our path grew vivid in color and glittered with fat, impossible drops of dew. No one remarked on the changes until suddenly we stood in a corridor of trees so immense that it would take more than three dozen linked arms to encircle one of their trunks, and a yellow flower bigger than my head suddenly flung itself into my path.

"Where are we? It feels like there's someone here," Glisette whispered.

"You see this too?" Kadri asked, cupping an enormous white flower with purple leaves and a spattering of pink freckles.

I realized then that the sun was creeping away from its center point in the wrong direction—that *we* were moving in the wrong direction. We were supposed to be walking north with the sun bearing down on our left by now. I had been meticulous enough to use a guiding stick for most of the journey, but today the sun glared so brightly through the canopies that I hadn't. Somehow I'd managed to veer us off course.

A massive dark shape cantered between the trees straight ahead. Panic beset me until I realized it was a horse. The markings on his hide revealed that it was one the blights had commandeered. Last we saw those horses, they were wild-eyed and tormented. But this one swung his head to blink lazily at us. His gleaming black mane and tail had been plaited into neat nets strung with flowers. He flicked the tail in lethargic satisfaction before trotting forward and greeting me with a wet nibble on the forehead.

"How—?" I started.

A vine crawled over the toe of my boot with a life of its own, lashing around my ankle. Rustling behind me suggested that the others were encountering the same problem. I struggled to pry the sinewy green bonds from around my limbs to no avail and ripped out my dagger before it was too late.

"Don't cut them," Mercer said. "The fair folk won't take kindly to that."

"Fair folk?" the other three of us echoed.

"Fay," he said. "Fairies."

A bubbling laugh with a touch of malevolence danced through the wood. One of the vines slithered around my neck. My every instinct told me to rip it away, but Mercer said, "Stay calm. If we don't put on a show, they'll get bored and set us free. I think."

A clean whistle bit through the birdsongs. Far from perturbed by the sentient vines, the horse circled around and trotted back the way he'd come. When a vine decided to slide across my eyes, I couldn't take it any longer. I thrashed violently.

"Mercer Fye." At the sound of the melodic but thistly male voice, the creeping vines relented. "You're punctual."

TWENTY-SIX

EVEN when the vines fell slack, disencumbering myself turned out to be no easy feat. The skirmish ripped off the bandage covering my stitched wound, which started it throbbing again.

Finally, I wriggled my lower half free of the entrapment and turned my attention to our host. He was a tall man, even taller than Mercer, and slender, with tapered ears and cunning eyes the color of murky green lake water. His long hair was ash blond in the shadows and gold as honey in the light, and the veins that corded his sinewy frame were deep green rather than blue or purple. He wore a loose-woven rugged green tunic and robe.

"Forgive me, friend. I do not know your name as you know mine." Mercer took a wary step that positioned him between the newcomer and the rest of us.

"Theslyn," the stranger replied, petting the horse's muzzle. The animal leaned into his touch. "I'm here to welcome you. But the mortal will not be allowed to enter without drinking the nectar. And you all must bathe."

"Where are we?" I asked. My voice seemed loud.

"You'll never be able to find it again, so the name matters not."

"The hidden fay dwelling," Mercer answered. "Wenryn."

With the edge of a smile on his face, Theslyn turned and started forward.

"Are we in danger?" I whispered to Mercer as we followed him.

"The fay are complicated creatures, but they're not treacherous. We're not in physical danger."

"What other kind of danger is there?"

"I would urge you to relax, Lady Braiosa," Theslyn said. "The nectar works best when one is receptive to it."

"I'm merely confused," I replied. "The fay are supposed to be extinct. I know many descendants, fairies who perform simple charms, but..."

"We fair folk have our ways of lingering in the ancient places."

"But...why are you showing yourselves to us?"

"We are flowers that bloom in the night," he said over his shoulder. "For only the stars to see."

Mercer's eyes narrowed to slits.

"Did my grandmother come here? Juniper Braiosa?" I asked.

"The more questions you ask, the less they'll tell you," Mercer said in a low voice.

We came upon a meadow bordered by gigantic trees. The other five horses that had escaped from the blights grazed alongside speckled deer.

"Have you happened to see a large deerhound?" I asked Theslyn, considering for the first time that Calanthe might have been set loose rather than stolen. "Gray, female?"

"I regret to say no," he responded, but he didn't sound invested in her fate. "Did you lose her?"

"She was taken, I think," I said darkly.

"It's clear you've seen difficult times. Here, you have no choice but to lay aside your burdens."

Mercer's eyes shot to mine. It wasn't exactly a warning look along the lines of *Let's take him down and get the blazes out of here*, but it communicated a level of distrust, which made me restless as we drew near a stream.

Theslyn approached a twisted tree with a wooden spout tucked into one of its many folds. Beneath the spout sat a wide wooden bowl filled with a sticky orange liquid. He dipped a dainty ladle shaped like a leaf into the tree nectar and turned his clever eyes on Kadri. A hard green hope ripened in the back of my mind. Could this ancient magic do as much for her as a Healer?

He brought the ladle to Kadri and, without even the dawn of a question on her lips, she let him tip the nectar into her mouth. She drank deeply, gripping the handle to serve herself at her own pace, until Theslyn laughed and said, "Don't be hasty, my delicious darling. A little will restore the color to your cheeks. But too much will poison you with happiness, which you will miss after you leave. The ache inside would be too great to bear."

"Valory," Mercer said, beckoning me forward. "You're next."

"You three will be given some later," Theslyn said. "It will cloud your minds, and your minds must be keen."

"For what?" I asked.

"I'm afraid we must be going," Mercer said firmly, clasping Kadri's hand to pull her along. She looked thoughtful and dazed. The blush in her cheeks rushed back like a blooming flower.

"I'm afraid you *can't* be going," Theslyn said. Other green-clad figures stepped out from the trees, all of them tall with tapered ears and ash-blond hair. I thought of Ellen, who was a tad plump and rather short, like the other fairy descendants I knew. Those with enough pronounced magic wielded wands made of wood from the forest. These full-blooded fairies looked nothing like them and carried no wands, and that alone unnerved me. As they were surrounding us, the disparity made me feel nothing short of threatened.

But Mercer didn't seem prepared to resist. He only frowned.

"Rynna, they're all yours," Theslyn said.

A woman with waist-length hair and freckles stepped forward. The netted green garment that clung to her body was even more artfully arranged to hide the essentials than the pink-and-silver confection Glisette had worn to the banquet in Beyrian. Her veins were green like Theslyn's, though slightly fainter, and there was something feline about her features. She approached Kadri and swept my friend's dark hair behind her shoulder. "The sickness is still within her," she said, pressing her thumb fearlessly to the unhealed sore. "She'll need more nectar, or Malyrra will expel her."

"Malyrra?" I said, unable to resist despite Mercer's warning. "My grandmother went looking for Malyrra. Did she come here? Juniper Braiosa?"

"You know what will happen if I give her more," Theslyn said to Rynna with an arch of a fair brow, ignoring me.

"And I know what will happen if you don't," Rynna said. Her green eyes were as sharp as skewers.

"What will happen?" I asked.

"The same thing that's already happening," Theslyn answered. "She'll die. The nectar will save her, but at a cost."

I bit my lip as Theslyn slid the ladle through the nectar again. He gave it to Rynna, who brought it to Kadri's lips. Unlike Theslyn,

Rynna didn't take the ladle until Kadri had emptied it. The sore on her neck became nothing but a scar.

A dense brick of fear in my chest cracked, crumbled to grains, and blew away. But there were still enough bricks inside me to build a wall. What had happened to Grandmum? Did she make it to the fay dwelling? Was she here now?

Rynna gave the cup back to Theslyn and began unlacing the neck of Kadri's tunic. "What are you doing?" I demanded.

"Undressing her to bathe," Rynna answered.

Kadri giggled and stumbled sideways a step. Rynna righted her with traces of an amused smile. This drunken, tittering version of her brought out by the nectar only made me miss the healthy and sharp Kadri even more. But at least it would wear off...the blight disease wouldn't have.

Rynna slipped off Kadri's tunic. Mercer had the manners to look away, but as another fay woman approached to work off his clothes, I nearly lost my own sense of decorum. "Can I go downstream?" he asked.

"Human men are so high-minded," the woman replied, beckoning him along in answer to his request. "So protective and possessive of the womenfolk. It's part of what makes you fun to play with, that bashful nature...."

"Lyssa..." Rynna warned, leading Kadri into the stream. "Malyrra wants to see them. You can play with them after."

Glisette set down Kadri's bow and quiver and undressed herself, more excited to bathe than she was nervous to lay down weapons and disrobe around strangers. She stepped into the stream without needing to be ushered. Meanwhile, Rynna handed Kadri off to Theslyn and approached me. "Come try the water, my dark little duckling," she said, cupping my face as she towered over me. Her scent was flowery and earthy and ancient. I sent a glance to the untended weapon beside me. "The weapons will be yours again when you leave," she added.

Resigned, I began unlacing my tunic with my right hand. Rynna noticed the wound on my left but said nothing and let me be. When I stepped into the water, which was just cool enough to refresh but not shock, I surrendered completely, using an aromatic leaf to scrub myself clean. Seeing me peel back the bandage to look at my swollen, leaking wound, Rynna returned to force it under the water, scrubbing it vigorously, as though the stitches didn't exist, or as though she didn't care that they did. I bit back a cry and snatched away, slipping on the mossy rocks underfoot.

"You have to be clean, and that's infected," she insisted, but she massaged my hand with more care now. "I'm sorry," she added. "It's been a long time since I felt pain."

She gave me light brown linen undergarments and an open-weave green dress that clung to my body like a nightgown. I tried to wriggle down the jagged front hem, which ended at my thighs while the back cascaded to my bare ankles.

I joined the other three, who had been lent variations of the same materials, and we followed Theslyn upstream into a haven bursting with flowers. Knotted trees formed hollow, earthy dwellings with curtains of vines strung across their entrances. Fern-green eyes watched us from every nook and shadow, and the grass was as soft as fur between my bare toes.

"You look nothing like the fairies I know," I said to Theslyn.

"Fay and humankind were not always fond of each other," Theslyn replied. I found myself glancing at Mercer, who wore a frigid expression. "Each side frowned upon copulation between fay and humans, but ours less so. Those of us who dabbled learned to choose the humans whose traits would cover our tracks: short, rotund, plain. That way, our mixed offspring did not face the danger of being murdered or abandoned in the woods when humans suspected fairy blood. Over time, the fairy magic became diluted enough that humans began to accept the species they knew to be 'fairies' and forgot those of us who lurk in the deep wood."

I thought of the captive redheaded fairy the Moth King had sent to Ambrosine. Tilmorn had said she was full-blooded, but I wondered if that had been a lie.

Rynna stepped out from a cavern at the base of one of the ancient trees. "Malyrra will see them now," she said. "But leave the foreign girl with me. She can barely stay upright."

Kadri hiccupped in response, and again I noticed the genesis of a smile on Rynna's face. I didn't like it. I couldn't decide whether the expression was amused or predatory.

"I'll go with her," Glisette muttered before following Rynna. "I think you two are the guests of honor."

"They'll be fine," Mercer whispered, nudging me along as Theslyn beckoned us into the maw of the tree, where steps led to a mossy pedestal that looked a bit like a throne.

On the throne sat Malyrra, whose hair was as white as winter snow on a clear day, her skin the color of the tree that sheltered her. One of her eyes was dewdrop-blue, the other burnished gold. She didn't look like an old woman, but by the dignity of her presence I

knew she was centuries older than what even the oldest elicromancer I personally knew would call young.

"Malyrra survived Emlyn Valmarys's first reign," Theslyn said.
"We fairies change with every season, and from day to night, like
nature itself. When he laid waste to the fields and forests, it confounded her faculties. She can only live in the trees and close to
the earth, where her body and spirit do not have to fight as hard to
adapt to changing conditions."

A warm, pleasant breeze swirled in the mouth of the cavern.
Both of Malyrra's eyes flickered green before turning blue and gold
once more, though this time on opposite sides. Old folklore did
say fairies changed with the seasons, their skin darkening in the
summer while their eyes became the color of a bluebell. In autumn
their hair turned fiery red, and some people still teased redheaded
children, calling them the fruits of the fairy autumn harvest cele-
brations. Pulling their hair was said to bring good luck.

Malyrra shifted on her throne and spoke in the old tongue.

"I will speak for her," Theslyn said. "She doesn't know your
language."

"Does she know my grandmother?" I asked, desperate for
answers.

Malyrra spoke again, and Theslyn translated. "She came here
recently," he said. "We told her what her kind had awoken. And
then she left without drinking the nectar. She did not say where she
was going."

"Why did she come to you?" I asked. "How did she know you
were here?"

"The elders of Darmeska can be trusted," Theslyn answered on his own. "They know enough of our history to respect our secrets and ways. Your questions, though, will tire Malyrra."

I sealed my lips. Malyrra began again, her tone hollow and dark.

"'Emlyn Valmarys was my grandson,'" Theslyn translated.

Mercer and I turned to each other in awe.

"'His mother was a fairy,'" Theslyn went on, speaking over her as he translated. "'His father was an elicromancer. The union of an elicromancer and a fairy was entirely unheard of...the power that child would wield could destroy kingdoms. But my daughter fell in love with an elicromancer. Even we fairies, who do not judge, tried to stop her. She hid her pregnancy for several moons, then made herself scarce in the woods and gave birth alone. She brought the child to our dwelling here and was never seen again. Perhaps she knew what she had done. The father was executed by his own kind.'"

Malyrra paused and resituated herself. I sensed a deep ache in her bones, in her very marrow.

"'We knew we could not keep the child," Theslyn continued. "'We do not have many rules. We live within the framework of nature. We respect it. But otherwise, we are a whim-driven folk. We knew that if we could find an elicromancer who would accept Emlyn and hide his secret, he could be trained and learn to restrain his power. We found a man and woman, elicromancers who agreed to take him and raise him as their own in seclusion, to keep him away from the source of all elicrin power and help him practice control.

"'But not so many years later, the rumors penetrated the woods. We heard of a man who called himself Lord of Elicromancers, a man who indiscriminately murdered creatures of every species. A dark feeling pierced my soul. I knew that it was Emlyn.

"'Elicromancers and mortals made many attempts to vanquish him. They did not succeed until they struck the bargain with sea witches. The time-walker arrived and rescued the one the elicromancers had chosen to sacrifice.'" Her shifting eyes landed on Mercer. "'She made a sacrifice out of the elicromancer leader, disemboweled him, tied his innards in knots as he suffered. To complete the contract, the time-walker had to penetrate Emlyn's lair. We hid in the wilds to protect our own, but she found us and sought our help.

"'We sent three of our own as fairy slaves to be traded for reward. The time-walker posed as a traitor to her elicromancer kind. Together they won him over, and the fairy "slaves" prepared a feast, disguising the innards as food for Emlyn and his men. The sea witch magic took hold immediately, and Emlyn and his servants became like stone, trapped around their banquet table. Their mountain court became a tomb.'"

My mouth dropped as Theslyn and Malyrra spoke. Callista *had* done what needed to be done—what we'd asked of her and far more. Malyrra's voice seemed to scratch over the text of my history books, scrawling horrid details in the margins of the pages that boasted of my forebears' heroics.

"'Afterward, elicromancers cleared mortals' memories of Emlyn's atrocities. They hid the contract in his lair and set traps to thwart anyone who sought it. I vowed that, should Emlyn ever rise again, my people would help end his reign forever. And that is why we have taken you in, and your grandmother before you. You are welcome here. It is a safe place, for the time being, and our nectar heals wounds inside and out.'"

Once she finished speaking in Old Nisseran, Malyrra's eyes fluttered closed. Theslyn touched the back of her hand with his long, slender fingers. "She needs rest now."

"Thank you for helping us," I said, with a slight bow. Mercer said nothing and left the tree dwelling without another word.

"Make yourselves at home," Theslyn said to me, watching Mercer with an impassive expression. "Eat and drink anything you wish, and go anywhere you like. But don't drink too much of the tree nectar or you will regret it."

"Thank you," I repeated, and followed Mercer into the sunlight, my thoughts reeling. The fairies were minding their own business, some picking fruits as others arranged them on massive platters. Some wove clothing, and some carried laundry from the streams and hung it on branches to dry. They were busy, but also unhurried, free of worry or strain.

"You might have shown her a touch of respect," I said, catching up to Mercer. "She wants to help us."

"Her kind retreated to safety while Valmarys tortured and killed thousands of innocent people, even though he was *one of them*. They hid in their haven while the rest of us kept fighting to keep this realm from perishing at his hand, while others designed a plan to take him down. The fay are selfish and capricious and have no sense of responsibility."

"I think they do, but...just different from ours," I said. "If their calling is to maintain a place like this—to refuse to let darkness and human ambition and evil touch this little pocket of the world—who's to say that's not a noble cause? It's certainly proved useful for us. And they helped Callista…finish things," I added euphemistically.

"That whole bit was rather startling, wasn't it?" he asked.

"I found it encouraging."

He quirked a brow.

"Callista is a famous hero," I explained. "You saw for yourself that she was noble and good, and she risked her life to save you. The heroes carved in stone and written about in books seem so immaculate, as if they've never had to dirty their hands to seize victory. But Callista was ruthless when she had to be, terrifyingly so. Your vision of me depicted bloody deeds. Now I know that…"

"One can be ruthless for good reason?" he supplied. "I didn't suspect you would act out of malice or evil. Not in the least. But it's difficult, once I see something like that in someone's future, to unsee it. I'm afraid for you, what you will endure…"

"Don't fear for me," I said, squeezing his arm. He looked down at my hand. If we could rid ourselves of our hounding fears for even a moment, would other feelings race to occupy the vacancy? I studied him, trying to guess what emotion he felt. His hair was tousled and damp. His dark, straight eyebrows and fathomless eyes brought intensity to an otherwise sprightly face. Feeling indulgent, I pored over little details: how the sculpted curves and peaks of his lips offset the strong cut of his jaw, how fine and feathery the hair was that bordered each of his ears. The most thrilling detail was something that had changed, something in his eyes: our linked gazes possessed something mighty all of a sudden, like a glare of sunlight off a mirror.

A vertical line worked its way between his eyebrows, and embarrassment overcame me in a hot wave. I dropped my arm and looked around for Kadri and Glisette. I found them sitting with Rynna at one of many long slabs of gray rock positioned at the far side of the dell. Others were setting platters of fruit, vegetables, and breads on the rock tables along with flagons of wine. I glanced up to see a pink dusk settling in. The birdsongs were giving way to beetle chirps, and a flute seamlessly joined the entrancing ballad of a peaceful spring evening.

"I wish I didn't have to worry about anything," I found myself saying.

Mercer opened his mouth to reply, but Theslyn beat him to it as he passed us by. "Then don't," he said, flashing me a mischievous look. "Come. I think your friend may forgive us after he sees how we welcome our guests."

"Shall we?" Mercer asked, surrendering to the allure of food and wine. No one could resist after the journey we'd endured, regardless of prejudices.

Other fair folk crowded around the table, laughing and talking and drinking and sipping juice from succulent fruits. By the time Mercer and I arrived, there were only two seats left to claim, so I nestled between Glisette and Rynna.

"There you are, dark little duckling," Rynna said, handing me a small wooden cup of nectar. "That should heal your wounds."

I glanced over her at Kadri, whose eyes shimmered. She bit into a fruit with relish and leaned in to whisper something in Rynna's other ear. They laughed together and Rynna stroked Kadri's raven hair. This wasn't the Kadri I knew—in fact, this was the furthest she'd wandered from her recognizable self—giggling and enamored of someone she had just met, and a woman at that.

"What else will it do to me?" I asked.

"Not much," Rynna answered, turning back to me. "That's just enough to bring you to the cusp of euphoria for a short while. You'll need a little wine to help it last the night."

I looked across the table to Mercer, who sat next to Lyssa, the one who had bathed him earlier. She offered him a cup of nectar. I doubted he would partake at all, until he gave me an encouraging nod and took a drink. I did the same. It tasted like honey and fruit juice but better than both, sour and sweet and divine. It slaked an inner thirst I didn't even know I possessed.

The wheel of dour thoughts and worries spinning in my mind slowed and dropped off its axis. Before I knew it, the last taste was gone. I licked it from my lips and heard myself asking for more.

Rynna laughed. "You don't need more. Look around. You will see and want everything. Oh, let me pull those out."

She released Kadri and cradled my hand, yanking concisely at the stitches with her fingernails as the bite wound healed. I felt an uncomfortable tugging but no pain as the cut sealed itself into a tight scar. Rynna wrapped her arm back around Kadri and whispered to make her laugh again, a deep and wholesome laugh that suddenly made everything feel all right.

"The lights are lovely," Glisette said, tilting her head back to look. I followed her gaze to the floating constellations of small incandescent lanterns, anchored by some carefree bit of magic.

It was as if an invisible second eyelid had peeled from my eyes and now I could see beauty in everything. The fruits were cut to resemble flowers, and I bit into edible flowers that tasted like aromatic fruits. The wine was oaky and round. I tore into an open-textured bread filled with berries and nuts and found it softer than the softest pillow beneath my thumb. When I met Kadri's eyes, she no longer seemed drunk or lost, but alert and rightfully enraptured by everything around her.

It occurred to me that in spite of Fabian's good looks and charm, Kadri had never claimed to desire him. And Fabian didn't seem to expect desire. She implied that they had an arrangement that worked for them both. She had not felt threatened by his attraction to other women, but by what the attraction might cost her. And now I saw everything it *could* cost her: not just a future as queen, but the freedom to be herself, knowing her husband wouldn't abandon her for it.

Maybe she wasn't the furthest from herself that I had seen—maybe before this awakening, I had wandered the furthest from *me*.

When I'd had my fill of food and Theslyn reached over to replenish my wine, I glanced up and saw Lyssa perching on Mercer's lap, pressing her hips into him and splaying her hands on either side of his face. Her plump lips were a hair's breadth from touching his, and his broad hands hovered over her. It took several seconds for dismay to cut through the haze of wonder in my spirit, and when it did, I didn't know how to receive it.

"Aren't elicromancers forbidden?" Mercer asked, breathless. He was resisting her, but whether it was out of disinterest or a desire to prolong pleasure, I couldn't say.

Lyssa slid her fingers along the chain holding his elicrin pendant, skimming his neck and chest. How was it that she had so easily and swiftly won the right to touch him? Had I only to try to be permitted? Why did that possibility feel so inadequate and hollow?

"We're forbidden to copulate," Lyssa said into his ear. "But not to touch. Doesn't that make it all the more fun?"

"I told you to stop worrying."

I looked up and saw Theslyn next to me in Glisette's former seat. Glisette was dancing under the lights.

"That's like telling me to stop breathing," I said, lifting the wine to my lips almost as a reflex. I cleared my throat and twirled a dainty yellow flower between my thumb and forefinger. Theslyn watched me. "Why did Rynna call me a dark little duckling?"

He laughed. "Did she?"

"Yes."

"I don't know about the duckling part," he said. "But you *are* dark."

I tested my lips for a last taste of nectar and forced myself to study the grains in the gray rock instead of looking back to Mercer.

"There are those who only hold mornings inside them, and they are happy and simple," Theslyn said. "But you, my darling, hold the night with its wild mysteries and twinkling secrets. If you would wear the cloak of darkness more proudly, you would be surprised at how it augments your beauty." I noticed that his eyes had taken on a peculiar brightness in the twilight—one of the many ways the fair folk adapted, I supposed.

Theslyn's warm fingers trailed along my forearm. I closed my eyes and thought of the relish with which I'd broken the necks of the blights. The power had felt exquisite.

Something inside me had changed. But Mercer's vision had

made me fear that change. I had locked it out in the cold, yet it knocked and knocked, a persistent peddler selling self-acceptance at a price.

Theslyn faced me, straddling the bench. "You are a beautiful human," he said, using a curled knuckle to tilt my chin. I leaned into his touch, finding myself receptive to it, even eager for it. With my encouragement, he brushed his thumb across the dip in my bottom lip. I blinked my eyes open, entranced by his mystical beauty.

The journey his lips took to reach mine seemed like a century of torment, and even when they touched, his damp mouth, tasting of nectar, barely brushed across mine. "We do not hide our desires here," he whispered as we shared breath. "We give them the freedom to guide us."

With another affectionate stroke of his knuckle along my chin, he slipped away, flinging a meaningful glance across the table before joining the crowd.

Breathless, I followed his fleeting look to find both Mercer and Lyssa gone.

Leaving the balmy glow of the feast, I wandered into the trees until the lights from the revelry faded to a soft glow. My steps were unsure, as though I might be floating instead of walking. I found a tree whose mossy, twisted base looked like several nurturing arms inviting me in, and sat down, and curving myself to its cradle.

As the nectar began to wear off, the claw of Mercer's rejection didn't just sink into me. It dug deep, dredging up past hurts: Ander accusing me of killing Ivria, his eyes two shields of fire instead of refuges of brotherly love; Rayed setting me up to look guilty of Brandar's death; my father abandoning me when he could no longer let the palace walls hem him in, and my mother's subsequent abandonment of me during my grief for the thrill of fresh passion; Ivria touching her toes to the Water when she knew I would suffer unimaginable sorrows without my sister at my side.

I heard the rustle of steps in the soft undergrowth. A few of the fairy lights seemed to have pursued Mercer and bobbed over his head as he approached. I stood up.

"I resisted Lundy touching me like that so many times because... because it wasn't right," he said. "And now I—it's not as if I want *her* specifically. The touch of a woman is something I didn't even know I desired so fiercely before, in the midst of the terrors—"

"I don't know why you feel you need to explain this to me, Mercer," I said, but when I got around to uttering his name, my rigid tone became unconvincing. It was a savory shape in my mouth, magic dancing on my tongue.

He shut his lips like someone shutting a door in the midst of undressing, embarrassed. "Um," he said. "I don't know why, but I felt as though I'd wronged you...perhaps I mistook your..." He trailed off.

A silence yawned, but the nocturnal insects and hoots of owls raced to fill it. "I thought you didn't like what you saw," he finished.

I looked up at him and found a steady, heated gaze that could liquefy gold. "I *didn't* like it," I said, my voice quavering with the power of the plain truth. "I don't want anyone else to touch like you that."

"And is it because *you* want to touch me like that?" he asked huskily, propping his hands on the tree behind me. His breath skimmed down my neck and ignited every nerve in my body. "At the outset of our journey, I lay awake at night imagining it, even though I didn't want to. My dreams of you feel so real they might as well be visions. Tell me you want me."

"I want you," I whispered, my breath hitching as the hollow of his hand found its way to the back of my thigh.

"Your wrath withers grass and crumbles stone. Think of what your joy could do. . . ." He grazed his lips against the base of my neck and whispered, "Your *ecstasy.*"

Unwilling to wait any longer, I crushed my lips against his, drawing him close so I could feel the heat of his skin through the meager fabric of our tunics. We intertwined, one of his arms encircling my waist and the other cradling my nape, his touch like velvet. My hands gripped his face before sliding down, grappling to pull him ever closer. My lips and tongue fought to taste the cool spring of his mouth more deeply, spurred on by his clear desire to devour me.

"Valory," he whispered, my name a seal of fervor on his lips. "Look."

I released him just enough to turn my gaze to the surrounding twilight. New, pure white blossoms erupted from the spindly tree branches above. The mossy trunks spurted bright yellow flowers and the enchanted lights danced about them. The trees themselves bowed away from us, clearing a black sky holding a ripe, full moon, which the stars themselves seemed to gaze upon with awe.

Mercer laughed and collected me in his grasp once again. I knew that no matter what came, I would hold this moment forever, unchanging, an ever-burning lamp of goodness to light the path ahead.

❧ TWENTY-SEVEN ❧

A CATLIKE stretch worked its way through my limbs, filling me with shivers of delight. Even when the effects of the nectar had waned, every touch and kiss felt like a step into uncharted lands of wonder, at least before sleep caught up with us.

Wriggling a little, I realized I was lying on a bed of leaves. A smoky fragrance flitted along a crisp wind. I curled my arms under my chest to retain the warmth of sleep. But as the musk of a new dawn flooded my senses, I felt that something was not right. This morning was, in some way or other, not what I had anticipated.

It wasn't that Mercer was far away. I could hear his breaths, somehow distinct. No, it was that I'd fallen asleep engulfed in the perfume of flowers and greenery. But this morning smelled like cool dampness and overripe fruits browning on the ground. The leaves beneath me crackled and whispered.

I opened my eyes, clearing away the fog of sleep as I rolled over. A woman with auburn hair, tapered ears, and golden eyes peered down at me. I gasped in alarm before recognizing Rynna.

"I wondered if you'd ever awaken," she said, but there was no trace of teasing in her voice. Worry threaded her every word.

I looked up to see Glisette and Kadri sprawled nearby, also stirring. The bedding of leaves beneath me was a fiery mound of scarlet, orange, and yellow. "What happened?" I asked.

"We hid you from the summer fires," Rynna answered.

"Valmarys scoured the northern stretch of the forest looking for you and burned as he went."

Her gaze glided beyond me. I followed it to a clear border ahead between the healthy, autumnal forest and a gray landscape of scorched earth.

Splaying my hands over the dry leaves, I rose to my feet. The haze of the nectar lingered, but with every step I took toward the destruction, my head cleared while the air grew murkier, stifling. The trees, stark black and white, many of them felled, flaked ashes to the wind. I paused at the border and drew my fingertip across a blackened tree. It left a charcoal stain on my skin.

"Did we sleep through the whole summer?" I heard Glisette demand as I turned to rejoin the group.

Mercer kicked a dry branch and sent it reeling to crack against a tree, reverting to Old Nisseran curses to express his anger. "Was this the plan when you took us in?" he demanded, whirling on Rynna.

Keeping her composure, Rynna answered, "We heard Valmarys had come to the forest looking for you. That's when we chose to intercept you and brought you to our dwelling, to keep you safe during this bout of his temper. The fairies of long ago, Malyrra included, swore to help you when the time came."

"But a whole season passed," Mercer said, his voice echoing in the abyss of shriveled forest. "What other horrors has Valmarys wrought in that time?"

"You don't have to like it, but we have fulfilled our duty," Rynna said, trudging back several steps to retrieve loaded packs for each of us. I realized I wore my own clothing, which had been washed and mended. My dagger sat in the sheath at my hip. We'd been unclothed and dressed and lulled to sleep like infants.

"Believe me when I say I wish I could come with you," Rynna went on, turning a melancholy smile on Kadri. "But I would perish in the burned forest after a short time. We may be immortal, but we are not a hardy folk when our surroundings suffer."

"My heart feels torn in two," Kadri said, grimacing against unshed tears. "I feel I've left my home behind yet again, but it hurts far more than before."

Rynna cupped Kadri's face. "We had to give you too much of the nectar to keep you alive. That's where this sadness comes from. It will worsen the farther you go. Sometimes you will forget it. Other times it will pierce you like an arrow. But you are alive."

"Will I ever be able to come back?" Kadri whispered.

Rynna shook her head. "I don't know. When this is done, return to the forest. Keep going until you are lost, and continue on. I will do my best to bring you back to Wenryn, but no mortal has ever been permitted to stay. I make no promises." She slid a beautifully crafted bow and a quiver full of arrows with striped green-and-black fletching from her shoulder. "Theslyn and I made this for you. The other didn't suit your draw."

She pressed the fay weapon into Kadri's hands. The smoke-tinged wind played with her auburn hair as she slid her fingers along Kadri's jaw and leaned in to bestow a chaste kiss on her lips. "I'm afraid I must leave you here," she said, pulling away slowly. "I sense the Water lies near, at least whatever remains of it, and two ancient powers crossing can be dangerous." She looked at me. "We brought you as far as we could."

"Thank you," I said, but my voice grew weak as I looked across the wasteland. I wondered how else the realm had suffered. Beyond the forest, did the fairies know what was at stake? I doubted Ambrosine's uncle and his tolls had even crossed the fair folk's minds.

I could only be comforted by the indisputable truth that no one in Arna—especially not King Tiernan—could be seduced by tawdry riches. Arnan royals took too much pride in their positions to desert responsibilities for love of jewels and silk.

"Theslyn wanted me to give you a message, Valory," Rynna said. "He said 'Don't forget your cloak.'" With a few doelike strides, she nearly melted into the vivid colors of the wood. "May victory be yours."

When she was gone, Kadri fell to her knees, dropping her bow and quiver on the rustling leaves. "I don't belong to myself, but to Wenryn. I'll never be happy again."

I knelt beside her and wrapped an arm around her shoulders. Staring ahead at the charred wilds left in the Moth King's footprint made me want to weep too, and made for a stark contrast against the fleeting euphoria of the fairy dwelling.

"I know the magic in the nectar is strong, but you are stronger," I whispered. "And you're alive, which is more than we thought to hope for before the fair folk took us in."

I looked up at Mercer and the memories rushed back, bringing color to my face.

Only my mother and Ivria had ever spoken to me about fleshly desires, and their explanations had been nothing if not parsimonious and proper. I'd learned more from what my mother hadn't wished me to see than from what she willingly shared. I had not been taught to lay my feelings bare to a man, and certainly had no idea how to approach one in the aftermath of passion. It seemed impossible to compose myself when I harbored the memory of his hands plunging into my hair and peeling the fay clothing off me, my thumbs stroking his hipbones through his thin shirt.

"We need you, Kadri," Glisette said, dropping to kneel beside us. "We need you more than you need Wenryn."

Kadri sobbed, wiped a tear, and stretched to seize the grip of her new bow. She slung the quiver strap over her shoulder and wobbled to her feet.

The four of us stared down the path ahead.

Scattered fires still burned in the deserted wasteland, violent orange waves consuming what little life remained. As we walked, I could feel the beginnings of a ravaging cough in my chest. We were drinking the water too quickly—and we certainly wouldn't find a clean source here.

I thought back to our first night, how the compactness of the map had made our journey seem as straightforward and simple as a line of black ink cutting through the forest to Darmeska. I had not projected hunger, sickness, entrapments, betrayal, thirst. My appetite for redemption had led me to believe I would somehow master my power and be ready to face my enemy by the time we arrived, like a lady running late to a ball, lacing her bodice in the carriage.

I glanced at Mercer. Anger punctuated his movements, and what few words he had uttered since Rynna left us. Glisette began to cough, a wretched sound that reminded me of an ash rake scraping along a stone hearth. Soon, a ghostly creaking groused over our heads and we noticed a swaying tree just in time to for each of us to jerk forward or back. It fell with a mighty thunder and stirred up ash that brought on more coughing.

"Everyone all right?" Mercer rasped as he skirted the debris to circle back to us. He caught my chin. My eyes watered from the haze as I looked up at him. "We can't go on like this," he said, voice booming in the stillness of decay. "We need to go around the forest."

I loosed a fathomless sigh, a sigh that told our story thus far. "Then let's cut straight west. We're closer to the coast than the hills. I think...."

"Rynna said we're near where the Water used to be," Kadri said. "Can't you know where we are based on its location?"

"It moves throughout this region of the forest," I said. "One of the many ways it tries to thwart the attentions of the unworthy."

"At least, it *used* to do that," Glisette said, but any obloquy that might have been implied was devoured by a dry cough, and we both knew that old thorn had lost its sting. It was more observation than affront.

"Either way, it's not of much help to us," Mercer said. "Let's cut straight west. We'll escape this eventually."

The rest of us mumbled our agreement, but no sooner had we started forward than we noticed a sprawling patch of live evergreen trees just ahead.

"The fires must have missed that stretch," Mercer said. "There may be fresh water somewhere in there."

The thought of filling our skins forced me to bury any suspicions that arose. My plate and goblet had always been full. But now I realized how far a person would go, how much they would risk, for a drop of water or a nibble of bread. I was suddenly grateful for Arna's time-honored tradition of allowing first-time convicted thieves to become Realm Alliance soldiers rather than headless bodies.

The border between the burned forest and the healthy patch was distinct, as if the living trees and grass had been scooped up as a whole and gently transplanted. The evergreens were so dense that I had to lower my head and wrestle with the supple branches as they flicked my cheeks. When I finally pushed through, I found my toes at the edge of a hollow of jagged black rocks.

"This used to be the Water," I whispered, my eyes skimming across the familiar clearing, snagging on the rocks where I'd found Ivria's body. Kadri drew level with me, and Glisette used her magic to bend the trees out of her path.

"Well, that's perfectly useless," she said.

"The portal," I gasped, looking across the pit to a pile of gray stones. "They destroyed it."

"Why wouldn't they?" Glisette asked, watching me circle around to stand in front of the rubble. "Who needs a door leading to nowhere?"

As I stared at the crumbled stones, I thought achingly of my mother, Ander, Ellen, Knox. What would I have found if the portal had still been standing and I had dared to pass through? My royal family members seduced by wealth and guarding treasure like greedy dragons, ordering about half-fairy slaves? Or worse, empty halls, bodies strewn across the floor, their blood all but invisible against the red carpet?

"We have to keep going," Mercer said softly, pressing his warm, large palm to my cool, small one.

I was turning to follow him when I caught a glimpse of something wooden buried amid the ruins of the portal. Detangling my fingers from his, I bent down to lift one of the heavy stones and found the carved box, the one that once held Callista's amethyst elicrin stone, peeking through a crack. I gasped and lifted away another stone.

"What is it?" Mercer asked.

When I was able to extract the box, I breathed, "I think King Tiernan put this here."

There was no other reason for it to be neatly tucked away amid the rubble. Who did he want to find it? Or had it been left here carelessly?

I opened the lid, hoping it contained the diadem, a tool to see through my enemy's cunning and lies. But it was empty. My fingers explored the velvet lining in case the precious artifact—even more precious than it had initially seemed, now that I'd met its original owner—might be concealed by a spell, but there was nothing.

"Come on," Mercer said. "We should find water."

"But why—?" Before the question took shape, the corners of the box started expanding within my grasp.

Mercer acted quickly, striking the box from my hands and yanking me back, assuming it was some sort of trap. When the box hit the ground, it rolled onto its side and continued to grow until it was roughly the height and width of a doorway.

It was a portal.

The purple velvet bunched up like a curtain. Fingers trembling, I reached out, daring to gather its edge so that I could steal a peek at what lay beyond. My heart thrummed as I wondered whether

King Tiernan might have done me the favor of creating a portal straight to Darmeska, hoping to spare me the last difficult leg of the journey and its unknown dangers. But with a nudge further I could see familiar paneled walls, a canopied bed, and a vanity inlaid with gold.

"It's my room," I whispered in awe, thrusting the curtain open.

"We're close enough to Darmeska now that to risk getting trapped in Arna would be downright imbecilic," Kadri said. "I almost died wandering the woods—I am not letting us get trapped here after all that."

I knew she was right. But I felt a tug to the other side that I couldn't resist.

Glisette pushed past us, crossing through and tiptoeing to my drawers. "I need stockings without holes."

I stepped in after her, amazed to be back in my own home, comforted to see it exactly the same, without a speck of dust. That meant Ellen and the other maids had been busy at their usual tasks. It was almost enough reassurance to allow me to turn my back on it...almost.

"We don't know whom we can trust right now," Mercer said from the other side. "But we can take the box with us in case we get desperate."

I could sense him leaning back into his old relentless efficiency. "King Tiernan must have left this here for a reason," I said.

"Maybe it was for someone else," Mercer said, taking a single step into my room. "We're just a few days away from Darmeska." He tilted my jaw with a curled finger until I was looking into his golden-brown eyes. "I'm with Kadri. It's not worth the risk."

"Neither is dying of thirst," I said, forgiving Glisette for having spent longer at the summer cottage than necessary. "I'll wait for my maid in the common room and ask her to fill our waterskins. I will hide and speak to no one but her." I looked past him to Kadri. "I swear I won't stay long."

Mercer released me and massaged the bridge of his nose. "Fine. I'll hold you to that." He stalked back through the portal to collect the empty waterskins. "I'm coming with you. Glisette, Kadri—stay here and be ready to run. If anything, *anything* feels the slightest bit awry, we're coming back and breaking this box to bits."

Kadri nodded. Glisette slammed my drawers shut, squeezing back between Mercer and me with two pairs of clean stockings. "Don't be long," she said, and pulled the curtain closed.

From this side, it looked like an ordinary window dressing.

"The common room is through here." I crossed my bedchamber, pulse aflutter, and peeked into the shared antechamber.

It was empty, but it should have *felt* emptier. Embers burned in the hearth. My first thought was that my mother or Aunt Sylvana came to sit and dwell on the ghosts that haunted this room. But then I saw the perfume bottle on the table, the slippers by the door to Ivria's chamber, the door itself flung open to reveal a new covering on Ivria's bed, rumpled and slept-in.

This made me uneasy, but I wouldn't say so to Mercer, who already looked apt to throw me over his shoulder and carry me through the portal. Who would so carelessly invade Ivria's space? Why hadn't Ellen or one of Ivria's old maids tidied the bed and put away the shoes? Most mornings, Ellen was so keen to straighten up after me that she'd start making the bed while I still occupied it.

I hurried across the suite toward the double doors leading to the corridor, but stopped, shocked to see Calanthe lying on her pallet.

She leapt up to lick my face and nuzzle against my chest, whining and whimpering with delight. I dropped to my knees, my laugh muffled as I pressed my face into her wiry coat. "How did you get here?" I whispered, pinning back her ears in disbelief.

An innocent question born of sheer wonder but followed by an alarming realization: the person who had plotted against us had been here.

"What is going on?" Mercer asked as Calanthe nearly knocked him over in glee.

I hurried to press my ear to the door. Gentle, birdlike laughter drifted down the hall. I thought I heard my mother's voice, her words indistinguishable, and cracked the door.

I heard light footsteps. Ellen turned the corner at the end of the corridor, carrying folded sheets from the laundry. I stepped out despite Mercer's whispered protests.

Ellen's mouth fell open and she bustled forward, casting a sideways glance at the open door of the ladies' tea parlor, from whence the laughter bubbled. Eyes snapping wide as hedge apples, she motioned for me to hurry back into the room.

"What are you doing here?" I whipped my head in the other direction. The warm voice with its deep timbre had the power to make this place feel like home again—or rip all hope of welcome away from me.

I found Ander at the top of the stairs, wearing his finest clothes. The emotion on his face was indecipherable, and for a moment I feared I would see a light igniting in the depths of his carnelian elicrin stone.

He started forward. Mercer, who had stepped out beside me, tensed to intervene. "Ander, please!" I said, my voice breaking in desperation, but he opened his arms, and with a gasp of joy I felt him sweep me up. I linked my arms around his neck and wept into the elegant wool covering his shoulder.

"Valory," he whispered. "Every day I've regretted what I said to you. I'm so sorry."

"You were grieving." I buried my chin in the dark curls at the back of his neck. "I never blamed you for it. I only missed you."

He set me down, and we were both beaming. "How did you get inside?" he asked, his gaze fixing on Ellen.

"Um," I said, fearing what his question insinuated and what it might mean for my maid. "I know this place front to back. You know that."

He laughed, and I felt relieved. Ellen ducked her head. "Shall I prepare her room, Your Highness?" she asked.

"Yes, of course," Ander replied. Ellen slipped past Mercer, not meeting my eyes. I couldn't blame her—I was an outlaw, wanted by the Realm Alliance.

"I see you've brought a friend to the wedding." Ander turned a stiff smile on Mercer, the look of a protective older brother surveying his sister's suitor. My spirit leapt with glee. But then his last word sank in.

"Wedding?" I repeated, entertaining dark fears of trunks arriving from a lord in the Brazor Mountains....

"Your mother's," he clarified. "That is why you risked returning, isn't it?"

I wanted to fixate on the word *risked*, but worry for my mother won out. "Who is she marrying?"

Ander laughed again. "Who else? Victor."

"Oh," I said, glancing back at Mercer to show my relief. "Ander, listen: Glend Neswick is a Summoner, a traitor. He—"

"We know what he is. Everything's under control. Just try not to stir up trouble, and you'll receive the welcome you deserve." Ander squeezed my arm reassuringly. "I've been summoned to greet a few overly punctual attendees. Borrow anything you need for your guest from my wardrobe and if anyone asks, say you're both here by my invitation. There's much to tell you, but we'll get around to that." He smiled. "My father sent me up to see if your mother is ready. Will you make sure she's hurrying along?"

"Of course."

With another gratified grin and a tight embrace, he strode back toward the staircase leading to the principal floor.

"We're going now," Mercer whispered from behind me. His words tickled my ear, arousing vestiges of desire. His hands reached around my waist.

"But my mother," I said, turning in his embrace and gripping his forearms. "I have to see her...."

I trailed off, an unsettling realization emerging. The relief of knowing that the Moth King had not lured her into a mysterious betrothal had blinded me to an aggravating truth.

"What's wrong?" Mercer asked.

"The only reason my mother never married Victor in the past is that he's not noble. He doesn't have land or a title. Marrying him would force her to abdicate her bid for the throne—and mine."

"Not to trivialize your birthright," he replied, "but your claim to the throne is not our greatest concern. This could be an intentional distraction, a snare set by the Moth King."

"Or maybe there's a simple explanation," I countered. "Perhaps King Tiernan bestowed land and a title on Victor so they could marry."

I felt even more acutely the need to speak to my mother and garner reassurances. I imagined my happiness as a cup that Ander had filled to the brim by greeting me with fraternal warmth, but I couldn't quite contain it. It leaked, drop by drop, from a secret hole in the bottom. "She's right there," I said, gesturing to the parlor from where the laughter had come.

"You can't—" Mercer began.

"Wait for me in my room," I interrupted, peeling away from him. "Ask Ellen to fill the waterskins. I'll be along shortly. I promise."

Clearly miffed, he stepped back inside and swung the door shut.

I padded to the open doors of the parlor. My mother sat at the center of a gaggle of ladies, wearing a wine-red dress, her rich dark hair woven in braids and curls. The others wore gowns of pure, soft white: Grandmother Odessa, Aunt Sylvana, and a few courtiers, including Jovie Neswick.

What was Jovie Neswick doing in my mother's boudoir on her wedding day? Was it charity? A response to the poor girl's family falling to ruin when her father's shameful deeds had been made evident?

Jovie was the first to notice that I wasn't another clothier or servant. She smiled, surprised. "Ameliana," she said, calling my mother by her first name, "look who's arrived!"

"Valory!" my mother gasped, parting the little crowd so she

could embrace me. After all my worrying, I longed for the warmth and comfort of her arms, but felt only the rib-gouging pressure of her structured bodice. "How did you get here?"

"You're marrying Victor?"

"Darling, we love each other," she answered dreamily. "Don't look so shocked."

"They've been carrying on their lurid affair for years," Odessa said. I'd never been permitted to call her Grandmother to her face, but Ivria and I had developed the habit in private. "They're finally doing what they ought."

I opened my mouth to bring up my birthright. Odessa of all people should have known what was at stake, and had assured my mother in the past that marrying Victor would be unwise. But I noticed that Odessa's ametrine elicrin stone had disappeared from her pale, youthful throat. Her grayish eyes looked distant as she combed her fingers through my mother's artfully arranged tresses. I shut my mouth.

"Come with me," my mother said, ushering me out the door. "We must find you something to wear."

When she shut the door behind us, I said, "Please tell me King Tiernan has given Victor a title."

"King Tiernan," she repeated, attempting to pull me across the hall to my room. "No. No, he didn't."

"Then why are you marrying Victor?" I asked, resisting her. "Don't you know what this means?"

"Darling, isn't the throne the least of your worries? With the extended age of surrender, you never would have been queen in your lifetime anyway." Her tone was vague and casual, but her gray eyes pierced, setting me on edge. She gripped my wrist, digging her nails into my skin.

"But I—" I started, and she dug in harder, as if to silence me. "What's wrong?" I whispered.

Aunt Sylvana emerged from the room, the others shuffling behind her. My mother schooled her features into a calm expression.

"The guests will be arriving soon, Ameliana, and we must not keep them waiting," Sylvana said.

"You can look in my wardrobe for something to wear, Valory," Jovie offered. "I'm happy to have you as a roommate."

"Roommate?" I echoed.

"I'm in the room across from yours," she said, as though it had been vacant previously. "I always envied the pupils who lived in the dormitories together, how much fun they must have had." She cradled an emerald jewel around her neck—the abandoned elicrin stone she used to wear to balls. "I'll see you down there."

I glared at Jovie. My mother released me, leaving marks on my skin. "Valory, *hurry*, dear," she said. "It doesn't matter what you wear, as long as it gives you the freedom to *move*. Sore feet and cumbersome skirts are no excuse to avoid dancing at your own mother's wedding. Now, *go*. Quickly."

The hidden meaning of her commands and their urgency alarmed me. Her order was veiled enough that I could choose to obey the surface meaning rather than the deeper one she truly wished to convey, but I had to *hurry* and I had to *go*.

I darted across the hall and slammed the door of my suite behind me. The compulsion of her command was satisfied, though I knew *she* wouldn't be.

"Something's not right, Mercer," I said, crossing the room to meet him. "I think my mother is being forced to marry."

"By whom?" he asked, unfolding his arms.

"I don't know. Someone behind her in line for the throne, perhaps? Otherwise, what would they have to gain?"

"We are on a mission, Valory. You saw the forest. That will be this whole realm if you don't kill Emlyn Valmarys, and soon. We've already wasted enough time."

"I just need to understand what's happening," I insisted.

"And when you understand it, you'll want to stay long enough to stop it."

"Where's Ellen? Maybe she can explain."

"Filling our waterskins."

"We'll ask her what's amiss."

"No, Valory," Mercer said, catching my arm and pulling me back to him. "You are imperiling our whole mission."

"Our victory is certain. Isn't that why we're on this horrible journey in the first place? Can you not abide a short delay for something so important?"

Mercer slid his hands from my shoulders to my hips. I felt that pull in my body again, that feeling as if he'd fastened a hook deep in my belly to draw me toward him. He bowed his head to kiss me, his mouth warm on mine. Heat consumed me from the inside out. I considered the soft surfaces nearby, every silky cushion where I might invite our bodies to touch skin to skin, where I could see him propping himself over me and peeling off my tired clothes lace by lace and button by button. It was just a fantasy, of course, and that realization was punctuated by his pulling away just as I melted into him.

"It's not certain," he whispered, stepping back.

"What?"

"When I said I saw you stabbing the Moth King in the heart, I lied. I did see you destroying his court. But I didn't see the moment of victory I described. My visions don't coddle me. Sometimes they show me more than I care to know, other times they show me just enough to point me in a direction, to help me put pieces together and take action—"

"You aren't certain that I kill him?" The tone of my voice frightened even me. Mercer winced against the barely controlled rage.

"But I knew it, from the moment I met you," he said. "You were in other visions, visions that showed me your power. You needed to believe it was certain to come with me. I was going to tell you the truth: that I believed but didn't *know*. But you were so insecure, so unsure of yourself, with so little command over your power or desire to use it—"

"So you took the choice away from me? Why tell me? Why now? Why didn't you just keep parading me north, your little fool on her supposedly sacred mission?"

"Because I couldn't keep lying to you, not after we..."

"It took putting your lips to mine to grow a conscience?"

"You can be furious at me when we're back in the woods. You don't ever have to speak to me again. But I know—not because I've seen it explicitly, because I have faith in you and your power—that you will kill Emlyn Valmarys. He will be nothing but a pile of ash to tread on when you're done."

"He's not the one who should fear my wrath right now," I growled, the power deep in my bones coming to life.

"Valory…" Mercer tried to touch a lock of hair that hung in my face. I wanted to break his fingers but settled for pulling away.

"Go," I said. "Go back to the woods and tell Glisette and Kadri the truth. See if they will still risk everything to deliver me to Darmeska."

He hesitated, the pain on his face plain to see. I felt bereft and broken, but indignation deformed these feelings into a pounding anger that could strip this palace to its ancient foundations.

"You're the only one who—"

"I said *go*, you deceitful worm," I whispered, each word sharper than the last. Mercer stalked back to my bedchamber. Through the open door, I saw him enter the portal and yank the curtain shut behind him.

❧ TWENTY-EIGHT ❧

COLLECTED myself, exhaled the anger, and abandoned the suite that no longer belonged to me, or even to Ivria's memory.

I had changed into a plain black dress with an ivory panel down the bodice, a bit too simple for a wedding. It pained me to select from Jovie Neswick's gowns when they occupied Ivria's wardrobe, so I'd chosen the first one I touched. I still wore my boots underneath and secured my dagger at my hip.

I couldn't imagine remaining here with everything that had changed, but neither could I cross back through the portal to rejoin the others on a mission whose ending was up to interpretation. I was a vagabond, a wanderer, like my father, on a desperate pilgrimage to nowhere.

Would Kadri and Glisette give up on the quest now that Mercer had returned to tell them the truth? Would they come through the portal and leave everything we'd fought for behind, hailing carriages to their respective homes, nestling in the protective bosom of wealth and status while the realm wasted away? Would Mercer continue charting his course, alone, and meet his fate facing the Moth King?

My anger renewed at the thought of hidden lies beneath our intimacy, and I thrust these questions from my mind.

Guests in elaborate formal wear packed the receiving hall. Whispers and stares abounded as a servant ushered me to an open seat next to Ander at one of the two high tables flanking the throne.

"After you left for Beyrian, I wondered if I would ever see you again," Ander said as I settled in, his hand fitting over mine. "I wondered if I would have a chance to apologize for accusing you. I know you were only trying to save Ivria. When I started hearing rumors, I realized how my resentment over your mistake might have fed unfounded suspicions. I should have stood by you from the beginning. I should have gone with my father to the Realm Alliance to defend you."

Long-sought solace overpowered my uneasiness. I squeezed his hand in return.

"You don't have to worry about the Realm Alliance coming after you," he went on. "Their policing of elicromancers has gone too far. I will not let the rumors stand in my court. I know you're not capable of what they say."

I was reluctant to clarify whether he was referring to my character or my competence.

"You can clear your name and, of course, stay here where you belong," he added.

His affirmation should have brought me such comfort. *Ander doesn't blame me. He'll help everyone understand the truth. Arna is still my home.*

But these assurances didn't settle well, and I couldn't ascertain why not.

I chanced a look around for the first time since entering the receiving hall. Jovie sat across from me, her tawny hair as tightly constrained as ever, the overture of a smile on her lips.

With a start, I realized that Knox sat directly to my right. He stared rather studiously into his wine goblet, refusing to look at me.

"Knox."

"Valory." He compelled his eyes to meet mine. "No one mentioned you were planning to come."

"It's my mother's wedding." I jutted my chin as though I had known about the event all along.

A brunette woman with a spattering of freckles leaned around him. I recognized Elythia Carrow, the elicromancer beauty Ander had been dancing with just before I'd followed Ivria, unknowingly, to the place of her death. "How sweet that you returned for your mother's wedding, Your Highness," she said, with no trace of irony. "Last I heard, you were exiled to Darmeska."

She intertwined her fingers with Knox's. His cheeks flamed, but he didn't spurn her touch.

"As I understand it, you were good friends with my husband before...at the academy," she went on, catching herself before mentioning the Water. "I had my ceremony five years ago, so I didn't meet Knox until...well, it was at Valory's birthday ball, wasn't it, my love?"

"You're married?" I asked.

"With a babe on the way," she answered, sculpting her dress to emphasize a rotund belly.

Knox swallowed hard. I seized up a bit, disturbed by how much time had passed while we slept in the fay dwelling, how unexpectedly my friends and family in Arna had made use of that time. Nothing seemed to make sense. In fact, neither Knox nor Jovie should have been seated at the high table. They weren't royalty.

For the first time, it occurred to me to look at the familiar dark-haired man on the throne. I felt like a torn flag flapping in a stormy wind, and King Tiernan's dignified expression would stake me to solid ground.

But it wasn't King Tiernan who sat on the throne.

It was Prosper. Neswick stood nearby, wearing a pure white tunic.

No.

I turned back to find Jovie watching me keenly. I thought I saw a glimmer of light in the jewel around her throat, but it had to be a reflection of the chandeliers glancing off its many facets. And Knox too wore a gray elicrin stone that looked suspiciously similar to the one that had allowed me to recognize Brandar's mangled body in the dawn light at Beyrian. Was it a trinket, a trophy? Or was there more to it?

"Where's King Tiernan?" I asked Ander.

He didn't seem to hear me. He was speaking to Melkior's grandfather, Vesper.

Out of the corner of my eye, I saw Knox give a single firm shake of his head. I gripped his arm. "What's happening?"

"Stop asking questions," he muttered.

Was he afraid? Or was his good-heartedness a shell that sloughed off with friction? I had spurned his advances and ruined his future. Perhaps he simply didn't want to act as my personal town crier, bringing me abreast of the latest court happenings.

"Just tell me where King Tiernan is," I whispered. But I shut my mouth as a cold certainty overcame me.

I will not let the rumors stand in my court, Ander had said. *His court.*

As the younger sister of childless King Tiernan, Odessa was meant to succeed him before her son, Prosper. Under no circumstances should my uncle be king right now.

The stringed instruments stopped merrily plodding along to take up a more solemn and dignified tune. My mother emerged from the far end of the receiving hall, her joyful expression stilted. A somber Victor waited at the foot of the dais. I looked from him to Prosper, who wore a smile of quiet conquest. My gaze shifted to Ander, who stroked his chin complacently. Everything felt wrong, so wrong.

My mother's face changed, and I realized I had risen to my feet. Prosper's gaze slid to me and I felt its iciness like a knifepoint protruding from soft snow.

Someone behind me tripped and spilled liquid down my collar and around my throat. I gasped as I tried in vain to mop up the red wine with a cloth napkin. The ivory bodice of my dress was soaked through and seemed to fasten to my skin.

Sniggers of laughter surfaced and even the musicians stumbled for a few beats, distracted by the spectacle. I whipped around and found Melkior grinning with triumph. He had done it on purpose.

I wanted to shrivel and disappear, or shed my skin and crawl into someone else's—become anyone besides Valory Braiosa.

I shoved Melkior. He stumbled drunkenly back and fell in front of everyone. Ander stood and loomed over him, and for a moment Melkior looked truly terrified. "Get out," Ander said, and Melkior scrambled away.

"I'll go clean up," I muttered.

"Should we stop the ceremony and wait for you?" Ander asked. The suppressed laughter had jolted to a mysterious halt.

"Um, no," I said, bewildered, embarrassed, frightened. "No, please continue."

Hiding the stain with crossed arms, I hurried out of the receiving hall, my boots clunky on the marble. I knew my mother could not come after me.

In the secluded corridor, I let the panic wash over me. I wanted nothing more than to flee, to go back through the portal to the dead, blackened woods, even if it meant facing Mercer and our fruitless mission.

This was not my home. This was not my family.

Meandering footsteps and a hiccup announced Melkior's pursuit, and with a breath to calm myself so I could refrain from breaking his neck, I looked him in the eye. "What do you want from me?"

"Lower your voice," he whispered, glancing over his shoulder, suddenly quite sober. "You have to leave."

"Not without answers," I whispered harshly.

"You want answers?" He yanked me down the hall toward the stairs. Even though it was *Melkior*, I felt inexplicably safer with every step.

"Where are we going?" I asked, struggling to keep pace with him as we ascended to the upper floor and turned toward the men's wing.

"There are only five members of the Conclave now," Melkior snarled. "They no longer just decide the fate of elicromancer pupils. They decide *everything*. The end of the Water was the end of the equitable Ermetarius reign. Our family was only noble so long as there was a Realm Alliance to hold them accountable. Why do you think Ander is able to pardon and reassure you, when the Realm

Alliance wanted you in chains? Prosper, Ander, my father…they've taken control."

"That can't be," I whispered, the stain on my chest growing cold. "Where's King Tiernan? He wouldn't allow this."

"He has no choice."

"What do you mean?"

"I mean he's been overthrown."

"Dead?" I asked, dread slicing through my belly.

"Nearly."

"What—?"

"I'm taking you to him." He flung stringy hair from his eyes as he beckoned me to hurry. "There is no age of surrender now. They will keep their elicrin stones for as long as they want and find excuses to confiscate them from any challengers. They're going to slip control of Nissera out from under the Realm Alliance. The Summoners have infiltrated our government and the Ermetariuses have welcomed them because they have the same goal: to end restraints on elicromancers, to live forever, and to rule forever, unchallenged. Even if it means they must bow to a demon."

"Valmarys?" I asked, stopping dead merely because my legs seemed to forget how to function.

"Yes," he hissed.

The truth dawned like a garish sunrise. Jovie Neswick wore a retired elicrin stone. She had been trained and schooled alongside the realm's most promising future elicromancers. She used to snap quills in lectures from taking notes so furiously. And now her elicrin trinket sparkled with light and power—the girl most of us had treated like an intruder at the academy.

The Summoners didn't just believe Valmarys was a god. They believed him a god who could grant their wishes in exchange for loyalty, in exchange for raising him from his slumber and restoring him to power. Their wishes for immortality, for magic—for the status that accompanied both—had been granted by this tyrant who possessed the power to steal and bestow elicrin gifts. At least, they'd been granted by the tyrant's head servant.

When Valmarys returned, the Summoners had reaped the rewards of centuries of devotion.

And yet...Prosper sat on the throne and wore the crown. What sort of agreement had he struck with these impostors? How could Ander abide such atrocities?

"Not Ander," I whispered, resisting the boiling pressure of tears.

"Yes, Ander," Melkior spat. "He's among the worst because he doesn't know what a shit he is. Self-righteous bastard. He thinks no one knows that he's the father of Elythia's child, that Knox is being played for a fool. Ander turned his nose up at her until she and Knox married, then he changed his mind and had to have her. He appointed Knox to be a so-called crisis ambassador and sent him on a doomed mission to bring recovery supplies to Beyrian. Ander made me stay behind. Can you imagine? An elicrin Healer barred from stopping the plague! Instead, he sent Knox with two dozen men. Only Knox and three others returned, all ripe with the plague. I healed them. That's when Valmarys came and took my elicrin gift. He transferred it to Jovie."

"No, no, no," I muttered, lurching to catch up to him, latching on to his arm and forcing him to face me. "Is this some sort of morbid farce, Melkior?"

"Look outside and see whose soldiers guard the palace. It's not our guards or our branch of the Realm Alliance army. They've been summoned away to address the plague and the famine and the fires."

With my stomach tied in knots, I marched to one of the windows overlooking the courtyard. Men in white cloaks and tunics stood at attention around the perimeter—the perimeter of a new outer curtain wall that looked very unwelcoming to outsiders. Gray flags with white moth sigils fluttered in the breeze.

"What have they given Valmarys?" I whispered harshly, returning to rattle Melkior with my grip. "What did he want in exchange for leaving the Conclave intact, for keeping Prosper on the throne?"

"Elicromancers," he answered, continuing on until we stopped outside a set of grand double doors. Two guards wearing Valmarys's sigil stood at attention but subtly made way for us. Apparently, a few remained loyal. "Gifts to borrow at his whim. Several elicromancers went missing when the Conclave changed, among them the professors: Strather, Wyndwood, and the others. Of course, Valmarys expects the Conclave's loyalty, his sigil on the breast of every prince and guard. They acknowledge him as King of the Brazor Mountains, though he could have taken the whole realm without asking. But he gives them autonomy here. The Conclave can make and destroy laws on a whim. Valmarys pledged to defend Arna if the Realm Alliance ever regroups and attacks it. Blaming you for the realm's woes is what allowed them to get away with all of this when the Alliance was still powerful enough to stop them."

"They're not still powerful enough?" The question came from the back of my throat, almost like a sob.

"No," Melkior said, relentlessly honest. "Welcome to the new age, Valory. The Conclave is now Prosper, Ander, Neswick, my father, my grandfather...answering to Lord Valmarys."

He swung open the doors, revealing a dim, musty room with the curtains drawn shut. "This could be the last thing I ever do. But it was worth it to help you. You may be the only one who can stop them."

He gestured for me to enter. I stepped into the darkness, my eyes striving to adjust. Melkior entered and locked the door behind us.

A shape shifted in the corner. I blinked away the shadows and saw a bent form occupying an armchair.

"Come," the scratching voice said. At first, I thought it was age that shriveled the man. But as my sight fully acclimated, I distinguished familiar features, mossy eyes too sharp for such a hollow face.

"King Tiernan?" I whispered in disbelief.

"Yes," he rasped.

Hot tears finally broke my self-restraint. I fell to my knees before him. "What have they done to you?"

"Prosper didn't have the spine to murder his own uncle," Melkior explained. "So he took King Tiernan's elicrin stone. Neswick sucked the life out of him with his newfound power but stopped just short of killing him. Every day at dawn, Jovie comes and heals him only enough to let him live to another sunrise. Ellen takes care of him, but she isn't permitted to do more than clean the room and help him bathe."

My lip twitched with fury through my falling tears. "I'll kill those cruel bastards," I said, trembling, feeling the fire ignite inside me. *You walked through the blood to the steps of a dais and sat on the throne.* The refrain returned, vicious, lovely, saturated with fresh significance.

"I suspected treason…in their hearts," King Tiernan said through a feeble cough. Except for his eyes, he looked like a phantom of his former self: pale, wretched, and sickly. "Ivria knew something too. Callista's diadem allowed her to see her father's true nature, the resentment that had been fomenting for years. Prosper chafed against the restrictions my father and the Realm Alliance erected to govern elicromancers. Ivria couldn't bear the grief of knowing the man her father truly was."

"That's why she went to the Water?" I whispered, my anger dislodged by grief that left me feeling cold and paltry.

"It seems she would rather have risked death than watch her father create a new realm for elicromancers when she knew in her heart she wasn't meant to become one. She couldn't confront corruption within someone she loved, so she passed the burden of truth on to you."

"My birthday gift," I muttered. "She hoped that I would do what she couldn't…expose the truth."

I remembered my fleeting glimpse of a white-cloaked figure that night at the academy. A Summoner knew that Ivria knew something. They had been watching her.

"I didn't know about Ivria when I took the diadem from you," King Tiernan explained. "I was attempting to confirm my own suspicions. But the more I discovered within the short time I possessed it, the more I understood Ivria's state of mind on the last night of her life." King Tiernan's wrinkled, pale eyelids shut over his bright eyes and he dragged in a rattling breath. "I didn't know what Prosper and Neswick were planning. I saw mere hints of the truth, shadows behind smiles, whispers behind words. I hoped to discover their full intentions and expose them to the Realm Alliance. But I did not know how far their plans reached, how their motives and the realm's disasters were so intimately intertwined."

I grew light-headed. This insurrection had not been born of opportunism. Prosper had not simply used the cover of the Moth King's chaos to cast off the irksome restraints of the Realm Alliance. He had banded together with Neswick and the Summoners to *create* the opportunity. The sedition had risen from the inside like an infection in the blood.

Neswick had always known, from the legends of his ancestors, that Valmarys could bestow power on those who helped resurrect him, and take it from those who displeased him. But Neswick must have needed an elicromancer's help to break through the magical barriers protecting the tablet. He and Prosper must have joined forces to wrest control from the Conclave and the Realm Alliance. They capitalized on the chaos to extend the age of surrender, chipping away at restraints while they waited for the Lord of Elicromancers to regain his footing. With Valmarys on their side and the Realm Alliance castrated, they could take power from anyone who resisted their cause and give it to followers who proved loyal. They didn't even need the Water anymore.

But in order to agree, Prosper had to have thought he would remain in control, that Emlyn Valmarys would be a tool, an ally, not a master. If he had known what Valmarys could do, surely my uncle, however corrupt, would have found a less compromising way to seize power.

Prosper had pretended to be gracious when he sent me to Darmeska, but he was hoping that my absence would allow the blame for Valmarys's crimes to land upon my shoulders. Then chaos descended—the plague, the traps—and they no longer needed me as a prop. When Valmarys learned of Mercer's vision, I became disposable in every way.

"They'll look for her soon, Your Majesty," Melkior said, cutting through my horrified astonishment. "The wedding has begun."

"The wedding, yes," King Tiernan said. "Prosper is treating his mother and sister like children with toys, confiscating and returning their elicrin stones based on their compliance. He believes he's being gracious. He says he solved your mother's marriage quandary by taking her birthright, freeing her of the 'burden of choice' that had prevented her from uniting with the man she loved. He could have changed the laws to strip them all of their rights and powers, but he fancies himself a compassionate leader."

"And Ander welcomed Valory as though she were toothless," Melkior growled.

"They are confident," King Tiernan said. "Confident they can snuff out any attempts to revolt against this new order. The system of repurposing elicrin stones has made the loss of the Water inconsequential to them. They've made Knox their new Neutralizer, reanimating Brandar's stone with magic stolen from another Neutralizer. If Knox is loyal, they'll promote him to a seat on the Conclave."

The king's eyes sparked with the secret we held, the secret Brandar had taken to the grave.

"So Ander is acting as ordinary as possible hoping I'll just… accept all this?" I demanded. "Fall in line, become docile for the sake of my safety and my mother's? Pretend that nothing has changed?"

With tremors running down his arm and fingers, King Tiernan reached to place a featherlight hand on my shoulder. "I know what you crave to do. But you must pull this diseased tree up by its strongest roots, not just break its branches."

"Kill Valmarys?" I asked, gripping his fragile wrist.

"Yes."

Mercer's false prophecy slammed back into focus. Why hadn't Neswick, who knew about the vision, ordered me killed on sight when I arrived here? The premonition had nearly resulted in my death twice already.

Before I could begin to ponder this, distant footsteps sounded.

"The portal is for you," King Tiernan whispered. "It will open only for you, taking you only where you want to go. I sent you a missive months back, explaining where I hid it and how it functioned. I suppose you never received it. Thankfully, I enchanted it against prying eyes. Darmeska is fortified by magic, but the portal can bring you nearly to its gates. Finish this."

"We have to get out of here," Melkior whispered, tugging on my arm.

"I will avenge you, Your Majesty," I vowed. "You will rule again."

"I doubt that," King Tiernan said. His frail hand landed on the crown of my head. "Melkior, you are our witness."

When King Tiernan's intentions struck me, my mouth fell open.

"I, Tiernan Anthony Ermetarius, true King of Calgoran, hereby name Valory Ermetarius Braiosa my heir apparent. Calgoran's wounds will be your wounds, its victories your victories, its peace your peace. You will prosper as queen and woman if you do these things: provide for the hungry and the weary and the bereaved. You may stand."

These words were intended to be spoken amid joyous revelers, but somehow they were more precious whispered in the shadows of rebellion.

No longer trembling, but blinded by tears, I rose to my feet. A soft pattern of knocks sounded on the door: the loyal guards alerting us to danger, no doubt.

Melkior drove me out of the dark room before a profession of humbled gratitude could form on my lips. "Take the other way," he said, shoving me farther down the hall instead of back the way we'd come. "Play dense. Do whatever you have to do to escape."

"Thank you."

"Thank me by escaping alive."

With that, Melkior hurried off, along with any argument I had ever had for calling him my least-favorite cousin.

❦ TWENTY-NINE ❦

SOFTLY treading on the pads of my feet, I hurried back to my room. In spite of Mercer's bold-faced lie, which bared my shameful naïveté, I knew I could have confidence in his motives, and that I needed him to finish this. Glisette, Kadri, Mercer—they were mere steps and a flick of a curtain away, if they hadn't already decided to abandon the journey and close the portal.

I hoped not. I needed that portal.

At last I approached the door to my room, breathless, my spine tingling with the suspense of a pursuit. But Ander appeared behind me at the top of the stairs, blocking the brightness of the chandelier above the landing just as my hand touched the doorknob.

My stomach knotted in terror. I had once trusted him more than I trusted my own mother. He was goodness, humor, strength. He was high-minded and gentle. But that was before he'd had reason to show his claws.

Now that they were exposed, I could no longer imagine him soft-pawed and protective.

"That imbecile," he said, advancing. "Are you all right? I know it must have been embarrassing."

"I—I'm fine," I stuttered. "Melkior was just drunk."

"He's always been dreadful to you. It's a struggle to take the high road with him, but I've tried. Are you changing or should I escort you back?" He offered me his arm. Everything inside me wanted to pluck out Melkior's accusations about Ander like picking gristly meat from a stew before taking a bite. What if Melkior was wrong about what Ander knew? What if Ander was oppressed just like my mother and grandmother, silenced, too afraid of the cost of defying those in power?

I had to know the truth. I couldn't speak of what Melkior and King Tiernan had shared—no, I couldn't endanger the life of my king, nor the cousin willing to risk caring for him in this backward regime.

"Ander...I heard that Lord Valmarys invaded and conquered Darmeska unchallenged. Is it true?"

He wrinkled his brow. "Not conquered. Brought under new leadership."

"That's my family, my father's home. My grandmother is an elder, if she's even alive—"

"Darmeska is not its own country, Valory," he interrupted matter-of-factly, dropping his arm. "It's a city of Calgoran. It retained its independence for so long thanks to the graciousness of Calgoran's kings. The residents of Darmeska still have a home, and the items of historical value will be well tended. Valmarys only requires that the elders step down. No need to be dramatic."

Step down. I couldn't imagine Grandmum stepping down. "And...what if someone refused?" I asked. "To step down?"

"Valmarys is the King of the Brazor Mountains now, by royal decree. To defy that would be an act of treason. And treason is treated the same everywhere, isn't it? There should be no surprises for anyone. Lord Valmarys is level-headed and fair. I'm sure he has given the elders a chance to adjust to their new roles."

"Do you not see what is happening to our kingdom, our home?" I demanded, straining to see a glint of emotion beneath the hard, handsome mask. "Valmarys is killing innocents, sabotaging rightful authorities, endangering everything we hold dear."

"We all know who is the *real* architect of Nissera's terrors: the plague, the disaster in Beyrian, the fires in the western woods. You reek of smoke and ash. One could chart your journey on a map alongside these catastrophes. Meanwhile, Valmarys has been nothing but honorable and decent."

"You think I'm the enemy? Moments ago, you said—"

"Not you. Mercer Fye."

Dread snaked through my veins.

There was a reason Ander had asked for only one extra setting at the high table even though I'd brought a guest.

But I'd watched Mercer retreat to my room, to the portal. He was safe in the woods, as long as no one knew what lay behind the curtain. And Glisette and Kadri were safe with him, waiting for me to return. *Stay there, all three of you*, I begged. *Don't come after me.*

"You're under his spell, Valory," Ander went on, frustration clear in his resounding voice. "You've never swooned and sighed over men, much less allowed them to take advantage of you. I could scarcely believe you would align yourself with Fye while his dark magic ravaged the realm. I wanted to believe that if you ever returned to us, his grip over your mind would loosen. But you're positively wrecked with worry over him, aren't you? Ivria would be so disappointed in your weakness—"

A hard slap bit the air like the crack of a whip. "I'm not the one she would be disappointed in," I snarled. Only when I stared at my own hand, the palm red and stinging, did I realize what I'd done.

Ander's nostrils flared as his cheek turned scarlet where I had hit him. He was the crest of a wave about to crash, the swing of a hammer that would strike its target with cold accuracy. "I thought I could break his spell by welcoming you here, by reminding you that your loyalty should be to your family and your home, not to a dark elicromancer terrorizing the realm. It's proving more difficult than I would have guessed for you to admit you've been fooled... unless you haven't been fooled. Unless you really are what Neswick says you are."

"No," I said, looking him in the eye. "I'm not."

He took a pause, soothing his temper. "Then I will give you one more chance. Go change—into something appropriate for a wedding, this time—and return to the celebration. Without causing a scene, you will spend time with your family and friends. You will pay obeisance to your king and his viceroy, Neswick, and you will return to your rooms after the celebration. Ellen will care for you, Jovie will befriend you, and I will determine when you have proved yourself worthy of your freedom."

One more chance. Was it a true threat? What might my cousin, my brother, do to me if I didn't comply, didn't close my lips and pretend nothing was awry?

How I longed to spit in his face, to grip his jaw and dig my nails into his skin and tell him King Tiernan was the only one who deserved obeisance, and that I was his rightfully proclaimed heir.

But I had only to flee to my room to leave this hellscape behind.

I would return and toss Emlyn Valmarys's head at Prosper and Neswick's feet in lieu of obeisance.

I clutched my stained bodice, feigning embarrassment over the commotion I'd caused. "I—I'm so confused, Ander," I said softly, bereft. "My mind feels broken. You couldn't imagine the horrors I've seen these months."

"I know," he said, his hands on my shoulders. "But family is family. You just need a little Arnan food and wine to remind you where you belong. Mercer Fye will never hurt you again."

Something about the last declaration made a shock of dread ring through my body as I twisted the handle. Ander strode away. I slipped inside, pressed the door closed, and heaved a breath of relief.

"I've the perfect thing for you to wear."

I whirled to find Jovie sitting on a chaise, Ivria's violet gown draped over the cushion beside her. Two guards in gray and white stood at her sides. With amber eyes like saucers and a button nose, she didn't look capable of cruelty beyond rejoicing in someone else's academic failures. But I could feel hostility emanating from her every pore.

"I asked Ellen to mend it for me," she said, fingering one of the fabric flowers. "When Ivria wore it to your ball, I thought it was the most splendid gown I ever saw. It would be such a waste for no one to wear it again. Ivria would agree."

A growl ripped out of me and I charged. I could kill Jovie and her guards with a flick of my wrist as I'd cracked the blights' bones.

"For every hair you harm on my head," she said, not even

flinching, "my father and his men will discover a new form of torment for Mercer Fye."

I halted just an arm's reach from her, breathless, as if someone had pounded my lungs with an iron fist. Calanthe, occupying her pallet in the corner, jolted alert.

"My Master wants him delivered alive," Jovie said. "But he didn't say in what condition. Do you think he will care if his special guest still has a tongue? I don't think he'd mind the loss of fingers or genitals. But he might want Mercer to keep his tongue so they can chat. They are very old enemies."

"Where is he?" I demanded, barely able to spit out the words for the shock of paralyzing fear that rang through me.

"I'll take you to him." Jovie stood fluidly and brushed past me, smelling of Ivria's perfume. I realized that the back of her white dress was cut in two panels that fluttered as she walked—like the wings of a moth.

I couldn't help glancing at the doorway that led to my bedchamber and the portal beyond. What if she was lying? What if Mercer was safe, waiting with Glisette and Kadri beyond the curtain as I'd thought? I could kill Jovie and her guards and flee.

But what if she wasn't lying? What if Mercer had come back through the portal out of concern? The guards could have come for him, or he could have gone looking for me and been caught.

The realization sank in: Mercer wouldn't have left me, not even after I'd raged at him.

My fears were confirmed when Jovie held her hand out to a guard, prompting him to fish a streaky gray-green elicrin stone on a black cord—Mercer's elicrin stone—from his pocket and hang it over her finger.

Struck with anger and horror, I wanted to rip at her tight braid until I drew blood. Jovie and I were both small, but journeying on foot had made me more sinewy and sturdy, and I couldn't resist designing dozens of attacks. But for every one of her bones I fantasized about breaking, every scream I dreamed of drawing from her lips, I thought of Mercer breaking and screaming. I'd been so horrendously foolish to come here. I should have been imagining Darmeska when I opened the portal, the end of this tiresome road. But I had thought only of home.

"Why haven't you or your father killed me?" I asked Jovie as we started down the hall, the guards flanking us.

"The Master hasn't decided whether we can fully trust the Ermetarius men. If we kill you on a whim, your family—namely, Ander—might revolt, and we would have to kill them too. But I don't *want* to kill them, and their gifts may prove useful to the Master. So I must furnish a credible reason, and your attempting to help a known murderer and criminal escape from the Conclave's clutches..." She smiled crookedly. "Well, *I* won't even have to kill you for that."

"You know I'm not who they say I am."

"Do I know?" she asked, the pupils of her normally soft eyes sharp needle points as she whirled on me. "I don't know much about you, Valory, except what I've observed from the distance you always forced between us. We could have been nonmagic mortals together if you had simply admitted you were no better than I, that you didn't deserve a seat in the academy any more than I did. If you had, I could speak to your character, maybe even convince the Master to chain you up rather than have you killed outright. He cherishes those of us who believed in his resurrection after our ancestors hunted the contract for centuries to no avail. I have the power to persuade him. But you never stuck your neck out for me."

She clearly relished lording this delicious revenge over me—revenge for crimes I hadn't realized I'd committed.

If she hadn't threatened Mercer, I might have felt sympathy for her.

"Valmarys isn't divine, Jovie," I said as we walked on, jogging down staircases, crossing paths with only guards—never anyone I could trust to help me, if anyone would even dare. "He's just an elicromancer fay whose right-hand man can take and give elicrin gifts."

Light bloomed in her elicrin stone and she roared, "*Nagak!*"

The spell swept me off my feet and knocked me against the wall. Pain wracked my head, back, and limbs as I slumped to the floor with a groan.

"Blasphemy," she hissed, casting her shadow over me. But without inflicting any further damage, she whipped around. "Come on, Valory."

I trembled as one of her nearby guards dragged me to my feet and shoved me forward. I staggered on, and soon we reached the arched metal door leading outside, to where the palace straddled the Roac River.

The water rushed by under the looming blue shadow of the monstrous building. We walked alongside the river, stopping at an iron gate. Jovie swung it open and I smelled the dankness of a stone stairwell leading to the dungeon below. When she closed the gate behind us, I realized how far I'd strayed from the portal. Imagining returning to it alive, with Mercer in tow, seemed an impossible fantasy.

I had never visited the dungeon before. The chilly, dripping passages smelled as wretched as expected. The pallid torch flames stood no chance against the dank, dark caverns.

"Why aren't you a member of the Conclave?" I asked Jovie, suppressing the shiver that longed to scramble up my spine as we passed filthy prisoners slumped in their cells. I told myself that their crimes were reprehensible, that a just king had been the one to pen them here like pigs. But behind scraggly beards and stale smells, I recognized faces of courtiers and guards, people from my old life in Arna.

Jovie's compact shoulders tensed. "I hold an even higher position as the favored servant of the Lord of Elicromancers. If we asked it of him, my Master would put an end to conclaves and kings. But Arna is our home, and we couldn't have resurrected our Master without King Prosper's help. We let them play at their politics knowing who is truly lord and commander."

"Have you seen him? Valmarys?"

"Masked and cloaked," she whispered in awe, clutching her elicrin stone. "When he rewarded me for my devotion with my gift. He was glorious."

Tilmorn, I thought. I wished I had destroyed him at the summer cottage.

Dampened voices echoed as we shuffled down slick steps. I could hear the river overhead. Drops trickled onto my scalp.

A long hall stretched before us. Neswick stood outside a cell, his elbow propped casually on his opposite arm as he stroked his beard. I heard distant, tired breaths, shuffling soles, a moan of pain. My heart constricted in terror.

Jovie shoved me forward so I could look inside the cell.

Uncle Prosper stood on the other side of the rusted metal bars, blood splattered across his face and his gray-and-gold doublet.

So this was the dawn of the new age of Arna: ruled by a king who would leave his sister's wedding to make an innocent prisoner bleed.

And bleed he did. When I saw Mercer's face in the shadows, every last drop of hope was wrung out of me. He looked even worse off than when I had first found him. He slumped over on his knees, blood matting his sandy hair. His face was almost unrecognizable with cuts and bruises.

"Mercer." I gasped out his name and clung to the bars, my legs buckling beneath me. He had lied to me, but he was mine to punish how I saw fit, with belligerent arguing—not with violence and bloodshed.

His swollen lips formed my name, silently at first before he managed to find his voice. "Valory has done nothing wrong," he gasped, blinking up at Jovie. "The prophecy isn't true. I lied to her, hoping she would work with me to kill Valmarys."

Prosper hesitated.

"A pathetic lie," Neswick said. "Carry on, my king. Just remember, Lord Valmarys wants him turned over alive."

Prosper turned to Neswick. "This monster set blights on my realm. He torched half the forest. Lord Valmarys will understand his king taking a share of the vengeance."

"I doubt he considers you his king," I said to Prosper, my eyes fixed on Mercer's face. "Nor are you mine."

Prosper clenched his fist, but instead of punishing me for my words, he dealt a kick to Mercer's ribs that made him cry out and nearly collapse.

"No!" I screamed, and every metal bar screeched as it bent until each empty cell in the musty corridor looked like a mouthful of jagged teeth.

"I will kill you if you hurt him again," I said, my vow broken up by heated breaths.

"Summon Knox to neutralize her." Prosper's voice was even as he spoke to two guards, who hurried to do his bidding. My uncle barely looked a day older than Ander and was nearly as handsome, but his eyes were more distant than they'd ever been, their gray light muted like a snowy sky. I had always thought Tiernan cold for keeping everyone at a distance, including his family. Now I understood that it was not apathy or indifference that made him aloof. It was wariness.

"You are cleverer than I thought, feigning a return to your senses," Ander said from behind me. "But you never lost them, did you? You knew what you were doing all along."

I turned to find him poised in the open doorway, his anger palpable. The air was fraught with it. His elicrin stone brightened and body armor slowly crystallized over his skin.

I turned inward, digging for that pulse of power in my deepest parts.

"I advocated for your welcome here even though you don't belong anymore." There was an easiness to Ander's stride, a certitude of his own righteousness. His cruelty did not have a tinge of wicked glee as Melkior's always had. He was like a dignified marble statue of an ancient warrior come to life—and the result was terrifying.

Jovie seemed to find his disapproval of me most satisfying. She set loose a wicked smile that reflected her most cherished ambitions coming to fruition.

Ander advanced until he loomed over me, faint torchlight glinting off the impenetrable crystal shell forming over his hands, arms, chest, and neck. "I wanted to believe you had not embraced your darker side," he said. "But Father was right. Neswick and Jovie were right. You're not a fool. You're not a victim. You're a traitor."

He struck me across the face with his hard fist. My nose cracked, pain burst from behind my eyelids, and a scream of rage rang through my aching ears—Mercer's. My teeth seemed to rattle loose in my head. Blood pooled in my mouth as I fell to my side on the damp, cold floor. I tried to connect with the power inside me, but the pain was like a wall, as solid as the rock-hard coating on Ander's skin.

"I'm relieved you see now, Oleander," Jovie said.

"You know, you are very little like your father," Neswick mused, traipsing into view, his belly lapsing over his belt. I thought he was speaking to Ander, but I blinked through the pain and found him looking down at me. Blood spilled onto my lips as I tried to move, to speak, to be anything but a helpless wretch floundering on the floor. I heard the clattering of Mercer straining at his chains.

"Yes, I knew Leonar Braiosa," Neswick said, answering my unspoken question. "He was one of the best mountaineers alive. I paid him to act as my guide and help me scale Mount Emlefir. I was searching for the artifact of lore that would raise Emlyn Valmarys. I suspected it lay hidden in the ruins of my Master's court, but no one, not even among my devoted clansmen, knew exactly where his court lay."

My eyes fluttered closed. I could not abide such pain. Neswick's every word was a chisel striking my temple.

"Your father did not ask who I was, or what I searched. I don't think he cared. Our Summoner legends said there were magical traps around the mountain tomb. Anyone who managed to enter it would go mad. Touching the contract would burn the flesh. Attempting to read the runes would blind the eye. I explained to your father the perils of the mission, but he was not dissuaded. He found a way inside. Yet his carelessness cost him: he emerged blind and babbling, his hands blistered with burns."

I recalled Grandmum's explanation of my father's encounter with Summoners before he died. Neswick wore a mask and withheld his true name but could not help sharing hints of his dogma. *Coward.* Blood leaked down the crease of my lip.

"I accepted my mission as futile and followed Braiosa, hoping he would lead me back down the mountain to the safety of the nearest village. But lunacy made him erratic and hasty. I lost track of him and wandered for two days before I spotted smoke from a small fire against the dusk. There I found your father, his eyes lucid in the firelight." Neswick's laugh was dark as he peered off into an unknown distance. "He was roasting a rabbit on a spit with his hands neatly bandaged. He had fooled me, taking the artifact and leaving me to wander the wilderness. After so many centuries, with their makers long dead, the protective spells had faded. Your father was neither mad nor blind. He burned his own hands to make me think the legends were true. And from the pack beside him jutted an item that gleamed in the twilight. The resurrection text had lain in that cave, unguarded, for years."

I thought of Grandmum during our carriage ride to Pontaval, how her insistence on telling me nothing about the Summoners had led me to act out of ignorance and knock on Devorian's door. She, like the elders of Darmeska before her, was tight-lipped and dutiful to a fault, hoping Evil would hold less power if its name went unspoken. She didn't even know what creature the tablet summoned until she consulted Malyrra. Magic secrets of old had been guarded too closely—but left untended. The sea witch was right: our collective human memory was weak.

"He had taken what belonged to me. So I attacked, inflicting severe wounds, but Braiosa managed to escape with the tablet. I earned these for my struggles." Neswick pushed up the sleeves of his white doublet, revealing burn scars that spanned the lengths of his forearms and snaked around his elbows. "My Master would see what I had endured for his sake, that I continued to devote my life to his return after being thwarted time and time again. It is only fitting recompense that we sacrifice Leonar Braiosa's daughter in the name of the immortal rule of the Lord of Elicromancers."

Neswick seemed gratified by the symmetry, which should have enraged me. The wounds he had inflicted had ultimately caused my father's death. But his account brought me a strange sense of peace, for my father hadn't faced his mortality stumbling along in aimless isolation. After laying eyes on the tablet, he must have known it was a thing that could only yield evil—and that Neswick would use it without restraint. My father had died for a cause, fighting in flames and glory to bring the tablet to Darmeska, where Grandmum and the other elders could guard it with elicromancers' help.

But elicromancers couldn't always be trusted to keep dangerous secrets. Prosper had helped create the protections, or at least knew which ones had been used... and he had helped Neswick and the Summoners break them to steal the tablet.

I refused to give Neswick the satisfaction of anger. "Ander," I begged, though I could barely form the words. "I'm not the enemy. They are. Please..."

"If you could have seen these two lying to the Realm Alliance," Neswick huffed. "Master deceivers. Jessa Veloxen was under their thumbs and content to remain there."

Ander's eyes slid from Mercer to me, from Jovie to Neswick, and finally, to his father, who gave him one sound nod that said, *Finish this.*

"Heal her, Jovie," Ander barked, despite his father's encouragement. "I don't want her to go like this."

"She's a traitor."

"Yes, a traitor who deserves death—but a swift and painless one."

With a sigh of annoyance, Jovie complied. The hem of her pure white gown had picked up filth along the dungeon floor. It swept over my cheek as she leaned close to me, fading in and out of focus.

Power surged from her elicrin stone. The pain gradually ebbed, and my nose cracked as it righted itself. My teeth wriggled firmly back into their sockets.

I swung my gaze to Mercer, who dripped with sweat and blood. Fates, how handsome he was, even half wrecked by torture. His bright eyes begged me to save myself, whatever the cost, though all I wanted was to torture Jovie until she healed him too. My heart ached with such fierce anguish I knew I couldn't contain it.

The pain gone, my power and I connected, two fingertips touching on a cold, dry day, quarreling lovers' hands meeting in reunion. *There you are*, I thought, and jerked my wrists to break them all.

But their elicrin powers provided a shield, and I could feel my strength ram into it. Blights were one thing. Even with elicrin gifts, they were weaker, half alive, easy to break.

Jovie's arm snapped and she emitted a horrifying squeal as bone protruded through flesh. Shock passed over the others' faces, which I savored, but it wasn't enough. After a moment of agony, Jovie recalled that she could heal herself and did so, wincing, sobbing with panic as bones, ligaments, and flesh rearranged.

You can do better, I thought. *Break them.*

I didn't understand the flash of steel through the air, Prosper pinning Mercer's hand to the wall, until my uncle's dagger slammed down and severed the smallest finger of Mercer's left hand, eliciting a cry of pain that hurt infinitely worse than the merciless blow to my face.

"Attempt anything else with that perverse power of yours and he'll lose more than fingers," Prosper spat over my scream of horror. "Finish this, son."

Ander gripped me by the throat, cutting off my sob with his impossible strength. His gray eyes winced nearly imperceptibly. As I began starving for breath, I wondered if, for only a moment, he considered that he might have aligned himself with traitors instead of against them. But perhaps he'd already wandered too far down this path, clawed through too many tangled thorns to turn back.

The panic set in, the ache of reaching, striving, laboring for air, the pain crushing my rib cage and the back of my throat. My fingernails slid along the crystal shell of armor that guarded Ander's hands and fingers, finding no purchase. No doubt he viewed strangling as more merciful than beating me to a pulp, but it didn't matter how he chose to do it. My own family had been poisoned against me and would not spare my life.

An arrow zinged through the damp air with a metallic whiz as it crossed through the bent bars and embedded itself in Prosper's shoulder. Neswick barely dodged a subsequent shot aimed at his chest. I recognized the green-and-black-barred fletching of Kadri's new arrows. Hope coursed through my veins.

Ander dropped me, leaving me rasping for air as I pressed myself against the wall to clear a path for Kadri's arrows.

Glisette aimed a spell at Prosper, but even while weakened by the blow Kadri had dealt, he was quick to call out, "*Sokek sinna!*" The spell made a glimmering shield billow out from his sun-bright elicrin stone. It stretched from wall to wall, embracing Neswick in its protection.

While Ander and Glisette locked each other in a duel, shouting and deflecting Old Nisseran spells, Jovie lurched toward the safety of Prosper's shield. But I couldn't let her slip away so easily. I latched on to her braid, tearing a thick lock loose. She screamed and wrenched to face me, yelling the first few syllables of a spell that would have turned my blood to lead. She truly had studied elicromancy with a purpose, but her reflexes weren't swift enough to match her knowledge. One of Kadri's arrows pierced her neck and bright blood issued forth.

Neswick lunged to catch his daughter and pulled her behind the safety of Prosper's shield, urging her to heal herself before the wound turned fatal. Her hand frantically found the shaft of the arrow amid the slick fountain of blood, and her flesh began to mend.

"Take him to the Master," Neswick commanded his daughter. Her healing skin broke the arrow and shoved it out of her throat as easily as it had gone in. Gasping, Jovie stumbled toward Mercer.

"Wait!" Prosper cried, the crimson stain on his shoulder growing. "Heal me!"

But Jovie scooped up Mercer's elicrin stone, which she'd dropped in the scuffle, and pressed it into Mercer's hand so she could spirit him away with her, materializing and leaving only the dismembered bit of bone and flesh from his finger behind.

I roared into the subterranean shadows, the agony of loss wrecking its way through me.

A wail of wind whipped through the dungeon, snuffing out the torches, catching the slick moisture on the stones to form icy pellets that tore at my skin.

"Valory!" Glisette called. She bared her teeth and trembled with the effort of using her gift at half force while holding a shield against the bright spells that lashed out of Ander's elicrin stone. I ducked my head, fearing that one of the spells Neswick was clumsily spouting might actually work. As Kadri's arrows bounced off Ander's impenetrable form, I threw myself toward the two figures illuminated in the darkness by the barrage of spells. At exactly the right second, Glisette let down the shield to let me slip past, raising it again just in time to thwart Ander's crystal-clad fist as he slammed it down.

"Go back through!" Glisette called over her shoulder. "I can't hold the shield for long. I'll be right behind you."

Kadri and I whipped around and took the stairs three at a time. Daylight and fresh air had never felt so precious as when we emerged from the bowels of the palace and reached the gate leading to the river. Stealthy, silent, Kadri jogged alongside the roaring water and kicked open the cracked door to the palace, where a guard lay on the scarlet stairs, two green-and-black arrows sunk in his chest. As Kadri stopped to rip them out, a shape shifted in my peripheral.

Kadri nocked an arrow before I could even look the oncomer in the face. But when I recognized him, I stayed her arm. "Wait!"

It was Knox—Knox the Neutralizer. All three of us froze. Knox's expansive chest rose and fell, every breath the cusp of a life-altering decision. The dilemma—*her or me?*—passed openly over his features. Then he tendered a brusque nod so subtle that one could argue it had never happened.

"Come!" I yelled, and Kadri and I started in the direction of my chamber, where the portal awaited.

❧ THIRTY ❧

A FTER Glisette scampered through, the passage to my room shrank behind her, barely shutting out a final blast from Ander's elicrin stone. Glisette panted from the pursuit as the portal packaged its immense magic into the carved wooden jewelry case.

Our breaths heaved in the quiet. A thin layer of colorless smoke idled overhead.

"Mercer told us the truth about his vision," Kadri said after a stunned moment had fled by. "He thought you would return sooner. He was afraid you would put yourself in danger, so he went back to find you."

I clamped a hand over my mouth. "He'll die because of me—"

"No, he won't," Glisette said. "We are going to do what we set out to do, and save Mercer in the process."

"I thought you two would have left," I said, barely managing to get the words out in full voice.

Glisette bent to pick up the box and handed it to me. "What Mercer did was wrong. But we have no choice. We must go on as though nothing has changed."

"Mercer may have deceived us, but he would die to save any one of us," Kadri agreed. "And I know you can kill Valmarys. I don't need a prophecy."

I wept—out of loss, out of joy, out of utter desperation for this journey to be over.

Kadri pulled me close and held me still against her. Glisette joined in, but instead of embracing us, she clamped her hands around both of our napes and leaned in close. "We finish this now or die trying," she vowed.

"Are we ready?" I asked, palming tears away and holding up the box.

They set their jaws and nodded.

I opened the latch again. Within seconds, the road to Darmeska stretched before us. Beyond rolling slopes quilted with autumn hues and evergreens, white and silver crests jutted into a cloudy sky. The vast fortress city hunkered in the folds between the foothills and the mountains with their fog-ringed peaks.

We stepped through, our soles rustling over crumpled leaves and pine needles.

It seemed Valmarys had refrained from ravaging the land he'd chosen as his domain. What did that mean for the citizens of Darmeska, Grandmum among them? Were they safe, as Ander believed, or wanted to believe? Or did they dwell in the darkness of terrors more insidious than fire and flood?

It seemed we ought to have one night's rest, nestled in the wood like little hatchlings before daybreak would shove us from our perch. But every thought of Mercer enduring further torture lit me with urgency.

When the portal closed, Kadri swung her quiver off her shoulder to count her sparse remaining arrows. Glisette dropped her pack to comb her hair into a braid. I'd managed to scoop up my clothes on the way out, and now ripped off Jovie's dress with the spite of scraping manure off a boot.

While I shrugged into breeches and a tunic, my imagination

populated the road ahead with guards and blights. A sense of hopelessness fluttered over me like the first snowfall of a long, brutal winter to come. Darmeska was an impenetrable fortress, or at least, it was intended to be. And beyond facing servants of the Moth King—blights, Summoners, unwilling souls he might have forced to do his bidding as Tilmorn had forced us to do his—we knew precious little of how our enemy operated. One day he was playing games with Ambrosine, plucking delicately at the seams that held Nissera intact. The next, he was a tempest, burning the forest, his rampage tinged with impetuousness.

"Tilmorn accounts for a large portion of his power," I said aloud as we set off down the road. I dug into the pack Rynna and the fairies had filled, finding brightly colored fruits, bean pods, and bread. I had to be at my strongest to storm Darmeska. "We know that, at least."

Looming rock walls soon closed in on either side of the passage. As they towered ever higher, I felt ill at ease. I scanned the ridges on either side, expecting to see living shadows among the boulders.

"There's someone lying in the road," Kadri said, readying her bow. I tore my eyes from the ledges and saw a lifeless body sprawled across the path ahead.

"It could be a ploy," Glisette said.

"Stay back, Kadri," I said. "It might be diseased."

Kadri nocked an arrow while Glisette and I paced cautiously forward.

The man in the road was dead. The grainy dirt held a dark brown splotch of blood and the air smelled foul. As we neared, I could see a bloodstain darkening his tunic. Two streaks of white war paint formed the image of a moth stretching from eyes to jaw. Surely his assailant had left by now, but it was worth a glance around. An enemy of our enemy might be someone worth meeting.

But all I found were more victims. A few slumped against the rock face, their blood trailing like rich brown paintbrush strokes. One of their severed heads had rolled into a ditch. All of them bore the same white war paint.

A figure dressed in black separated from the trees up ahead. Kadri's bowstring creaked snug—until she recognized her brother.

"Rayed?" she said, letting her guard down as she darted to greet him, but I lunged to restrain her.

Rayed held both arms high in surrender, but his sword hung ready at his belt and he paced steadily toward us.

Glisette's brows shot down over her eyes, one of them sliced through with a gleaming pink scar.

Kadri struggled free of my grip. "Rayed, why?"

"I know I have amends to make," he said.

"And why should we give you the chance?" I demanded.

"You may never pardon me, but…" He unbuckled his sword belt and took a few more steps to present the weapon to me. "I offer my sword to your service."

I took the opportunity to relieve him of it, scanning the foliage for signs of a ploy. I saw nothing but turned inward to stoke my power, just in case. "Explain yourself," I said, cradling the sheathed weapon. "Give me good reason not to use this against you."

He faced Kadri, remorseful, and she looked ready to launch into his embrace.

"The day after we arrived in Beyrian, Prosper Ermetarius threatened Kadri." Rayed's eyes were red as he turned to her. "They threatened to torture and kill you, to dump your dismembered body in a ditch. No one had ever spoken to me like that, dared to describe such brutal and beastly acts...." He shook his head as if to be rid of the memory. Mercer's tormented cry filled my thoughts. I believed Prosper could be as vicious as he had advertised to Rayed.

"I thought I had the gall to kill anyone who dared threaten my family. But when it came to it, I was too afraid to defy him."

"You could have told someone," Kadri said. "He would have had his elicrin stone confiscated, regardless of status—"

"Don't be so sure. For years, I suspected that Prosper was installing people loyal to him on the Realm Alliance and the Conclave. But I didn't have proof, and wouldn't have known how to expose him. I had no idea which of my colleagues might act at Prosper's pleasure. So I obeyed him. What he asked of me didn't seem terrible...not at first."

Unwelcome pity poked holes in my resolve. Kadri's large brown eyes swam with regret.

"What did he want?" I asked. "Your vote to extend the age of surrender?"

"That, and to plant seeds of doubt about Mercer, then convince you to leave in a hurry that morning. I didn't know they were going to kill Brandar. His death rattled me, but I still obeyed out of fear and tried to stop Mercer from leaving with you as they asked. When Kadri returned to Erdem, I was relieved; I could tell the Realm Alliance the truth, even if it meant sacrificing my life. But Kadri's maid suspected she had gone after you instead of leaving on the ship." He looked at his sister. "So I pursued the blights hunting you. I didn't catch up until your wounds from the ambush slowed you down. Then I knew the actions I'd taken to save Kadri had only put her in harm's way."

"We found your pin at the summer cottage," I pressed.

"By the time I arrived, Prosper was there with his men, stealing your supplies. I tried to kill him, but he overpowered me and took me prisoner. He was so certain that his men would kill you that he took Calanthe and left without even waiting to see what happened."

"He had no reason to think we'd escape Tilmorn," Glisette said. "We barely did."

"Prosper materialized away, leaving his elicromancer guard to kill me. But the guard saw my grief and showed me mercy, dragging me with him for days as he tried to work up the nerve to get rid of me. I convinced him to release me. I came here to wait for you, but I long ago lost hope that you would ever walk down this road." He looked at Kadri again. "I'm so sorry."

She leapt forward and threw her arms around him. They embraced until Rayed stepped back and asked, "What's become of Mercer?"

"He was taken captive," Glisette answered, so I didn't have to.

With a lump in my throat, I clenched the scabbard. "We've all made mistakes." I thrust the weapon back at Rayed. "And we all must redeem ourselves."

A breeze stirred the trees, a breeze that smelled of smoke and the distant nip of snow.

From the next hilltop, we could see the city. Though I had visited Darmeska many times, staring at the mountains from afar made my knees weak. They were enormous, infinite, dense with hidden pathways and eternal secrets. Their crests pierced a morning fog that didn't seem to mind the spurts of harsh wind.

The city stood against a mountain, a mighty fortress with age-old cliffs at its back. A bridge cut across a ravine to the massive gates. In Callista's time, this had been the city where elicromancers gathered, feasted, prepared for battle, passed on their stories. Now it was the home of mortals who revered the history of their magical ancestors—but not enough to brave the Water and repeat it.

Except for the sentries dotting its ramparts, the city looked the way it always had. But a lofty sash of fog drifted away, severed by a muted sunbeam, to reveal a metal tower of fantastical proportions, looming over the monumental fortress like a specter.

My heart raced. The tower somehow looked more ageless than the mountains from which it sprang, an overbearing, otherworldly parasite. The tower was truly elegant in its detail, with spires, peaked arches, and glass panels that threw light in sparkling prisms.

"Oh," I breathed, craning my neck to glimpse its highest spire.

"As close as I've dared go, I can't tell if there's life behind those walls," Rayed said.

"Why build on top of a sprawling city only to exterminate all of your subjects?" Glisette pointed out.

"True. The sentinels are mortals," Rayed went on. "Expendable in Valmarys's eyes, no doubt."

"There are so many of them," Kadri said, certainly thinking of how few arrows bounced around in her quiver. "Around the wall, at every balcony, every tower. We'd need an army, we'd need *ten* armies—"

"Just to lay siege to it," I marveled. "Let alone storm in and take over."

"Then perhaps it's a good thing we don't have ten armies," Glisette said mischievously. "We don't need to lay siege or kill every soldier. Valory just needs to get inside. I think we can do that." She sighed. "Don't look at me like that, you've had plenty of time to prepare yourself for this."

I thought of Prosper striking Mercer across the face after he was already wounded beyond recognition, of Mercer's swollen lips forming my name. Tendrils of power came to life inside me. Each pang of longing I felt for him was a strand of muscle I would flex to crush Emlyn Valmarys.

"Are there any secret entrances?" Glisette asked.

"It was built to be impenetrable," I answered. "It's fortified with magic too, even more so than the palaces in the capitals."

"I see," Glisette said. "Well then, I need to get closer and see if there's water in the ravine."

"Wait! Is this it?" Kadri asked. "Shouldn't we discuss strategy beyond getting Valory in there?" She jabbed a finger at the tower, and the angle of the gesture somehow made the task seem more preposterous.

"There's no getting around the fact that we're only four people," Rayed declared.

"Essentially, try not to die, Valory," Glisette said, retying her golden hair. "We came all this way for you after putting faith in a farce, so don't embarrass us."

Sensing we could preamble for eternity to avoid going anywhere, I steeled myself and started down the hill, passing into its shadow. I curbed my speed by dashing from tree to tree, hoping to obscure my approach. The others caught up near the base of the fortress, where a stone bridge spanned a deep ravine and led to solid wooden gates set in a massive stone wall. I had only ever seen the gates wide open.

We stopped within a mad-dash distance of the bridge. "Lie down and brace yourselves," Glisette said, her elicrin stone brightening.

A fierce, freezing wind carved over the slope, catching our tunics, tearing leaves and branches off trees, and making the trunks sway and groan. I lay prostrate while Glisette's wind sliced over us. I dared to lift my head, cheeks stinging with windburn, so I could see what she accomplished.

Glisette's whole body shook as she drove a powerful wave of frozen water into an arc over the gate. For a quiet moment, there was a sparkling wall of ice, a magnificent sculpture rivaling the tower in its artistry.

But Glisette yanked her hands back, tearing away the ice sculpture, and with it the gates as well as an enormous chunk of the brittle wall, opening up a path to the stone bridge, which she left intact. The rubble crumbled into the ravine with a deafening thunder.

I could see commotion, people inside the city walls rushing to find the source of the damaging power. White-painted servants of the Moth King peered into the distance. It encouraged me to see so many survivors—men, women, and children. It meant Grandmum could be alive. It meant there was hope.

"Impressive!" called a deep, smooth voice. I sat up and turned to see Theslyn trotting downhill toward us, Rynna beside him. Their faces were ashen, the hollows under their eyes deep. Their hair was a dingy black, but I could see streaks shaded with auburn. Their journey through the wastelands had taken a toll on them.

"I suppose we're stronger than our excuses implied," Rynna said before any of us could comment, extracting a gorgeous, elaborate knife from her belt. Theslyn wore a bow and quiver stacked with arrows, more than a dozen of which he offered to Kadri.

Cries from the city made me snap my head around. A few brave Darmeskans had dared to cross the bridge, but guards had sent arrows piercing their chests. The victims toppled, one stumbling off the bridge into the expanse.

Kadri and Theslyn each nocked an arrow in unison and took aim at the Moth King's archers. They let their arrows fly, striking down the two posted nearest the bridge.

"No matter what it costs, we get Valory to that tower," Glisette said.

Mingling fear and grit churned up a glorious swell of power inside me. Glisette, Rayed, Rynna, and I hurried forward as a pack and started across, Glisette casting a shield of protection at the helm.

But a horde of Darmeskans found the nerve to attempt crossing to freedom, like floodwaters bursting a dam. A rain of arrows slashed through the air in response. I watched in horror as they struck innocent people, piercing their chests, their eyes, their necks, spraying blood in the air. Disturbing cries of suffering wrenched out of them. The lucky survivors moved as a nervous herd, desperate to reach the other side. Glisette had to draw in her shield, leaving room for them to go around it, forcing us to file behind her. Beside me, a figure fell off the edge, howling as she became nothing but a shadow hurtling into the ravine. I heard a young boy crying out for her. More victims were plucked off, and the frenzied stampede became even more desperate.

An arrow whooshed past my ear to take down a white-painted sentry perched on the wall, alerting me to Kadri's presence on my left. Theslyn stepped up on my right and released an arrow that sent another of the Moth King's soldiers into the abyss. Refugees had begun to pile up, jamming against Glisette's shield. Glisette had no choice but to drop the shield entirely so they could pass.

Someone pushed by me, throwing me off balance until the ravine reeled below me. Regaining my composure, I reflexively drew my dagger, but what could I do? Attack the very people we hoped to save?

"Calm *down*!" Kadri yelled to the crowd, to no effect. "Calm down or all of you will die!"

A large man with a gray beard pushed past me and I lost my footing, stumbling and landing on my side. Someone stepped on my elbow and another kicked my chin. I longed to lash out at these people, who didn't seem to care that we were risking our lives to save them.

But I could imagine the Moth King peering down at this spectacle from above, high enough that these flesh-and-blood humans looked like nothing but swarming gnats. He would not see fear or hear the screams of the sufferers. He would see people turning on one another, helpless enough to show their primitive underbellies, and if I gave in I would be one of them.

"That's about enough of this," I heard Rynna say. She seized my elbow, effortlessly lifting me to my feet, and charged down the center bridge, baring her long dagger in front of her. A head taller than everyone else, with flaring, golden eyes, she seemed to bring some back to their wits. "You're killing each other like rats!" she yelled, driving me through the crowd until my soles landed on the dirt at the other side, past where the gates had stood just minutes ago. Now standing within the citadel walls, I looked ahead at the cobblestone streets that branched to either side of the front entrance to the fortress itself, an imposing great hall. Rynna wheeled around to glare at me. "You can't be so soft."

A group of soldiers surged out from a side street to attack the fleeing Darmeskans. Rynna jumped into the action.

Kadri caught up to me. "We can't save them all."

"I know," I said.

An arrow jetted between us, narrowly missing both of us. The crowd, the city walls, the windows and doorways of the great hall were haunted with white moths painted on faces, and everywhere the soldiers aimed there were violent bursts of blood, cries of suffering. Impaled bodies on pikes waited at the entrance to the fortress. I couldn't bear a closer look at their features; the number of them matched the number of elders, and I would die where I stood if I found Grandmum among them, her flesh a feast for ravens.

The Darmeskans had been permitted to live, but only in the shadow of death. Children had looked up at these corpses. My stomach heaved. My path, an unavoidable path toward the Moth King, cut through a forest of twisted remains.

Kadri loaded another arrow and pointed it at a soldier charging her with a sword. But he was barely more than a boy, and his white-painted eyes looked vague and distant. As he raised his blade,

I thought of the compulsion Tilmorn had placed over Glisette and me. "Kadri, they're Darmeskans!" I called, but too late. Her arrow hit its mark and a red flower bloomed on the boy's chest. Awareness appeared in his eyes as he dropped his sword point-first and stumbled into her.

"Do you know how to use that knife or not?" Theslyn demanded, nudging me hard with his elbow.

"They're Darmeskans. Innocent people compelled to kill us!"

"Will gawking at them break the enchantment? You have to kill the one who enchanted them. So do it!"

I looked up at the looming tower and brushed away the strand of pity that remained for my attackers, drawing my dagger. Blameless victims or willing soldiers, I couldn't discern, so I started toward the steps of the great hall. People who had not been compelled to fight darted from their hiding places toward the bridge, trying to escape their captors in this city of shadows and death.

A soldier with a knife lunged to stab me in the ribs. I dodged and he followed the arc of the failed blow, leaving his neck vulnerable. I sank my blade into his jugular and felt warm blood rushing over my fingers, heard him choke and gurgle out his last breaths.

Piercing flesh was too easy, like stabbing a ripe fruit. I ripped out my knife and shoved him to the ground. Another fighter closed in from behind and gripped my fist, staying my blade. I lashed and kicked, skimming his shin with my boot, but he was strong and turned my hand so that the dagger pointed toward my own heart. I gritted my teeth and resisted, but the lethal point trembled closer to my fragile flesh. . . .

Closing my eyes, I invited the Water's power to the fore. All it took was a twitch of two fingers and the magic lashed out of me, snapping the bones of the hand and arm that clenched me. If flesh was no more than a tender peel, bones were dry stalks of wheat.

The man screamed and retreated. I darted through the maze of bodies, up the steps toward the six soldiers guarding the doors to the great hall. I looked not at their features but at the moths splayed in cracked paint across their faces. When I raised my hands in front of me, my dagger dripping bright blood down my knuckles, I thought of each man as nothing but a pillar blocking my path, a pillar flaunting the enemy's emblem. My wrists snapped outward and the pillars cracked and collapsed, falling to either side. Swords clanged tersely on stone.

More compelled Darmeskans advanced from behind them. Glisette appeared at my side in a flurry of blond waves, panting, shallow cuts shining like latticework on her pale skin. Her elicrin stone shot light and flung three of them down the hall, cracking them on a statue with lethal force. Having made my job easier, she drew her sword again and lunged away from the great hall's entrance back into the streets. I hoped most of the lucid Darmeskans had managed to escape across the bridge, but the persistent howls and sobs of terror suggested otherwise.

Facing the remaining attackers, I tested my power again. What I didn't break, I pierced and jabbed. Warm life flooded over my hands and sprinkled my face. One of the soldiers clawed my cheek like a cornered animal and I deepened the stab into his chest in vicious vengeance.

Finally, I faced an empty, vast hall.

The Moth King's tower eclipsed whatever light should have

fallen through the high windows. The men Glisette had sent flying back with her spell had struck a stone statue of Queen Bristal and King Anthony surrendering their elicrin stones with peaceful smiles. Bristal's cupped hands had broken off and lay on the floor as if pleading.

Only when the quiet fully cocooned me did I realize how loudly the battle raged outside: my friends against the soldiers, the soldiers against their own people.

I burrowed deeper into the silence, passing lucid Darmeskans daring to scurry from hiding places. The fortress was immense, the halls and rooms within its walls as complex as the city streets, but I had explored enough to know how to go up and keep going up, beyond meeting chambers, residences, and libraries to secret rooms holding dusty artifacts stale with old magic. I could feel the spirit of this ancient place, stalwart, unruffled, drafty with mountain wind creeping through cracks. As I walked on, deeper, higher, my legs burning but my breaths calm, the smell of stone and timber gave way to the bite of mountain wind and iron.

From the topmost level, there were cold stairwells leading to a mountain plateau, unscalable from below. I shoved open a creaky door and looked across a metal bridge spanning grass and rocks, connecting the fortress to the looming tower of its new ruler.

It took all of my self-control not to crane my neck and look up to see its austere form stabbing into the heavens.

"You're a flashy sort of fellow, aren't you, Valmarys?" I whispered as I walked. "Men who like the idea of power tend to erect monuments to themselves. But you're just a half-fairy, half-elicromancer man in a tall tower. Glisette would probably accuse you of compensating for inadequacies."

Though light humor eased the terror in my chest, I heard a cry of suffering, Mercer's, echoing from the heights, glancing off the mountain cliffs. The terror came rushing back full force.

There was no door to the base of the tower, just a gaping entry. I swallowed hard as I stepped inside, expecting to be bombarded. Instead I found myself alone in a glass chamber. The chamber closed, jolted upward, and carried me into the dark belly of the looming bastion. I pressed my bloody hands against the enclosure, panicking and short of breath. The dark walls soon slid away and were replaced with glass revealing the view. Clouds shrouded Darmeska below. My belly and knees seemed to drop out from under me as I continued upward.

I was out of my element. I could break bones with a twitch, but I could not send a glass room whirling through the air. The Moth King was bigger, grander, greater, smarter than I.

Chilling images raced through my mind as I imagined standing in his presence. Would he look like a blight, decayed by his dark deeds? Would he be a fork-tongued ghoul, a giant shadow man in a cloak with eyes like glowing coals?

The soaring prism came to a smooth halt and a pane of the glass chamber slid open.

Vast stairs led toward a platform with a magnificent back wall of glass laced with intricate metalwork. Faint clouds muted the sunlight from gold to silver.

Two guards stood at either side of the glass door that had opened for me, but both of them seemed to look through me as though *I* were made of glass, and therefore I didn't move to attack. One simple mistake could demolish any chance of victory.

I had no choice. I started up the stairs, daring to look beyond the deadpan faces of the soldiers. The moment I crossed the threshold, the prism plummeted.

I was trapped in the Moth King's lair.

❦ THIRTY-ONE ❦

WHEN I reached the platform, a long banquet table stretched before me. At the far end, a figure sat silhouetted against the light.

Could this be Emlyn Valmarys? So ordinary and human in shape? I recognized Tilmorn's bulky, stoic form standing at his right side. On his left, Jovie wore a silky white dress that clung to her curves.

"Welcome," the sitting figure said. The greeting was so bizarrely mundane I wondered if I could be dreaming. "Come in, please, Valory. I plan to keep this most inevitable of encounters amiable. I am far more powerful than you, and yet you are said to be fated to end my life. I feel neither of us would benefit from an altercation."

The surge of intensity that had seen me this far skittered away, leaving me small, weak, cold with the dampness of others' blood. My mouth was dry. I swallowed to bolster the frail confidence in my voice. "You sent blights to kill us. You ravaged the forest. Forgive me if I am not convinced you seek a civil encounter."

"That was before," he said, rising to his feet. He was tall. As he came closer, I could make out his features. There were no signs of decay, despite his dark elicromancy. His long hair was glossy black. He did not have tapered ears like the full-blooded fay, but his eyes glittered a crisp silvery blue to match the sky. His cheekbones were harsh, his lips thin. He wore an elicrin stone of rough coppery red streaked with iridescent blue. Above all, he was ordinary-looking, someone to whom I might not have given a second glance were he a face in the courts of Arna.

The lilt in his voice proved that he had only recently tried this language on his tongue, that he must have absorbed it by some magical means other than omnilingualism. There used to be a girl in my tier who could memorize absurd amounts of information. She had received her elicrin stone just after Ander. I wondered if hers was one of the many powers Valmarys had borrowed.

"Before what?" I asked, my magic vigilant inside me again, longing to react to every step he took.

"Before I realized: neither of us has had any peace since I returned. We have been living in fear of each other. When Glend Neswick told me your name, I wanted to destroy you so that you couldn't destroy me. I couldn't stop dwelling on the vision. Until it occurred to me how miserable I was, how I had stopped enjoying the pursuit of my passions because I was thinking of you always, like a tormented lover, ransacking the realm to exterminate you. And you, how miserable you must have been carrying this task of murdering me, thinking you would meet some beast far worse than any storybooks have told. So I have decided to close the distance, to light the lamp that makes the shadows less frightening. Instead of running from you, I have, like you, decided to look destiny in the eyes. And to have a conversation with it. I much prefer to learn than to lash out in violence. Won't you sit and join me?"

He gestured. The table was set for two. Tilmorn strode around and pulled a chair out for me. The Moth King retreated to his own seat, thin and willowy compared to his strapping right-hand man.

I noticed that despite standing by her master's side, wearing an elicrin stone as she'd always dreamed, Jovie did not look happy. Valmarys dismissed her with a flick of his finger and she stalked away, her glare hateful as she disappeared down a side corridor lit with bluish light.

"My favorite pet thinks I'm too fascinated with you," Valmarys said. "She argues there is nothing special about you at all, that you came upon your elicrin power by chance. Ivria, however, she regards highly, and regrets that her sorrowful death made you mighty."

I would kill that hypocrite Jovie, make her a pincushion like the Darmeskans I'd been forced to destroy. But this creature knew too much about me, and I knew so little about him. Before I lashed out, I would need to learn.

A corner of my mind acknowledged that the meal laid out for us looked enticing. A hearty portion of fish with silver-white scales was drizzled with an aromatic yellow sauce and garnished with radish roses. If this was a dream, it was an odd dream indeed.

I cooled my temper, perched on the edge of my chair, and surveyed the Moth King's features again, searching for something I could use. He focused his attentions on the meal, using elegant cutlery to carve small bites. Tilmorn hovered at his side again, his smoky elicrin stone winking with readiness. I examined his eyes, hoping to find a secret message of awareness, some sign that he would help me, but saw nothing.

I dared to slide my gaze away from them. Glass chambers lined the walls from front to back. They reminded me of display cases that held jewels and artifacts in the palace's relic room in Arna, with three solid sides and a transparent front. Beyond the glare of bluish lights on their surfaces, I could see that what lay inside each separate case was not an object, but a person.

A new terror pierced my heart. The captives were elicromancers—wearing stones around their throats—and Tilmorn was a trader of elicrin gifts.

It was a collection.

The Moth King could try on elicrin gifts like jewels. And he wore them until they dulled. Because he borrowed others' gifts, the dark magic he performed affected *them*, not him. Each elicromancer showed signs of dark magic decay. Small ones—a festering sore, a discolored eye—but the Moth King hadn't been in this age very long, and he had already created stains and marks that no Healer could reverse.

There was no question in my mind that it was in my best interest to dine rather than fight.

I didn't see Mercer, but I dared not search for him. The Moth King could not see how I cared for him. In my mind, love had always been an advantage. It meant friendship, protection, loyalty. Now, I saw it differently: an exposed vein, a weakness, a chink in my armor that could not be revealed.

"The food isn't poisoned," the Moth King said. "How petty would that be?"

"Pettier than pretending to be Ambrosine's doting suitor?" I asked.

"You can't say someone is pretending if you do not know their intentions," the Moth King said. "I have not told a lie since I returned from my nap. Tilmorn, would you please give the lady a napkin to clean her knife? We're attempting to enjoy a meal."

Tilmorn stalked over to unfold the silk napkin at my elbow. My hand shook as I accepted it from him, accidentally brushing his broad knuckle. I wiped the keen blade and hilt of my knife. It was not the deadliest weapon I possessed, so I forced myself to part with it, sheathing it at my side and taking up the dainty fork. If eating would make the conversation last, I could gain an advantage. The second I dared use my power would be the point of no return. If I failed to break him as I'd failed to break Prosper, Ander, Neswick, and Jovie, it would be the end of me.

I separated the scales from the meat and took a small bite, testing it, my eyes on the Moth King. A flutter of fluid movement drew my gaze to one of the glass chambers. This one was filled with water and its occupant turned out to be a sea maiden, though she looked nothing like the beautiful one I'd encountered off the coast of Beyrian. Her eyes were the size of small plums and red-rimmed. She was silver and white, hunched, her upper body thin and her fluke translucent and ragged. The webs between her fingers were so protracted that her hands resembled fins. She remained still, staring at me, until she snapped at me with horrid eagerness, revealing sharp teeth.

"A cold-water sea maiden," the Moth King said. "If you extract a creature from its natural habitat, over time it develops new traits to survive. During my prior reign, I relocated her ancestors from the south sea to the northern ice caves, and there, as I expected, they became more carnivorous over time for lack of edible plants. Those with paler features survived the predators, as they were less easily seen, and the survivors bred until most of them looked like this."

I recognized the scales on my plate. They were the same

silver-white of the sea maiden's. The hair on my arms prickled, and I fought to keep down the nibble I'd already consumed.

"I appreciate narratives of transformation, the process of meta-morphosis," Valmarys continued. "The elicromancers who raised me were supposed to teach me and care for me, but they vacillated between treating me like a son and a captive. At times they wanted to kill me so I wouldn't become as powerful as they feared. They isolated me in the mountains to keep me from the Water, but also to protect me from other elicromancers. They loved and hated me, and I loved and hated them. They could be delicate, obsequious almost, and sometimes gave me everything I wanted. Other times they denied me food and water, as though the problem of *me* would simply fade away." He took a thoughtful bite and swallowed. "I began to understand the devices people use to manipulate one another. By trying to keep me weak and dim-witted, they had made me strong and clever. I escaped them, and ever since, I've been fascinated by what causes creatures to change, to grow stronger, to peel back pretenses and invite the truest self to the surface. That's what I've attempted to accomplish with this realm, studying and manipulating the natural and the supernatural to produce the most dynamic results. I am Nissera's most ardent admirer and its most avid pupil."

"You're its oppressor."

"You can't study a moth's intricate pattern unless you pin down its wings."

But if you grind it to a pulp... I thought. However, I would not pique him yet. I needed to learn more about him, to locate a weakness before I acted. "Is that what you were doing with Ambrosine? With my family? Stimulating transformation?"

He smiled, but it was not an evil smile. It reminded me of a professor pleased by a pupil who cared enough about a droning lecture to pose a question. "By inviting true natures to the fore. Naïveté, vanity, blind ambition. Yorth was too welcoming to outsiders, so open-minded and unwary. Their border security was lax and they were slow to suspect strangers. And Volarre's royals, with their love of fine things, were too easily mesmerized. Oh, and the Ermetarius family, so proud and puff-chested! But they helped my devotees restore me to power, so I let them cavort about in their paper crowns, spoiling everything with the corruption that lay dormant in their hearts for so long." He paused, then beckoned me, mysterious. "I like to coax creatures out of hiding."

My breathing hitched as I feared he would show me Mercer as a blight, as a wrecked, tortured, unrecognizable creature. I warily followed him to the back wall of glass, chancing glimpses at the cases holding motionless elicromancers. A knot formed in my throat when I recognized Queen Jessa, Professor Wyndwood, and Professor Strather. Small patches of decay crept over their skin. Each face that wasn't Mercer's drove dread deeper into my soul.

The elicromancers were still, watchful, their eyes too blank for silent pleas. They were compelled into frozen resignation.

Valmarys faced the cliffs spanning from the base of the tower toward the distant western sea. It was too far to view from Darmeska or even the surrounding cliffs, but this tower reached so high that I could see for leagues and leagues. As he looked out,

Valmarys didn't seem worried I would attack, but Tilmorn's watchful eyes bored holes in the back of my head.

I stepped up to the window, feeling I stood on nothing but a thin wisp of a cloud, and could not look down for the height sickness that came over me.

The Moth King flicked his fingers. A glass chamber dislodged from somewhere in the tower and glided off into the distance. It held two thrashing, panicked sea maidens with bright green flukes.

A massive shadow started rising up in the faraway sea, the water rushing off it. I squinted and made out an array of lashing black and blue tentacles, followed by red eyes and jaws so gigantic that each tooth looked to be the length of a longsword only the mightiest warrior could wield. As the sea creature rose, it revealed an armor of black scales.

The maidens were bait.

The mammoth creature emerged from the sea, gripping the distant cliffs with clawlike limbs, hiking closer as the water slammed the rocky shore in its wake. The glass chamber holding the maidens halted, far enough from the shore to draw the monstrous thing inland.

I knew what would come next, and barely averted my eyes before the monster tore the writhing sea maidens to shreds.

"You should see his father," Valmarys said. "An ancient thing, lurking beyond time, trapped by a sea witch's spell as I was. This one isn't as powerful, but he pleases me. His ancestors bowed to no man, nor even to time itself, but now he submits to both. I lured him from the south and he surfaces each morning for his treat."

Valmarys turned to look down at me, licking his thin lips, clearly relishing the awe on my face as I watched the creature retreat into the distance and sink back into the depths. This explained the destructive wave that would have sunk the whole city of Beyrian if not for the elicromancers. I wondered if he'd conspired with Neswick to orchestrate the disaster on the day Prosper was meant to hold the vote.

Either way, like Kadri, I would never set foot on a ship again.

"I must boast that I possess an intuitive understanding of innumerable creatures, humans not the least among them," Valmarys went on, motioning for me to return to my seat before gliding back to his own. Tilmorn slid out my chair again, his rugged face wiped clean of emotion. "To lure them out of hiding, to change them, to train them…that is a triumph indeed. Look at Glisette and Ambrosine: two sisters cut from the same cloth, both vain and languorous. But when trials come, one rises to the occasion, steps out into a perilous world, while the other retreats into a mirror. I sharpened opposite edges of the same blade. Ambrosine is a pustule of foul qualities draped in silk and feathers, while Glisette lets her lovely skin become marred for the sake of heroism. And you, no one expected much of you, accepted only because you were your cousins' lapdog. No one would dare lay a finger on Valory Braiosa when Ander and Ivria waited around the corner to defend her honor… yet here you are, storming my tower, breaking bodies with nothing but the flutter of an eyelash. It was interesting to see how pitting Darmeskans against you might change your approach. And it was interesting to see that it didn't."

The blood on my hands was starting to dry, congealing into a crust. My skin twitched with the longing to scrub it off.

"Forgive me, but are you crediting yourself for others' bravery *and* downfalls?"

"I pull strings you don't see, Valory Ermetarius Braiosa."

"And what is the meaning behind your dark deeds? To rip down dominions and cause chaos?"

"Dark deeds?" he demanded. "What are my offenses, Valory Braiosa? Tell me what crimes I committed to have earned hundreds of years of imprisonment in the mountain and the spite of a girl who has only grown stronger for the challenges I have thrown in her path."

Underneath the coolness, there was a hint of petulance in Emlyn Valmarys's voice that reminded me of a greener Melkior. He did not seem to enjoy being accused of atrocities, despite committing them without restraint. He set down his fork, pursing his narrow lips in displeasure, and the clouds seemed to darken behind him.

"Shall I start from the beginning?" I demanded, gulping down my fear. "You declared yourself a king when there is already a King of Calgoran—"

He couldn't listen to even one of his wicked acts before rushing to his own defense. "What makes a man a king? Hundreds of years ago, one of your ancestors was the most powerful man in the region and therefore named himself sovereign, drew boundary lines, and claimed lands. Maybe his subjects liked him or perhaps they hated him. It didn't matter. He was powerful and wealthy enough to maintain the self-imposed title, and the lines he drew became his country's borders. Since I have returned, I have approached sovereignty with civility."

"Civility? You're holding the people in this city captive." My voice cracked. "You tormented and killed the elders, forced people to murder against their will—"

"I began my conquest of Darmeska through legal procedures, securing my right to this fortress and the lands around it by permission from the King of Calgoran. A ruler is entitled to treat defiant subjects however he sees fit." He tapped his finger hard on the table.

"You received permission from an usurper," I growled.

"He wears the crown and his people call him king."

"You kidnapped elicromancers. You took them from their families. You're holding them hostage—Tilmorn among them."

"Tilmorn is like a brother to me," Valmarys said. "He's the only person I've ever been able to trust."

"There may not be chains on his wrists, but that hardly means he isn't a prisoner."

He leaned back in his chair. "That's what Mercer Fye wants to believe."

That name sent fire through my chest, an engulfing indignation. The Water inside me undulated forward, a heavy, off-kilter thing, ready to take control of my body. I pondered using it, ending this when Valmarys least expected it. But when I batted through the murk of fury to look at him again, I caught him studying the flicker of renewed rage in my eyes. I blinked it back into hiding. "You burned the northern stretch of the forest," I went on. "You sent blights to Yorth."

"That was a bit much, I admit. As I said, I've gone wild hunting you. I let fear rule me to the point of obsession. But I believe you and I can be diplomatic. My proposition is both practical and generous: I will agree to let the people you care about go free, even

Mercer, who deserves to die, if not to be imprisoned for an eternity himself. I will give you vengeance against your uncle and seat you on the throne of Calgoran, if you wish. I will not destroy the land as I have, or set any more blights on the realm." He shifted to cross his legs. "But, in return, Darmeska and the Brazor Mountains must remain my domain, a new, separate kingdom that is mine to name and rule. I must be permitted to continue my studies and experiments without challenge, granted that neither you, nor anyone you care about, nor your precious court will be involved. We can live in harmony in our separate spheres."

"And if I'd rather snap you in two?"

"If you refuse, or try to hurt me, Tilmorn will kill Mercer. If you try to hurt Tilmorn, well, you'll be lighting your own funeral pyre."

I looked at Tilmorn again, cold, impenetrable. It was impossible to believe he was ever the man Mercer had described.

"We will subvert prophecies and make our own futures," Valmarys went on. "How does that strike you?"

I stared at him, confused. Thrones, crowns, riches, titles, they had to be trivial to him. If he wanted omnipotence, he could have it. If he wanted to rule Nissera with an iron scepter, he could have killed the royals. So what did he want? Freedom? Freedom to do whatever he desired, to treat Nissera and all of its creatures like a board game, to strategize against the powers that be just to see what exciting things might happen when he knocked over the pieces?

I thought of my father, abandoning our family to trudge through the mountains, exploring the unexplored. After he had scoured every inch of stone and shadow in the north, he would probably have set out to sea, looking for new lands or godlike creatures slumbering in the deep. The world had been too small for him.

And the world was too small for Emlyn Valmarys. But instead of looking to tame the restless fire in his soul, he started other fires.

How could one best a man so removed from feeling, so intent to flee boredom that he turned living creatures, humans, fairies, elicromancers, sea folk, into personal subjects of study?

"Well?" he asked.

"Jovie brought Mercer to you," I said, leaning back in my chair and crossing my arms. "I want proof that he's alive before I agree to anything." *And that you haven't tormented him enough that I'd die just for the privilege of striking your arrogant face.*

"Fair enough," he admitted, pushing back from the table.

Tilmorn held up a hand and wordlessly took the light from Valmarys's elicrin stone. *This is it!* Everything in me screamed it.

But I wasn't quick enough. Barely had I noticed that the exchange was underway before Tilmorn had bestowed a different light upon the Moth King's stone.

I might have missed my chance, but the exchange revealed something vital: Valmarys could hold only one power at a time.

He didn't just keep the collection of elicromancers to use as puppets, preventing dark magic from leaving its mark on him and Tilmorn. He needed them as vessels. Perhaps even Tilmorn could hold only a limited number of gifts—though he possessed multiple ones after taking Glisette's from her, so I couldn't count on that weakness.

Perhaps Valmarys did not want to store his entire collection with one person who could betray him?

Whatever the answer, one thing was clear: Tilmorn was the fire. The Moth King was just the wind that chose its direction.

Kill Tilmorn. Without him, the impostor king will be far easier to kill.

But Valmarys must have had some kind of power before Tilmorn. How else would he have won the loyalty of Mercer's noble older brother? And he was already killing and conquering when he summoned Tilmorn.

The Moth King waved his hand and a compulsion slid over me. My muscles relaxed. My hands dropped to my sides.

I was too late. He had been exposed for a brief, glorious moment, and now he wielded the worst power of all. Maybe the compulsion was his originally, and Tilmorn offered him the amusement of trying on different supernatural endowments.

"Just a precaution," Valmarys said, brushing past me. My feet followed him. He led me to one of the glass chambers I hadn't yet seen.

When we stepped in front of it, my heart leapt with joy. Grandmum leaned against the wall, her papery eyelids shut in rest, her chest rising and falling. Her faded red hair was matted with blood. Rage bloomed like a vicious thorned rose in my chest, but I couldn't move, couldn't speak, couldn't reach. I could only watch.

"Your grandmother values her dignity more than anything else. She was given the choice to surrender her city to save you. I was only testing her. But do you know which she chose? No doubt she wanted to choose you. She cares more about you than those little specks of flesh down there. But she knew her legacy would hang on that decision. Her *pride* hung on that decision. Ultimately, she chose her city, and therefore herself. Is that not fascinating?"

He knocked on the glass. Grandmum's eyes flickered open in alarm. "She's part of the agreement, if that's what you want," he added, since I was unable to ask. "As for *my* grandmother, I would feed Malyrra to the majestic sea beast if I could find her."

I hated him. I wanted to break every bone in his body, slowly, listening to the crack of each one like a skilled musician plucking pure notes with satisfaction.

But I couldn't help considering the proposition. Grandmum would be safe. Mercer would be safe. My mother, Kadri, Glisette, Tiernan, Ellen would all be safe. I could rule Arna. I could rebuild the Realm Alliance, take Valmarys down with a proper army.

But would it be worth it, existing in a world otherwise ruled and tormented by the Moth King? Would he even stay true to his word?

I looked into Grandmum's sober, pale eyes and knew the answer.

"If she's not enough to convince you, maybe this will," Valmarys said, beckoning me along. He had misinterpreted the hesitation he saw in my eyes, thinking Grandmum was not enough of a prize to sweeten the deal. Considering how much he seemed to understand about manipulation, he didn't know a thing about humanity.

Valmarys led me back to the banquet table. "Tilmorn," he said, and with a wave of his hand Tilmorn slid a section of the floor away. A glass chamber rose up, bearing Mercer, who wore glowing magical chains.

My heart constricted with such agony, such joy, such longing, a parade of emotions too strong to hold without fearing I'd rip in two.

I was searingly aware of his every wound. But the bruises and cuts weren't fresh. The injuries had occurred at Prosper's hand. Yet one of his eyes gleamed milky white with just a tiny black freckle of a pupil.

The Moth King had forced him to use dark magic. The coward Valmarys could force others into the throes of dark elicromancy while he remained unscathed, gadding about and bringing ruin. He must have tried to force visions out of Mercer, perhaps regarding his encounter with me, and whether I could be defeated. There were parameters to most elicrin gifts. Going beyond them could often give you what you desired, but at a cost.

I wondered if Valmarys's foray into prophecies had led him to believe there was no destroying me. Why else would he try to strike a deal? I could imagine a thousand scenarios in which he could kill me. Right now, as he compelled me, he could throw me off the tower and be done with it.

Mercer had maintained that his original vision was true— that I was the glorious savior who would make Valmarys face his reckoning—even in the face of torture.

Mercer's endurance was the reason the Moth King wanted to strike a deal with me instead of trying to murder me.

I felt freedom in my facial muscles again, though my hands were still pinned at my sides, as Valmarys lifted part of the compulsion. "What do you say?" he asked.

I could no longer toy with the idea, and I could no longer stall him. I would have to decide. If I turned down Valmarys, he might enjoy morphing Mercer into a festering shell of an elicromancer. He might kill him and Grandmum immediately.

I could accept the proposition. Mercer would hate me. I would be a traitor. But he would be alive. He wouldn't be a blight.

I looked at Mercer. One of his eyes was still the color of barley wine, rimmed with deep purple. I felt the loss of the other's beauty more acutely. "Don't, Valory," he said hoarsely. "Not for me."

I loved him. I would do anything for him, defy his wishes, even nullify all he'd worked for, just to save him. But when I opened my mouth to comply with the Moth King's demands, I couldn't.

Valmarys's pale blue eyes fell into the shadow of his black brows. He knew my verdict.

"Tilmorn," he said. "Kill him. But make it last. Use your hands."

I lurched, but my will rammed against the barrier of the compulsion. "No!" I screamed, and Valmarys waved a hand to close my mouth again.

Tilmorn, who stood with his hands behind his back and shoulders relaxed, strode forward, opened a glass panel, whipped away Mercer's bonds, and hauled his younger brother out by the collar.

Tilmorn threw Mercer back into the glass chamber, shattering it. Mercer slid across the floor, his head striking the table. Before he could stand, Tilmorn crushed Mercer's wounded hand beneath his boot. Mercer cried out, the worst sound I'd ever heard. I wanted to save him, to heal him, to stroke his hair. The pent-up rage inside me was torment.

Mercer managed to stand, draping his hurt hand at his side. He gritted his teeth. "Tilmorn," he said, but before he could make his plea, Tilmorn smashed a ruthless fist into his face.

Mercer spat blood and charged out of desperation, his boot soles crunching glass. He tackled Tilmorn with the brute strength of one good arm, slamming his brother to the ground, thrashing him. But Tilmorn used both legs to launch him away, crashing him against one of the other glass-fronted chambers that held the elicromancers.

"*Rethir!*" Mercer cried, the word tearing out of his throat with such devastating sorrow that I knew it could only mean "brother."

The Moth King smiled a crooked smile. He was confident in Tilmorn's loyalty—maybe too confident. A flicker of some sort of awareness crossed Tilmorn's eyes, but the Moth King was watching *me*, relishing my incapacitation, punishing me for not taking the coward's way out.

My power began to work to break the compulsion. I'd tried to pick a lock in the palace with a hairpin once, and that was how this felt: finagling, a secret struggle in the dark. All it would take was the right pressure at the right point and the door would creak open. Tilmorn had left the Moth King with only one gift: the compulsion. If I could render it useless, this would all be over.

While the fight raged around me and blood began to sprinkle the floor like warm raindrops—most of it Mercer's—I yanked at the coils of power inside me. But they didn't break me lose.

I needed my power more than ever. I would have to disregard the compulsion, let the presence inside me speak for itself and act on its own whim. Perhaps if I concentrated hard enough, I could crack the Moth King's bones one by one until imminent death blazed in his eyes.

I summoned the Water's mighty power so that my fingers and toes curled with it and my vision went black. But when I sought hold over Emlyn Valmarys, he was like a slippery, quivering thing that I couldn't quite grip.

Yet I felt pulses of other living things, orbs of bright elicrin magic throbbing in the dark, the warmth of gifts nesting in their stones. I could see each elicromancer, feel their essence. The Water had already chosen them, let them pass unharmed—so echoes of the same entity inside me could not destroy them. If I had taken my time with Prosper and the others in the dungeons, I might have been able to see that their elicrin power blocked them from me. The blights had still only been shells of elicromancers, and Jovie an elicromancer in pretense alone. That was why I'd managed to break her arm. Neswick had kept a safer distance, otherwise I might have injured him as well.

But these elicromancers had already survived the Water, and therefore it could no longer destroy them.

Destroy. Transform. Destroy. Transform.

When I opened my eyes, the Moth King's blue eyes were wide, aware, alarmed like a snake before a heel strike.

Destroy. Transform. Destroy. Transform, and...

The visceral coldness of that night at the Water with Ivria overcame me. I thought of the uncertainty of that moment, the way everything seemed to pause when Ivria's toes skimmed the surface, as if the whole forest watched with bated breath.

Destruction and transformation were only the *results* of the Water's true power: its power of *choice*. The Water was sentient, decisive. It was the purveyor of every gift, and killer of those who dared approach it undeserving.

The Water chose me to carry on its legacy, which meant it chose me to *choose* who was worthy. I had become the Water.

I closed my eyes again, tuning out Mercer's screams. Acting out of anger and sadness was not the way to use this gift. Mercer had been right.

The hot rage inside me turned cool and devious, icy waters lapping at a winter shore. I saw each elicrin power as a pulse of color: blood red, forest green, smoke gray, vibrant purple, incandescent yellow, blue-streaked orange, even a faint sparkling white that must have represented Jovie's.

But as the colors began to throb brighter in the dark, my feet strode forward, obedient to the Moth King's whim. My eyes shot open and I watched as a glide of Tilmorn's finger made the glass wall along the back of the tower slide away. My pace became a run, and my tired legs drove me toward death with treasonous enthusiasm. I heard my name break free from Mercer's throat, the desperation, the passion, the beautiful fragility. Mountain cliffs waited for me below, jagged mandibles eager to snap my small body.

I leapt over the edge, suspended in the clouds for just a beat before I careened from the heights.

THIRTY-TWO

THE fall lasted as long as a blink. I didn't feel pain, just the cold roughness of a surface beneath my splayed fingers and prostrate body. I was afraid to open my eyes, afraid to see my own corpse, broken and maimed beyond recognition.

Something hard scraped against my sternum as I shifted, and sensations of icy moisture skimmed across my back. Softness tickled my ankles. My bones didn't feel broken. My skin didn't feel torn. *Why is the land of light so cold?*

Perhaps I didn't deserve to enter it.

I dared open my eyes. *Maybe this is Galgeth. The place of dark spirits. The underworld.*

But soft, white shadows surrounded me. I propped myself up, realizing that I wore a gown. I looked and saw the jeweled neckline of my birthday dress, the shining silver-and-cream skirts twisting around my legs.

I glanced around, hoping to see Ivria, but found only the shadows of ghostly trees and heard only the whisper of falling snow. But the whisper took shape and formed words.

It was a voice, neither male nor female. *You were chosen before time.*

My breath was deafening in the hallowed quiet. "For what?"

Humankind erected gates, enchantments, decrees. Our power has been depleted over the ages. We are weary of being used. You are the new vessel, more powerful than any elicromancer. You are the essence of elicrin power, its curator, its steward.

"What are you? Are you a god?"

The voice laughed gently, but no answer came.

The silhouettes of trees fled like wisps of smokes. My dress ripped away in a violent wind, revealing my ragged clothes underneath. The ice, however, remained as a pedestal beneath my feet. Mountain crags rose up around me. I heard the echo of my booming voice and the silky laugh resonating over the sunlit cliffs and peaks.

I whirled around. The Moth King's tower loomed behind me, across an expanse of ice that pulsed with vivid colors. Fear-stricken faces stared at me from the topmost floor.

I took a step in their direction and found my feet steady on the ice. I closed my eyes as I walked, seeing more in the darkness than I could in the light, elicrin powers blinking above pounding hearts. I felt myself nearing the edge of the ice and opened my eyes again to peer at the whirling depths below. But the ice spread to catch my step, and I looked up, feeling my face brighten with a gleeful smile.

I closed the distance and took an easy leap back into the tower room.

Valmarys backed up. "Tilmorn!" he called.

But my soul reached out to Valmarys's elicrin power. It curled out of his stone as a tendril of fog, snaking into my mouth and nostrils like a breath as I strode toward him. One look at Mercer's bloodied face and I felt no pity for the powerless man staggering away from me. I unsheathed my knife, seized him by the collar, and thrust the blade into his heart, happy to make Mercer's lies become truth.

For all the talk of Emlyn Valmarys's greatness, his flesh tore as easily as anyone's.

Valmarys dropped to his knees, sputtering. I would have thought a clean stab through the heart would make death instantaneous, but Emlyn Valmarys suffered at my hand.

Tilmorn cried out in sorrow. Every surface of glass in the room exploded, raining broken bits that sliced my skin. The sea maiden slipped out in a rush of salty water, a shimmering corpse on studs of broken glass.

Tilmorn charged to catch the Moth King as he slumped over. Gurgling, twitching, Valmarys pointed to the corridor.

"Jovie!" Tilmorn roared.

Soft footsteps crossed broken glass. Jovie looked around the corner, emitted a sob, and rushed to the Moth King's side. She took his hand to heal him, whispering, "Master." But I closed my eyes, locating the pulse of light in her chest, and yanked.

Jovie gave a strangled noise as I ripped out her stolen gift. She swayed on her knees for a moment, her eyes blank, her chest an open cavity as though I had ripped out her heart. Her mortal body was not strong enough to withstand the rescission of power.

I felt an odd sorrow as her lifeless form collapsed inelegantly over the corpse of her dead master. Like me, Jovie had dreamed of being an elicromancer, of being accepted rather than mocked. Like me, she had longed to put her doubters in their place. If I had been raised to believe in someone who could give me whatever elicrin gift I desired, would I have raised him from the grave, no matter the cost?

In death, she looked like a stunned child, but I remembered

how she had plagued me with taunts of Mercer's torture. No one would ever hurt him again.

My gaze skimmed across the broken glass, the bodies that had fallen limp when Tilmorn exploded the chambers with his temper.

"Grandmum."

I darted to the farthest cage. Her hair fanned around her. Her lips were parted, already emptied of their last breath. An old woman, no matter how tough, no matter how strong, should never leave this world in bloodshed. She should have died in a warm bed, with her loved ones around her and peace in her heart. But she was gone. Tilmorn's rage had killed her.

Grandmum. She was warmth, wisdom, honor, the gentle laughter of a warm fire, the scent of briarberry tea, and pages of ancient books telling heroic stories.

I sank to the floor, a violent sob building inside me. Even in victory, something Grandmum would have been proud of, I felt a stain spreading on my soul, one that would last forever.

I blinked back at Tilmorn, who looked around as if seeing for the first time. Horror eased into his expression and he looked at his bloody hands as though they belonged to a stranger. I bared my teeth and prepared to strike, instinct taking over.

"Valory, no!" Mercer called, the plea muffled by swollen lips and blood pooling in his mouth.

A dozen emotions crossed Tilmorn's face at hearing his brother beg for mercy on his behalf. His ire faded to confusion and then to a grief beyond words. He yanked off his elicrin medallion and slid it through the broken glass. It stopped just a hair from my fingers splayed on the floor.

Mercer shoved himself off the ground and staggered toward me. Hot tears filled the cuts streaking my cheeks. He fell to his knees and gripped my shoulders. "Valory," he said, tipping my chin with his good hand. "You have every reason to kill Tilmorn, but if you love me, as I love you, you won't. He did not choose this. He chose Lundy and me, but that choice was torn away, just as Ivria, your father, your grandmum were torn from you. Take out your wrath on those who *choose* corruption. Give Tilmorn a chance to redeem himself."

"I don't want it," Tilmorn rasped. "I don't deserve it. I only ask that you kill me quickly."

I swallowed hard, bent to brush a featherlight kiss on Grandmum's forehead, and planted my hands on the floor. When I rose, glass shards from the broken cases trickled like raindrops.

I scooped up the chain of Tilmorn's elicrin stone and crossed the banquet room toward him.

He kept his head bowed as I stood over him, but I waited for him to find the courage to look up at me. I took in a deep breath, extracting the gifts nestled in the gray facets of the stone. I exhaled Melkior's healing gift, which Jovie had taken, and slid the chain back around his neck.

"You have work to do, Tilmorn Fye."

THIRTY-THREE

MID the aftermath of the battle, helpers emerged. The great hall became a refuge for the wounded. By nightfall, the survivors had located their loved ones, alive or dead. White paint was scrubbed from faces. Across the bridge, funeral pyres blazed against the onset of night. I said my farewells to Grandmum and welcomed the darkness, knowing that the shadow of that horrible tower would not loom so fiercely when it came.

Tilmorn had donned a hood and healed everyone who could still be saved, but some died awaiting his touch. Glisette was nearly one of them. She had been skewered by arrows and lay writhing on a blanket. Rayed and Kadri hunched at her side as she whimpered and groaned, her wheat-gold hair streaked with blood and damp with sweat.

"There, there, beauty," Rynna said, rushing to tip a cup of nectar to Glisette's lips. Glisette nearly choked on the viscous liquid, but she managed to swallow and collapsed back on the cot. "There isn't enough to go around," Rynna whispered. "Feign dying a little longer."

After he had done all he could to help, Tilmorn found his way back to us. I didn't look at him as he sank down. He had healed Mercer and me on our journey down from the tower in the glass chamber, but Mercer's damaged eye remained white as an eggshell.

"They fear me," Tilmorn whispered, sweeping his gaze over the Darmeskan victims.

"They will see who you are without Valmarys," Mercer said. "They know what it's like to be trapped in the shadow of his cruelty." The lump in his throat bobbed. "Tilmorn, what did he do to you when you left with his men so long ago? Do you even remember?"

Tilmorn didn't speak for some time. The soft fires burning in metal pits throughout the hall projected shadows on his comely face. "I'd nearly forgotten. But when he died, the worst of it came back to me. He brought me to his court and took my elicrin stone. He kept me in a dark cave, isolated from everyone and everything. Except, he had a Healer. He would... he would pry off my fingernails. He would bleed me out. One time he even sliced the beard off my face, and the flesh with it. And then he would heal me, and reassure me that he wouldn't do it again."

I shuddered.

"He told me that he would torture and kill you and Lundy if I ever tried to escape. But if I committed myself to his service, did everything he asked, he would keep you safe. Then... he started to tell me about how you had turned your back on me. How you both had forgotten me, that you barely waited a week before you made love to my wife and put a child in her. He insisted he was the only person I could trust."

Mercer hung his head, sobbing. I had already been rent into a thousand pieces, and now each one of them rent in half.

"He stopped hurting me," Tilmorn went on. "But he told me the story of what you had done, why you deserved to die, over and over.

I did as he asked, always, at first because I wanted you and Lundy to live even though I hated you. And then he treated me so kindly, like a brother. He made me believe you had set out to destroy me and that he was my defender. When we awoke from the darkness in the mountain, he promised me the world. He said my family had died. He compelled me to forget you, and it wasn't until Valory killed him that I could...see you for who you were."

"What was his elicrin gift?" I couldn't help asking.

"He could hide himself well."

"Like a Clandestine?"

I heard a wry, dark chuckle building in Tilmorn's chest. "No. Nowhere near as interesting as that. He could integrate into his environment if he wanted—which he never wanted. It's odd. I think the fairies and elicromancers, fearing he would grow to be too powerful, somehow molded his desires. When he finally killed his elicromancer guardians and escaped to the Water, he was expecting so much and received so little. After that, he had to prove them all right somehow, justify their fear and hate. Or all that torment would have been for nothing. He turned to torture and manipulation to feel powerful."

"He was just an Obscurer?" I demanded. Growing up, I had been taught that no elicromancer was "just" anything, that every one was useful in his or her own way. There was a time when I would have longed to show an affinity for obscuring, even if it wasn't the kind of elicrin gift that birthed legends. But for a man who had ravaged a realm...it was an astonishingly plain one.

"Tilmorn," Mercer breathed, wiping a tear with his thumb. "You should know that Lundy was with child, but he wasn't mine. He was

yours. I loved them and cared for them, but I never touched her...."
He lost his voice to unuttered sobs. It took a moment for him to
recover it. "Valory tells me that Halmer grew to be a war hero."

Tilmorn didn't look at his brother but stared at the fire instead
as tears filled his eyes. He clapped a hand on Mercer's shoulder
before standing and wandering into the night.

"I'm sorry I lied to you," Mercer said, turning back to me.

I managed to smile. "Maybe...maybe I killed the Moth King
because you told me I could. Maybe you have an even greater gift
than prophecy: you say it and so it shall be."

I slept little through the night. In my dreams, King Tiernan shriveled into a lifeless corpse. My mother smiled, her lips held in place
by a clothier's pushpins. Prosper struck Mercer's face over and over
until his bruises became festering sores. Ander opened his arms to
embrace me only to stab me in the gut, explaining it was for my
own good. Ivria and Grandmum stroked my face and whispered in
my ear, giving me violent ideas of how to take down the new order
in Arna.

Mercer's arm pressed against my shoulder. He looked at me out
of the corner of his white eye. "Are you sure you don't want me to
come with you to Arna?"

"You should go with Tilmorn to Yorth. They need all the help
they can get clearing the plague. And Tilmorn needs you to help
him remember who he is." I gulped. "Besides, I don't want you to
see me do what I have to do."

"I *have* seen you do it," Mercer reminded me. "And I know now why you must."

I turned to him, lacing my fingers into the soft, sandy hairs at his nape. "You'll come to Arna as the Queen of Calgoran's lover, nothing less."

"Summon me at your leisure, my queen," he said against my lips, catching me up in a kiss.

"So this is it?" Glisette demanded, looking from Mercer and me on one side to Kadri, Rayed, Rynna, and Theslyn on the other. "The heroes disband for now?"

"I'm afraid we have a long road of recovery ahead," I said. "But we can't rebuild while the realm's enemies hold power."

"Will you go back to Wenryn?" Kadri asked Rynna and Theslyn.

"Yes," Rynna answered softly.

Kadri pursed her lips, making a valiant attempt at nonchalance. With a bursting laugh, Rynna gripped the back of Kadri's neck and drew her against her, sliding her lips over Kadri's. "But not until after we help you in Yorth," she amended.

"And then what?" Kadri asked. "I must marry Fabian, if he'll still have me."

"But Kadri, you can't marry Fabian when—" Glisette started.

"Someone will need to sign parchment while Fabian is busy naming newly discovered islands after himself." Rayed sighed.

Rynna smiled. "The Queen of Yorth can make diplomatic visits to the deep woods."

"But...but what if I can't bring myself to leave Wenryn?" Kadri asked.

"Then you won't leave," Rynna answered, her gold eyes sparkling with mischief.

"Rynna…" Theslyn warned, though he hung his arm casually around Kadri's shoulders as he spoke. "You know we can't keep humans."

"I'm not a pet," Kadri said, laughing, her dark eyes resplendent as she looked from Theslyn to Rynna. "And just because you can't keep me doesn't mean I'm not yours."

"Well, now that I feel as though I've eaten a whole platter of sugar cakes, I suppose it's time I return to Pontaval," Glisette snorted. Though she had claimed months ago to be uninterested in ruling, I could see the fantasy playing behind her eyes, the glint of a jeweled crown within them.

I extracted King Tiernan's portal from my satchel as Tilmorn hiked up the hill to join us.

"I'll see you all in Yorth in two weeks' time," I said. "Be ready. Rebuilding the Realm Alliance will not be easy."

I unlatched the portal and it did as I wished, opening to the wooded spot along the sea where I'd practiced my magic. Tilmorn's eyes barely grazed over mine as he stepped through. He hadn't been able to look at me yet.

Mercer touched his forehead to mine. "Be careful," he whispered, and followed his brother.

After saying her goodbyes to Rynna and Theslyn, Kadri embraced me. "I'll see you down there," I said against her shoulder.

"I think when the tower's gone, they should build a statue of us in its place," Glisette mused when only the two of us remained.

She propped her hands on her hips and flashed me a wry smile as I opened her portal to Pontaval. "Let's hope they don't make it to scale, or everyone will know how short you are."

"Let's hope they don't depict you as horrid and bedraggled as you look right now."

Glisette's exiting laugh was tinged with annoyance.

❧ THIRTY-FOUR ❧

FEAR hung over Arna like a fog. The city practically reeked of it as I pushed open my windowpane and looked out on the stone wall that bordered the palace.

That wall should have made Arna's leaders look strong and unapproachable. Instead, it made them look nervous. It was a hastily constructed eyesore, nowhere near as magnificent as the royal residence it protected. Curling the blue-streaked bronze elicrin stone in my fist, I exited my bedroom, not bothering to make my footfalls land softly on the carpet.

I caught the hum of voices bubbling from the upstairs ladies' tea parlor and strode down the corridor. Two guards in the Moth King's livery rushed to attention. I flicked my wrists and snapped my way up their spines. When they collapsed to the floor, I looked up and found the cracks running up the walls, the ones I'd made when Melkior had taken Calanthe from me. Then I stepped over the pair of corpses and shoved open the tea parlor's doors.

Aunt Sylvana and Elythia shrieked in surprise, but my mother's and Odessa's eyes went wide with something that looked like perilous hope. A rustling in the corridor announced the approach of two more guards. I waited until they laid hands on me, jerking me away from my family. Without even glancing over my shoulder, I felled both guards.

Sylvana screamed again as their bodies toppled. Only she and my mother still possessed elicrin stones, and I imagined their ownership was rather tentative.

"Is King Tiernan alive?" I asked.

No one dared speak except my mother, who shook her head and finally found her voice. "Without a Healer, he died last night. He was very ill."

I cursed viciously. "You were told he was ill?"

"That's what we were told, dear," Mother said, dancing around the truth.

"And Melkior?"

"Alive," Sylvana answered. "Though he'll have to prove his loyalty to the true king if he wants to sit on the Conclave."

"There will be no Conclave," I said. "There will be no king." I closed my eyes and summoned Sylvana's power from her ruby elicrin stone.

"What's happening?" she asked as I breathed in her Confounder gift. I wouldn't use it, however; I wanted everyone to know what I was doing and why. But I let it settle inside me before I turned and strode away, hearing the rustle of skirts as they followed. "What did you do to me?" Sylvana demanded.

My footfalls seemed to echo across the kingdom as I charted my course to the receiving hall. The thuds of guards' falling bodies and gasps of shock followed me like drumbeats, until I turned around and only Odessa and my mother lingered behind me, because the others had fled. They both nodded, urging me on.

At the far end of the receiving hall, Prosper sat on the throne, leaning his right elbow on the elaborate armrest, the gold crown poised atop his dark, thick waves. His left arm hung limp in his lap, and it pleased me to ponder the pain he must have endured without an elicrin Healer at his disposal.

Neswick sat at his right hand, Ander at his left. The rest of the Conclave perched nearby. They had the air of men who had sat in power since the beginning of time.

Their elicrin stones caught the light of the overhead chandeliers and flickered with exuberance that their trained faces were too stately to reflect. They were holding court, little fake kings in their toy palace, and relishing every second of it.

My boots streaked mud across the pristine marble tiles. The nobles seated in the hall cast glances at me over their shoulders, ranging from derisive to leery.

Ander noticed me before the other members of the Conclave. His lips parted in surprise. I unhooked my cloak and dropped it as I approached. The flesh on my arms prickled with anticipation.

I held up Valmarys's elicrin stone. "Your master is dead," I said, tossing it to the floor.

Gasps traveled through the crowd. Prosper pressed his shoulders against the upholstered red velvet of his borrowed throne. His gray eyes darkened as they landed on me.

"How courteous of you to come straight to my court and confess to murder," he said, beckoning guards from the corners of the room. "Now my men don't have to hunt you down."

I let four guards seize me, two of them yanking my arms behind my back while the other two planted themselves in front of me, blocking my way.

With a thrumming yet patient exhilaration, I closed my eyes and shrugged my shoulders, stretching and loosening the muscles.

A guard dropped dead with each movement. The thuds resonated through the receiving hall.

A feral smile crept across my face. I opened my eyes and found the Conclave members leaning forward in their seats, alarmed.

"Knox!" Prosper called, his voice nearly cracking.

The five men sat back in their chairs, more comfortable now as Knox's pale gray elicrin stone swirled with reluctant white light. I let him wrestle with his guilt, face the hard choice. He had an unborn son to think of, or at least so he thought. But soon his reluctance turned to clear frustration. "I'm sorry, my king," he whispered, breathless, confused. "I can't extinguish her power."

Prosper looked apt to lash out at him.

"Oh, it's not his fault, though I know you have reason to believe he wouldn't hurt me," I said, striding forward, clasping my hands behind my back.

"Valory, stop!" Ander said, attempting to halt me with a firm hand. He was clearly accustomed to the effectiveness of the gesture. "You can ask for mercy."

"The truth is that I'm not like you," I went on, ignoring him. "You see, not only am I more powerful than all of you, but I am the *rightful* heir to King Tiernan's throne. Melkior will tell you."

Melkior sent me a look of combined admiration and murderous intent for exposing his loyalties. He cleared his throat. "King Tiernan named Valory heir before he died. He made me witness."

"My uncle has been ill, and in no state of mind to appoint a new heir," Prosper huffed, rising. "The line of succession has long been established."

A crack raced out from my toes, splitting the dais in half,

crawling up the wall to the ceiling. The massive chandeliers over-head swayed with a metallic clang, threatening to drop.

Prosper's elicrin stone brightened, but I ripped out his power with a yank of my fingers. One by one, I plucked their powers away, leaving only Neswick's and absorbing the others with delectation.

I relished the rustle of panic and confusion. "I'd wager you didn't think the age of surrender would come so soon," I said, skimming my gaze across the men's faces and landing on Neswick, my father's murderer. "What about you, Neswick? You figured you had many more years ahead of you, didn't you?"

"I—"

I tore away his elicrin gift before he could answer. His chest burst open as I revoked the power that never should have been his. Vaguely, I heard screams, but some sounded more riveted than fearful.

Ivria, forgive me, I thought as I drew my knife. Prosper had plotted against his own family, twisting his flesh and blood into submission. And he deserved the same treatment.

He drew his ceremonial sword, wincing from the pain plaguing his opposite shoulder. I wondered if he'd ever truly used a sword the way Mercer had. He attacked, his lunges graceful and his strokes decisive. I leapt back as he swiped the blade and ripped my tunic, drawing a thin line of blood from the skin over my ribs.

Prosper laughed. I closed my fist and crumbled his sword to dust. Then I drove forward, plunging my knife into his belly.

"For King Tiernan," I said as my uncle's blood rushed over my hands.

Ander cried out, his stiff boots squeaking as he dashed to catch his father. Prosper gasped and gulped, blood seeping to the corners of his mouth and staining his shirt. Melkior's grandfather stood to attack. I twitched my fingers and broke him like a twig.

Ander released his father to charge at me, slamming me down and knocking the knife from my hands. My shoulder hit the floor at an angle and I felt something inside me rip and crack. Violent pain demolished my body. The dangling chandeliers whirled above me. To be reminded of pain was to be reminded that I'd inflicted so much of it in Darmeska.

But anger clawed its way out of the devastation in my heart. The Ander I once loved as a brother had changed, leaving this husk behind. The Conclave was diseased, regal on the surface and rotten at the core. It had to be uprooted. Blood had to be shed.

Fighting for breath, I propped up on an elbow. Ander kicked me in the face. My mother rushed forward to help me. "Stop, Ander!" she managed to command with calm. "Don't hurt her and she'll spare you. We all know this wasn't your idea. Right, Valory? Don't you know that?"

My mother's eyes pleaded with me to spare him. She hoped to salvage as much of her family as she could.

"You will never rule Arna," Ander spat at me. "The people won't allow it. Everyone knows you are a disgrace, a murderer. They know you killed Ivria and you will never be forgiven."

I stood up, my shoulders lopsided, and studied the faces in the crowd. Staggering a few steps, I picked up my knife and faced Ander again. "Many years ago, one of our ancestors named himself sovereign, drew borders, and claimed lands," I said, echoing the

Moth King's words. "Maybe his subjects liked him or perhaps they hated him. But it didn't matter. He was powerful enough to maintain his standing." I looked him in the eyes. "But I don't deserve to rule purely because I can take the throne, do I? Fortunately, King Tiernan named me heir. I am queen. And you are nothing."

Ander reached for his sword to strike me down, but I plunged my knife beneath his collarbone. He fell to his knees, moaning in anguish. Panic permeated his expression, and a small, insignificant part of me wanted to say I was sorry, that I loved him. The words nearly tore out of my throat.

Aunt Sylvana lunged for me, clawing, screaming through her tears. I held her wrists until the fight left her and she sank down next to her dead son. I let her go.

My left arm hung limp. But I swallowed the pain and looked at my mother. Her eyes were wide and replete with reverent horror.

"Ander will have a son," Sylvana snarled, looking up at me through her dark curls. She and Ivria looked so much alike. Her gaze shot back to Elythia, who gulped, waiting to see what I would do. "The throne rightfully belongs to him."

I stood and stepped over Ander's body, my soles treading heavily in his blood. Melkior's father scurried away. I walked down the crack running over the dais and mounted the crooked, blood-spattered steps, turning to face a court of awestruck eyes.

But they would learn to trust me. I would do right by these people.

The Realm Alliance would prosper. Only the just and good-hearted would earn the right to be elicromancers.

I sat on the velvet throne and leaned back, testing it for fit.

My bloody fingers tapped on the scrollwork of the gilded wood as I draped my arms over the armrests and crossed my legs. Melkior strode forward and brazenly picked Prosper's crown off the floor, wearing his same smug smile as he advanced to place it on my head.

My voice boomed through the hall. "The bastard is welcome to fight me for it."

❦ EPILOGUE ❦

GLISETTE

A FRAGRANT breeze sifted through the rosebushes crawling up to the balcony. I shielded my eyes to look down at the courtyard where Ambrosine shuffled to the coach, wearing a sage-green dress with draping strands of pearls. She turned back at us, glaring daggers through a pearl-studded lace veil held in place by a crown of pink roses.

She looked ridiculous, especially with the servant trailing behind her, nearly collapsing under the weight of her favorite mirror.

"Do you think she'll be happier in her new life?" Perennia asked.

"I hope so," I sighed. "I know we'll be happier without her."

"You shouldn't say that."

"Maybe the responsibility of motherhood will give her a greater sense of purpose."

"Uncle said the King and Princess of Perispos are both kind and lovely. I hope they can manage to be patient with her."

"Let's hope the daughter's not *too* lovely," I said, recalling how Ambrosine had ripped that gorgeous gown away from my reflection. "She might tear out the girl's heart in envy."

Perennia managed to laugh. "No matter how she tortures her new stepdaughter, she'll never be half as ruthless as you."

I pinched her arm.

"Ouch! See?"

I smiled, but my smile faded quickly. Ambrosine's envy was

something I might once have found satisfying. We traded in it. We looked so alike that all it took was losing a bit of sleep or waking up with a blemish for one of us to surpass the other in beauty. It had always been a harmless rivalry. But the way she had glared at me as she pressed that gown of sparkling twilight to my neck...

"We lost her somewhere, didn't we?" I asked. "Somewhere between Mother's and Father's deaths, Devorian leaving, Uncle threatening to give us away like tokens to various dukes and earls... she lost hope. She was always praised for her beauty. She clung to it when it seemed there was nothing else left."

Perennia wiped away a solitary tear as we watched the coach rattle through the open gates. "Why don't you ask a Healer to tend to that scar when you go to Yorth?" she asked with a sniffle, turning to me so she wouldn't have to see Ambrosine disappear in the distance.

I sipped from my goblet of blush wine and smacked my lips once in annoyance. "Because I don't mind it. Do you?"

My lovely little sister shook her head, offering a neutral shrug. "Actually, in a way, it makes you look more like a ruler...as if you earned it."

I set down my wine and absentmindedly stroked the tight scar stretching from my eyebrow to the apple of my cheek. In truth, it reminded me of him, of what we had endured together. But the vibrant longing for Mercer that I'd felt on the journey had seeped away when I'd seen him and Valory together. I'd never caught his eye, not beyond a passing lustful glance, the type of glance that he'd rerouted from Kadri or me to his true quarry. Even I could not compete with the strong hold Valory had over him.

A trace of the longing burrowed in my chest. The familiar, soft fire inside me burned, making my knees feel limp. I would have to set my sights on one of Ambrosine's handpicked and eager male attendants.

"Should we use the mirror to peek in on Devorian?" Perennia asked. "I've been checking on them every day."

"Them?" I demanded.

"There's a girl visiting. Her father was a merchant who lost his fortunes when the wave destroyed the port in Beyrian, and he thought he could salvage valuables from the abandoned palace—"

"I don't care about her father! Who is she?"

"She's just a girl. A bit plain, but her family calls her Beauty."

"That's cruel of them if it doesn't suit her."

"Well, her face is pleasing enough, but her neglectful toilette doesn't do it justice. At first I worried for her safety. You know how Devorian can be. But I think...I think he's come around. She was afraid of him for a little while, and he was holding her captive—"

"Captive?" I demanded, storming toward the doors.

"No! Stop! They're friends now." Perennia hurried in front of me to block the balcony doors. I'd grown strong, and she was as dainty as a teacup, but I would never touch a hair on her head. "She's changing him. I wonder if she has the power to break the enchantment. Maybe she could change him back, and he could come home—"

"Well, if he does, I hope he remembers that I'm older than him and I have the right to be queen."

Perennia folded, opening the doors for me and floating across the room to lift the filigree mirror off her vanity desk. "I doubt you'll let anyone forget that, Queen Glisette."

I winked at her. "All right. Show me the beast."

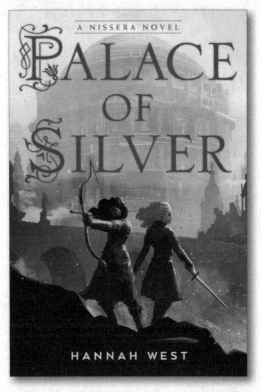

An uneasy peace reigns now that the Moth King has been vanquished. Valory, Kadri, and Glisette are newly crowned queens. All should be well.

But then a dangerous uprising led by elicromancer-hating rebels gains momentum. Rot spreads through the Forest of the West Fringe, sickening the fay. And Valory goes missing. Facing enemies on both sides, Glisette and Kadri must reckon with the role of magic. How far will they go to defend their power—and can they build an uprising of their own?

Hannah West intertwines the tales of *Snow White* and *Bluebeard* with the imaginative world of Nissera for an exhilarating follow-up to *Realm of Ruins*. Don't miss the next installment!

@HolidayHouseBks • HolidayHouse.com

ACKNOWLEDGMENTS

It was a joy and a riveting challenge to revisit Nissera and see how it had changed over a century, to tell a new story in this familiar world. I owe so much to the people who encouraged me to take the journey.

My deepest gratitude goes to Sally Morgridge, editor at Holiday House, who I've come to see as a friend through the years since our first call about *Kingdom of Ash and Briars*. You have always been so attuned to what these stories need, and your wisdom, humor, and empathy hearten me. We're the same age but I still want to be you when I grow up.

As the dedication implies, this book simply wouldn't have happened without my husband, Vince, who was patient through my many late nights and frazzled days of wrestling with a first draft on deadline, something I'd never done before. You spoiled our fur baby when I was too busy, and you never doubted that I would hand over a story we would both feel proud of.

As always, endless gratitude goes to Sarah Goodman (Mama Sar), my critique partner, sweetest of sweet rabbits, and dearest friend. I'm looking forward to drinking half-and-half sweet tea and discussing young adult books with you even when we're old and gray.

I also owe a great deal of thanks to Kelly Loughman at Holiday House for believing in the promise of this return to Nissera and hashing out ideas with me in the early stages. You helped shape those scattered ideas into a story.

My humblest thanks to Logan Garrison Savits and Sarah Burnes of The Gernert Company, who championed the very first novel I ever wrote and continued to believe in the magic of elicromancy.

My deepest thanks to the delightful people at Holiday House who have worked hard to help this book reach its potential, including Kevin Jones, Mora

Couch, and Hannah Finne. Thank you to the marketing and publicity teams, with special thanks to Terry Borzumato-Greenburg, Emily Mannon, Faye Bi, and Emily Campisano.

Praise to Art Director Kerry Martin and artist Daniel Burgess for yet another striking and unbelievably beautiful work of cover art, and to Jaime Zollars for your enchanting illustrations.

Credit also goes to hawkeyed copyeditor Barbara Perris, who did an incredible job.

I also want to thank Kali Katzmann, beta-reader extraordinaire, best friend since forever, and the type of compelling person you base a character on without realizing you're doing it. And to my other best friend since forever, Brooke Buchanan, who exchanged angsty middle school writings and fangirled over fictional boys with me.

Thank you to Johnny Wink, Monsieur Clin d'Oeil, for pulling me aside and telling me I could do this for real. And thank you to Jody Persson, fellow river nymph, for your quandary-solving literary insight.

Thank you from the bottom of my heart, Mom and Dad, for leading to my love of books (shout out to Dad's theatrical voices for *The Little Mouse, the Red Ripe Strawberry, and the Big Hungry Bear*). Thank you, Douglas, for loving fantasy stories and convincing me to play with real swords in the woods even though it turned out to be a not-good idea.

Thank you to all the dear friends and family who have supported me. It says a lot about my community that there are too many of you to name, but know that I am grateful for every one of you.

And my most profound thanks to everyone who read and loved *Kingdom of Ash and Briars*. I got to stay in my beloved fairytale world a little longer because of you.